P9-DFZ-777

THE YEAR

THE COLORED SISTERS

CAME TO TOWN

THE YEAR

THE COLORED SISTERS

CAME TO TOWN

Jacqueline Guidry

WELCOME RAIN PUBLISHERS
New York

Printed in the United States of America by Blaze I.P.I.
1 3 5 7 9 10 8 6 4 2
First edition June 2001

Library of Congress Cataloging-in-Publication Data
Guidry, Jacqueline.
    The year the Colored Sisters came to town / Jacqueline Guidry.—1st ed.
        p. cm.
    ISBN 1-56649-200-9
        1. Girls—Fiction. 2. African American women—Fiction. 3. Race relations—
Fiction. 4. Louisiana—Fiction. 5. Racism—Fiction. 6. Nuns—Fiction. I. Title.
    PS3607.U54 Y43 2001
    813'.6—dc21

                                                    2001017372

CONTENTS

TO MICHAEL

PROLOGUE

There comes a time when you learn your world, how you will live your life, how you will fit your life into the lives of people around you. You learn where you will draw the line, what you will sacrifice, and what you will protect. For me that time came the year I was ten. From summer 1957 to the following spring I watched as events overtook us all, my own family and others in Ville d'Angelle too. I'm not claiming to have learned nothing since I was ten. I am saying some of my greatest wisdoms came to me in that year, the year the colored sisters came to town.

I

CHANGE-OF-LIFE BABY

NOT A DAY WENT BY that July without someone saying, "Hot enough to fry eggs on a sidewalk." Living in the country the way I did, I didn't have much chance of finding anyplace to fry eggs except Mama's skillet. But I wasn't too put out about missing that chance, because even town children didn't go around breaking eggs on sidewalks. Nobody's mama would abide wasting good food to prove up a saying, true or false. Even Willie LeBlanc's mama would draw the line there. Least I expected so, though it's hard to tell for sure because Willie is one of those change-of-life babies who, more times than not, leave their mamas with addled brains.

Tante Deacy was having herself one of those change-of-life babies come New Year's. Didn't neither me nor Mavis know exactly what "change-of-life baby" meant, though I had my suspicions.

Mama liked to break through the roof when she got wind of it. "Why, in the name of all that's sweet and good, did she go do a fool thing like that?"

I was curled on one end of the sofa, Mavis on the other. We both had library books in our hands, but neither of us was looking at words. Mavis twisted strands of her hair, the same shade of brown as mine but still long and straight because Mama didn't allow permanents till a girl turned nine.

There was nothing but a frame, no door, separating us from the kitchen where Mama was cleaning supper dishes and Daddy taking apart the mixer that had gotten in mind to work on nothing but slow speed. I hoped Daddy could figure it out because Mama'd said cakes did not get baked with slow-speed mixers.

Mama's pies are good. But they're nothing to compare to her Double Chocolate Devil's Surprise, which I could eat every single day of the year and which we hadn't had since before school let out. I asked her once why it's called Devil's Surprise and she said it tastes so good, it'd take the devil to Heaven, where he'd sure be surprised. That made as much sense as anything, so I guessed Mama was right about it, as she is about most things. Some days I worry over whether I'm learning fast enough to know everything I'll need to be a grown-up myself. But then I remind myself I'm not close to being a woman and I'm shoving things in my brain fast as I can, so I'm pretty sure I'll be ready when my time comes.

Our house is built for eavesdropping, which does help my education along. Mama'd reached the rinsing-off part of dishwashing. With the water running, I couldn't hear voices. Mavis looked up at me. "Wait," I mouthed.

I was right. Soon as the water turned off Mama was back, just like Ozzie and Harriet after commercials.

"The three she's got are more than a handful. Believe me." Mama swatted her dishrag over some innocent plate. "For God's sake, little Austin's two years older than Mavis." A plate clanged, so now she was stacking dried dishes in the cabinet.

"I think a new baby is fine. Proof Everett isn't ready for the grave yet." Daddy laughed at his joke, though I didn't get it. Mavis grinned, but she didn't get it either.

"Go ahead and make your jokes, Floyd Dubois. But I tell you this, a change-of-life baby is nothing but hard work and sorrow and I don't just mean in the having of it, though Lord knows that's going to be hard enough on poor Deacy."

"Just joking, Hazey. That's all." He wasn't in an arguing mood, else he would've called out her full name—Hazel.

Tante Deacy's baby would mean changes for everybody, because those type babies always change the lives of every person they touch. Mavis and I, just being that baby's cousins, might not get changed much as Tante Deacy's own boys, but we were relations and so we'd be bound to feel some of the winds of change that new baby'd be blowing. Maybe we'd get around to building the extension Mama'd been talking about for long as I could remember. I could stop sharing a room with Mavis. Course I'd get to move out, since I was oldest. Mavis'd have to settle for the used-up room. That'd be a fine change, so I hoped that's what Tante Deacy's new baby had in mind. As it turned out, though, that baby was thinking of a whole lot more than separate bedrooms for me and Mavis.

"Little Miss, you get that tub water ready," Mama called to me. Mama only called me that around the house and only some of the time. She says only dogs, poor white trash, and coloreds call themselves anything but their God-given names. Why did Mama come up with Little Miss for me, Baby for Mavis? I know she's not a dog and I know she's not colored and I know she's not poor trash, though she is white. Daddy never would've married a dog, or a colored or trash neither.

"Vivien Leigh, put that book down and get to the bath," Mama called again. She didn't bother coming to the door. She knew I'd still be sitting on the sofa because I'm the type child always has to be told twice to do anything. That's not my fault. I inherited those lazy Dubois genes. I heard Mama say so herself to Tante Deacy.

Mavis is too young—just finished up first grade—to tell whether she got that particular gene. I hope not. Somebody's got to have the get-up-and-go to keep our room clean and other such things.

"Vivien Leigh, don't make me leave this kitchen."

Time to move now. "I was just finishing my chapter." I'd been best reader in fourth grade and Mama was so proud of that, she never stayed aggravated when I'd been reading.

Our bathtub is the biggest I've seen—round with not a single sharp edge and almost deep enough for swimming. Mama kept it scrubbed clean and white. Four claw feet hugged the floor, making the tub look as if it could run out the house anytime it got tired of bathing people. Mama was after Daddy to put in one of those modern tubs, maybe a blue one with a shower attached like Tante Deacy's. But so far Daddy hadn't obliged. That was fine by me. I hoped his Dubois laziness kept him from obliging for a long, long time.

While the tub filled, I squirted toothpaste on my brush. After I rinsed, I stared at my teeth, nearly straight as Scarlett O'Hara's. I'm named after the girl who played her in *Gone with the Wind*.

"Why don't you name her Scarlett and be done with it?" Daddy'd wanted to know.

"Cause Scarlett is a white-trash name," Mama'd said. Course I hadn't heard that myself, but Mama'd told me enough times. She saved me from a white-trash name. Sometimes I wrote SCARLETT DUBOIS on my notebook sheets. I liked the way the name looked. But I never told Mama, not wanting to worry her into one of her headaches over her own child flirting with becoming white trash.

By the time I stepped into the tub the water'd reached the top drain hole, which prevented overflowing. I turned off the faucet and leaned against the back of the tub that curved exactly right so I could rest my neck and head easily. The shimmery blanket of water stopped just below my neck. I swished water with both hands, then closed my eyes, thinking about Tante Deacy's change-of-life baby and waiting for Mama to yell at me to stop playing and start washing.

When I woke next morning, Mavis was already out of bed. Since this was Thursday, Aussie was helping Mama, and that meant Marydale was here too. Marydale was Aussie's change-of-life baby, and Aussie always said that baby was worth all her other five girls put together and then some. She made change-of-life babies sound better than Mama's Christmas gingerbread. I wondered Mama didn't want one herself. I'll probably be getting myself one of those change-of-life babies when I'm grown.

Marydale was Mavis's best friend. Daddy turned red, nearly broke into a sweat, when Mavis said that, because whites aren't supposed to have coloreds for best friends. But Mavis was too young to know that. When I get discouraged about all the things I don't know, I look at Mavis and shake my head at all she's got to learn. Mavis never gets discouraged about being ignorant, though. She's too young to know how little she knows.

Mama and Aussie were cleaning closets today. I could hear them in Mama and Daddy's room. They were talking too softly for me to understand what they were saying, but every once in a while Aussie's laugh leaked through the pores of my wall. When something hit Aussie funny, she gave this low-pitched laugh from deep in her stomach, her belly shaking a little just before she let it out. By the time the laugh leapt out her throat it was so deep it sounded like a man's. But that didn't bother Aussie any. Colored ladies don't mind sounding like men.

"Vivien Leigh, get out of bed this minute." Mama rapped twice on the wall. Sometimes I think Mama can see right through walls, no trouble at all. How else could she know I was awake and ready to get up?

Mama's good about letting me and Mavis sleep late as we want in summer. Not like Clorise Mouton, whose mama kicks her out of bed at six-thirty every single day, no matter it's Saturday or summer. I'm sure Clorise has to get up at six-thirty on her birthday.

"I won't abide a girl in bed at nine-thirty." Mama said that for Aussie's benefit, then rapped again. "Hear me?"

"Yes, ma'am," I called back. I stretched. I was wearing baby-doll pajamas, which are close as you can get to nothing without actually being there, and the fan was blowing right on me. Still, I could tell it was going to be another one of those fried-eggs-on-a-sidewalk days. Only question was who'd be the first to say it.

Aussie and Mama were ready for their first cups of coffee when I was still finishing my Sugar Pops. Mama handed Aussie a cup from the mug tree standing in the corner of the counter. Daddy says Mama should give Aussie one special cup so we won't chance getting colored germs. Mama says fellow who's full of germs as my daddy shouldn't waste anybody's time worrying over getting a few more, colored or not. I don't ever use those tree mugs, so doesn't bother me any.

"Ever seen a girl so lazy she's still eating breakfast at ten o'clock a.m.?" Mama asked Aussie.

"No, ma'am," Aussie answered. "Never did see that, me." She shook her head, then sipped coffee.

Mama and I waited because we knew more was coming.

"Now I think on it, that's nothing but a lie and Aussie don't tell no lie. I got to set this right."

"You know someone who ate breakfast later than ten o'clock a.m.?" Mama dragged out the time like it was the most interesting thing she'd had to think over in many a day.

"Yes, ma'am. That sure be right." Aussie looked at Mama, serious as anything, though all three of us knew something funny was coming.

"Tell me, Aussie. Please tell me someone has a worse burden than me."

"Yes, ma'am. Worse for sure. That be God's truth."

"You listen up now, Vivien Leigh." She looked over at Aussie. "The girl doesn't have problems listening. When she feels like it, that is. I'm grateful at least her ears are working models."

"That sure be something to thank the Lord for."

"Course I'd be even more thankful if the Lord saw to it that she listened and minded more than when the feeling happened to come over her."

"I hear that," Aussie said.

I wondered how old you had to be before grown-ups stopped talking over you as if you weren't there. I scooped the last three floating Sugar Pops with my spoon, then poured more cereal into the leftover milk. I never could figure the right amount of milk to go with a bowl of Pops.

"You remember Ti-Boy, my cousin used to live with Henry's sister?"
Mama nodded.

"That Ti-Boy didn't know morning light. Never home after dark. He be gambling and carrying on like he be Satan, him."

"Guess that's why Henry's sister threw him out," Mama said.

"No, ma'am. The boy went and got himself rich with that Los Vegas gambling. He still be there, him."

"That doesn't sound so bad," I said.

"Read one of that boy's letters, you. Plain pitiful. The boy got so much money, he stuck on what to do with it all. Him, he worry sick over money. Can't get half enough sleep, him. Too worried for his money."

"You watch yourself not to be getting into that kind of worry," Mama said.

Aussie grinned, her top lip pulled up, showing purple gums.

"I want to know what you think of this coffee cake Deacy sent over," Mama said as if she'd forgotten all about me and my late habits. Course I knew that hadn't happened. Mama wasn't the forgetting sort.

Aussie took a bite and chewed, her eyes closed, her tongue making little sucking sounds. Mama and I watched till she swallowed. "Need more cinnamon, less sugar." She pronounced judgment the way God would on the Last Day—so sure, no one could brook opposition.

"Deacy always had a sweet tooth. Recipe calls for half a cup sugar, she throws in three-quarters just to be sure."

"Taste to me that what she done here."

"She's gotten herself so sugared up, poor old Everett can't stay away," Mama said.

"Look to be. Yes, ma'am, look to be. You get that cake away from Aussie." Aussie pushed her plate toward Mama, then let out her belly laugh. Mama joined.

"What's so funny?" Worst thing about not being grown is not understanding half the things adults laugh over.

Mama and Aussie, didn't neither one of them look my way. "What's so funny?" I said again.

Mama was laughing so hard now, she was losing her breath. "Get that cake off my side of this table," she said between spasms of laughing.

Aussie pushed the cake to Mama, then Mama pushed it back to her. Back and forth that cake traveled across our kitchen table till it finally rested right in the middle. I stared at it to make sure I wasn't missing something. Then I looked at Mama, Aussie, Mama again. Grown-ups get these spells is about all I could see. Hope it never happens to me, but maybe that's the only way you know you're grown. You act demented and nobody but another grown-up can put any meaning to what you're doing. Some days being grown doesn't sound quite as tempting as others.

I'd finished my second bowl of Pops before Aussie and Mama got their right minds back. They were quiet for once, finishing their coffee refills, so

I offered something new to talk about. Mama always said to steer conversation to pleasant topics when you have guests for eating. Aussie didn't exactly count as a guest, her being colored and all, but we were eating. "Aussie, did Mama tell you the good news about Tante Deacy getting herself a change-of-life baby?"

Mama looked at Aussie. Aussie looked at Mama. I couldn't tell who cracked first, but those two ladies were runaway trains, past anybody's control, even their own. I ran out the back door because this morning, even Mavis and Marydale would be better company. I'd nearly reached the willow before I stopped hearing Aussie's laugh, which was the carrying kind as well as the deep kind.

Mavis had gotten two trowels from the toolshed back of the house and she and Marydale were digging themselves a hole under the willow. It was a good place to dig because the wavy branches would curtain them from the sun all day.

"Mama know you digging this close to her willow?" I asked. Mavis stuck out her tongue. Marydale did the same and shook her head at me, her plaited hair waving every which way. My question must've sounded grown-up as I'd wanted.

"Well?" I stuck out my hip, though it was too bony to look much like Mama's, and put a hand on it.

"Mama don't care about this old dirt," Mavis said.

"Mama'll care if you break up those roots. Don't you know roots are a delicate thing?" I stared off at the Blakes' cow pasture and hoped I looked disgusted as Mama when Daddy lit up a cigar. "You two are the dumbest pair of little bits I've ever seen."

"Your mama won't be caring when we show her what we dig up," Marydale said.

"What's that?"

Mavis kicked Marydale's foot, but not quick enough to stop the words. Marydale was one of them fast-talking colored girls. "We digging up some gold. You help and we let you have some."

"I guess you will seeing as how it's my property you're digging on."

"It's my property much as yours," Mavis said.

"Been mine longer."

That got Mavis. She puffed her cheeks till she looked like a stuffed chipmunk. Marydale whispered something in Mavis's ear that shrank her cheeks back to regular size.

"If you want to help, that's okay. If you don't, stop bothering or I'll tell."

No doubt that was true. Mavis Dubois was the biggest tattle anyone'd ever had the misfortune to be related to. "Why should I waste my time digging for gold that isn't there?"

"Why isn't it there?"

"How should I know? It's just not, that's all."

"We'll see." Mavis went back to digging fast as she could. She didn't look at me, didn't look at Marydale, just kept digging.

I ran to the canal back of the house and sat on the bank, throwing clods of dirt and rocks into the water. I had a crazy sister digging for gold, a crazy mama laughing herself sick over a piece of coffee cake. Far as I could tell me and my daddy were the only fully sane ones left in this family. And some days I wasn't sure about him. I hoped Tante Deacy's change-of-life baby changed some of my family's craziness into something better.

I dug in the dirt bank with a stick, though I wasn't fool enough to expect I'd find gold. Only babies like Mavis and Marydale were dim-witted enough to think that.

Did change-of-life babies ever change things for the worse? I'd never thought such a thing possible till this very minute. When Mama was having a sane moment, I'd ask. That is one of the most important tricks I've learned. If you wait for the exact right moment, you can ask anybody anything and not get into a sliver of trouble over it. Mavis doesn't know that yet. If she was ever nice to me for more than a minute, I'd share that secret and others too. Mavis is certainly nothing but an irritation half the time and more. Still, she's my sister and I do have obligations of teaching her what I know.

"Hot enough to fry eggs on a sidewalk," Mavis called at me from behind her willow curtain. She only said that because it's what she'd heard so many grown-ups say. Mavis was as good a mimic as anybody when she wanted to be.

"Just don't eat one of them eggs is all. Eat one of them eggs and you die." I ran alongside the canal, away from Mavis so I could pretend not to hear her calling, "Why?" I didn't know why sidewalk-cooked eggs were bad for you. I just knew they were. Mavis would have to take my word for it. I was closer to being grown, to knowing the whole world. She knew that well as I did. Even Marydale knew that and she was nothing but colored, though her mama was the smartest colored lady I knew.

"That Aussie's got herself a brain," Mama'd say more times than not after they'd done their cleaning.

"Aussie's okay for being colored like she is," Daddy'd say back.

"Not her fault she was born with that piece of bad luck."

"Not my fault neither." Daddy liked getting the last word. Most times he didn't with Mama. But Mama never had anything to say when Daddy said wasn't his fault Aussie was colored because that was the truth and even Mama couldn't say anything to the truth.

I wondered if colored brains looked different from white brains. Surely they must. Another question I'd have to catch a grown-up in a good mood to ask. I crawled under the barbed-wire fence to the Blake pasture to chain clover flowers. Next summer I'd chain Deacy's baby a whole crown of clover so she—least I hoped it'd be a she—could be queen of change.

Once that baby started working her powers, she'd prove to us all that she deserved a clover crown and more. Course, on that July morning, that was just one more thing I didn't know yet.

2

COLORED SISTERS AT CHURCH

NEXT SUNDAY MORNING Tante Deacy's baby started working its changes. I never expected a baby, not even born yet, to stretch its tiny fingers far as the church, but that's just what happened. It was my turn for the aisle seat, so I saw them first. Mavis said she spied them before me, saw them crossing themselves with holy water at the back of the church because she had her head turned. That might be true since Mavis doesn't know proper reverence yet, which is why Mama has to keep an eye on her, jerk her back to her holy duty at least three times each Sunday. Mavis might've caught sight of the colored sisters first, but hers was a cheating look and couldn't beat mine, the first honest look.

Those sisters marched up the aisle, calm as could be, and sat in the left center section, fourth pew from the altar, with three white nuns who taught at Holy Rosary. Nuns could pretty much do anything they pleased, but none of them had ever pleased to bring colored sisters into a white church. They wore flowing gowns and wide square-toed clogs and covered their bald heads with veils—nuns shave their heads twice each month and every day during Holy Week. Thick rosary beads, fit for whipping, hung around their middles, nuns being too holy to have waists, which are sexy and which it is against Catholic rules for nuns to be. No one dared go up against nuns. So no one tried to throw the colored sisters out of church that first Sunday.

I could tell the sisters belonged to the same order as our school nuns because they wore the same navy habits. They were probably traveling to some God-appointed destination and resting up at the convent before continuing on their way. Everyone knew nuns could not stay in motels. It was another of their rules. I'm sure some people wondered why they didn't stay with the other colored nuns and go to colored church services. But no one said anything. They were nuns, after all.

A few more people probably wondered whether Father Strauss would serve them Communion, him being the sort hates mixing with anybody below his class. But since that pretty much included all of us, I guessed he wouldn't see the harm in giving the Host to a couple of little colored sisters. Besides, he never touched your tongue when he gave communion. If he had, it would've been the certain ending to that Sacrament for a lot of people.

"Wonder where the colored sisters came from?" Mama asked when we'd edged out the church parking lot and were on the way home.

"Don't care where they're from, just so they're going back," Daddy said.

"Sisters don't check with Mister Floyd Dubois about where to go to church." She waved her church fan, the fancy one with pink flamingos that closed with a gold clasp.

Daddy grunted but didn't say anything. Not even Daddy could feel like fussing in that heat-trap car. Except on Sundays I liked our car, all black and smooth, inside and out. Mavis and Mama and I washed it each Saturday so it sparkled for Sunday church. About once a month we vacuumed, and then Mama rubbed oily stuff on the seats to keep them soft. That was the day we waxed the outside too. But all the washing and waxing in the world couldn't take away the hotness that liked to suffocate us on those summer-Sunday church rides. Mama wouldn't let any of us roll down windows more than a crack, because it might mess up the hair she'd had fixed at Claudette's Beauty Salon the day before. Didn't bother Mama that it was ninety and climbing and that her daughters were near to melting with heat. She was not having her dollar-twenty-five 'do mussed because some people couldn't stand a little warmth, which everyone knows is good for you or else why would Doc Joubert prescribe it for anything ailing the old folks—arthritis, chest pains, upset stomach, didn't matter what.

When we pulled into the driveway, Daddy had to stop short of the carport because Cleo was sprawled out right in front of it. He honked, but Cleo didn't move. She had lazy Dubois genes, even though she was only a cat.

"One of these days I'm running over that damn cat. See if I don't," Daddy said. He leaned on the horn, but Cleo stood, or laid, her ground.

"I'll get her. She's just sleeping," I said. Mama pushed to the dashboard so I could squeeze out her door.

"Cat's deaf, if she's sleeping," Mama said.

Daddy let go the horn. I scooped Cleo, who blinked twice and yawned in my arms. I passed a hand across her back, down to the tip of her tail. She was the blackest cat I'd ever seen and strangest too, but not strange as Daddy said. There wasn't sense to him saying she was a witch cat. I was too old to believe in witches, though she did have her ways. Still, she was mine and I loved her, which is normal because, like Mama says, person always loves her own.

About ten minutes later Mama called from the back door. "Little Miss, stop fooling with that cat and come help me."

I stroked Cleo. She didn't purr, just looked at me as if she couldn't puzzle why I was petting her.

Mama called again and when she called a third time, I nestled Cleo under the willow shade, then ran into the house. Tante Deacy and Uncle Everett and their three misbegotten sons were coming for dinner, so Mama'd need me to set a fancy table, stir up the dressing for potato salad, maybe taste stuff to make sure everything was all right.

Tante Deacy and Uncle Everett just had to get themselves a girl this go-round. Those three boys of theirs didn't know up from down and didn't care either. T.J. thinks he's Mister Smart Stuff because he'll be in high school come September. But that high school'll let anybody in because T.J. is the dumbest boy I know and I know plenty of dumb ones. Being in high school won't change that any, far as I can see.

Malcolm is two years older than me and nearly always in a sour mood. When we were little, he asked me to drop my panties to show him my privates. I wouldn't unless he'd show me his first. He dropped his pants and I got a good long look. Then it was time for me to show, but I turned chicken and ran away. By the time he found me I was eating chocolate chip cookies in Mama's kitchen. Course he couldn't say anything about my privates in front of Mama. All he could do was eat cookies too. But he never did get over being irritated with me. If I had to like one of my cousins, I guess it'd be Malcolm, except it's hard to like someone who's always scowling at you. Maybe he's afraid I told someone about his privates. But who would I tell? Mavis? She'd run to Marydale with that story faster than anything and I'm not about to share my own cousin's privates with a colored girl.

Austin is a year younger than me and more of a pest than Mavis, which a normal person might not think possible. But it is. He is also the most spoiled child I know and doesn't even have the excuse of being a change-of-life baby. Maybe Tante Deacy's new child will straighten out Austin and his brothers too. But that's a lot of weight to put on a little baby, maybe more than even a change-of-life child can bear. Still, someone who could put colored sisters in a white church before even getting itself born might just be able to do it.

When I got inside, Mama was frying chicken and Mavis was stirring egg yolks and oil for the potato salad. I gave her a dirty look. She knew that was my favorite job. She smirked and stirred faster so Mama wouldn't take the bowl away on account of her being too slow.

"Table needs fixing," Mama said.

I knew I'd get stuck with the lousiest job. But no use complaining. I pulled out the kitchen table and got the leaves from the hall closet. "Can't Mavis help with the chairs at least?"

"Mavis is busy," Mama said.

Mavis clanged her fork against the side of her bowl to show how busy she was. She didn't fool me any. "I'd of had that dressing done twenty minutes ago," I said.

"Too bad you couldn't bother coming when I called so you could've done just that," Mama said.

I stomped to the shed to get the extra chairs, which I saw I'd have to be lugging by myself. I ignored Mavis's smirks each time I carried a chair to the kitchen. One thing Mavis Dubois cannot stand is being ignored.

When our company arrived, I ran ahead of Mavis to see if Tante Deacy's stomach pouched. It didn't, still flat as Mama's. I wasn't surprised, it being a long way to the new year, but was still a little disappointed.

All through dinner Mama pushed food, but just on Tante Deacy. The rest of us could starve far as Mama cared. "Another piece of chicken, Deacy? How about more dressing? Potato salad? Mavis made that salad herself."

Course that was a bald-faced lie. Mavis no more made that potato salad herself than she crowed the sun up the sky. But everyone oohed and aahed themselves sick over those potatoes, which could've used more celery and less pickles according to my way of tasting.

"I was wondering why those potatoes tasted so good," Uncle Everett said. "Need to have you give Deacy a few cooking lessons, why don't you."

"So now it's my cooking that's the problem." Tante Deacy didn't have a joke in her voice.

"Among a string of other things I'm sure no one at this table needs to hear," Everett said. My uncle had a soft voice, but it carried a long way. He buttered another roll, then used it to clean his plate.

T.J. giggled, which sounded ridiculous coming out a boy close to six feet. T.J. took after those tall Menieres on his mama's side, which I hoped I might take after too. Malcolm glared at me as if it was my fault his mama and daddy weren't getting along.

I cleared my throat, grown-up-like. "It'll sure be nice to have a new cousin come next year."

T.J. giggled again. The boy was a true fool even though we were related.

"Real nice to have a baby around," I repeated, in case folks had missed my first comment. "I'll be old enough to baby sit, if you need me, Tante Deacy." I knew she wouldn't trust her change-of-life baby to one of her boys.

"Be nice if you helped around here before you started offering your services elsewhere," Mama said.

"I'll be needing all the help I can get all right," Tante Deacy said.

"You saying I'm not enough help for you?" Everett asked.

"All she's saying is you've done your part and now other folks can help just as well," Daddy said. He grinned, but Everett didn't grin back.

"Floyd, stay out of this," Mama said, her eyes black as a hurricane night.

"Out of what? I'm congratulating old Everett is all. Can't a man congratulate his wife's brother-in-law without someone getting bent out of shape?"

"Congratulations. Yeah. Sure." Everett pushed back from the table so hard, his chair rammed the kitchen wall and rattled pans on the stove.

"You don't have to break this house down," Deacy said.

"As if I'm in the habit of breaking homes?"

"I didn't say that."

I hoped she wouldn't start crying, but she sounded pained, like she might.

Nobody said anything. Even T.J.'s giggles stopped. Everett looked at the floor as if he couldn't think whether to get up or stay where he was, crushed against the kitchen wall. Deacy looked at Mama. Mavis chewed her chicken leg, smacking her lips against the bone between bites. Those smacking noises were the only sound in our kitchen. Even I couldn't think of anything to say to make things better.

When Mama stood, I jumped, surprised. She grabbed plates and carried them to the sink. That broke the spell and everybody started talking at once. Daddy took Everett out back to see the new riding mower he'd gotten from Sears even though Mama'd told him she had a mile-long list of things she needed more than he needed a soft spot to settle his butt when he was supposed to be working. T.J. tailed after the men as if he'd been invited, which of course he hadn't. Mavis and Malcolm and Austin ran out to find trouble.

"Vivien Leigh, aren't you done yet?" Mama asked.

"Almost." I'd been too slow and now I'd be stuck with the dishes. I scraped the pecan glaze off my yams to save for last, then ate one slow yam bite after another.

"Bring your plate and the rest of those platters when you're done. Hurry up about it."

I swallowed the last bite of yams and stuffed the pecans in my mouth all at once, hardly daring to believe my lucky break. But I looked behind me and there was Mama, done with dumping leftovers from plates into the paper sack Daddy'd burn with the rest of our trash later. Now she turned on the faucet to fill one side of the sink with soapy water. Next to her was Tante Deacy, twisting a towel, ready for wiping. For no reason I could see, I was being spared kitchen duty.

I cleared the table quick as a flash and stacked the dirty dishes on Mama's side of the counter.

Tante Deacy sniffed twice, but since Mama stood between the two of us I couldn't see her very well. "You got yourself a cold? Hope your change-of-life baby don't catch it," I said.

Deacy moaned like I'd punched her belly, dropped her dishrag, and rushed to the parlor.

Mama gave me a disgusted look that I did not, in any way, deserve, then wiped her hands on her apron. "Don't just stand there. Get busy." She hadn't washed a single dish. My lucky break had broken, leaving me with a stack of dirty plates and pots that'd take half the afternoon to clean.

In the parlor Deacy rested her head on her arms, folded across the back of the sofa. She and Mama weren't much alike, though they were sisters. Mama's hair was brown, like mine and Mavis's. Deacy's was mainly black with a few streaks of gray. Mama tended to be the bossy type. Deacy couldn't manage to boss her own children and if a person can't boss her own children, she can't boss anybody. But they were sisters and you could see it in their eyes that darkened to black in the same way when they were feeling strongly in some way or other. You could see it in the way the bridges of their noses wrinkled when they laughed, their mouths stretched thin when they were angry. They were surely sisters, alike and different, but always sisters.

Mama wasn't saying anything loud enough for me to hear. Far as I could tell she was just rubbing Deacy's back, though she might've been saying real soft words because Mama can get her voice quieter than anyone I know. Many a time I've eavesdropped and gotten everything Daddy said, clear as if he were talking in my ear. I knew Mama was talking too because he'd stop, every so often, like you do when you're listening. But try as I might I couldn't hear her words.

"Get busy in there," Mama called. She couldn't see me pressed against the door frame but still knew what I was doing.

"Water's too hot," I said.

"Heard of cold?"

I dragged myself to the sink and turned on the cold faucet. Now I couldn't hear or see. I turned off the faucet soon as it was safe to do without risking Mama calling out that must've been the tiniest bit of cold anybody ever needed in dishwater. But even with the water off and me washing dishes quiet as a silent prayer, I couldn't hear what was going on in the parlor. I could tell Mama was talking, but that's about all I could tell. Dirty dishes were coming between me and my own education. Things you need to learn to be grown, adults discuss when they think you can't hear.

I had half a mind to make Mavis help with cleanup. But she'd just carry on till Mama'd stop conversing in the parlor altogether and start yelling in the kitchen. These dishes were all mine and no getting around it.

By the time I finished the last platter Mama was back in the kitchen, drying to make room for me to put pots in the drainer. I watched her out the corner of my eye. She didn't look upset, just far away, like she was too busy thinking to bother with me.

"Mavis should be drying," I said. More times than not Mavis got out of work by looking small and pitiful. Nice, if you can get away with it.

"I suppose," Mama said, still not paying any real attention to me.

"It's not fair," I said. "How come I do all the work around here?"

That jerked her back to me. "That's a new one. Wait till I tell Aussie, 'Miss Vivien Leigh does all the work around this house.' Aussie'll be laughing so hard, she won't be able to pass a broom, much less get any real work done. Course with you doing all the work around here, there's hardly any need to have Aussie coming. Hardly any need at all."

My mama sure could carry on about not much of anything. But at least now I had her attention so maybe I'd find out what happened in the parlor during my dishwashing. "Tante Deacy okay?"

"Well as you'd expect under the circumstances."

I nodded seriously, wisely I hoped. I liked Mama treating me like just another grown-up. But now I had to be careful. If I asked too many questions, she'd remember who I was—Vivien Leigh Dubois, nearly ten, going into fifth come September, not grown, not even close to driving.

"It's her change-of-life baby," I said. That much was easy to guess.

"Nothing's that pretty baby's fault. That's what I told Deacy."

"Sure." I kept scrubbing the pot I'd cleaned to shining at least two minutes ago.

"That big sister of mine never could see plain day shining in her face."

"I didn't know that about Tante Deacy," I said. Now I was really confused and tried to think of a question that would clear me up but wouldn't remind Mama she was conversing with a child.

"Lots you don't know, Little Miss."

That much I did know and didn't need reminding about my general ignorance. "Looks to me like Tante Deacy and Uncle Everett aren't getting along again. That's all and since they've been doing that, off and on, long as I can remember, what's the big deal?"

"The big deal, Vivien Leigh, is marriage. Marriage is a big deal and when you're older, you'll know what I mean." She folded her dishrag, poured coffee into two mugs, and went back to the parlor.

I finished the pots, then ran outside, but didn't join Mavis and Austin and Malcolm right away. Instead I sat on the back steps, plucking splinters from the underside of the railing. My change-of-life cousin was going to be smarter than all three brothers, which wasn't saying much in itself. But that baby might be near smart as me. She hadn't even gotten herself born and she'd moved colored sisters into Saint Stephen's, Tante Deacy into the parlor crying like a baby, and Uncle Everett ramming chairs against the kitchen wall. No doubt my change-of-life cousin would be a girl. She had too much get-up-and-go to be nothing but another Comeaux boy.

3

COLORED
GOLD

ALL WEEK TEMPERATURES climbed higher and higher
till we were living in a bowl of heat. The air was hot and still. Nothing had
the energy to move. Even Mavis hung in the house, face pushed against a
fan. She didn't bother nagging Mama to let her walk down the road to
Marydale's, too melted with heat to want to play in a house with only two
electric fans. With it being so hot, a person didn't want to have to fan her
own face, wanted the electricity to do it for her.

Mavis and I'd both finished our library books and begged Mama to take
us to Lafayette for new ones. With the windows rolled down and Mama
going a fair speed, the wind'd blow our faces and cool us much as a glass of
iced lemonade. But Mama said no, she had to finish some baby Jesus costumes for the Altar Society's annual week of special Masses, which was just
twelve days away, so stop bothering her. Since her excuse had to do with
an Altar Society affair, we knew there was no use pushing for library books
or anything else for that matter.

When it came to Altar Society business, everything else had to wait.
Mama was second vice president of the society. She joked that was just a
fancy way of saying she was in charge of the dirty work other ladies couldn't
be troubled with. But there was nothing dirty about sewing new dresses for
the statue of baby Jesus at Saint Stephen's. I think the ladies gave Mama

---

that job because they knew what a good sewer she was, how careful and exact she'd be with a baby Jesus dress. No crooked seams or loose buttons or shaky sequins for Mama. She did things right and those Altar Society ladies knew it.

If Mama had to pick a week to keep us from new library books, though, this was a good one for me. I'd checked out eleven books I'd found myself. But number twelve was *Jane Eyre*, which the librarian said she thought I was old enough to enjoy. I didn't open the book till I'd finished my other eleven, even read a couple of those twice because I had no faith in what a librarian would recommend. I'd only taken the book to be polite and didn't have intentions of reading it. But by the end of the week I was ready to try even a librarian's recommendation.

I'm a big-enough person to admit I was wrong about that book. *Jane Eyre* was about the best story I'd ever read. Better than *Black Stallion* and all the children of black stallion that followed. Better than *Heidi*. Better than anything. It was romantic and tragic and had a happy ending, almost more than you could expect from one book. I read it four times and liked it better each time, which goes to show how good it was because I'm tired of most books after two readings. But even the fourth time, I cried enough to need three Kleenexes when Jane left Rochester because she couldn't stay with a man who had another wife even if that wife was a lunatic locked in the attic so she wouldn't burn the house down, which of course she did anyway. Rochester going blind trying to save his crazy wife from the fire she'd started herself was perfect too. Jane couldn't marry someone with less morals than she had. Burning his eyes out showed Rochester knew how to do the right thing much as Jane did. They could marry knowing they'd each do the right thing when push came to shove.

Sometimes figuring right from wrong isn't easy. Other times right is staring you in the face but, if you're a weak person, you don't choose it. You choose the other even knowing you're doing wrong. I am sad to admit to being that sort of person. I would've married Rochester right off. But I would've made sure his crazy wife had everything she needed, would've visited her every day, might even have taken her on Sunday-afternoon walks, if she wasn't acting too crazy. I'd still have known I was doing wrong, stealing a crazy lady's husband, but I couldn't of helped myself. Maybe Tante Deacy's baby will change that about me, change me from a girl who only knows right some of the time and does it even less of the time to a girl who knows right all the time and does right all the time. Maybe that baby'll stop me turning my head to wrong whenever it suits me. I wouldn't mind that kind of change because I sure would be happy to marry a Rochester someday, even if he was blind.

Between reading *Jane Eyre*, thinking about Rochester, and worrying over Tante Deacy, I didn't have time to bother with colored sisters. But there they were, already sitting in the left center section, fourth pew from the altar, when we arrived next Sunday. From now on folks would call that the colored sisters' pew, seeing as how they'd sat there two weeks running. Since they were already kneeling and praying when we got there, I didn't get to see the looks they got when they walked up the aisle, but I imagined people weren't happy. Two weeks of colored nuns in a white church were more than most folks would be able to stand. Still, they were nuns, so nothing could be said about it.

I was sorry I'd made us late. It isn't often you get to watch colored sisters parade up Saint Stephen's, relaxed as if they really belonged, which of course they didn't. But making us late was the only way I could be sure Mama'd let me wear my pale blue dress from last summer. Besides, Mavis had the aisle seat this week and would've gotten the better view and never let me forget it either, her being that type of gloating sister.

"What are you digging for?" Mavis had said when we'd been getting ready for church that morning.

I rummaged through the back of the closet I shared with her, looking for my favorite dress from last summer, figuring it to be the coolest thing I owned that was presentable enough to pass Mama's inspection.

Mavis was ready first, as usual. Mama still allowed her to wear sundresses to church so, naturally, that's what she wore. I had plenty of those myself—cotton print, spaghetti straps, open bars across the back. When you reach a certain age, you can't wear those type things to Mass, Mama'd explained last summer. I'd bragged about my being "that certain age" to Mavis every chance I'd gotten. But last summer'd been extra cool and this summer certainly wasn't, so now I was paying for all the bragging I'd done and was ready to trade being "that certain age" for a flimsy sundress. I knew better than to even try getting away with that, but maybe, if I timed it right, I'd get by with the blue sleeveless I'd worn most Sundays last summer.

"What're you doing on my side?" Mavis asked.

I am the only girl I know ready for fifth grade in less than two months, turning ten in less than one month, who does not even have a closet to call her own. Some days I wouldn't mind sharing a room with Mavis forever, if only I could have my own closet.

"Stop touching my stuff. Stop or I'm telling."

I stuck my head out the closet because I knew tattletale Mavis would be good on her word. "I'm looking for *my* blue dress, if you must know."

Mama sometimes pushed things from my side of the closet to Mavis's, where they waited for her to catch up to the size I wasn't anymore. Sure enough, back of Mavis's skirts and blouses and dresses was my blue one. When I turned around with it, Mavis was sitting cross-legged on her side of our bed, watching me like I was a new picture at the Roxy.

"That thing don't fit you anymore." She knew well as I did why Mama'd hung the dress on her side of the closet.

"It's way too big for you," I said. I stripped to my underpants and slipped the dress over my head.

"That dress is too short."

I looked down. The dress had hung below my knees last year. Now it was an inch and a half above, but still felt good as I remembered. Sleeveless. No collar, just rounded neck. Loose as a tent. If I spread my legs, I could get a breeze that'd cool all of me except my privates, which were covered by underpants. I wasn't taking that dress off now, even if it was on the short side.

"Girls, five more minutes," Mama called from her bedroom.

I sat on my side of the bed, across from Mavis and cross-legged like her.

"Mama won't let you wear it," Mavis said.

"We'll see," I said.

"I know she won't."

I crossed my arms and looked at her but didn't say anything.

"I'm right, you know," she said.

I still didn't say anything.

Mavis jumped off the bed and hopped around the room, first on one foot, then the other. I stared after her but didn't say a word. I sat tall, imagined looking like this Indian girl I'd seen in a John Wayne movie—ready for anything, afraid of nothing.

Mavis stopped hopping. "Hope she makes you wear the orange plaid," she whispered, then ran out the room. That orange plaid dress was the ugliest, hottest thing I owned and Mavis knew it. Mama'd gotten the material on sale. The reason it was so cheap was no one would think of dressing someone in material ugly as that. Sometimes my mama gets blinded by the idea of saving money and can't see ugliness staring her in the face.

About two minutes after Mavis left our room, Mama called to me. "Time to go."

I didn't move, just set my face sterner like John Wayne's Indian girl.

Another minute went by. "You're going to make us late," Mama called.

I nodded slowly. My plan exactly.

"Vivien Leigh, get out here now. Right now," Mama yelled.

I unfolded my legs lazily and stretched off the bed. I smoothed the front of the dress, forcing it to hang low as possible. I took one tiny step after another till I was out the bedroom and in the hall where someone might see me, then walked regular to the parlor.

"Anybody seen the keys?" Daddy asked.

"You looked in the can?" Mama asked back.

"Don't know why I should, seeing as how things are never where they're supposed to be in this house."

"Just look."

I crossed my fingers the keys wouldn't be in the black-eyed peas can Mama kept on the kitchen sill. The hubbub that'd follow would stop Mama noticing me. But my luck didn't hold. The keys were right where they were supposed to be and Mama saw me clear.

"What do you think you're wearing?"

"My blue dress," I said, trying to sound as if wearing clothes from a year ago was the most normal thing in the world.

"From last summer," big-mouth Mavis explained, as if explanation were needed.

Mama opened her mouth to say something, then gave me a dirty look instead. She shook her head, knowing it was too late to expect me, a real slowpoke when I have to be, to change. "You take that dress off and give it to me when we get back," is all she said, nudging us out the door.

In the back seat I stuck out my tongue at Mavis, which I don't usually do, being too grown up for such foolishness. But this was one of those occasions when words weren't enough.

After services we were almost home when Daddy said, "Must be going to stay the summer."

"Looks like," Mama said, waving her blue Chinese patterned fan, which wasn't fancy as her pink flamingos to my way of thinking but which matched her aqua dress better.

We pulled into the drive and under the carport. Cleo was probably sleeping under the house, where it was cool and damp and dark. I used to go under there myself sometimes when I wanted to think.

"Somebody needs to show those coloreds where their church is," Daddy said.

"Somebody like you?" Mama said.

"Maybe."

"Floyd! They're sisters, for Heaven's sake," Mama said.

"Never said different."

"Nuns have their special God-given orders and nobody, certainly not a Mister Floyd Dubois, can tell them different." Mama pushed open her door. "Like to see him try. Him trying to order a holy sister around. Some days, Mister, I don't know what gets into you."

Daddy followed Mama into the house, mumbling, "All I meant was it don't seem right. That's all I…" The screen door slammed on his last words.

Mavis climbed into the driver's seat and clicked the turn signal on and off, turned the wheel and honked the horn, but not often enough for anyone to bother coming out to stop her. I thought about following Mama and Daddy into the house, but decided to wait my turn for the wheel. It'd be too hot for any real fighting inside.

I let Mavis have three more honks before I started in pestering for my turn. She whined but after a last honk scooted to the passenger side. I was bigger and meaner and she knew it.

If I stretched my legs and sat on the tip of my tailbone, I could barely touch one of the pedals and peek through the steering wheel to see where I was going. Daddy'd promised I could drive in the pasture when I could see out the window and press pedals at the same time.

"Daddy's sure in a bother about those colored sisters," Mavis said.

I made a sharp left with the wheel, gunned the accelerator, then braked hard, imagining a white rabbit scurrying across the road. "He's always in a bother about something. If it wasn't nuns, it'd be something else, us more than likely. You ought to be grateful to those Negro nuns." I gunned the accelerator again and beeped the horn twice.

"I think Daddy's right." Mavis leaned her chin on the dash and squinted at something I couldn't see. "Them coloreds have no right being in our church every Sunday like that. It's not like they don't have their own church."

"They are nuns, Mavis Ann Dubois. They have God-given orders." I sat up straight even though my foot couldn't touch the pedals anymore. "Mother Ignatius says us whites brought the coloreds from Africa and they didn't want to come anyhow, but now they're here we got to treat them right."

"Mother Ignatius is a Communist," Mavis said. She only said that because she'd heard Daddy say it. If a big shot did something he didn't like, he'd say the Communists were behind it. Far as I could tell Communists were running every northern city, had taken over most of Texas, and were knocking at Louisiana's door. But truth be known I wasn't exactly perfect-paper positive what a Communist was, even though I knew a lot more than baby Mavis.

"You're too dumb to know a Communist from a pile of cow poop." One thing I knew for sure. Mother Ignatius was no Communist. It was a nun rule—sisters cannot be Communists or they'll go straight to Hell without so much as a how do from Saint Peter.

"Know what Marydale says?" Mavis asked.

"I don't care what some little colored girl has been telling you." I pushed over to the passenger side to give Mavis another turn at the wheel. "Marydale hasn't said a true thing since the day she was born cause she's a change-of-life baby." Some days I worried my own cousin would lie much as Marydale, but Mama'd said in some ways change-of-life babies were all different, just like regular babies. Some of them lied, some didn't. She was sure Deacy's baby'd be one of those truth-telling babies.

Mavis honked once and turned the wheel left, then right. "This time Marydale's telling the truth. She double-dog-dared me to ask any other colored kid or even grown-up and see if they didn't say the same and I did." Mavis looked prouder than sin, showing me up. "I asked her mama and her mama said Marydale was telling God's truth."

"Sure, her mama'd say that."

"Aussie does not lie. Ever. Mama says so and you know it." She honked again.

"So out with it." I leaned against my door as if I couldn't care less.

"Marydale says their church has real gold trimming on the altar and real gold crowns for the Virgin Mary and baby Jesus. That gold's worth so much money, they could sell it and get enough to build a brand-new, fancier-than-all-get-out church. They're sworn to keep the gold secret so some no-account white trash don't come stealing it. Marydale swore her oath last year."

"So what's she doing telling you?"

"I'm not white trash," Mavis said. "Besides, she tells me stuff. Don't tell anybody, cause it's secret."

"She tells you stuff. You tell her stuff. So what?"

"Those colored nuns have a plenty fancy church to go to without bothering ours," Mavis said. "So I think Daddy's right." She honked five times, then jumped out and ran into the backyard before Mama or Daddy could shoo her out the car.

I stayed a while longer, turning the wheel and thinking about all that gold.

4

TALK, TALK, TALK

WHEN I WOKE UP THURSDAY, I had the sweet luxury of being all alone in bed. Thursdays were the only days I knew for sure Mavis would be out from underfoot, since Marydale would be here, supposed to be cleaning with her mama, though Marydale never cleaned a thing in her life and got away with it too, her being a change-of-life child.

Aussie or Mama, couldn't tell which, was running the sweeper in the parlor. Looked like a light cleaning day. The only time Mama bothered with the sweeper on an Aussie day was when she wasn't going to tackle any big cleaning job like windows or closets. Too hot for real heavy cleaning, even for Mama, who'd put her housecleaning up against anybody else's and come out a tie, the very least.

I rolled myself over to Mavis's side, which was much cooler than mine, meaning she'd been up a while. Nothing like the promise of Marydale to get Mavis moving. I was sure if I looked out the window, I'd see those fools under the willow, digging for gold that wasn't there because if it had been Daddy would've dug it out years back. Marydale's one dizzy colored girl if she thinks my daddy's sharing gold off his property with her, anyway. Depending on how much there was, I might share some seeing as how she did so much of the digging. But my say wouldn't be the final word in gold sharing. That final word'd go to Mama and Daddy, just like all the other final words in this house.

I yawned, stretched some more, thought about reaching for a library book, then thought different when my stomach growled. Breakfast dishes were soaking when I got to the kitchen. Mama was dicing green peppers, probably for some recipe she was planning for supper. I took my time eating cinnamon toast, slowly pulling off the crusts, keeping the soft centers for last, chewing each bite to mush. I knew those dirty dishes had my name on them.

Sure enough, minute I swallowed my last bite Mama started in on me. "Dishes in the sink need cleaning," she said as if she was talking to no one in particular.

"None of those dishes are mine," I said. I'd already washed and dried the knife I'd used for buttering my toast. Why couldn't the rest of my family take care of their own dishes, same as I did?

"Girl saying the truth, Miz Hazey," Aussie said.

I looked up, surprised because I hadn't heard Aussie come in and double surprised that she might be taking my side in this.

"Well I hope to God I haven't raised myself any liars," Mama said. She swept her cut peppers into a container and put it into the icebox. I wondered what those would go into. Nothing that would be much good, seeing as how I hated green peppers on account of they gave me gas.

"Girl's not a liar, her. That be for sure," Aussie said. She settled in the chair across from me.

"Hardworking girl too," Mama said, pouring the last of the coffee into two mugs, putting one sugar lump in hers, two in Aussie's.

"I didn't know that, me," Aussie said.

Mama sat next to me and handed Aussie a cup. "Sure enough. Don't you know this girl does most of the work around here?"

"No, ma'am. Aussie didn't know that, her."

"She told me herself and you know I don't raise liars."

"That be God's sweet truth," Aussie said. She sipped coffee, but a laugh trying to sneak out her mouth crinkled skin around her eyes. I was in for some business, no getting around it.

"Why do I have to do all the work around here? Why? It isn't fair. Not one bit fair." Mama did her imitation of me in a high-pitched, singsong voice that wasn't close to what I sounded like.

"Girl said that, her?" Aussie asked.

"Sure enough," Mama said.

Aussie shook her head. "You sure be wasting your money on Thursdays. Yes, ma'am, you sure be. Paying Aussie to clean house when this poor, sweet, truth-telling girl work for free."

"I'm a sinful woman is all I can say."

"For what you throw away your husband's money?"

"Hard-earned money too," Mama said.

"I hear that," Aussie said.

I pushed toast crumbs from the edges of my plate to the center, mounding them in the middle, listening to these foolish ladies, one of them my own mama who didn't even have the excuse of being colored.

"Forcing my own flesh and blood to slave her life away," Mama said, continuing her litany of sins.

"God help your soul, Miz Hazey. God help it."

"Amen," Mama said. "Amen to that." She took another swallow of coffee. "Don't just sit there, making a liar out of your mama, Vivien Leigh. Get to those dishes while Aussie and I finish our coffee and be ladies of leisure," Mama said.

"That be us all right. Ladies of leisure," Aussie repeated. She loosed that deep, rumbling laugh that sounded like a church bell, low and loud.

Mama laughed too, though hers wasn't big as Aussie's.

If a person had to be stuck with dishes, breakfast was the meal to do at my house. None of us Dubois were big early-morning eaters so, most times, all a washer had to clean were a few spoons, bowls or small plates, coffee cups or juice glasses. No pots or pans, which any regular dishwasher can tell you are the worst. Some mornings, though, Daddy decides he's in the mood for bacon, eggs, grits to keep his cornflakes and toast company. Lucky for me this wasn't one of those mornings.

I let out the cold water where the dishes had been soaking and ran warm with more soap than I needed because I like bubbles covering all my dirty dishes and my hands too. If Mama and Aussie hadn't been at the table, I would've squeezed soap between my hands and blown huge bubbles all over the kitchen. Mama wouldn't abide such foolishness in front of her and especially not in front of visitors or strangers, though Aussie didn't exactly fit in either category.

I stroked the dishes and bowls with my bare hands. That didn't count as real washing. I'd have to pass the dishrag over them for true cleaning. I wasn't sluffing my duty, just enjoying the smooth feel of my hands filled with bubbles and warm water, rubbing against china, though not real china, which only came out for Christmas, Easter, and other fancy occasions.

Mama and Aussie hummed behind me. I barely listened. The chores they talked about doing when the hot weather broke didn't interest me at all. But my ears perked when I heard plans for fig preserving. I loved eating fig preserves much as I hated making them. That'd be the one day of summer Mama'd wake me and Mavis early, before sunrise. We'd drive out to Mama's oldest aunt's house to climb the fig trees in her backyard. Deacy would be there and, if she was lucky, at least one of her sons. Often as not Tante Deacy'd be stuck picking those figs herself, though I'm sure she didn't have the eating to herself come winter.

After we picked all our bushel baskets could hold, we'd come home and do the canning. Heat up the kitchen like a piece of Hell but end up with enough preserves for us, Deacy, Aussie, and Tante Yvette, Deacy's and Mama's aunt strictly speaking, but the closest thing to a grandmother me and Mavis and my worthless boy cousins had on our mamas' side because our real grandma, Yvette's sister, died when I was two. Malcolm says he remembers her fine. The boy is lying, of course. Just wants to have something over me. T.J. remembers her and Malcolm should be satisfied with that, T.J. being closer flesh to Malcolm than to me. But Malcolm wants to be the middle of everything, even the middle of remembering. Comes from being the middle child, I imagine.

"They were back again," Mama said. "Two Sundays in a row now."

"That's what it be for sure," Aussie said. When I turned back to the table to get my toast plate for washing, Aussie was grabbing a second powdered doughnut from the package Mama'd opened for the two of them. White confectioner's sugar circled Aussie's mouth, turned her into a Halloween mask, a ghost face just beginning.

"People are wondering. You know how people are," Mama said.

"Yes, ma'am. I know people and that's for sure."

"Daddy wants to know why they're not going to the colored church." I eyed the three doughnuts left in the carton and turned my plate, still on the table, in a small circle.

"Them sisters are following the Lord's word," Aussie said. "He show the way and they got to follow."

"No matter what. Just what I told Floyd." Mama's fingers inched toward the treats, then back to her coffee cup, maybe remembering about Marydale and our needing that third doughnut for her. Course if there wasn't enough treat to go around, Mavis'd share, a bite for her, a bite for Marydale, a bite for her till that tiny doughnut was all gone. Mavis was too young to know about colored germs. Even if she did know, she didn't care. Half the time I think the girl forgot Marydale was colored.

"Them colored sisters think they're better than our colored folks. That's what they're thinking, going to the white church that way," I said. I pulled the doughnut box closer to me, though not so close it'd seem I was claiming them for my own, stopping Mama or Aussie from another treat if that's what they wanted.

"Vivien Leigh, haven't I raised you better than to talk about holy sisters that way?"

I went back to the sink, scrubbing my plate as if it was a greased-up pan.

"Well, haven't I?" Mama insisted.

Sometimes Mama asks questions I have no idea how to answer. Was the answer, "Yes, ma'am, that must be how you raised me cause if it wasn't, I wouldn't of said what I said"? That's not what she wanted to hear. Was the right answer, "No, ma'am, somebody else has been raising me when you weren't looking, so what I said isn't your fault"? Neither answer made sense. Left with yes and no both wrong, I kept my mouth shut.

"I expect an answer, Vivien Leigh." Mama's voice was hot as the air that pressed down on all of us, though it was only ten-thirty, not even close to the real hot part of the day.

"Yes, ma'am," I mumbled.

"Girl only be a baby, Miz Hazey," Aussie said.

I jerked my head around to give Aussie a dirty look that said I wasn't anybody's baby. But I didn't say anything to go with my look because I knew she was trying to help me out.

"Girl's old enough to know right from wrong, how to talk the right way about holy sisters, God chosen and above us all, coloreds and whites alike."

"Right and wrong, she not always so easy to see," Aussie said.

"That's right," I said. "I get confused about that myself sometimes."

"Most times, far as I can tell," Mama said.

"I know colored sisters belong in a colored church, same as the rest of colored folks. Isn't that right?" I was on solid ground there. "We've got to treat coloreds right, like Mother Ignatius says. But that doesn't mean we've got to let them in white churches. Let them go to their own churches like all the other coloreds." I pulled the plug from the sink, ran water to drain the last suds out the bowl, then rinsed my hands and wiped them on my shorts, which were still clean, since I hadn't been outside yet.

"If you were half big as your mouth, you'd be full grown and that's a fact," Mama said.

I leaned against the icebox and slid down, my back pressing against it till I was sitting on the floor, waiting for the okay on those doughnuts.

"Them sisters go to our church. Same as they go to yours," Aussie said. She passed her tongue over her top lip, swiping at her powdered-sugar mustache.

"They've been to church at Saint Paul's?" Mama asked, surprise in her voice and on her face.

"Six o'clock evening services. Two weeks running."

"Are you sure they're the same sisters? Could be different visiting sisters," I said.

"They be the same," Aussie said, sure as she was pronouncing judgment on one of Mama's experiment desserts.

"Why they going to evening Mass when they've already been to morning Mass?" Nobody I knew, not even sisters, was made to go to two services a day, not even on Sunday.

Aussie wet the tip of a finger and passed it around her lips, then licked that last bit of sweetness.

"Person can't ever get too much holy blessings. You know that," Mama said.

I looked at Aussie, waiting for the real explanation. But she didn't say anything.

"I don't know what all the fuss is about anyhow," Mama said. "Colored sisters aren't hurting a thing at Saint Stephen's. Not a thing."

"Not hurting a thing," Aussie echoed.

"Folks just like to talk is all."

"Talking is all some folks do," Aussie said.

"Some folks think they'll dry up into raisins if they can't talk," Mama said. She ran water into the mugs she and Aussie had used and left them soaking in the sink.

"Talk, talk, talk is all some folks know," Aussie said. She pushed up from the table and followed Mama to my bedroom, where one of them'd run the sweeper and the other one'd do the dusting. The noise of that sweeper would drown out their words for a while. But when the sweeper cut off, they'd go back to their talking. Words, back and forth, glided in the space between Mama and Aussie. So many words, person would think they had nobody else to talk with the rest of the week when they were apart. Those ladies were fine ones to talk about other folks' talk.

I grabbed the leftover doughnuts and ran outside to find Mavis and Marydale. I could've kept the treats to myself and those girls never would've known the difference. But I'm not greedy, least not when it comes to powdered doughnuts in a box.

The two of them were under the willow, just as I expected. Their gold hole was big enough to bury a cat. Only tools they had between them were Mavis's plastic sand bucket and shovel and an old wooden spoon, so they'd gotten quite a bit done. Daddy'd had a fit when he'd spotted his trowels next to the willow and had forbidden Mavis from using a single thing from his shed. The yelling she'd gotten was still fresh enough in her ears to force even Mavis into obedience, at least for now. I wondered whether Mama'd seen the hole yet. I thought about telling on them but decided to save the news for when I needed it, which, with Mavis, could never be predicted.

"Got a treat for you girls," I said.

"What did you bring?" Mavis called, sitting behind her willow curtain with her legs crossed. The girl wasn't satisfied with knowing she had a treat. She had to know exactly what the treat was so she could decide whether to reach up for it.

"You want a treat or not?"

"Well, what is it?"

"Sure," Marydale said. "Mavis and me ready for a treat."

"Tell us what you brought." Mavis's cheeks were beginning to puff out.

I wasn't looking for midget-sized trouble this morning, so I brought the doughnut box out from behind my back. "I choose first since I brought them."

Both girls nodded. They knew fair. Mavis's cheeks shrank back to normal. The girl is part chipmunk, I'm sure.

"Marydale, you seen those visiting nuns at your church?" I asked when I'd eaten all but the last bite of doughnut.

"Marydale doesn't know why those colored sisters bother with Saint Stephen's," Mavis said.

"Saint Paul's be good as Saint Stephen's," Marydale said.

"Better," Mavis said. She was thinking about all that gold.

"When they leaving is what I want to know." I dropped the last bite of doughnut in my mouth and sucked my fingers clean.

"Leaving when the Lord give them the word, cause they're sisters," Marydale said.

"Holy sisters," Mavis added.

"They got the calling from Jesus and they following his word. Don't nobody but God know when those sisters be leaving."

"Just God," Mavis said.

"God and Tante Deacy's change-of-life baby," I said. I dug a toe into the dirt piled next to their gold hole. A few clumps trickled into the hole, enough to make Mavis's cheeks start puffing.

"Watch that. Watch it or I'll tell."

I gave her a disgusted look. I was the one going to tell on her about this hole, but she was too backward to know it.

"Miz Deacy's baby got nothing to do with them sisters."

"She's the one called them here to my way of thinking." I pulled my toe out the dirt pile slowly so none of it fell into their precious hole.

Mavis and Marydale looked at each other to see whether this was something they should believe. They swiveled their heads toward me in the same instant.

"That baby can't be calling nobody cause it's not got itself born yet and them who's not born can't do nothing," Marydale said in one quick breath, with Mavis bobbing her head up and down just as fast next to her.

"You sure don't know much about change-of-life babies for being one yourself," I said.

"She knows more than you," Mavis said, cheeks puffing because I'd insulted her friend.

I parted the willow curtains. "That change-of-life baby brought those sisters here and she's the only one knows when they'll leave or what they've got to do before they leave." I dropped the willow curtain and stepped into sunshine too bright and too hot for so early in the day.

5

LOOKING FOR ANSWERS

I LET MY BOOK SIGH CLOSED and rolled from my stomach to my back. Sometimes I got awful tired of summer, though I wouldn't admit to something so foolish without getting a serious secret told in exchange. Long day following long day, time stretching thin and flat in the heat. I missed my school friends—Clorise and her stories, Lena and her jokes, even Willie and his strange change-of-life ways. They were town children who got to visit each other whenever they wanted, least that's what I imagined. We were country people and country children don't go tramping to other folks' houses whenever the notion hits them. So Mama says. Oh to be a town girl, even for only the summer. Frying a breakfast egg on the sidewalk would chase boredom out anybody's head. Maybe fry other things too. Chickens, hot dogs, burgers. There might be no end to what a person could cook on an August sidewalk in Louisiana. Not that I'd be eating any of that. Still, town children had it easy, surrounded as they were by so much available entertainment.

"Vivien Leigh, you want to ride Aussie home, then go to Deacy's a while?" Mama called from the kitchen. Aussie could've walked home easy as anything, her house being just down the road about a quarter of a mile. Even Mavis and Marydale walked it. But Mama insisted on the driving each week. Made Daddy pick up Aussie each Thursday morning, while she drove Aussie home each Thursday afternoon. "Person does for you, you do for them," is how Mama explained it. She didn't listen to Daddy fussing over wasted time, wasted gas.

By the time I got to the car Marydale and Mavis were hugging the two side windows in the back. I hated the middle seat, but that's where I was stuck. I hoped Aussie would invite us in for some treat, but she didn't, probably because Mama was there. Mama seldom went into Aussie's house except for Christmas, maybe a First Communion. Even I visited more times than that, course not near often as Mavis did.

Mavis begged to stay but didn't fuss too much when Mama said no, she was going to visit her aunt and cousins and that was that. If Mavis had her way, she'd move in with old Marydale. That's how dumb Mavis was.

T.J. was sitting on the front steps, pitching rocks at the china ball tree at the edge of his drive. That boy was too slow to take any advantage of being a town child.

"Where's your mama, T.J.?" Mama asked.

He turned a blank look on her as if she were asking the way to Mars. "Inside, I guess. Maybe out back."

Mama hurried inside, shaking her head at such stupidity, probably amazed as me that the high school'd let in someone dumb as that. Anybody can get themselves an education nowadays and that's God's truth.

Mavis ran to the swing hanging from the pecan tree back of the house. If she was lucky, Malcolm or Austin wouldn't of heard the car and beat her there. I'm sure those boys never touched that swing unless me and Mavis were around. My cousins were born selfish, would die selfish unless Tante Deacy's change-of-life baby pointed them in a different direction.

I sat next to T.J. and grabbed a handful from the rocks he'd piled next to him. Boy wouldn't of thought to offer me any himself. He stared at the rocks in my hand but didn't say anything, because he knew better. My first rock hit the tree dead center. I looked over at T.J. to make sure he'd seen.

"Where's Malcolm and Austin?" I didn't hear any screaming from the backyard, which meant the boys weren't out there and Mavis had the swing to herself.

"Around," T.J. said.

"I could figure that for myself." I threw a second rock, which barely managed to graze the lowest branch on the left side of the tree. I threw another one against the lowest branch on the right, pretending that's what I'd intended all along.

"Uncle Everett home yet?"

"It's not six, is it?"

"Thought maybe this was his afternoon off." Everett worked at the IGA, unloading trucks, running a cash register, stocking shelves. He was assistant manager, but far as I could tell that just meant he did whatever Mister Alan didn't feel like doing. At least he got off one Thursday afternoon each month, which was more than Daddy could say about his job checking oil tanks.

"I think next week's his day off. Or maybe two weeks coming." He shot a rock that hit leaves at the top of the tree.

"You ready for school?" If he admitted to being tired with summer, I might do the same.

"It's a ways to go."

"You start in three weeks," I reminded. Public school always started the Monday before Labor Day. Holy Rosary didn't kick in till the Wednesday after. Catholic children were not in as sore a need of educating as public children, though you couldn't prove that looking at T.J. and Malcolm, who'd gone to Holy Rosary through sixth and then switched to public because Holy Rosary didn't go to seventh. Couldn't tell it looking at Austin either even though he was still at Holy Rosary, be in fourth come September. That boy needed more educating, not less.

T.J. walked to the china ball tree, went down on all fours to pick up the rocks we'd thrown. I went over to help without him even asking. "Mowing machine hit one of these rocks, it could fly up and kill a person," I said.

"Don't be stupid."

"Nothing stupid about getting knocked up the side of your head with a rock going a hundred miles an hour. Dead. You'd be dead as dirt, if that happened."

"Don't bother me with your stupid stuff."

"You're sure the expert on stupid," I said. "If you say it's stupid, it must be stupid," I said slow and sassy. I dumped the rocks I'd picked in a pile next to the steps, then went in to see if Mama and Tante Deacy had anything interesting going because T.J. sure didn't. Probably never would, poor boy.

They weren't in the kitchen, drinking coffee, where I'd expected to find them. I followed voices to Deacy's bedroom. She and Mama sat on the bed, folding towels. I sat at the vanity, opened Tante Deacy's jewelry box, and decorated myself with the fanciest things I could find. Deacy always was one for dressing herself fancy, Mama says. She and Everett used to dress up and drive to Baton Rouge for supper and dancing. Once they spent the night in a swank New Orleans hotel. That was before they got plagued with those boys. I couldn't quite imagine Everett looking fancy, but I could see a fancy Deacy in my mind every time I fiddled with her necklaces, bracelets, earrings, brooches, all her beautiful things.

"Don't tangle those necklaces," Mama said.

"Vivien Leigh's always careful," Tante Deacy said.

I smiled at her smiling at me in the mirror and circled a pearl necklace three times around my neck, then pinched matching earrings on my lobes.

"You been to Doc Joubert yet?" Mama asked. She folded a wide pink towel that looked soft in the mirror.

Deacy buried her nose in a towel, smelling cleanness same as I did sometimes when I folded towels. "I'll go soon."

"When?" Mama was never one for letting things slide, even other people's things.

"Soon."

"Baby can't wait too long." She snapped a washcloth in the air, then folded it into quarters.

"Baby's fine." Deacy folded a rose towel into even rectangles. "I'm fine. Boys are fine. Everything's fine and dandy."

I noticed who she'd left out of that listing of fine same as Mama. I took all the bracelets out and lined them up, darkest to lightest, but I worked softly, wanting to hear more, not wanting to scare the ladies into quiet.

"Everett still acting the ass?" Mama asked.

I swallowed a giggle. "Hi, Uncle Ass." Mama'd skin me if I said that, but it'd sure be hard not to next time I saw him.

"Hazey, don't," Deacy said.

"The man's being an ass. No getting around it this time." Mama flapped another washcloth, louder than the first.

"We had our family. You know that. We weren't counting on another." She patted her belly, which pushed out a little but was still flatter than most women's. "T.J. in high school. Only eight more years before Austin graduated. We could see the end."

I nodded agreement. If those boys were mine, I'd be counting the days till they were out my house too.

"Never an end to being a parent," Mama said.

"That's true. *End's* the wrong word. No end to being a mama." She passed a hand across a towel, gently smoothing one place over and over. "We could see the boys on their own is what I meant. The house cleared out. Things more peaceful is all I meant."

She was thinking about those fancy dances. The dresses she never wore anymore. The golden fineries she hardly ever bothered with. I bit my tongue to stop from saying I understood it all.

"Everett's still adjusting is all. He'll come around."

"Takes two to tango. You remind him," Mama said.

"Everett doesn't need to be reminded about dancing."

"One thing about your Everett. He always was the best dancer on the floor."

"The best," Deacy said, such a faraway smile on her face I guessed she heard a band playing in her head just for her.

When we got home, the letter was waiting. Mama hardly finished reading it before she was on the phone to Deacy, who hadn't gotten hers yet and made Mama read every single word twice. After that Mama called up must've been every one of the Altar Society ladies. Some had gotten the letter, some not. Mama read that letter out loud so often, I practically had it memorized.

"I don't even want to see what Floyd's going to be like when he reads this," Mama started off saying to Deacy and ended up saying to every other lady she called. I couldn't hear the other end of the conversations, but from what I could tell each lady said something close to the same about her Everett or Sam or Carroll or Joe or whatever husband she happened to have. Seems the men were going to be particularly worked up about this. Why, I don't know. They weren't the ones going to be staring at colored teachers all day.

The welcome-back-to-school letter never actually came right out and said two new teachers would be Negro. But it hemmed and hawed enough so there was no doubt that's what it was meaning. First and fifth, my grade, were the ones supposed to be having colored sisters. I couldn't come close to imagining having a colored for a teacher. Getting ordered about by a colored. Getting your hand whacked by a colored. It was all too much to imagine.

But if I had trouble getting this picture straight in my mind, Daddy sure didn't. Mama'd waited till we'd finished supper and she'd stuck me and Mavis in the kitchen with dirty dishes before pulling out the letter. Daddy is always more likely to yell on an empty stomach than a full one. But even Mama's lemon meringue pie, Daddy's favorite, which she'd baked up that afternoon when she finally got off the phone, wouldn't be enough to quiet Daddy when he saw that letter.

Mama started off easy. "Girls got their back-to-school letter today," she said.

Daddy was in his recliner, flipping through *Popular Mechanics,* which had arrived that day. Mama should've waited. She knew well as me that Daddy did not like being bothered the first chance he had to read a new *Popular Mechanics.* But Mama wanted the news out and over with.

"Here. Read it."

I was washing dishes so quietly, I heard the letter rattle, passing from Mama's hand to Daddy's. I looked at Mavis, who was drying soft as I was washing. She rolled her eyes but kept quiet.

We waited for the explosion. The letter wasn't that long. He could've read it four times by now. We waited and waited. Finally, when I thought I'd explode myself, Daddy let out the loudest "shit" I'd ever heard. I dropped the plate I'd been cleaning. Good thing it landed on the dishrag, else it would've broken for sure.

That first "shit" was followed by more, just like Mama and her friends had predicted. "Shits" were flying in houses all across town right now. Anywhere a Holy Rosary child lived, curses filled the air. Even homes without Holy Rosary children, where the news had reached, would be filled with shouts of aggravation and more. All those words, flying out open windows, floating up the sky, a cloud of curses, all aimed at two colored sisters set to teach in a white school. That change-of-life baby was doing itself proud.

"What the hell is this world coming to? That's all I want to know," Daddy said when he could finally manage more than "shit."

"Guess the convent had trouble getting nuns for Holy Rosary, this being such a little school, out-of-the-way place and all," Mama said, her voice easy as if they were talking plans for Sunday dinner.

"Trouble, hell. If they want trouble, this'll give it to them."

"I'm sure they didn't have any choice."

"There's always a choice. Always."

I was already old enough to know that wasn't right. Sometimes choices aren't free for the asking.

"Close the school. Maybe that was the only other possibility," Mama said.

"Then close the damn school. Do it, if it comes to that."

Mavis waved an arm in the air and hopped on one foot. I could've told the fool girl we'd just get sent to public instead. But I let her be because at least she was hopping quietly.

"Don't talk foolishness, Floyd," Mama said, her voice still easy.

"Coloreds trying to teach whites. That's the foolishness."

I pulled the plug from the drain and rinsed the sink best I could with the dribble of water I ran so I could still hear the parlor talk.

"It's not right, Hazel. You know that well as I do."

"Sure," Mama said.

Even I knew this wasn't right.

"What'll happen next? That's what I'm wondering," Daddy said. "Colored nuns in the church. Colored teachers in the school. What's next? Niggers sitting next to Mavis in school. That's where it's all heading. I'm telling you right now, that's where things are heading."

Mavis grinned wider, hopped wilder around the kitchen, bumped a chair, which would've fallen if I hadn't been there to catch it. Girl couldn't see a thing wrong with doing her spelling lessons next to a colored, especially if that colored was Marydale.

"Maybe it's temporary, just till they can get white nuns in here," Mama said.

"What's wrong with those nuns anyway? Whoever heard a nun saying she wouldn't go someplace? Mother Superior says 'go,' a sister goes. Isn't that how those things work?" Daddy asked.

"Far as I know," Mama said.

"By the time they find white sisters it'll be too late. Damage done and everything too late."

"It might not be so bad," Mama said. "They're nuns after all. Well educated."

"They're coloreds. Nothing more. Nothing less."

"They've been called to do the Lord's work," Mama said.

"Then let them get called to some little colored school. Let them do the Lord's work there."

I waited for Mama to say something back, but she didn't. She knew well as Daddy that colored sisters belonged in a colored school, in a colored church, saving colored souls so's they'd be welcomed in the colored side of Heaven. No one had ever told me about Heaven being split in two, colored on one side, white on the other. Catechism books never showed half of Heaven white, the other half colored. But how could it be any other way and things still be right and perfect, which is what Heaven promises to be?

"Something's going to have to get done is all." Daddy slammed his recliner to the floor.

I sat at a kitchen chair where I could see into the parlor. The book opened on the table in front of me could've been closed just as easy for all the attention I paid it. Daddy paced the parlor, so bothered he couldn't sit any longer. His neck creases were ringed with sweat and half moons of wetness showed at his armpits.

Normalwise Daddy wasn't much for getting riled in the middle of August, especially an August hot as this one. But this was serious. This was bigger than our school, for sure bigger than first and fifth. Like Daddy'd said, if colored sisters could move in on a white school, who knew what would happen next? Before you knew it there'd be coloreds at school, in church, even using the drinking fountains at Chaisson's, the high-class clothes store where Mavis and me only went for Christmas and Easter out-fits. Drinking right after a colored. Just thinking about catching colored germs gave me the creeps.

Daddy paced back and forth while Mama watched, not saying any-thing, which must've meant she agreed because she never was one for keeping her feelings to herself, especially when she thought Daddy was going wrong.

"Give a colored an inch, he'll take a mile every time."

Mama must've looked doubtful about that one, though I couldn't see her face from where I was sat.

Daddy stopped pacing to stand in front of her. "Take Marydale."

"Marydale's got nothing to do with any of this. Less than nothing."

"Starts off she's here when her mama's cleaning. Fine. Nothing wrong with that. Nothing wrong with her learning her mama's job cause she'll be doing same thing someday, more than likely."

Mavis had stopped hopping. "Marydale's flying helicopters when she's grown," she said in a low voice so Daddy wouldn't hear.

"Next thing I know I'm as likely to find Marydale as Mavis or Vivien Leigh when I get home. Here more than she's at her own house." I could've told him Mavis was over there much as Marydale was over here. But he was wound up enough without that piece added to it.

"Marydale's a child, for Heaven's sake," Mama said.

"Never said different. We gave an inch, she's taking a mile. Same as any other colored. That's all I'm saying."

"The girls entertain each other. Keeps Mavis out of my hair. So don't worry about it."

"Maybe I should be worried, should do something."

Mavis slid to the floor and pulled a bare foot up so she could pick off loose skin around her toenails. She pretended she wasn't listening anymore, but I knew better. Her eyes squinted like they did when she was leaning over a sheet of subtraction.

"Just you imagine a roomful of Mavises, all under the spell of some colored sister." Daddy was pacing again. Even though he wouldn't have any kids of his own starting school, he was more doubled over by the idea of a Negro in first than he was about me having one in fifth because kids in first were too young to know there's something wrong with having a Negro teacher when you're white. You could look at Mavis and tell that. This summer she'd stopped telling people her best friend was colored, but we all knew she'd rather play with Marydale than anybody else.

"As I see it, there's nothing to be done about it, so you might as well calm yourself," Mama said.

"Nothing to be done? That's what you think? Nothing to be done? I'm thinking different, thinking something sure has to get done." He sat on the sofa next to Mama. "Question is what."

He was quiet a while, thinking, I supposed. Mavis hadn't moved from the floor but now her legs were stretched out and she was leaning against a cabinet, still as she ever got.

"I'll call Everett. See what he hears at the store," Daddy said at last.

"Everett has home business to take care of. He doesn't need to be messing with this."

"He hears things at that store." Daddy didn't bother with a joke about the change-of-life baby. Most times he acted as if it was the funniest baby ever when Everett's name was mentioned.

He picked up the receiver and dialed. I imagined the ringing in Deacy's kitchen where she kept her phone. Daddy covered the mouthpiece. "We got to think on doing something about Marydale too. Don't need a colored girl on our place so much." He turned back to the phone, held it a long time, but no one answered. You'd think at least one of those no-account boys would be home, not to mention Tante Deacy or Uncle Everett. But they weren't. All Daddy got for his dialing and his waiting was the ringing in his ears.

"You girls finished in that kitchen?" Mama called.

"Yes, ma'am. All done," I said. That was only true for my part. Half the dishes still sat in the drainer. I got up to finish drying and saving them. Mavis sat on the floor, still not moving. But her cheeks were puffed so round she looked like a balloon liable to float to the ceiling any second. Her eyes squinted into narrow slits. No messing with Mavis right then. But the girl better not make a habit of leaving her work for me to do. I was doing her dishes because I was being generous tonight. No other reason. "Don't make a habit of this," I whispered so Mama wouldn't hear.

She didn't act as if she'd heard me any more than Mama had.

In the parlor Daddy was dialing again, bound to find someone with an answer tonight. But even I could've told him some answers can't be had for all the dialing on earth. One look at Mavis said that plain as anything. But either Daddy didn't know or wouldn't admit that. He just went on dialing, looking for answers he might never find.

6

BABY WITH THE DANCING FEET

BY THE TIME DADDY GOT HOLD of Everett, Mama was shooing me and Mavis to our room. Didn't matter since we could still hear the whole thing clear as if we were on the parlor sofa instead of on our bed. Daddy was talking loud as a snare drum in a Mardi Gras parade.

Mavis and I promised each other to stay up and listen to the goings-on. But Mavis was snoring by ten. Girl can't keep problems in her head long enough to worry her awake past bedtime, even in summer. Mama would've licked me good if she knew I was up till Daddy and Edwin Sonnier hung up close to midnight. I listened to it all from my bed, Mavis snoring in one ear, Daddy fussing in the other, my ears too unbalanced to even consider falling asleep.

"We pay good money for that school," Daddy said at least fifty times that night. "We don't have to stand for such things, my friend," he said.

Only time Mama said anything was when Daddy let slip about those colored sisters being nothing but niggers, nuns or no nuns.

"Mister, you watch that," Mama said. "This is a Catholic house, not some heathen bar. Sisters are sisters and don't think God forgets that. Coloreds need sisters same as anybody else."

Daddy didn't say anything back and, even though it didn't calm him down any, he didn't use *nigger* again. Seemed you couldn't be a nigger if you were a nun, but I couldn't quite figure which Commandment said so.

Between phone calls Daddy kept up his pacing, back and forth in front of Mama darning socks on the sofa. "Nuns or no nuns, things are getting out of hand. What's next? That's what everybody's wondering," he said over and over.

Around eleven I got up to go to the bathroom, pressing myself against the wall when Daddy shifted in my direction. But he was too worked up to notice a speck like me.

When I got back to the bedroom, I shifted the fan at the foot of our bed so it was hitting me more than Mavis, though I still left some air blowing on her. She was snoring and not sweating, so that little bit of fan air was probably more than she even needed.

I was surprised to still be so hot this late at night. Usually by bedtime the air cooled so a person could breathe without her lungs feeling like they were taking in nothing but fire and flame. Not this night, though. Daddy afire in the parlor. Men, maybe some ladies too, afire all across tiny Ville d'Angelle, town people and country people alike. It was more than the air could take on top of regular August hotness.

By the end of the night Daddy was part of something called Concerned Citizens for a Decent Education. I liked the sound of part of that—Concerned Citizens—and thought I might be one when I got old enough. Far as I could tell the Concerned Citizens were going to beg money from everybody they knew till they had enough to drag Miss Boudreaux out of retirement to teach first. They knew they didn't have a chance of raising enough to cover someone for fifth too, so they didn't bother trying. I guessed the grown-ups figured we were old enough to take care of ourselves. I fell asleep thinking how it'd be to have a colored sister standing at the front of my classroom in less than a month. I wondered if she'd be bossy as regular white sisters. Me with a colored boss. Impossible to even imagine.

I got up early, not even nine, but Daddy'd been gone for a good while anyhow. No one got to Daddy's job later than seven-thirty without Mister Jack, the boss, asking if the man was sick or if someone had died to make him so late. Mister Jack said it like a joke so everybody laughed, but everyone knew it wasn't a joke.

The sky was dark, sun hidden by gray clouds that promised rain before noon. It was still too hot and too clammy, but those clouds held out hope of relief.

A note on the kitchen table said Mama'd taken Mavis grocery shopping. I was to do the dishes, make my bed, and dust the parlor if I had time. Course I knew right away I wouldn't be having time for any dusting, would probably barely have time for the bed that was half Mavis's so why should I be stuck with the making of all of it.

I was almost done my first bowl of Sugar Pops when Marydale came flying through the back door, looking for Mavis. I expected her to leave after I explained Mavis was grocery shopping and only God and Mama knew when she'd be back. But Marydale sat herself down across from me.

"Me, can I have some dry?" she asked and pointed to my cereal.

"Okay by me. Get one of the mugs and I'll pour you some."

"Don't need a mug," Marydale said and proceeded to pour herself a pile of Sugar Pops on the table in front of her.

"Your mama taught you better than that."

She popped her Pops, one at a time, into her mouth and snapped her teeth down on each one. "Your table, she be clean."

Couldn't argue with her there. If Daddy'd been home, he would've told her we wanted our table to stay clean, didn't want colored germs spread all over our table, not even little-girl colored germs. But I was too polite to say that.

I poured more Sugar Pops and watched them float on my leftover milk. "Aussie'd sure be aggravated if she knew her sweet Marydale was eating off some table, even the cleanest table in Heaven."

Marydale didn't answer back, knowing I was right as could be. She just kept popping those Pops.

"You hear the colored sisters news?" I asked.

"Sure. I seen those sisters at church plenty, me. I told you that."

"I'm not talking church. I'm talking Holy Rosary School."

Marydale stopped chomping Pops. This was news to her, I could see.

"Holy Rosary's getting itself two colored sisters come September. One for fifth, one for first. Except the Concerned Citizens are getting Miss Boudreaux to teach first so I don't know what that colored sister who thinks she'll have first will do with herself."

"You be sure?"

"Course I'm sure. Wasn't my own daddy on the phone half the night organizing this Concerned Citizens club?"

"I never heard of no Concerned Citizens, me."

"You never heard of colored sisters at Holy Rosary neither. But that's true as can be. I've got the proof."

"What proof you talking?"

I told her about the letter and even got it out the holder on the kitchen counter where Mama'd put it after last night's ruckus. Marydale didn't catch all the words, her being a seven-year-old shrimp like Mavis. But she got enough to know I was speaking nothing but God's own truth.

She finished her pile of Pops but didn't reach for more. Marydale was one amazed little colored girl. "Mama sure be surprised," she said.

"Everybody's pretty surprised." I carried my bowl and spoon to the sink and added them to the other dishes soaking. One of these days I want somebody to tell me why I'm the only one in this family always stuck with dirty dishes. But since those dishes looked to me like they could use more soaking, I went back to sit across Marydale.

"I'll be having myself a colored sister for fifth," I said.

"Same as me." Marydale grinned like she'd put something over me.

"I expect my colored sister'll be smarter, better trained than the ones at your school."

"I expect she'll be the same. No difference at all. Sisters get trained the same cause they's called by the same Lord Jesus, Amen. Might be those Holy Rosary white sisters be teaching my school next year. Might be this just the beginning of everything getting flipped upside down and backward."

"White nuns aren't having anything to do with Sacred Heart Elementary. Don't waste your brain thinking different."

Marydale got up for the dishrag to wipe her crumbs from the table. Looked to be a well-set habit with her. Made me think she was accustomed to eating off a table whenever she felt like it. Her being a change-of-life baby meant her mama let her get away with lots more than she'd allow an ordinary child.

"Could be the start of whites going to Sacred Heart, coloreds to Holy Rosary. Everything all mixed up. Mavis and me'd be in the same class." She flipped the dishrag into the sink.

"Over my daddy's dead body and don't forget it."

Marydale hopped on one foot from the sink to the table and back again, looking like a colored version of Mavis. "This here be the beginning of change."

I was afraid she might be right. Change-of-life babies are known for knowing more than ordinary folks in ways so mysterious they don't understand it themselves.

"Change, change, change," Marydale chanted, hopping across the kitchen like an out-of-control kangaroo. She landed next to the table, poured a handful of Pops for the road, then hopped out the door, maybe hopped herself all the way home. Nobody'd think anything of it, just another silly colored girl is what folks'd think. When you're colored you can act wild and crazy as you want and people don't think a thing about it, just figure you're acting colored. Far as I can tell that's about the only good thing about being colored, but it's better than nothing.

I was half through the dishes when the rain started. I scooped a mound of suds and played it back and forth from hand to hand while I stood at the back door, watching heavy drops smack the ground. Mavis and Marydale's hole would fill up fast, turn to a muddy mishmash. But soon as the rain stopped those girls'd be out there digging, hoping the rain had loosed some gold. They'd dig even knowing they were getting filthier than sin, knowing they'd be in big trouble with Mama and Aussie. Those girls don't know enough to act different so as to keep out trouble's way.

Rain hammered the tin roof now, loud as cymbals. Lightning cracked the sky in two. I was sure glad I hadn't gone shopping, stuck carrying grocery sacks in this downpour. With the rain, Mama'd be late getting home. I figured I had at least an extra hour. Still, I did finish the dishes and made my bed before I took up my book. I was rereading *Black Beauty*, which I liked to do every so often to let myself be sad. Cleo curled against me on the sofa. I scratched behind her ears with one hand and held my book with the other. I showed her the picture of Beauty as a colt when everything was fine and easy.

"Things'll get bad pretty soon," I warned Cleo.

She purred, saying she didn't care what happened to some horse in a book. Like most cats, Cleo was selfish. Only thing she wanted was a soft bed, a saucer of milk and bowl of tuna for a treat every once in a while, and regular food and water. Long as she had that, she didn't care about anything else.

"You're just lucky you're mine. You're dependent on humans, same as Beauty," I told her.

She turned up her nose as if to say, Am not. Then she swished her tail, chased it in a quick circle before landing in a ball against my folded legs. Cleo was full of herself, saw her life set with no chance of anything bad catching up to her. Cleo had no gratitude for me keeping up with her wants like I did. But in spite of her sassy attitude, I didn't think about missing her food, not even for one day, to teach her a lesson in appreciating her good fortune. She was mine and I knew how to watch over her, better than Black Beauty's owners watched over her for sure.

I was deep into a good, but not especially sad, part of my book when Tante Deacy called from the kitchen. "Anybody home?"

"Me," I said. I dog-eared my page, then went to meet her.

"Didn't you hear me calling?"

"I was reading."

She shook her umbrella out the back door, then placed it, opened, on the kitchen floor to dry. "I brought you folks some cucumbers and lima beans, but I can't carry them and the umbrella too."

"Want me to?" I liked lima beans with butter and salt and pepper, though I didn't much care for cucumbers.

"They'll wait till this rain lets up." She checked the coffeepot, but it was empty, so she made some up fresh.

"Your mama have anything to quench a sweet tooth?"

"There's some lemon meringue left," I said. I'd been hoping for some of that pie for lunch but didn't say anything when Deacy lifted the entire wedge to her plate. She was the one carrying what might be the only change-of-life baby our family'd ever get. She was entitled to all that pie and more, much as she wanted.

"Where's Hazey?"

I told her.

"So you're stuck home all by your lonesome."

"I don't mind." Outside, rain beat the house.

"Doesn't look like it's ever letting up." She carried a forkful to her mouth. "Hope the sackers all showed. Everett hates sacking when weather's like this. Not the sacking so much as the carrying to cars. By the end of a day like this he's drenched to bone. Just drenched."

"Might could catch his death." I'd heard that from Mama often enough to know the danger of too much wetness, particularly rain wetness. Course, I'd never actually known someone to die from rain. But that's not to say the danger was any less real.

"More likely I'll catch my death from his nastiness. Everett's a good man. Don't ever say I said different."

"No, ma'am," I said.

"But the man is a bear from the time he walks in the house till he turns out the lights and starts snoring when he's had to carry groceries in the rain."

"Rain'll probably stop soon. He'll be dried off before he gets home."

"Won't matter. Nowadays dry won't matter at all." She pushed the plate away, leaving the back crust and a thin line of lemon and meringue.

"Can I have your leftovers?"

"Sure. Fine."

The part she'd left was my least favorite, but it was better than nothing.

"Don't know why I'm wasting time worrying over Everett staying dry. Least if he comes home wet, he'll have a decent excuse for his foul mood."

Tante Deacy talked to me like I was closer to grown than to child. That was only one of the reasons I liked her so much. "Uncle Everett still put out about this change-of-life baby?"

She smiled. "Those ears don't miss much, do they?"

"Everybody knows about your baby," I said.

"Well, not everybody. Least I hope not everybody." She patted her stomach, which pouched a little.

"So Uncle Everett's still mad," I said.

"Mad. Worried. Amounts to the same thing, though he won't admit it."

"Why?"

She shrugged. "Who knows? Maybe cause it's easier for a man to admit being mad than to admit being worried."

"Worried over what?" Uncle Everett should be happy to be getting himself a change-of-life baby. Some folks don't appreciate good luck when it's knocking them up the side of the head.

"Money. More times than not, when a man's worried, money's at the center of it."

I never bothered over money. It was hard to see why anyone would. "Don't you have enough money?"

"Plenty. Even with this new baby, we have plenty. That's what I keep telling your uncle. But does he listen? No, ma'am. In one ear, out the other. Might as well be talking to a stone wall."

Or to one of your half-wit boys, I thought to myself.

She went to the sink to wash off her plate. That was one more thing I liked about Tante Deacy. She didn't treat me like her personal slave. She dirtied a dish, she washed it herself.

"Maybe we could give you some money when the baby comes."

She smiled. "That's real generous of you, Vivien Leigh. But it wouldn't be enough, no matter how much you gave." She wiped her plate and returned it to the cabinet. "Besides, Everett's got his pride. Wouldn't take charity even from family, especially from family."

"Wouldn't be for him. Would be for the baby."

She came back to the table with her coffee. "Same thing, far as Everett's concerned."

"Guess you could always sell off some of your jewelry, if things got too bad." I hoped if things came to that, she wouldn't have to pawn the cameo locket she'd promised me. The locket held a strand of black hair that had been the first curl cut from my grandmother's head when she'd been a baby, much younger than me. Then I thought of something just as bad, maybe worse. If that change-of-life baby was a girl, as I well suspected it would be, Tante Deacy might forget all about her promise to me. A change-of-life baby decides she wants something, a locket or anything else, there's not much anybody can do about it. But I wasn't letting go that locket without a fight.

"If you have to sell the cameo, promise you'll give me first chance at buying it." My savings amounted to eighteen dollars and seventy-six cents at the present time, not enough to buy a locket off anybody and I knew that. I just wanted Deacy reminded about who was supposed to get that locket when she got tired of staring at it in her jewelry box.

"Honey, I'm not selling anything. Everett'd starve first." She folded the dishrags, the washing one and, next to it, the drying one. "Listen to that rain, will you. Angels crying their eyes out this day. You ever hear that, Vivien Leigh? That rain means an angel's crying?"

"Don't know what an angel'd have to cry over." I'd never heard of stacks of dirty dishes piling up in Heaven.

"Bet even angels have their bad days." She walked back to the door as if she was getting ready to leave. But she didn't unlatch the screen, just stood watching rain pummel the earth. Nothing angelic about it at all.

"Remember, I get first chance at the cameo," I said.

"What?" She turned back to me, her brows pulled into a puzzled look. "What's that you say?"

Sometimes grown-ups, even grown-ups I like, don't pay me half a bit of attention. "The cameo locket," I said again. "You promised me the cameo locket."

"Sure I did. I know that." She came back to the table and sat across from me. "Get your mama's polish and I'll do up your nails."

I ran to Mama's bedroom and got the supplies out her left dresser drawer—cotton balls, pink polish that Mama pretended was hers but that only Mavis and me ever used, remover in case of mistakes, mine or Tante Deacy's. At this rate I'd never have time to dust the parlor.

I splayed my fingers on the table, opposite Deacy. She'd start with my pinkies, first the left, then the right. Next, the ring fingers. Left, then right. She'd work her way down till, finally, even the right thumb glowed fresh pink. Deacy was the only person I knew who went from hand to hand, back and forth that way. Mama said it wasn't a normal way of polishing, normal was do one hand and when you finished it, do the other. Didn't matter if you did right hand first or left first. One was normal as the other.

What wasn't normal was switching back and forth between hands as if you couldn't decide which should be done first. "I feel so sorry for that bare hand when you do it your way. Poor naked little fingers, orphan nails. This way seems the fairer," Deacy would say back to Mama. Neither of them thought about changing to the other one's way. They were Meniere women, set in their ways and not easily agreeable to anybody's suggestions for change. I expect I'll be the same when I'm grown.

"If this baby's a girl, I'm painting her nails every single week," Deacy said. She passed the brush over my first pinkie with careful, narrow strokes. Only a thin line of polish had to be wiped off my cuticle.

"Even when she's a baby?"

"Especially when she's a baby. Tiny little nails. Won't take more than a teardrop of polish each."

"What else will you do, if that baby's a girl?"

"Sing her lullabies and brush her hair, a hundred strokes every night. Show her how to paint her lips with raspberry juice."

"Dance? Don't forget to show her how to dance."

"I'd never forget that part. Course any girl coming from me and Everett will be born with dancing feet. No question about that."

I listened to the rain, not so battering now, offering some promise of ending, though not right away. And while Deacy worked her way to my thumbs, I dreamed about her change-of-life girl, the baby with the dancing feet.

7

LET A LITTLE
TIME GO BY

THE RAIN DIDN'T STOP all that day or night. I fell asleep with the window gapped open for fresh air, but not all the way so the floor wouldn't get soaked. Rain danced on our tin roof, stepping smart and fast like Tante Deacy's baby would once she got herself born.

By morning the rain had ended, leaving everything clean except for that hole, nothing but a mud pit back of the house. Before I'd even finished breakfast Marydale came over and she and Mavis went right out to make more of a God-awful fiasco.

I stared out the window over the sink while I washed my bowl and spoon. Daddy was fooling with the car, changing oil or some such thing. He loved working the car when he got a Saturday off, about every six weeks or so.

Cleo rubbed against his legs while he hunched over the engine. She did it to annoy him, knowing he found rubbing particularly aggravating. Cleo is the type cat cannot pass up the opportunity to aggravate, especially to aggravate folks who don't care for cats in general and her in particular, which pretty much described my daddy.

I went out to save Cleo from her own evil intentions. Daddy'd kick her away soon. Not hard, but a kick all the same. Then she'd get her feelings hurt and run under the house, *boudeeing* the whole day. She learned that from me because I used to pout just the same when I was younger. I went under the house for lots more reasons than just pouting, though. I went to think, to be alone, to hide from the heat and sometimes from Mama.

I feel sorry for people up north who live in houses set flat on the ground, no spaces between earth and floor. Where do those northern children go when they want to escape? What place do they have for private thinking?

"Want to help?" Mavis called when I passed her spot on the way to the back shed where Daddy had parked the car to be close to his tools.

"Why should I? You paying me or what?" Course I knew the answer, so I didn't get annoyed when Mavis gave me a look and nothing more. Still, the girl was getting old enough to learn manners, which includes answering when you're asked a question.

"Digging be easy this day. Ground good and soft," Marydale said. "Hardly feels like real work."

"Hardly looks like real work, even when dirt's hard as rock," I said.

"Don't bother us or I'm telling," Mavis said.

Marydale leaned in to Mavis and whispered something in her ear. Mavis giggled. Then Marydale did too. I knew they wouldn't tell me what was so funny, so I didn't take the trouble to ask. Who cared what they were laughing at?

While I walked over to Daddy to have some grown-up conversation, I checked the zipper on my shorts, the buttons on my shirt. Everything was closed proper. Who cared what those silly girls had found to laugh themselves sick over?

"What you doing?" I asked when I reached Daddy and Cleo.

"Changing plugs." His head was bent into the engine, muffling his voice.

"Thought maybe it was the oil." Daddy said before I get a driver's license I have to know how a car runs, how to take proper care of it. I'm not excited about learning any of that and am hoping he'll change his mind or forget about it by the time I reach fifteen. So far all I know is you've got to change oil regularly, though I don't know how to go about actually doing the changing. I also know to check air in the tires and to keep water in the radiator. But I don't know how to actually do those things either. I won't be fifteen for a long, long time, so what does it matter?

"Where's Mama?" With Mavis and Daddy around, she hadn't bothered leaving me a note and I liked knowing where people were, keeping track of what's what, who's where.

"Fixing flowers at church for the Assumption."

The fifteenth of August was Monday, exactly one week before my tenth birthday. The Altar ladies would have the church spiffed up for the feast day. Mary's just about my favorite saint even if Marydale was named after her. One of my oldest wishes is that I get to crown Mary during the May festival when I'm a senior in high school. I don't know how the senior girl gets picked and it's too far away for me to start pestering Mama about it. Besides, the rules might change by the time I'm a senior. Whatever the rules, I hope I'm chosen. It would be a splendid honor for me and my whole family too. Even Malcolm'd have to wear a suit and sit up straight and watch while I climbed the special holy ladder set up behind the Virgin Mary's statue so the senior girl can place the golden crown on her head. Malcolm would be green, but I wouldn't care. It's not my fault he's a boy and everyone knows boys aren't allowed to crown the Virgin on account of boys being more sinful than girls.

"Think she'll be back for lunch?" I asked.

He straightened and wiped his hands on the maroon oil cloth, which had been resting on the strip of car metal in front of the hood. "You ever think about anything besides your stomach?"

"Sure." I scooped Cleo because I heard a kick coming. "I was just wondering when she'd be back is all."

"Nothing wrong with making sure you know where your next meal's coming from."

Seeing as how I'd just finished breakfast, I was hardly thinking about eating. But I didn't say that, since he seemed to be putting himself into a good mood without any help from me.

He handed me the keys. "Start her up. Let's see how she runs."

I laid Cleo against the back tire where the shade could hit her full and patted her twice to let her know she was to stay there. Course with Cleo, that message might or might not make a dent in what she actually ended up doing.

Behind the wheel, I pumped the pedal twice, then turned the key like I'd been taught. She started up smooth. I stuck my head out the rolled-down window. "Sounds good, don't you think?"

"Not bad," he said. "Rev her up some."

I pushed the pedal, but not all the way to the floor.

"Whoa. Hold it." He bent into the engine again, so I couldn't see his face or what he was doing. "Let go."

I waited for more instructions, touched my toes to the pedal while sitting straight. If I sat on a pillow, I'd be able to reach the pedal and see out the window, no problem. One day, when Daddy was in an especially good mood, I'd ask if a pillow would be allowed to let me drive the pasture. Didn't seem likely. But it'd be worth a try asking on one of Daddy's real good days.

"Kill her," he said.

I turned off the car and opened the door, easing my legs out slowly, imagining how it would feel to do this every day, just a regular thing to get in the car, drive around, pick up some milk or something else Mama'd run out of. I'd be a wonderful driver.

Cleo stretched awake from her nap. She'd stayed where I'd put her. A Saturday surprise.

Daddy dropped the hood shut. "She sounds all right."

I knelt next to Cleo and stroked her belly. "Why do we always call the car she?"

"Why?"

"Why not him? Why's it always a her?"

"Let me think about that one." He leaned against the car, cleaning his hands on the oil rag. "Boats, ships, planes too. Always she."

"Sure. Why is that, do you think?"

"Don't know." He paused, still wiping his hands and looking out toward the Guillots' house. "They're complicated is all I can think. Nearly complicated as women. One day some man said, 'This car's nearly confusing as Betty Sue down the road. Must be a female.' That's how it all started." He grinned, inviting me to grin back, to show how clever I thought he was. So I did. No harm in keeping on Daddy's sweet side.

He closed his toolbox and carried it to the shelf in the back of the shed. I scooped Cleo and followed. "One thing I want to know, Vivien Leigh."

"What's that?"

"I want to know if you're planning on being complicated as your mama."

I shrugged. "I don't know. I suppose."

"Take some advice. Don't." He walked back to the house, going the long way so he wouldn't pass Marydale and Mavis. He was no doubt put out by Marydale arriving so early, because it meant she'd be here all day or till he or Mama shooed her home. Also sounded like I'd missed a fight either last night from the rain drowning out everything or this morning from me sleeping late. I imagined it was more talk about the colored sisters but couldn't be sure. I did hate missing out on a decent fight, which, from Daddy's piece of advice, it must've been.

Mama was out of sorts when she got home. Shelby Mouton hadn't brought enough wisteria, which naturally messed up all the arranging Mama'd done in her head. No doubt Mrs. Mouton was too busy getting poor Clorise up at first light, even with it still being vacation, to bother remembering how much wisteria she'd promised to bring. Just went to show the evils of getting up too early. A person doing too much too early in the day wears out her brain, forgets things everyone else remembers without trouble. All this business about rise and shine with the sun may work for the birds but is dangerous business for human folks, as Shelby Mouton proved this morning.

Mavis and Marydale wandered in about noon, hungry and dirty. Their hands were so disgusting, Mama must've known about their hole. Otherwise she would've asked what they'd been up to, and she didn't. But before they could make it to the bathroom to wash off, Mama was all over their tiny butts. "Don't you girls use my good towels."

"No, ma'am. We sure won't be using them towels." Marydale nudged Mavis in the small of her back to get her moving. "No, ma'am. We'll wipe on toilet paper or something."

"Don't you girls go messing with the toilet paper either."

"No, ma'am. We sure won't." Marydale was probably wondering how to light a fire under Mavis to get her out that kitchen. I could've told her, nobody moves Mavis Dubois when she doesn't want to get moved, which is more times than I care to relate.

"Come on, Mavis," Marydale said finally. "We don't need to wipe, no. Just shake water off our hands, that's all."

"See to it you do your shaking in the sink."

"Yes, ma'am." Marydale's answer faded into the bathroom, where she'd finally pushed Mavis.

Mama's not the snapping sort most times, so she must've been as put out as Daddy about the fight I'd missed. Was almost, but not quite, enough to make a person want to get up earlier in the day.

Things weren't any better by late afternoon. Mama and I were weeding her spot along the side of the house. Hardly big enough to be called a real garden. A short row of tomatoes. Another of green peppers. Two zucchini plants, a couple of eggplants, three rows of okra, and two of green beans.

Daddy came out and stood at the corner of the house. He didn't say anything and neither did Mama, who wasn't one to get out-silenced any more than she was one to get out-talked. At least they were standing in the same general area. All day Mama'd been in a room and Daddy came in, she left. Other way around too. Daddy was in a room, Mama came in, he left. The rule was whoever got there last got to stay last.

Marydale left right after lunch. She remembered some chore her mama wanted done before evening. Course that was nothing but a Marydale story. She could feel the heat of a coming fight or a just-been fight and wanted to get out its way. Mama and Daddy were bound to pick up where the weather'd left off. Seemed to me we needed a storm in our own house to cool things down the way last night's rain had cooled things off outside.

After a while of standing by the house, watching us weed, Daddy moved closer to where I was kneeling. "Vivien Leigh, you want to go frogging in a bit?"

I looked over at Mama, waiting for her to say she wasn't cooking up pitiful frogs' legs tonight. But she didn't say a word, just kept plucking weeds as if that was the only thing a person could ever want to do.

"I'm helping Mama," I said as if Daddy was blind and couldn't see that for himself.

"We're almost done," Mama said, still not looking up from the weeds. "You can stop, if you've got something else to do." That was close as she'd get to saying I could go frogging with Daddy.

"You finish up the okra. We're not leaving for a while." He moved closer to my row, maybe to see how much more weeding I had left to do, maybe to see if he could get Mama talking. But he could've stepped on her hand, ground his shoe into her fingers, and Mama wouldn't of said boo unless she'd decided to talk again, which she would've decided on her own, no thanks to anything Daddy said or did.

I pulled another weed.

"I said you could stop." Mama, dark eyed as she ever got, looked at me as if I was acting wacky, still working when she said I could quit.

I straightened, but before I could get off my knees Daddy said, "I told you to finish that okra, Vivien Leigh. Hope you're not forgetting that."

"No, sir." I bent back to the weeds and waited for Mama to say she didn't want me messing with her garden and for Daddy to keep his big nose out of it. But she didn't say a thing. Mama's no fool and if somebody's willing to do her work for her, all's the better.

Daddy stood at the end of my last okra row, arms folded across his chest, staring at the Blake pasture. Two Jerseys chewed their cuds and looked back at Daddy, not showing any more interest in him than he did in them. He tried to look as if he'd gotten the best of Mama, put one over on her. But even I could see that wasn't so and I was nothing but a child.

After I finished the okra, Daddy and I drove to Ketchum Basin in his pickup. We knew this good spot for frog catching, best spot outside the Atchafalaya. The sun dipped behind the horizon as we drove. The sky was red and orange and gold, so bright it was easy to believe darkness would never come.

We didn't talk while we drove. Daddy didn't like being bothered when he was in his truck, which had a standard shift, unlike the car, which had automatic. That was why talking was okay in the one, not in the other. I watched him shift gears when we turned off the main road and onto the dirt road that led to our secret frog spot. I liked watching how he knew exactly when to push the lever up, down, across, the clutch in just right, out again. The knowing was a mystery but one I'd know too someday, so I didn't have to spend time thinking about it now.

When the trees along the sides of the road changed from oaks to cypresses, we were there. Daddy pulled far to the side of the road as he could without hitting a tree. I carried the two burlap sacks with pull-string tops that had lain scrunched on the seat between us. The ground was spongy under our feet, as if it would turn to swamp given a few more years. Water was just a couple of hundred yards from the car. We walked right up to the marsh, then sat on a large rock to wait for the frogs to start calling each other. Frogs are stupid that way. "Here I am. Come and get me," they say. If they kept their mouths shut, they'd live longer. But then maybe they wouldn't be as happy. When a frog's got to sing, a frog's got to sing.

"How many you figure we'll need?" I asked.

"Hard to tell."

"Think Mama'll cook them up tonight, if she doesn't have to do the cleaning or chopping?" Fried frogs' legs were a treat long as you didn't think what they looked like just a few hours earlier, croaking and hopping happy.

"With your mama, who knows?" He opened the top of his sack, getting it ready for the unlucky frogs who'd spend their last hours trying to puzzle out where they were.

"Mama doesn't like anyone interfering with her kitchen or her food plans neither."

"Too bad she's not the same when it comes to interfering with other folks' business." He pulled the drawstring tight. "Relative or no relative, some business is none of anybody else's business."

Now that change-of-life baby had my father and mother fighting each other. That baby was one powerful rascal.

"Mama just wants to help Tante Deacy is all," I said. I folded my sack into tiny pleats and kept my eyes on that so, I hoped, I wouldn't look too bold.

"Help is one thing. Sticking your nose in it is something else."

The first frog of the night peeped. Poor, stupid little thing. Daddy stood, loosened the drawstring of his bag, and started walking toward the croak. His shoes left soft prints in the ground. I extended my legs full length and placed my feet into the prints he left behind. I looked back at the trail we left, my foot inside his foot. It looked like a bizarre monster tracking the swamp, step by strange step.

That first frog sat near the water's edge, calling, calling. Down the shore another frog answered. I snuck up behind the first frog, grabbed him behind the neck, and dropped him into the sack Daddy held open. I was so fast, the frog was in the bag before he finished the peep he'd started on the rock.

We walked to the second frog and did the same. The frogs in the sack didn't peep loudly as you'd think they would. They were too scared, not knowing where they were, where they were going.

By the time we'd filled one sack Daddy'd had enough. Frogs aren't like fish where one or two will set you and your family fine. Some days Daddy could eat a sack of frogs' legs himself. Other days he wasn't that hungry and shared one sack with the rest of us. Today must've been one of his not-so-hungry days.

Though the sun had set, we didn't need lights till we turned off the dirt road onto the main one. I liked that about summer, the way day stretched into night, stealing time that should've belonged to darkness.

When we got home, Daddy took our sack into the toolshed. I left him to his work. Once I'd watched. Once had been enough. He told me frogs didn't feel a thing. The ax was too sharp and they didn't have enough nerve endings to feel pain. It was true not a single frog yelped when the blade hit. But some people are quiet no matter the pain, and so why can't frogs be the same? Daddy said I was being silly, acting like a girl. I didn't think Malcolm or T.J. or even Austin would act any different, but I didn't say that. Let Daddy think what he wanted. I just wouldn't ever stick my head into the shed after we'd been frog catching.

In the kitchen Mama had the batter waiting and was shredding lettuce for salad. The smell of boiled potatoes and carrots filled the room. "How many'd you get?" she asked.

"Sackful."

"Just one?"

"Guess Daddy's not too hungry." I snatched a potato chunk from the pot on the stove and sprinkled salt before I took my first bite.

"Why aren't you out there helping?"

I wrinkled my nose. She knew why.

"Just cause you're not watching, doesn't mean it's not happening."

"I know."

"See to it you don't ever forget. Just cause you're not watching, doesn't mean it's not happening." She repeated the words as if they were a golden rule, something to live by. I hoped she'd made extra potatoes cause I didn't have much appetite for frogs' legs this night.

By the time Daddy brought the legs into the kitchen, all cleaned and ready for the batter, Mama'd decided she'd had enough with being angry at him. She talked as if nothing had ever been wrong between them. He answered the same and to watch the two of them, laughing over something Edwin Sonnier had said, complaining about the parish not regraveling our road like they'd promised, you'd never think they were the same two who'd stood in the vegetable patch that very afternoon. But they were. Far as I could tell nothing had happened between the anger and now except a little time, which, I guessed, was all that was needed. Just let a little time go by and most everything will be all right.

I whispered that to Mavis when we'd settled in bed. "Just let a little time go by and most everything will be all right," I breathed into her ear so Mama and Daddy couldn't hear. She didn't say anything back, just turned to her side. I hoped she was thinking about the piece of wisdom I'd dropped into her head for free. But Mavis was just a young child, so who knew what she was thinking.

8

THURSDAY
QUEENS

BY THE TIME WE GOT BACK from evening church on the Assumption and finished supper it was close to eight, which meant Daddy couldn't call as many folks as usual. Every night since he became a Concerned Citizen he was on the phone, begging money. "Think of it being your sweet child starting school," he'd say. "Sure things are tight," he'd say. "Tight everywhere. But my friend, think on what'd happen if everybody said that. Think about it."

Some nights that's all he'd have to say to get the person to promise money to drag Miss Boudreaux off her front-porch rocker and into the first-grade classroom. Other nights folks said they'd call back later, which put Daddy in a bad mood because he knew, well as they did, they weren't ever calling back.

By a few minutes before nine Daddy'd only made three calls and all of them were the "I'll call you back later" sort. After he hung up the third time, he just sat on the sofa, passing a thumb back and forth against the edge of the table that held the phone.

"No luck?" Mama said. She sat next to him, sewing sequins on a baby Jesus dress.

"Man learns a lot about his town doing something like this," he said. He stared at the television where Marshal Dillon was giving some posse

---

what-for. Mavis sprawled in front of the set, her nose practically touching the marshal's so she could hear, Daddy having made her turn the sound down so he could do his calling.

"For what you let the girl sit so close to the TV? She'll need glasses before she's old enough to keep them clean. Another thing I'll have to pay for," he said.

"Nobody's saying we have to pay for Elsie Boudreaux ourselves. If not enough people give money, that's that," Mama said. She pinched another red sequin out her jar and threaded the needle through it.

"Who's talking about that?"

Mama went on as if he'd never said a word. "If you can't raise enough money, those first-graders will just have to get used to having themselves a colored teacher."

"Like the fifths," I said. I was curled on the stuffed chair with a book. But it wasn't that interesting and certainly couldn't win out over talk between Mama and Daddy.

Neither of them looked at me. Ignoring your own children: another amazing talent that comes with being grown.

"There's always public," Daddy said. The lines around his eyes were deep tonight. He looked too worn to pretend he'd been talking about Mavis and her eyes, which were plenty good enough, far as I was concerned.

"People want to be selfish, public'll have to do," Mama said.

"Or else they could just stick with Holy Rosary," I said.

"Holy Rosary with colored sisters." Daddy shook his head as if he still couldn't believe it. "Might as well be sending your children to Sacred Heart."

"Marydale says pretty soon the schools'll be the same. No difference going to Holy Rosary or Sacred Heart. Everything all mixed up." *Gunsmoke* was over and nothing but commercials were showing, so Mavis had sat up to throw her two bits into the conversation. If the girl had half a brain, she would've figured these particular two bits were bound to put Daddy in a sour mood. Some days it was hard to know whether Mavis was running with missing brains or just liked ignoring what her brain told her.

"Marydale's nothing but a colored girl. Get that through your head once and for all," Daddy said, his voice razor sharp.

Even someone with less than half a brain would've known to keep her mouth shut. But not Mavis. "She's a change-of-life baby too," she said.

"Don't talk to me about no change-of-life business either," he said.

"For God's sake, Floyd, let's not start that all over," Mama said.

There hadn't been any fighting since Mama and Daddy'd made up Saturday night. But Tante Deacy's baby was so powerful, even the mention of someone else's change-of-life child, and a colored one at that, could flame those ashes of fight into a knock-down drag-out.

"Come over here, Mavis," Daddy said, his voice real soft now.

Mavis got up slow as she dared, not knowing if she was going to get a spanking for being so dumb. I couldn't tell either. Neither could Mama, who looked up from her sewing to see what Daddy had in mind.

It seemed to take forever before Mavis crossed the few feet between the set and Daddy. He didn't hurry her along any. That could be a good sign for Mavis or a bad one. I couldn't tell.

When she finally reached him, he pulled at her till she was standing between his knees, then put a hand on each shoulder. She couldn't escape even if she'd had the nerve to try. "She is a change-of-life baby," Mavis said, sounding ready for a fight, though her bottom lip stuck out like she might start crying before she could bother fighting.

"First off, Marydale Arceneaux is the nicest colored girl I've ever known," Daddy said.

Mavis looked at him direct in the eyes, too surprised to stop herself.

"I mean that too. Yes I do."

"She's been my best friend forever."

No, Mavis, not that, I wanted to scream at her. Even Mavis was old enough and smart enough to know that was the wrong thing to say. But Daddy starting off so nice had tricked her into saying exactly what she was thinking, such a clear mistake, especially tonight.

Daddy took a deep breath but didn't reach to put Mavis across his knees for the whipping she seemed determined to get herself this night. "Marydale is nice, but colored. Don't forget that second part is what I'm saying. Colored." He dragged out the last word, hoping it would settle in Mavis's brain if he said it slow enough.

"I know," Mavis said.

"Come September you'll be in second," he said.

"Just a couple of weeks away," she said.

"That's right. You'll be a big girl. Second grade."

She stood up straighter. I don't know why. Even a total fool gets older each year. The accomplishment would've been if Mavis'd managed to stay young enough for first grade two years running.

"There's one thing I want to see by the end of second."

"No bad marks in conduct?"

"That'd be fine. But something else. I want you to look over all those nice girls in Holy Rosary's second and find yourself a different best friend."

Mavis's shoulders slumped. "No one lives close as Marydale."

"You can invite your new best friend over. Mama'll pick her up, bring her home if need be."

Mama raised her eyebrows on that one and went back to her sequins.

"Mama won't do it every day," Mavis said.

"A new best friend. That's what I want to see by the end of second. Not too much to ask, is it? Lots easier than perfect marks in conduct, don't you think?"

Mavis shrugged and wriggled her lips to keep from answering, because any words that came out now were bound to get her into trouble. Even Mavis was smart enough to know that.

Daddy reached out and rubbed her head. "That's my girl." He pushed her to the side, then went into the kitchen for a banana. From where I sat I could see him dropping strips of skin into the trash.

For once Mavis managed to stay awake longer than thirty seconds after her head touched the pillow. "I already have a best friend," she said to the ceiling.

"She's colored. Weren't you listening to nothing your father said?" I whispered back.

"Nobody needs two best friends." Even in the dark I could see those cheeks puffing.

Thursday Aussie didn't clean. She sent word through Marydale that she had to watch Evie's sick baby because Evie couldn't afford to miss work. Aussie'd taught all her girls, excepting Marydale, to be good workers. Evie in particular had herself a real good job in the Lafayette post office. Aussie didn't have a choice but to stay home and take care of her sick grandbaby. Little Aussie wasn't even close to a year and sure couldn't watch over her own self. Daddy didn't see it that way when he heard Aussie'd missed her day.

"So Evie's job's more important than Aussie's?" he said at the supper table that night.

"Evie's at the post office. She could get fired easy," Mama said. She flopped two spoonfuls of mashed potatoes on Daddy's plate and two pork chops, then went to the stove for green beans.

"What about Aussie? She think nobody'd fire her? That what she's thinking? If it is, you tell that colored lady she's thinking wrong," he said, then took a big bite of potatoes, yellow with melted butter.

"Aussie's been doing for us a long time. Did for my mama before she passed." Mama filled plates for me and Mavis and herself.

"I know all that," Daddy said.

"Then don't act like you're forgetting it," Mama said. She cut a bite of pork chop, scooped beans and potatoes on her fork, then opened her mouth for it all. Mama liked a little of everything from her plate to chew at the same time. Daddy ate one thing at a time. A bite of pork chewed and swallowed. A bite of beans next, chewed and swallowed. Last, the potatoes. Then he'd start the whole thing over. Mama said it was a leftover baby habit. Daddy didn't mind her teasing, just smiled and said food reached his stomach fast as hers reached her own, so what did it matter. Some days I ate like Mama, everything mixed. Other days I used Daddy's way, everything separate.

We were half done our meal when Daddy started up again. "Vivien Leigh's getting old enough to help out more around the house."

"What?" I said even though I had a mouthful of potatoes and beans. "I do plenty already."

"Girl's practically a slave. You forgetting that, Floyd?" Mama said.

"Oh, yeah. Almost forgot." He grinned at Mama, who grinned back, all the smiles coming at my expense.

"Vivien Leigh's a slave, nothing but a poor slave." Mavis joined the grinning.

"Shut up," I said.

"Watch that mouth, Little Miss," Mama said.

I stabbed my pork chop bone with my fork. Wasn't I entitled to defend myself? What had I done to deserve everybody picking on me?

Daddy was the first to get serious again. "Mavis could do more too," he said.

My turn to laugh now. When Mama wasn't looking, I crossed my eyes at Mavis. She tried to do the same but only looked disgusting, because her idea of crossing her eyes is rolling them to the ceiling till just the whites show.

"These girls start doing their fair shares, won't be needing to have Aussie here but once a month, maybe less," he said.

Mavis and I were surprised right out of being angry at each other and looked at Daddy first, then Mama to see what she'd have to say about that idea.

"Girls can't work like Aussie," Mama said. Her voice had that "subject-closed" tone that a person ignored at his own risk. Daddy never was one for taking the easy way, though, so I expected him to say more. But I was surprised for the second time that night.

All he said was, "Think about what I'm saying. Nothing needs to be done tonight. Just give it a think, will you?"

Even Mama couldn't say anything against that, because what harm could come from a little bit of thinking.

Saturday morning Mama decided we should busy ourselves cleaning house. Even Mavis got herself some chores, which I was happy to see because the girl is old enough to carry some weight, like Daddy'd said. Marydale came over about ten, but Mama sent her home. "Mavis has chores to get done before she does any playing this day," she said.

"What's she got to do, her?" Marydale asked. She leaned against the kitchen screen like my mama and her own mama had warned her against doing at least one million times.

"Help clean this whole house," Mama said. Her back was to Marydale while she saved dishes, else she would've told her to get off the screen.

"For what she have to clean the whole house, her?" Marydale asked, sounding as close to not believing Mama as a colored girl could get to not believing a white lady.

"Cause I say so. That's why," Mama said.

"How long that be taking?"

"How long do you think?" Mama asked.

"More than all the hours left in this day. That's for sure," Marydale said.

"You got that right," I said.

"Marydale, that you out there?" Mavis yelled from the bathroom, where she was supposed to be doing her business, but where I imagined she was making faces in the mirror, wasting time so she wouldn't have to start cleaning. All right by me because I wasn't starting till she did.

"It be me okay," Marydale yelled back.

"Come back here. Say hi," Mavis called.

"Marydale's not staying today. Hear me, girls?" Mama's words were a waste. Marydale'd already hightailed it to the bathroom and when those two girls got together, they heard nothing but each other. Pretty soon all you heard from that side of the house was giggle, giggle, giggle and I imagined the mirror was getting more than its fill of silly faces.

After she finished saving the dishes, wiping off the stove and counter, cleaning both sides of the sink, Mama remembered who was supposed to be cleaning this day and ordered Marydale and Mavis out the bathroom.

Those girls took their sweet time crossing the parlor, Marydale following Mavis, her hands shoved in the back pockets of Mavis's shorts. They shuffled along, step by dawdling step, like the shortest, slowest train in Louisiana, just engine and caboose.

Mama'd poured herself a cup of coffee and was sitting at the table by the time those two sashayed themselves into the kitchen. Mama didn't give herself a midmorning cup of coffee till she'd gotten some work done. Least that's what she did on Aussie's days. Saving dishes and slapping a rag over the counter, stove, and sink hardly counted for real work in anybody's book. Maybe that cup of coffee was a good sign, meant Mama wasn't really intending on cleaning the whole house, had just said that to scare Marydale back home where she belonged.

"Little Aussie doing better?" Mama asked.

"She still not be up to full shakes, but not so sick," Marydale said. She and Mavis had switched positions so now she was the engine and Mavis the caboose. Marydale didn't have pockets on her shorts, so Mavis had to settle for linking two fingers through belt loops. They choo-chooed their way around the kitchen while Mama sipped coffee and I waited for the cleaning to start.

"You think your mama'll be coming next week?" Mama asked.

"I know she be here next week." Marydale sounded surer than any colored girl had a right to sound. Like most change-of-life babies, she was born a know-it-all. I didn't usually hold that against her since it wasn't her fault.

"You tell your mama I'm thinking about figs for this week coming," Mama said.

"For Thursday, Miz Hazey?"

"Course for Thursday," I said. "Isn't that always your mama's day with us?"

"Long as I can remember. Thursdays always been the Dubois day," Marydale said. She and Mavis had stopped their train next to the screen door and were eyeing it with plans to disappear outside, if Mama wasn't careful. For once I was on the side of those foolish girls, because for sure if Mavis wasn't cleaning, neither was I.

"We're the queens of Thursdays," Mavis said. "Queen, queen, queen," she sang over and over, holding her hands over her head like a crown.

Marydale joined in, queening and crowning behind Mavis, who'd started high-stepping across the kitchen as if she were leading some sort of parade, which in a way she was, seeing as how Marydale was two-stepping behind her. I looked over at Mama to see if all this foolishness in her own kitchen was giving her a headache. But she didn't look one bit bothered, even smiled as if she was enjoying herself.

"Nobody's the queen of Thursdays in this house or anywhere else," I said.

Mama stopped smiling and carried her cup to rinse in the sink. "I guess Vivien Leigh's right about that. No such thing as queen of Thursdays."

"Nor of any other day of the week." I was staying ahead of Mavis, who'd just as soon be queen of Saturdays, Tuesdays, any day at all. Wouldn't matter to her, just so she got to be queen of some day.

"My mama be the real queen of Thursdays. Right, Miz Hazey?" Marydale had stopped her foolishness and stood quietly next to Mama.

"Don't talk more silliness, Marydale. Vivien Leigh's right. No such thing as queen of Thursdays."

"If there be such a thing, though, my mama, she'd be Thursday queen in this house. Right, Miz Hazey?" Her chin rested on her chest, but her eyes rolled up to meet Mama's. I couldn't figure what got Marydale so serious all of a sudden.

"We don't have queens in this country. Kings neither," I said.

"Too bad for us," Mavis said. She had the screen inched open with her foot and was signaling Marydale to follow. But Marydale wasn't paying her any attention. She was too busy staring up at Mama, waiting for Mama to agree Aussie was our Thursday queen.

"Time for you to be getting yourself home," Mama said. "We've got ourselves cleaning to do in this house this day."

Marydale walked out the door with nothing but a "see you" for Mavis. She was sure put out about Mama not making Aussie queen of Thursdays. I was just as aggravated because I'd been only a foolish queen away from a day not filled with cleaning. Mavis and I were stuck, and by the time Daddy got home from work our house was clean as it stood any Thursday. I dared anyone to say different.

9

No Choice
at All

AFTER A CUP OF COFFEE, Daddy took his tractor mower over to the Blakes to help cut their back pasture. Mister Blake had himself a mower too, which is where Daddy'd gotten the idea for his. Mama said the Blakes should've paid for at least half our mower since they were the ones going to get the most use out of it. Daddy said that just wasn't so and besides, nothing wrong with neighbors helping each other. What could Mama say to that?

We were late eating supper because Daddy'd wanted to finish mowing before he came to the table. So when Tante Deacy drove up, we hadn't even had a chance to clear the dishes, much less start any washing. She was by herself except for Austin, who only counted for half a person being so short and spoiled.

"Where's Everett?" Daddy asked. He had his chair balanced on its two back legs and was digging in his mouth with a toothpick.

"Who knows? Packing for all I know."

"Packing? For where? Where's Uncle Everett going?" I hated being the last to know something and no one'd mentioned any Everett trip to me.

"Uncle Everett taking a vacation?" Mavis asked.

"Course not, stupid." I wasn't sure where he was going, but I did know this wasn't about anything fun as a vacation.

"Don't call your sister names," Mama said.

I could've told her it wasn't my fault Mavis was born stupid. I was just stating facts, plain and simple. But Mama's lips were stretched so thin, I knew was no use explaining anything to her right now.

"He's really going," Mama said, more given truth than question.

"Tomorrow sometime." Deacy tried to laugh, but it came out strange. "I don't even know if he's leaving morning, night, or somewhere in between."

"Where's that goofy hole you been bragging on?" Austin asked. He'd gone straight to Mama's cookie jar and helped himself to a handful of oatmeals without so much as a by-your-leave. Crumbs sprinkled the front of his shirt. Austin was a slob, though he'd been raised better.

"It's a fine hole," I said before Mavis had a chance to answer. Sometimes sisters have to stick together.

"So let's see it."

Mavis pushed off her chair and headed out the back door, not bothering with whether Austin followed. Good for her.

"Imagine I could do one just as big. Bigger even." The screen door slammed on any more smart-aleckness that might've come out that boy's mouth.

Daddy finished with his toothpick, put it on the edge of his plate, then stood. "Oil needs changing in the mower. Just about enough light left to finish that up." He inched toward the back door like he was shamed about something, though I couldn't guess what. Mama didn't say anything, but I'm sure she knew what he'd done by the dirty look she threw his way.

"By all means, Mister Floyd Dubois. See to your mower, by all means."

He didn't answer because anything he'd of said, Mama would've twisted the wrong way. She was working herself into one of her moods, so no use starting a fight that wasn't absolutely necessary. Even Daddy could see that.

After he left, the three of us sat at the table, not saying a word, just staring at the dirty dishes scattered around us. I waited for one of them to say something. Tante Deacy. Mama. Didn't matter who. But they both just sat there, neither saying a word. This was not normal. I squirmed till my bottom rested on the edge of my chair and plopped both elbows on the table. Even that didn't bring Mama out her daze, though it could be she just didn't care since supper was over and it didn't matter how many elbows rested on the table. I was about to chase after Mavis and Austin. Even those two were better than eyeing grimy dishes and nothing more. But then Deacy decided she'd had enough of staring at dishes and not talking.

"I never thought he'd go," she said.

I thought about asking "where" again but decided my chances for learning more would be best if I kept my mouth closed.

Mama poured coffee dregs into the sink and started a fresh pot. "Look on the good side. He'll make enough for this baby and five more besides."

"No thanks. No more after this one." Deacy patted her belly.

"You need any work done, anything at all, you call Floyd while Everett's gone." Mama rested against the counter, waiting for the water to boil so she could pour it over the coffee beans.

"Sure. I'll call," Deacy said.

I'd been quiet and patient long enough. It hadn't gotten me anyplace. I still didn't know where Everett was going or why. "How long'll he be gone?" I asked at last, my tongue swollen from holding so many questions for so many long minutes.

"Gone long as he thinks money's the problem," Deacy said.

Water was boiling now, so Mama lifted the pot off the stove and poured a slow, steady stream that wouldn't drown the beans all at once. I never got tired of watching the grounds expand, soaking clear water, dripping rich brown coffee in its place. When the smell reached us, I took a deep sniff. Nothing like the smell of fresh coffee to make a person feel satisfied all over.

With Mama busy getting cups and saucers and pouring coffee, I chanced another question. "So where exactly is he going?"

"Lumbering. North Louisiana. The address says Monroe." She said that town's name with a voice that told anyone listening the town had nothing, less than nothing, to do with where her husband would be.

"Lots of money to be made in lumbering," I guessed.

"So some folks say. Money. Lots and lots of precious money." Her voice quivered. I hoped she wouldn't start crying.

Mama set the hot cups on the table, one in front of her place, one opposite, in front of Deacy. Steam puffs floated out the coffee. Even though it smelled good, I wasn't tempted, not at the end of an August day.

"Least you don't have to worry over Everett sending money home," Mama said.

"No. I don't worry about that."

"Some men leave town, all their wives get is a how-do postcard in the mail. Sometimes not even that much."

I wondered how Mama knew such things. Men leaving families like so much dirty laundry. Where did she learn all that?

"You don't need to worry over Everett on that account," Mama said.

"I'm not in the mood for counting blessings tonight, Hazey." Deacy's smile made her look sad and old. Most days she didn't look any older than Mama. Some days folks even took her for the younger sister, to Mama's mortification. That wouldn't happen this night because Deacy looked all of the seven years she had on Mama, plus some. The more I looked at her that night, the more it seemed to me the days of anyone mistaking Deacy for Mama's baby sister were over.

I got the rest of the story in bits and pieces and before Deacy and Austin headed home, I knew it all. Everett heard about lumbering jobs up north that paid three and four times what he got at the IGA. I don't know how he heard, but that doesn't matter because it's not what anyone would consider a real important part of the story. What is important is the way he got himself the names of a couple of lumbering companies and drove up on his last Thursday off and got himself hired and now was moving up there to make money for Deacy and their change-of-life baby and their three worthless sons. From where I sat, didn't seem Uncle Everett was doing anything so wrong. But I had sense enough not to say that to Mama or even Tante Deacy.

Daddy managed to make the oil change last till company was gone. The ladies had only left a cup of coffee in the bottom of the pot. The last cup is the one you have to drink slowly or else you'll swallow grounds by mistake. Some nights Mama offered to make a fresh pot even though that meant she'd be throwing out more than half of it at bedtime. Tonight she didn't offer and Daddy knew better than to ask, just carefully sipped what Mama and Deacy had left him.

As it turned out Everett didn't leave till Sunday afternoon. Mama dragged us to their house after dinner. I knew she didn't care about saying good-bye and good luck to him. But she wanted to be there in case Deacy needed her.

"Can't I go to Marydale's?" Mavis whined while she and Mama finished drying and saving the Sunday dishes.

"No indeed," Mama said.

"Uncle Everett'll be back most weekends, Austin says. I can say good-bye one of those visiting weekends." Mavis had never once been allowed to go to Marydale's on one of Daddy's days off. But she was never one to give up easy, especially when grumbling might get her over there.

"We are not going to say good-bye to Everett." Mama shoved a pot on a hook above the stove with enough force to rattle the pans already hanging. "We're going to visit Tante Deacy, your cousins. That's all. Nothing more."

Mavis kept quiet after that. Sometimes the girl gave hints of actually having a brain inside that head of hers.

No one said anything on the ride to town. Daddy drove. Mama stared out her side window. Mavis and I stared out ours. No one was upset with anyone, least not that I could tell. Just no one was in the mood for talking.

Uncle Everett's truck was parked in front of the house. A canvas tarp covered the back. I peeked under before joining the rest of my family inside. There was his toolbox, a plaid suitcase so faded you couldn't tell what the colors had once been, a cooler, once white but now gray and marked with splotches of yellow, and an ax, blade bright as a new day in the darkness of the truck bed. That was all. Nothing more. I'm not sure what I expected, but something more. Didn't seem a man could leave his family, even if it was only temporary—Everett figured he'd make enough to come back to Ville d'Angelle for good in a year or two—with only those few things in the back of a battered pickup. Far as I could tell Everett was the one should've been doing the crying that afternoon, not Deacy.

When I got inside, Tante Deacy was cutting a last slice of spice cake. Seems I'd heard tell spice was Everett's least favorite type cake. But I might be mistaken on that one.

"Just in time, Vivien Leigh," she said and handed me two plates, then picked up the last two from the counter. I followed her to the parlor, where everyone waited. I gave my extra plate to Austin and Deacy gave hers to Mavis. The boys were still in their church pants, dress shirts, and bow ties but had to sit on the floor because their mama didn't have enough parlor chairs for so much company. Deacy hadn't changed out her church clothes either. She wore a single strand of pearls. Her cheeks were flushed pink and her eyes were too bright. I hoped she wasn't running a temperature.

Only Everett had found the time to get out of his church clothes. He wore khaki work pants and one of his green IGA shirts. I didn't guess Mister Alan would mind if Everett wore an IGA shirt up in Monroe, Louisiana. Would be free advertising, if anyone from Monroe decided to move down to Ville d'Angelle, though I'd never heard of that happening.

I crossed my ankles to make up for wearing shorts, though they were clean and came with a matching shirt that I'd tucked properly. Mavis and I couldn't be blamed for not dressing fancy as our cousins. Who could know Everett's leaving would be occasion for Sunday church clothes and parlor eating?

"You boys about ready for school?" Mama asked, politer than she usually was to Deacy's sons. Parlor eating brought out manners in most people. Not in those boys, though. They didn't answer Mama. Just kept shoving cake into mouths.

"Answer your tante," Everett said.

"Leave the boys alone, will you," Deacy said.

"I am still their father," he said, his words clipped short, which made me think this was the continuation of a fight that had started long before we got there.

"No one's saying different," Daddy said, giving Mama a quick look. "Imagine T.J.'s ready to eye those good-looking high school girls. Just doesn't want to tell us old people about that." Daddy was trying to change the subject, get people picking on someone besides Everett. But T.J. didn't appreciate the effort. He turned red and stared at a spot on his right shoe.

Daddy was too taken with his cleverness to let go T.J.'s love life, which was an awfully hard thing to hold on to, it being completely nonexistent. "Got yourself a special girl, I bet," Daddy said.

T.J. couldn't take it anymore. He got off the floor. "Any cake left?" he said.

"No. Package of Oreos in the bottom cabinet," Deacy said. She felt sorry for poor old T.J., no girlfriend, not even the possibility of a girlfriend. Pity was the only explanation for her allowing two desserts.

Austin and Malcolm stared after their brother. "Last year Faye Fontenot told everybody she was my girlfriend," Austin said.

That was true. No accounting for Fontenot taste. Austin had been embarrassed into playing by himself every recess for two weeks. Only reason he brought Faye Fontenot up now was he was hoping for some of those Oreos.

"Always knew you'd be the Valentino of this family. Take after your daddy," Daddy said.

Even I could tell that was the wrong thing to say. Mama shot him a look that let Daddy know the error of his ways.

Daddy stood, pretending he hadn't noticed Mama's glare. "Anybody else interested in whether T.J. left some Oreos?" Both boys and Everett jumped up as if they suddenly discovered they were sitting on fire ants. Mavis got up too, but slower. They filed into the kitchen, one by one, looking like a fast-stepping funeral procession.

"Guess we should get these dishes out the way," Mama said.

I should've joined the Oreo parade. But Tante Deacy saved me. I say "me" because I would've been the one stuck with dishwashing even if I was a guest and shouldn't have to be doing work that rightfully belonged to those boys.

"No hurry about that," Deacy said, saving me the chore and the worrying over it too.

"So when's he leaving exactly?" Mama asked.

"It'll take him four, four and a half hours and he wants to get there before dark."

"Soon then."

"Soon." Deacy pushed her spice cake around her plate with her fork but didn't show signs of wanting to eat the half she hadn't gotten to yet. I'd never known Deacy to leave her sweets uneaten.

"Things'll work out," Mama said. "He'll be crawling back after a couple of weeks of hard beds, home-cooked meals fading to a memory, and nobody putting up with his moods. Before you have a chance to miss him, he'll be back."

I wondered whether Mama really believed that or was just saying it to get Deacy feeling better. For myself, I didn't believe a word. From the looks of Tante Deacy, neither did she.

"He won't let go the thought this baby was my idea. That I did it on purpose. Why do you think he keeps saying that, Hazey?" Deacy put her plate on the floor and leaned forward, cradling her belly like it ached. "Why do you think?" She frowned.

"Cause he's crazy. That's why."

I agreed with that. Anybody'd be crazy to get themselves angry and upset over the good luck of having a change-of-life baby. Deacy wasn't satisfied with Mama's answer, though. She kept frowning and leaning in to Mama. "How can he think I wanted this baby any more than he did? That this is any more my fault than his?"

Poor Deacy. Everett going up to Monroe was making her crazy too. I said the only thing I could think might make her feel better. "Maybe cause if he doesn't blame you, he'll have to blame himself," I said.

Both ladies stared at me, looking surprised I was still in the parlor. I snuggled deeper into the wingback chair Daddy'd abandoned. I tried to look so comfortable, no one would have the heart to make me leave.

"The girl's right," Mama said.

"You don't think I did wrong, chose wrong?" Deacy wasn't frowning, but still leaned forward, though she wasn't quite so bent over and had stopped cradling her belly.

"Listen to me, sister. You had no choice. Everett on one side. That baby in you on the other. That's no choice at all. None. Hear me?"

"What if he's really gone for good?"

"Then he's gone. No one would've taken Everett over that baby." Mama walked over to Deacy and reached for both hands and pulled her out the chair. "You did the only thing you could. Wasn't even a choice there. Hear me?"

Deacy dipped her chin to her chest slowly, again and again, hypnotized by Mama holding both her hands and staring at her that way. My mama can be a powerful woman.

Austin ran into the parlor, grabbed his mama around her hips. "Daddy says he's about ready to get started."

Mama let go of only one of Deacy's hands, holding the other so tightly I could see the knuckles whiten. Holding her that way, she led her out the front door, Austin and me following.

Everyone else was already gathered next to Everett's truck. No one knew the right thing to say or even the right place to stand or the proper thing to do with their hands. We shifted from place to place, foot to foot. We put hands in pockets and when that didn't work, on hips, and when that felt wrong, tried dangling them at our sides. None of it felt right. Only Everett stayed still, leaning against the driver's door and watching Mama lead Deacy to him. Mama led her right up to him before finally dropping her hand.

Deacy stood only a few inches from Everett. I know she could see his tiniest pores, the beginnings of the smallest whiskers. But she didn't reach out to touch him.

"You have the number. You need anything, you let me know," he said.

Her nod was so slight, it was easy to miss. But Everett must've been satisfied because he didn't push for more. He motioned each boy to him for a hug. "You listen to your mama while I'm gone. Help her out. Don't want to hear any bad reports on any of you. Hear me?"

They all mumbled promises about correct behavior, which were nothing but wasted words because those boys had no true intentions of changing their lazy, no-good ways.

Everett turned back to Deacy then and linked one hand through her pearl necklace, maybe remembering those long-ago Baton Rouge nights. "I'm doing right by us," he said softly.

She still just stood there. Not saying a thing.

He dropped his hand from the necklace and pulled her closer for a hug and kiss. But anybody with eyes could see how stiff she held herself. Must've been like hugging a piece of cardboard. Even her lips didn't pucker. "You take care of yourself," he said, then climbed into the cab and backed out the drive, waving once. Only Austin waved back.

10

A MEASURE
OF GOLD

WE STAYED LONG ENOUGH to make sure Tante Deacy
was holding up okay, then headed home because Daddy said he couldn't
measure in the dark. I didn't know what he was planning on measuring and
didn't care. Deacy's face, worn and miserable, was all I could think about.
I sure hoped that change-of-life baby knew what she was doing.

"Poor Deacy," Mama said softly as we pulled out the drive and into the
street. "Married to a fool," she said louder, daring any of us to say different, which none of us would, none of us being complete fools.

Daddy cleared his throat. "I've been thinking you might be right about
a bathroom. Won't hurt to measure for it, see what the estimate would be."

"Estimate for what?" I asked. I'd been spending so much time thinking
about change-of-life babies and colored sisters, I'd missed the goings-on
under my own roof.

"Estimate for adding a bedroom and den, small one, to the house,"
Mavis said.

My teeth like to fall out my jaw when I heard that. Mavis knowing
something so important when I didn't. Was enough to make me sick to my
stomach.

"How'd you know that?" I asked.

"I heard talk," Mavis said.

"You might've told me."

"I don't tell everything I know."

"There's not much to tell."

"I know much as anybody. More than you." Her cheeks started puffing, but what did I care.

"You girls keep off each other," Daddy said.

I crossed my arms and looked out my window, away from Mavis, that secret-hoarding sister who couldn't spell *share*, much less do it. When I thought of all the times I'd given Mavis important, useful information, I could've pinched her till she cried. Girl didn't know the meaning of sisterly love.

All four of us went to the shed to get Daddy's tape measure and spiral notebook he used for writing important things. We walked to a back corner of the house.

"Mavis, you hold this end and stand right here. Don't move an inch."

"No, sir." Mavis looked prouder than sin holding the end of an old measuring tape, the numbers faded to a pale gray.

Daddy pulled out more tape as he walked. "How much extra for a bathroom?"

Mama looked up at the sky as if the numbers were written there. I could see her figuring in her head. "Let's say nine by seven and a half, which'd be on the big side but give room for a towel chest."

"Make it ten by eight, just to be even," Daddy said as he kept walking. He stopped, turned around to face Mavis. "Vivien Leigh, get us some gardening stakes, the small ones we use for the marking strings."

When I got back, Daddy was adding lines and numbers to the sketch he'd drawn in his notebook. He shoved one of my stakes into the spot he'd marked with the tape, another one next to Mavis. "Let go your end now," he called. The tape zipped out Mavis's hand and disappeared into its holder.

"Want me to tie string between the stakes?" I asked. No need for Mavis to think she was the only one with an important job.

"Strings are a good idea," Mama said. "We'll see the whole thing better with strings."

"Just don't go tying them too tight. Men'll have to move them to do their own measuring," Daddy said.

"Sure," I said. So while Daddy and Mavis measured and hammered stakes into their marked spots, Mama and I cut and tied strings. It looked good when we finished, even without walls or floors or ceilings.

"What you doing?" Marydale surprised us all. We'd been too busy admiring our stakes and strings to notice her peeping around the corner. "I saw you got back."

"Want to play in the new part of my house?" Mavis ran to Marydale, grabbed her hand, and pulled her into my bedroom.

"This where the added-on part's going?"

Even the colored girl down the road knew more about my family's affairs than I did. I kicked a pebble that was right about where my bureau'd go. "Once this gets built, don't let me catch you two snooping in my room," I said. I thought Mavis'd puff up over who'd get the new bedroom but she just hopped over the string into the hall we'd marked. Marydale followed.

"Mama says I can have bunk beds when you move out," Mavis said, explaining in one quick sentence why she wasn't fighting me over the new room. She could have as many bunk beds as she wanted, far as I cared. A brand-new, never-been-used-before room was worth a dozen bunks.

"Mama says I can have a friend spend overnight when I get those beds," Mavis said.

Mama'd sure had to make a lot of promises to keep Mavis happy over getting that old used-up room.

"First overnight friend'll be me," Marydale said.

"That's right," Mavis said.

I threw Mavis a look that said not to be stupid, but didn't say anything. I didn't want to hurt Marydale's feelings even if she was colored. "You're lucky Daddy's back in the house," I said. Even Mavis'd know what I meant by that.

"We got any ice cream in this house?" Daddy asked when he got off the phone with Edwin Sonnier that night.

"Mavis and Marydale got the last of it Friday," Mama said.

"Piggies," Daddy said, but grinned and didn't show any meanness over a colored girl getting the ice cream his hard-earned money had bought. "What can you expect from two little piggies?" He sat on the floor next to Mama, who had a five-thousand-piece puzzle spread on the coffee table. Every once in a while Mama got it into her head to work a puzzle. Then for weeks and weeks no one could use the coffee table, which was a definite inconvenience. This one would be gorillas in some jungle when she finished.

"We did it," he said.

"Did what?" She was looking for all the straight-edge parts so she could get the outside frame done. First the outside frame, then everything in the middle.

"What have I been working on practically every minute these past weeks?" He jabbed Mama's arm till she looked away from her puzzle and at him. "Well?"

"That school foolishness," she said.

"*Foolishness* is the word, all right. Only not so foolish anymore." He paused, took a deep breath. "We've saved first grade. Got enough money and pledges so Miss Boudreaux's agreed to teach. Just for this year, but that's all right. We have a whole year to come up with something else." He paused again, maybe waiting for congratulations. But Mama just turned back to her puzzle, me to my book, Mavis to her drawing of her bedroom showing where she'd be putting those bunk beds.

"Well, don't any of you have something to say about that?" He said "any" but only looked at Mama.

"What'll happen to the colored sister who was supposed to get first?" Mama asked.

"No one knows. No ones cares."

"I just hope Elsie Boudreaux knows what she's doing."

"What are you talking about? She's a teacher, isn't she?"

Mama added two pieces to the pile she was building at the corner of the table. "Elsie Boudreaux never taught younger than fifth. You know that."

"Fine. So this'll be a piece of cake. What do you need to teach first? Know your A-B-C's, numbers to nine hundred ninety-nine. What else?" Daddy's good mood was fast disappearing.

"I just hope she has the patience for those little babies."

Daddy stood. "You beat everything. Know that, Hazel? You just beat everything." He went to the kitchen for a Jax, then came back. "If there were all these problems with Elsie Boudreaux, why didn't you say something before now?"

"Too much going on, I guess." She rubbed a hand across her forehead.

"Headache any better?" His voice softened to normal.

She shook her head.

"Maybe you're coming down with something."

"I'll take aspirin before bed." She swept a pile of oddly shaped pieces into the box, where they'd wait till she had the outside edge done.

"Miss Boudreaux'll do fine. She'll have to do. No other choice," Daddy said. He took a long swallow of beer.

"Except for that colored sister."

"Who could call that a choice?"

Mama didn't answer, just kept searching for the right puzzle pieces.

Next morning Mama dragged me out of bed at nine. I was disgusted. My birthday and my last free Monday before school started. I didn't count Labor Day, it being a holiday and who knew what'd happen on a holiday.

My last Monday for sleeping late and I wasn't given the chance to do it. The builders had come and gone while I slept. But now the bank man was due and he'd have to see all our house, including my bedroom. So not only did I have to wake up, I had to get out of bed, dress, and eat breakfast, all before the man arrived at nine-thirty. It was more rushing than anyone should have to do on an August morning that was also her birthday.

Cleo and I were sitting on the front steps by nine twenty-seven, three minutes early. But it wasn't the bank man who came tearing up our drive. It was Daddy.

The engine hadn't died before he'd jumped out the cab to stand in front of me. "Mister Kidder here yet?"

"Not yet." Anyone with eyes could see there wasn't a strange car parked in our drive, and bankers are not the hitchhiking sort.

Cleo sashayed over to Daddy's right leg and brushed against him. He pushed her aside, but not roughly, more from habit. "Good. Never be late when you're begging money. Remember that, Vivien Leigh." I waited for him to say happy birthday but he just went into the house to hunt Mama.

Daddy'd taken time special off work and would have to make it up late into the evening. But Mister Kidder must not have realized that because it was close to ten-fifteen before his red Cadillac pulled in the drive. Should've been green, money color.

"Sugar, your folks home?" He was tall and thin and every separate part of his body was that way too. His ears were pretzels against the sides of his head. His face was narrow, forehead and chin spreading too far on either end. Strands of spindly hair were pulled from one side of his head to the other, trying to cover his bald spot. Each arm and leg was so long and skinny, he looked like a stick. Fingers had skin stretched so tight, the bones showed plain. I couldn't see his toes through his shoes, but I was sure they were bony as his fingers.

Before I could answer, Daddy opened the front door. "Vivien Leigh, move out the way. Right in here, Mister Kidder." He held the door open while Cleo and I stood to the side.

"Hope you folks haven't been waiting too long."

"No, sir. Not long at all."

Before the door slammed shut on that lie, I followed them into the house.

"Something came up. Couldn't get away. You know how it is." The whole time he talked, he looked around the parlor. When he'd had enough of looking, he pulled a narrow notebook from his breast pocket and started scribbling.

"The place is kept up good. Just, it's a few rooms too small," Daddy said.

The banker nodded but didn't say more, just kept scribbling and walking around the room. Mama came out the kitchen where she'd been whipping up my Double Chocolate Devil's Surprise birthday cake and offered coffee.

"Too hot for my taste," he said. He wiped his forehead with a white handkerchief, but I hadn't seen any sweat. "Thanks anyway."

"We have lemonade. Don't we, Hazey? If we don't, she can make some up in a split. How about a glass of ice-cold lemonade, Mister Kidder?" Daddy said.

"Now you're tempting me. You surely are. But I'm running too late this morning. Business before pleasure. That's what I always say. Business first."

"Sure," Daddy said. "I feel the same. Always take care of business first."

"Let's see the rest of it."

"Sure thing, Mister Kidder. Right this way." Daddy led the banker through the house, room by room, bedrooms, bath, and ended back in the kitchen. The whole time, the banker scribbled and scribbled. I didn't think anyone could find that much to write about our house.

"Like I said before, place is kept up real good," Daddy said in the kitchen.

Mister Kidder crouched near the stove, inspecting the spot where linoleum had torn off a long time ago.

"That's just a little thing. I'll fix it right up, if it makes a difference. We still have linoleum in the shed I can use. Right, Hazel?"

"Sure," Mama said.

Mister Kidder stood, still staring at that one tiny spot. "The bank has to make sure its loans are safe. Owe that to our depositors."

Bankers wouldn't turn you down on account of one tiny linoleum mistake, would they? You wouldn't think so. But the way this man was bearing down on that spot, you'd think the whole loan turned on it.

"I could fix it up fine. Easy," Daddy said, and he could too.

"Looks like I have everything I need." He folded the notebook and returned it to his breast pocket.

"Want to look around outside? We have the shed, carport," Daddy said.

"No need."

"Isn't any trouble." Daddy especially wanted him to see the shed, all the tools hanging straight on pegs, nuts and bolts and screws in Mama's old mason jars, nails arranged by size in tuna cans lined in a square box, paint stacked neatly in one corner, rags folded, everything in a proper place. If

Mister Kidder could see the shed, he'd know we were the sort took care of our things, deserved that loan. But Mister Kidder wasn't interested.

"Seen one shed, seen them all," he said. He opened the back screen. Hot air pushed into the kitchen.

"Let us know if you need anything else," Daddy said.

"Anything at all," Mama added.

"Sure thing, folks." He looked over at Mavis and Marydale, working their hole near the willow. "Thought you only had two girls."

Guess he couldn't see Marydale too well behind those willow branches.

"Only one of those belongs to us. Other one is a neighbor girl," Mama said.

Daddy's lips parted, then closed. He'd thought better of explaining Marydale was a little colored girl, daughter of our cleaning lady, and didn't have any business spending as much time as she did hanging around our house. Daddy knew a banker'd think twice on giving money to a family with a girl who thought nothing of playing with a colored day in, day out.

Mister Kidder kept looking over at Mavis and Marydale as if, even with that willow curtain, he could tell something wasn't right.

"Sure you don't want to see the shed?" Daddy asked.

"Too busy." Mister Kidder patted his forehead with that white handkerchief again. He must've been able to tell just when sweat was about to pop out and swabbed before beads had a chance to show themselves. "Never enough time in a day."

"That's for sure," Daddy said.

"Course I'm also eager to get back to air-conditioning." He laughed, a hiccuping sound too shaky to be true.

Daddy laughed till Mister Kidder stopped. "Air-conditioning's a fine invention," Daddy said.

"Once you start with it, though, you can hardly stop." He patted his neck with the handkerchief. "Take my advice. Don't start with air unless you plan on putting it everywhere. Home. Work. Car. Everywhere."

"Yes, sir. Sounds like good advice and I'll take it. That's for sure."

"Air's expensive, but worth every cent."

"Every penny. Yes, sir, every penny," Daddy said as if any day he expected to get air-conditioning, at home and at work too. But you can't check oil tank gauges like Daddy did at work and be air-conditioned at the same time since those tanks are outdoors, not in.

Mister Kidder slid into his car, started the engine, then pushed buttons on the dash. "Feel that."

Daddy pushed a hand through the open door. "Cold." He sounded surprised.

"Darn right. Cold the minute you turn it on unless it's been sitting in the sun all day. Then it takes a while to cool down. You'd expect that, though."

"Sure. You'd have to expect that." Daddy rotated his hand so all sides could get some of that cool air.

"I should know something by Wednesday. You call then. If I'm not around, my secretary can help you."

"Wednesday," Daddy repeated.

Two more days before I'd know for sure whether I'd have my own bedroom, fresh and clean smelling, nothing to hint of Mavis.

"Evelyn's worth her weight in gold. Remember that about a good secretary. She's worth her weight in gold." He jiggled a hand as if balancing gold dust.

"Gold," Daddy said.

Reminded me of the gold Marydale claimed for her church. I never did check up on her about that one. Probably was nothing but another story from a change-of-life girl. Grown-ups'd laugh if I asked about gold in a colored church. Gold was for bankers and bankers' secretaries, not for coloreds, not even for a colored church.

"Your girls go to Holy Rosary?"

"Yes, sir. Sure do."

"Some mess happening at Holy Rosary." Now that he had cold air blowing on his face, he didn't seem in such a hurry to get back to business. Guess Evelyn could manage fine without him.

"We got the mess straightened. Least partways straightened." Daddy explained about Miss Boudreaux, who'd never taught first but who'd be lots better than any colored no matter if that colored had taught first all her nun life.

"That's all right then. Can't let coloreds take over."

"No, sir. Can't let that happen."

"Just look up north. See what happens if coloreds take over."

I waited for an explanation about what had happened up north. But Daddy and the banker just nodded at each other, neither seeing need to explain what they both already knew.

"The president has to look the papers over. But he'll go with my recommendation."

What would that recommendation be? I held my breath, waiting for Daddy to ask. But he didn't, maybe afraid to hear the answer he'd get.

"I do thank you, Mister Kidder. I do indeed. Yes, sir." Daddy offered a handshake, which the banker took.

Mister Kidder slammed the door shut, gave a short wave, then backed to the road.

Sure would be nice to have some gold of my own. If I did, I'd build a bedroom with shelves for my books and all my things. Wouldn't have need for a too-thin banking man roaming through the house to give his yea or nay. No need for me to worry over a small square of missing linoleum. No need to hope the banker wasn't thinking bad things about me or my family. With gold of my own, none of that would happen. But I didn't have gold of my own. Probably never would. So no use to thinking about what I'd do with it if I had it.

Daddy took two ham and cheese sandwiches with him in his truck. He'd eat on the way back to work so he wouldn't have to take off for lunch and could save a bit of makeup time that way. Wonder if bankers and their secretaries have to take time off for lunch or if they get paid while they eat? So many things to wonder over and all Mavis and Marydale could do was dig a hole for gold that didn't exist.

I relaxed on my bed in front of the fan with *Wuthering Heights*. The librarian had said I'd like it. It was okay but not close to *Jane Eyre*. The fan hummed air my way and soon I was too busy with Heathcliff and Cathy to worry or wonder over gold or bankers or what present I'd be opening after supper or anything else.

11

CHANGE-OF-LIFE LUCK

MISTER KIDDER WAS TRUE to his word. On Wednesday morning Evelyn told Daddy the loan was approved. Daddy called to tell Mama the news and she called Deacy to tell her. With luck, I'd be in my own bedroom, free from Mavis, come Christmas, a long time off, but seeable. Maybe Mama'd allow me an overnight during the holidays. If Mavis got one, I for sure would too. But I didn't know whether Mama'd just said that to stop Mavis's whining or whether it had been a true promise of something that'd really happen.

Tante Deacy drove up in late morning and caught me looking under the house, searching Cleo, who'd gotten angry for some cat reason and been under there since last night, only coming out for water when no one was watching. Just since I'd seen Deacy three days earlier, her stomach was pouchier.

"That cat's crazy, honey. Just leave her alone. She'll come out when she gets hungry."

"I didn't mean to upset her." I stood, wiped dirt off my knees and shins. "What'd you do?"

"I don't know. All I know is she's completely aggravated with me."

"Typical cat." She put an arm around my shoulders. "Come on in and leave her alone. Your mama's busy this morning?"

"I guess." Mama was always busy, even when she didn't seem that way to the normal eye. We found her paying bills at the kitchen table.

Deacy helped herself to coffee. "Everett called last night."

That got Mama's mind off check writing. "About time. So he made it okay."

"Says it's lots cooler in those woods." She grabbed one of Mama's unpaid bills and fanned herself. "Lord, we could use more rain." She fanned faster. "Never has been a summer hot as this one for as far back as I can remember. A crazy summer."

"So what's he say?"

"Got blisters on both palms and thumbs."

"Well, isn't that pitiful," Mama said, slow and sarcastic so anyone could tell pity was the last thing she was feeling.

"I told him to get himself some K-One ointment and bandage those blisters so they won't get infected."

"More advice than he deserved." Mama wasn't ever going to forgive Everett for moving to Monroe. He'd best not be begging advice off her because he sure wouldn't get any.

"Maybe," Deacy said. She patted her belly. "Maybe," she said again.

They got to talking about our loan getting approved and after that about the fig picking and canning, which'd happen tomorrow, so I went outside. It's bad enough to have to do all that work without hearing about it ahead of time. Feels like you're doing a job twice when you talk it through before doing it.

Mavis and Marydale had gathered sticks from the canal and lined them into different shapes inside the new parts of our house.

"What you girls doing?" I asked. "Why aren't you digging on that gold hole?"

"We're fixing up furniture," Mavis said.

When I looked closer, I could tell. Sort of. I could tell where they'd put the sofa and a coffee table. The rest were piles of sticks here and there. Course it all meant something to them. "Mama might want things different."

"We know."

"Don't put those stupid sticks in my bedroom either."

"They're not stupid," Mavis said.

"We got all the same size or close to same size. Wiped them good too. Wiped on pasture grass so's our furniture be good and clean," Marydale said.

"I wouldn't want to set my bottom on any of that furniture. That's all I know. And I don't want any of it in my room."

Marydale shrugged and turned back to stacking sticks in the bathroom. Was she working on a toilet or sink? No way to tell.

"Tomorrow's canning day," I said. I twisted the onyx ring I'd gotten for my birthday. I wore it on my middle finger, but Mama said it'd fit my ring finger by spring, maybe sooner.

"We know," Mavis said. Ever since it came out about her knowing plans for this house addition and me not, she'd been acting like Miss Know-It-All. But Mavis wasn't close to knowing it all, was so dumb she didn't even know how much she didn't know.

"Tante Yvette says there's lots more this year than last," I said.

"Be the hotness make those figs grow," Marydale said.

"That's it all right," Mavis echoed.

"Be them eggs-on-a-sidewalk days, day after day this summer, giving them good figs." Marydale picked up a load of seven or eight sticks and carried them to the den, squatting next to Mavis. "Too bad we didn't plant our peanuts this spring, us. Sure too bad we didn't do that."

"What peanuts you talking about, girl?" Cleo had inched her way to the edge of the house. Just the tip of her whiskers caught sunlight and gave her away. Even Cleo was tempted out her madness by talk of planting peanuts.

"Me and Mavis planning on growing peanuts," Marydale said, calm as when she'd explained their plan for digging gold.

"Nobody around here grows peanuts," I said.

"That's right. Everybody'll be wanting fresh peanuts and we'll be the only ones having them. Make us some good spending money. That be for sure."

"With all the gold you girls'll be digging up, what do you need with more spending money?"

Mavis knew I was making fun of both silly ideas. Her cheeks started puffing.

"Can always be using more spending money," Marydale said.

"I suppose." Cleo had crept all the way out and was sunning herself in a patch of light in the middle of my soon-to-be bedroom.

"Me and Mavis, we be coming up with more good ideas than we ever have time to use."

"You two are big thinkers all right."

Those cheeks puffed fatter and fatter. I wasn't even putting all my mind to insulting.

"You're just jealous," Mavis said.

"Of what, I'd like to know."

"Us. That's what." She stood from her pile of sticks and pulled Marydale up with her, not letting go Marydale's hand even after she had her standing. "You're jealous cause you don't have a best friend down the road who can come over most any day and think up ideas and do things."

"Sure thing. I'm boo-hooing jealous." I rubbed fists across my eyes to make like I was crying.

"Come on, Marydale. She's stupid as a mushy melon." They marched off to the willow, their two little bottoms swinging their aggravation all the way.

Would've been nice if Clorise lived closer. But at least she wasn't colored and that was better than having a dozen friends living all around my house. When would poor old Mavis learn that simple fact of life?

Cleo stretched, then walked my way, the whole time turning her head this way and that, pretending she didn't see me. I sat, waited for her to reach me. "Pretty baby. Such a pretty baby." I scratched behind her ears the way she likes. "Pretty girl. Pretty, pretty girl," I crooned. She lifted her haunches and waved her tail like a flag.

Some people say cats are nothing but wild animals who can't understand anything a person says. Though wild is true more times than not, Cleo understands every single thing I tell her and lets me know whether she's approving or not. She has her own ideas and her own ways of doing things, which is a big reason she annoys Daddy much as she does. He likes dogs— slobbering, barking, come-when-you-call-them, do-whatever-you-want dogs. Dogs are okay to pet. But they don't have minds of their own. Not like cats. If you're going to own something, isn't it better to own something with a mind than something without? Seems an easy question to answer. But Daddy likes obedience and devotion more than a thinking mind in his animals. One more reason he and Cleo'll never be on friendly terms.

Cleo climbed on my lap, her sign that she wanted to be petted. After about ten minutes she got tired of that and walked back to the corner of the house, turned in three quick circles, then curled in a ball to go to sleep. She was close to the underside of the house but not actually under there. That was to let me know she wasn't still irritated with me. Cats are clever creatures and not even Daddy could say different.

Mama opened the back door about the same time Deacy pulled out our drive. "I'm going down the road for bread and milk. Any of you girls want to come for a ride?"

"No, ma'am. We too busy for riding this day," Marydale called from behind her willow curtain.

"Don't forget ice cream," Mavis said.

"That's right, Miz Hazey. Don't forget you folks be out ice cream."

"Vivien Leigh, you coming?" Mama asked.

"Might as well." I brushed grass off my seat and followed Mama to the car. No use to staying behind with Mavis and Marydale and their gold-digging, furniture-building ways.

"You girls stay right there till we get back. I don't want any trouble while I'm gone."

"No, ma'am. Me and Mavis, we don't want any trouble us, no."

The Simoneaux Market was about a mile and a half from our house and didn't carry much, but sure was a convenience when Mama ran out of small things like milk or bread. It opened the year I turned four and has done good business ever since. The Simoneaux have three girls, three boys, a fair way of doing things. I don't know any of them well. Youngest two are in high school, older than T.J., and whoever heard of a high schooler running with a fifth-grader? No one, that's who. Still, those Simoneaux are real nice and have themselves a real nice store.

"You think it's lot of work owning a store?" I asked as we headed to market.

"Imagine it's lot of work. Sure is," Mama said.

We both had our windows rolled down so wind whipped our hair back and we had to speak louder than normal to be heard above the whistle of air blowing in our ears. "Doesn't look like much work. Not that I can see."

"Lots of paperwork. Ordering supplies. Keeping track of what's selling, what isn't. Stocking shelves. Paying for what you've ordered. Keeping the place clean. You never see a speck of dirt on that floor, no matter how many people track in and out each day. You look this time. See if you find a speck of dirt on those floors, shelves."

Mama glanced at me, though I couldn't see her eyes behind her sunglasses. She couldn't see mine either, since I had glasses on too. Mama kept two pairs in the glove compartment for me and Mavis to wear when we drove with the windows rolled down. She said those glasses were good protection from things flying into the car and settling in our eyes. I'd never had a piece of anything fly into my eye through the window, but no need to chance disaster. Some days I wore glasses to keep Mama happy. Other days I wore them to look like a movie star. Other days, like today, I wore them just in case flecks were flying around, looking for a place to land.

There were already two cars when we got to the market. Since there was only room for three on the gravel lot in front of the store, good thing we got there when we did or else we would've had to wait till someone left.

We could've parked on the side of the road, which is what Daddy'd done the few times that had happened to him. But Mama considered that dangerous business. Stupid too. Mama was never one to abide stupid or to look for danger when safety was as easy.

Mona, the youngest Simoneaux girl, was minding the register. "Morning, Miz Hazey."

"Morning, Mona."

"Hot enough for you?"

Mama didn't bother answering, walked instead to the bread aisle. It being Wednesday, she pushed aside loaves till she found the Evangeline Maid with red ties on the back part of the shelf. Each day of the week had a different-colored tie. That was the way to tell which loaves were freshest. Mondays were blue. Wednesdays were red. I wasn't sure about the rest of the week. Aussie was the one first found out about the colors business. She told Mama who told Deacy who told who knows how many people. No one bought old bread anymore, thanks to Aussie. Don't know why the Simoneaux still bothered putting the freshest bread on the back of the shelf.

Mama picked up a gallon of milk, then walked up and down the three aisles, eyeing shelves to make sure she wasn't missing anything. I followed behind, passing a finger on shelves every few feet, checking for dirt. I even checked the front counter next to the register. Clean. All of it, clean as anything.

"Girl, you sure are getting tall," Mona said. Mona tried to sound like her mama when she worked the register. Funny to hear an old woman's words come out a girl still in high school, though she would be a senior this September.

"She'd better be getting tall for as much eating as she does," Mama said.

"Vivien Leigh's a big eater?"

"Lord, Mona. Just thank God you're not the one paying her food bills," Mama joked, then opened her purse.

"I almost forgot ice cream. Vivien Leigh, pick us a half gallon of something."

I was happy to get away. Nothing worse than standing glued to a spot while folks make fun of you.

I picked Chocolate Supreme and brought it back to the counter, where Mona was already giving Mama her change.

"Chocolate your favorite?" Mona asked.

"Sometimes," I said. I looked at the floor. Not a speck of anything to be seen.

"Can't hardly keep ice cream in the house," Mama said.

"In this weather, who can?" Mona said.

"Mavis and Marydale'd eat a half gallon a day, if I let them."

"Aussie picked up strawberry this morning."

"Henry dropped her off," Mama said, knowing that's how it would have to be.

Mona nodded agreement. "She was walking back."

"Henry had to get to work," Mama said. Our family knew everything about Aussie and her family. Knew when Henry went to work. When Little Aussie was sick. When Evie got a vacation day. Thanks to big-mouth Mavis, I imagined Aussie knew nearly much about our family as we knew about hers.

"Guess Marydale's bothering at your house right now," Mona said.

"She's not much bother. Keeps Mavis out of trouble," Mama said.

"Mavis'll get tired of her soon enough." Mona pulled a cloth from under the counter and wiped the ring of wetness where I'd set down Chocolate Supreme.

"I suppose," Mama said.

"Oh, sure. We still tease Martin about how he used to spend more time with Lucky Gilbert than Lucky's own mama."

Martin was only a year ahead of T.J., but I was sure they weren't friends. Martin played football, basketball, baseball and was good at all those things. Poor T.J. was still trying to find something he was good at.

"I remember Martin carrying on like he was loony when the Gilberts moved to New Orleans," Mama said.

"That's right. Mama was nothing but relieved. I'll tell you that. Martin was close to eight, old enough to know better than hanging around with a colored all day." Mona leaned her bottom on the stool back of the counter. "Lucky sent Martin a letter once. But Martin never wrote back far as I know."

"Probably your mama wouldn't let him," I said.

"Probably not. I felt a little bad for Lucky, who was the nicest colored boy I've ever known."

"Aussie and her Marydale won't ever be moving to New Orleans," I said.

"Mavis'll outgrow Marydale before you know it," Mona said.

"I expect," Mama said. She pointed me to the door with a quick flick of her hand. She wanted me gone before I could say anything stupid like, Mavis says Marydale is her best friend. Or, Mavis wouldn't mind going to a colored school long as she could sit next to Marydale. But Mama didn't have to worry. I was much too grown up to say anything like that.

When we got home Mavis and Marydale weren't anywhere to be seen, not digging gold, not making stick furniture, not in our bedroom, nowhere.

"Didn't I tell those girls to stay put?"

"Yes, ma'am. You sure did," I said. Mavis was in trouble and I couldn't pretend sadness over it.

"You run to the canal. See if they're down there." She put away the milk and ice cream. "Well, get a move on, Vivien Leigh."

Mavis was the one did the wrong thing and I got yelled at. Just the way things always went at my house. I ran down to the canal back of the pasture. I only ran in case Mama was watching me from the kitchen window, not because I wanted to. This was the fastest I'd moved all that sticky hot summer and when I reached the canal, I was out of breath and so sweaty, my shirt stuck to my back. I hated being out of breath and I hated being sweaty and Mavis was the cause of my being both.

In public school teachers make you take physical education every day. You run till you're hot and sweaty and out of breath. Then you go to your other classes. Those public schools must be some stinky places. I'm glad Catholics do not believe in physical education.

"Mavis, Marydale," I yelled. I walked halfway up the Blake side of the pasture and yelled again. Then I did the same thing up the Guillot side. "Don't you girls be hiding. Hear? You're in enough trouble without hunting up more."

Low bushes grew all along either side of the canal. They could've been hiding, but I probably would've spotted them what with Marydale's bright yellow shirt and bright yellow barrettes at the end of each plait. Was Mavis wearing her pink shorts? Probably. She loved those shorts more than anything. Made Mama throw them in the wash every time she ran a load. Mavis sure was wild for those pink shorts. Why couldn't I remember whether she was wearing them today? I saw Marydale's yellow shirt clear as anything. But I couldn't find a picture of Mavis, my own flesh and blood.

I ran back to our part of the canal, yelling all the way. "Mavis, Marydale. We got ice cream waiting." I watched for one of them to pop out a bush I'd missed. "Chocolate Supreme," I called. "Chocolate Supreme," I said again, louder so they'd be sure to hear, no matter whose side of the canal they were on.

"Dear Lord," I prayed while I ran to the house, "please don't let Mavis and Marydale be kidnapped." I'd read the story of the Lindbergh baby that summer and knew all about kidnappings. But who in their right mind would kidnap Mavis? She was nothing but a bother and a big mouth, always meddling in other people's business. Kidnappers'd have themselves nothing but trouble if they snatched Mavis.

Marydale wasn't any better. She'd talk and talk and talk till those kidnappers'd have to cover their ears. Besides, she was colored. Whoever heard of kidnapping a colored?

Still, those pictures of the Lindbergh baby kept flashing in my head. No matter how fast I ran, I couldn't run from that sweet baby's face, smiling and happy because he didn't know how evil people could be or how some of those evil people would be after him soon.

"Lord, don't let those girls be kidnapped," I prayed again. Someone dumb enough to snatch two silly second-graders, one of them colored at that, was dumb enough to do just about anything.

Mama was on the back steps, shading her eyes with a hand. "Find them?"

I shook my head, too out of breath to say anything.

Mama rubbed her hands down each side of her dress. "Okay. Think, Hazel. Think."

Only time she called herself by her given name was when things were serious. I began crying, knowing my baby sister, who was nothing but a pest and a bother but my sister all the same, was gone forever.

"Stop that," Mama said so sharply, my tears dried instantly. "I do not have time for blubbering."

I swiped my nose on the underside of my shirt and sniffed twice. "Maybe we should call Daddy."

"No use to that."

"Then the police. How about the police?" Where was Joe Friday when you needed him?

"That miserable excuse for a sheriff is in some saloon drinking his fourth or fifth beer of the day."

Mama did not abide anyone drinking before two in the afternoon, no matter how hot the day.

"By the time Lafayette police get out here we'll have found the girls ourselves," Mama said.

Mama pulled keys from her dress pocket, then turned to the car. I followed. I didn't know where we were going but I wasn't staying home. If some maniac was out snatching children like Mavis and Marydale, I wasn't giving him a chance to add me to his collection of bagged girls.

I could see poor little Mavis, beaten and bloody. Marydale lying next to her looking the same. The both of them'd be holding hands, not caring if the whole world knew they were best friends. I closed my eyes to shut out those pictures, but they stayed. I sniffled, trying to hold back tears as I followed Mama. My poor baby sister.

"We should have one big funeral for the both of them," I said through a throat thick with uncried tears.

"Whose funeral you talking about?" Mama started the engine and glanced at me. "Don't be a silly goose. Only thing those girls are getting is the backside of my hand."

She was saying that to make me feel better. My sister was gone for good, but I'd see to it she'd have the best funeral Ville d'Angelle had ever seen. We'd pass the girls through both funeral homes, colored and white. We'd do the same for churches, get them blessed at Saint Stephen's and Saint Paul's. Keep those two coffins as close to each other in death as the girls had been in life.

"I made fun of her gold digging this morning," I said. "I think I called her a name."

"So what else is new?"

"I wouldn't of done it if I'd known this was her last day." Dear God, I promised, I won't ever be mean to Mavis again if you don't let that kidnapper kill her.

"Vivien Leigh, honey, Mavis and Marydale decided to go somewhere. Who knows where? But somewhere. All we have to do is find them." She looked left and right at the end of the driveway, trying to decipher which way the kidnapper went. "Stop all this morbid funeral talk. You give me the heebie-jeebies." Her voice was strong, trying to give me courage. But it didn't work.

Another thought came to me then. What if we caught the kidnapper before he'd actually hurt Mavis and Marydale? What if I kicked him where the sun don't shine while Mavis and Marydale ran to the car? The Lafayette paper'd probably carry a picture of me on the front page. Might even get myself on the TV news.

"Well would you look at that," Mama said.

"What? Where?" I hoped she'd spotted the kidnapper. But all I saw, coming down the road, was Aussie, Mavis and Marydale skipping in front of her. Even from this far away I could tell there wasn't any kidnapper in this story.

Mama turned the car back into the carport, then walked down the drive to meet Aussie. I was right behind her, intent on not missing one word of this story. We waited at the edge of the drive, Mama's arms folded across her chest, my arms folded across mine.

"Girls remembered I had me a half gallon strawberry from Simoneaux's this morning," Aussie said when they got close enough for us to hear without her yelling.

"That so?" Mama didn't unfold her arms and neither did I. A hunt for strawberry ice cream canceled any promise I made to God, to my way of thinking.

"Yes, ma'am. That be the truth. Girls got themselves so hot, all they was thinking about was that cold ice cream. Right, girls?"

"Sure, Mama," Marydale said.

"That's right, Aussie," Mavis said at the same time.

"Girls be planning on flying back here right after they done their treat. That right?" Aussie said.

"Yes," Mavis and Marydale said exactly together as if they'd practiced at Aussie's, which they might have between spoonfuls of strawberry ice cream.

"Girls be thinking, Miz Hazey won't mind we get us a little ice cream before she gets back. That right, girls?"

"Yes," they said, still as together as duet singers on some stage.

Mama wasn't moved. "Didn't I tell you girls to stay put while I went to the store?"

"Yes, ma'am," they said together. The both of them stared at their bare feet. They knew they'd done wrong.

"Didn't I say not to leave this house?"

They nodded. Marydale's lower lip trembled. She wasn't used to being in trouble.

"Mavis, you get yourself into the bathroom."

"I'm sorry, Mama. I didn't mean it."

Mama reached out and gave her a shove toward the house.

"I won't ever do it, ever again. I'm truly in my heart sorry." Mavis was bawling full steam now. Mama didn't spank often, but when she did, she gave you a long lecture first that felt worse than the actual spanking. I didn't know whether Mavis was crying over the lecture she'd get or over the spanking. We could still hear her even after she disappeared into the house.

"Girls didn't mean no harm, Miz Hazey," Aussie said.

"When I give an order, I expect to be obeyed."

"Yes, ma'am," Aussie said.

"I do not have time to worry over the ideas some colored child puts into my girl's head."

Aussie pulled herself straighter. "Both girls be wanting that ice cream, Miz Hazey," she said softly.

"I'm taking care of my girl. I expect you to do the same with yours." Mama turned, her arms still folded, and went back to the house.

"Yes, ma'am. I be taking good care of Marydale. Don't be worrying you. Not over that."

Mama didn't give any sign of hearing Aussie. When she opened the front door, Mavis's cries bounced down the drive, even louder than before because Mama's wrath would soon be upon her.

Aussie put an arm around Marydale's shoulders and turned her back toward their house. Marydale didn't look one bit worried. She had change-of-life luck and not even Aussie'd have the nerve to strike a change-of-life baby.

I 2

LIMITS

NOT ONLY DID MAVIS GET herself spanked, she couldn't watch TV for three days. Least that's how it started, but I imagined by the next day Mama'd forget all about it and Mavis wouldn't have to miss *Gunsmoke* or *Wyatt Earp* or *The Roy Rogers Show* after all. Still, even one night without TV was strong punishment far as Mavis was concerned. That girl liked nothing better than sitting two inches from the screen, hypnotizing herself with pictures. Half the time I don't think she paid attention to the story. She just liked watching those flashing pictures.

Clorise says she read someplace that one of these days everybody'll have color televisions. I don't believe it myself. I do believe Clorise read that, because Clorise does not make up stories, unlike some best friends I could name. What I don't believe is the truth of everyone having a color TV. But if I'm wrong and this should come to pass, no one'll be happier than Mavis Dubois.

Daddy wasn't as put out by the strawberry ice cream business as I'd expected. I thought he'd have a fit about colored influence leading Mavis down the devil's path. All he did was agree with the punishment Mama'd decided on, then tell Mavis to listen to Mama from now on, which, of course, Mavis agreed to do out loud. In her head I'm sure the girl had no intention of changing her stubborn, do-whatever-she-felt-like ways.

After supper Mavis went to our room. No one said she had to. But by then she'd worked herself into thinking this punishment was somebody else's fault, not hers. If Mama hadn't run out of milk and run to the store, she wouldn't of gotten in trouble. If I hadn't gone along for the ride, I wouldn't of let her and Marydale leave or at least I would've been home to tell Mama where they'd gone. I couldn't think of a reason for her to be angry at Daddy, but there was probably one, least in Mavis's brain. I know how that girl's devious mind works almost as well as I know my own.

Nobody bothered turning on the TV. We could have since Mavis wasn't in the parlor. But Daddy was looking over the newspaper, Mama still working her gorilla puzzle. The whole outside frame was done and now she was working on the forest. I sat on the floor, across the coffee table from her, helping find green pieces.

"Would you look at that Little Rock mess," Daddy said from behind his newspaper.

"What mess?" I asked, being polite enough to show interest, though I certainly wasn't obligated to keep an eye on what went on up in Arkansas.

"Governor Faubus wants to send in the state militia," Daddy said. "Like I always say, give a colored an inch, he'll take a mile."

I wasn't sure that was a sufficient answer to my question, but I was never one to let my end of a conversation drop. "That's sure what you always say, all right," I said.

"Arkansas doesn't have anything to do with Louisiana," Mama said.

My feelings exactly, but I was too smart to say that out loud.

"More than you think." Daddy folded the paper and laid it on the sofa next to him. "We don't watch out, Louisiana'll be next."

"Next for what?" I asked. Now that the danger, whatever it might be, was moving its way down to my state, I was more interested.

"You find more things to worry over than anyone I know," Mama said.

"Worried about what?" I asked.

"I'm not worried cause I know Little Rock isn't going to happen in Ville d'Angelle," Daddy said.

"What won't happen? What is it?" Sometimes I felt near to invisible around my own parents.

"Hand me your pile," Mama said. "Someone could get hurt with the militia."

I gave her the green pieces I'd gathered, then waited for her or Daddy to answer at least one of my questions. But they didn't. The conversation just continued around me as if I wasn't made of flesh and blood, was a spirit no one needed to pay any attention to.

"Someone could get hurt without the militia. No, sir," Daddy said. "Coloreds around here getting any ideas from Little Rock, all they've got to do is see how we handled Holy Rosary. That tells them people in Louisiana aren't letting things get out of hand."

"Colored sisters teaching in Little Rock?" I guessed.

"Not likely." He glanced at his folded newspaper. "Still. Shows what can happen if you let things go."

"Couple of colored sisters aren't enough to bring Little Rock troubles down on our heads," Mama said.

"That's just what Little Rock folks said. 'Won't ever happen here,' they said." He slapped his paper. "Well they were wrong on that one, weren't they?"

Mama fit two greens together, though she still didn't have a place to put them in the puzzle itself.

"There's a reason why things are the way they are. Coloreds here. Whites there. The reason is cause that's what works best. Some coloreds don't see it that way and I feel sorry for them. I really do," Daddy said.

"Why?" I asked.

"Cause they'll spend their entire lives miserable and dissatisfied that things haven't changed. And they won't change. Believe me. A hundred years from now Marydale's great-grandchildren'll still be going to Sacred Heart with colored sisters teaching them the ways of God. Mavis's greats'll be at Holy Rosary, staring up at some white nun's face. I'd bet you money on that one except I wouldn't be around to collect."

"Don't tell me you're predicting the future," Mama said.

"Nothing to predict. I'm just saying that's how things've always been. That's how they'll always be. The world needs limits. Always has. Always will. No trick to that."

"Maybe," Mama said.

"No maybe to it," Daddy said.

"What about that colored sister set to teach fifth?" I asked. "No one would've predicted her a hundred years ago."

"Or a hundred days," Mama said. "Vivien Leigh's got you there." She smiled at me from across the coffee table.

"That's just a slip that'll be gone come next September. I'll bet money on that one."

"Since when have you turned into such a gambling man? Bet this. Bet that."

"I'm not a gambler. You know that, Hazey. This is a sure thing. No gambling to it."

"Sounds like gambling to me," Mama said.

"Vivien Leigh, if I said to you: 'I'm betting the sun'll rise tomorrow morning. I want you to take the other side of that bet. You be on the side that says the sun won't rise in the eastern sky tomorrow morning.' Would you make that bet?"

"Course not," I said.

"Course not," Daddy repeated. "And why not?"

"Cause I couldn't win."

"And I couldn't lose." Daddy slipped off the sofa to sit on the floor next to the coffee table with me and Mama. "Same thing with betting coloreds'll be gone from Holy Rosary come next September. Both bets are sure things." He looked at Mama, expecting some agreement on her part. But Mama just kept concentrating on her forest, matching pieces until they fit.

"Here," Daddy said. He reached into his pocket and pulled out a handful of change, which he piled on the coffee table in front of me. "Count this, Vivien Leigh."

Mama looked up to see what Daddy was up to but didn't say anything.

I separated the money into quarters, nickels, and pennies. No dimes. Then I counted. Four dollars and fifty-three cents. I counted again to double-check. Four dollars and fifty-three cents. "Four fifty-three," I said.

"I'll make it four fifty to be even," Daddy said. He put three pennies back in his pocket.

"Even on what?" Mama asked.

"I'm betting you come next September, all trace of colored sisters'll be gone from Holy Rosary. This fifth-grade teacher'll be a fluke we'll talk about for years. But that's all she'll be."

"Put your money away, Floyd. For God's sake, we're not betting on anything," Mama said.

"Afraid you'll lose?" Daddy teased. "I can sure understand that. Wouldn't bet on the sun not coming up in the morning either, if I were you."

Mama put down the puzzle piece she'd been trying to match. "Get my purse," she said to me.

I jumped from my spot and ran to her bedroom to get her purse out the first drawer of the bureau where she kept it. When I handed Mama the purse, she reached in for her wallet. Daddy and I watched her count out four dollars and fifty cents, then push her money across the table to mix with Daddy's pile.

"Vivien Leigh, you'll be in charge of this bet money," Mama said.

"Never knew you to be a gambling woman," Daddy said.

"What I'm betting is this colored teacher'll be more than a fluke," Mama said. "She might be gone by next school year, but she'll leave something behind Ville d'Angelle won't forget, which, to my way of thinking, makes her more than a fluke."

"Now, wait a minute. How are we supposed to judge this bet?" Daddy wasn't teasing anymore. "I'm the one who said we'd talk about that teacher for years to come. Does that mean you win if all she leaves behind is talk?"

Mama didn't answer right away. She was thinking on how to be fair because that was one thing Mama always was or at least tried to be, though she oftentimes wasn't when it came to me and Mavis far as I was concerned.

"Has to be more than talk left behind," Mama said. "We'll need a judge."

They both looked at me. Not surprising since Cleo and I were the only other ones in the room and Daddy would never allow Cleo to judge anything having to do with him, being convinced as he was that she had it in for him. Even though I was the only judge possible in that parlor, I did not like the idea of being wedged between Mama and Daddy. No matter which way I judged, one of them'd be upset with me, probably for a long time.

"I don't think children are allowed to be judges," I said. "There might be a law against it." If there wasn't, there sure should've been.

"What do you know about laws?" Daddy said.

"That's only courtroom judges," Mama said. "If there's a law against children judges, it only applies in courtrooms. Not parlors."

"I don't know how to be a judge," I said. My mind was whirling, looking for an excuse good enough to make the both of them look elsewhere for their judge.

"Nothing to it," Daddy said. "All you have to decide next year is whether those colored sisters have left a mark on Ville d'Angelle. That right, Hazey?"

Mama nodded.

"What if part of town is marked, but the rest not? Who wins then?" This got more complicated the more I thought about it.

"I'll make this easy on you. If you find five people changed by those sisters, your mama wins. Just five." He looked at Mama. "How about it, Hazey? That fair or what? Only five people."

"I must be crazy betting money against my own husband, but okay. Five changed people and I win," Mama said.

"What kind of change, though? What counts as change?" I asked.

"That's for you to decide. You're the judge," Daddy said. He scooped the bet money into my cupped hands. "Put this someplace safe. I don't want you saying you've lost my money when I come collecting next summer."

"No, sir," I said.

"Don't be so sure you'll be doing the collecting," Mama said.

"Sure as the sun'll rise in the morning. Sure as that," Daddy said.

I carried the bet money into my room and dumped it on the bed, where Mavis was working on her bedroom drawings. You wouldn't think there'd be that many ways to put bunks in a room the size of this one. But Mavis had come up with seven and was working on eight.

"What's that for?" she asked.

When I told her, she shook her head. Even Mavis could see the foolishness of such a bet. "It'll be hard to choose."

"Impossible." I pulled out the box of shells Clorise had brought back for me from her vacation in Biloxi, Mississippi, summer of third grade and put the money on top of those shells. "No matter who wins, I lose."

"That's right," Mavis agreed.

After I saved the bet money, I went to the kitchen with a book. No use chancing going back to the parlor. With Mama and Daddy placing bets and making me a judge, who could guess what else they'd come up with. No use being in the middle of the next piece of confusion they'd be thinking up tonight. But I must just naturally attract trouble because I wasn't finished with half the first chapter when Daddy walked in to get himself some of that Chocolate Supreme.

"We got any cookies in this house?" he called to Mama.

"Look in the top cabinet," she called back.

"Where?" he said.

"Over the icebox," she said.

We've been keeping cookies in the cabinet above the fridge for long as I can remember. Why can't Daddy get that in his mind? He looks for cookies in the tin on the counter. If that's empty, all he knows to do is call Mama for directions on where to look next. Mama doesn't go around hiding cookies, putting them here one day, there the next. So why does Daddy have so much trouble remembering something so easy?

"All that's up here is oatmeal raisin," he said.

"Then that's all we have," Mama said. "Put water on for coffee, will you."

"You going shopping tomorrow?"

"Friday. You know that's when I always do my big shopping. Besides, tomorrow's canning day."

"That's right." He ripped open a corner of the oatmeal raisin package with his teeth, spit the plastic he'd torn into his hand and from there to his pocket. Mama was always after him to use the scissors from the utility drawer, but he said his teeth worked as well and saved him a trip across the kitchen, which Mama said wasn't far enough to count as a trip in anybody's book. Now he pulled out four cookies, though they weren't his favorites. Mine neither. But anything tastes fine with Chocolate Supreme.

"Get some Oreos and gingersnaps when you get to the store," he said.

"I'll remember," Mama said. She came into the kitchen herself, tired of calling from the parlor while she was trying to concentrate on matching jungle pieces that all looked too much alike.

"For someone who doesn't care for oatmeal raisin, you're eating enough of them," Mama said. She set up the coffeepot with beans and filter, waiting for the water to boil.

"Man can't enjoy a few bites in his own house without being hassled near to death," Daddy said.

"You sure are hassled day and night. Lord knows how you put up with it all." Mama leaned against the counter, still waiting for that water.

"Price I pay for marrying a Meniere girl. Those Menieres always have to have the last word on everything."

"That's true," Mama said. I could hear her smile even with her back to us, pouring water over coffee beans.

"You just be grateful you've got half Dubois blood in you, Vivien Leigh. Might cool off that hot-blooded, crazy part you got from your Meniere side."

I didn't say anything to that. This was all joking and fooling around right now. But if it turned serious without warning, I didn't want to be caught in the middle like I was with that judging business.

"So now we're hot-blooded and crazy too?" Mama said. She carried a cup of coffee to Daddy, still stirring the one sugar, which was all Daddy took in his coffee.

"What's it mean when you have hot blood?" Mavis asked. I guessed she'd finally managed to figure every single way to arrange those bunk beds.

"Tell the girl what hot blood's all about," Daddy said, grinning at Mama.

"You're the one brought it up. You explain hot blood," Mama said, carrying her own cup to the table and pulling out the chair next to Daddy.

"Think I wouldn't?" Daddy raised his cup to his mouth for a swallow. "That what you're thinking?"

"I'm not thinking a single thing, Mister Floyd Dubois." She crossed her legs, dangling a foot back and forth while Daddy watched. "I'm not thinking a single, solitary thing."

"Well, Mavis. Hot-blooded women are wild and amazing. Crazy. They want something, you better give it to them or get out the way."

"Mama's not wild and amazing," Mavis said, looking at Mama sipping coffee and swinging that foot.

"Goes to show you don't know everything about your old Mama. Now I could tell you..."

"You could tell nothing at all, if you know what's good for you," Mama said.

"I could tell you nothing at all," Daddy said. He winked at Mavis behind his hand.

"I saw that," Mama said.

"They can see through flesh too. That's another thing about hot-blooded women," Daddy said.

Mama laughed out loud at that one. "You're the crazy one in this family, Floyd Dubois. Our girls act crazy, it's coming from your side, not mine."

"Now, I can name some crazy ideas they've had that sure haven't come from me."

"Like what?" Mavis asked.

I shook my head but Mavis didn't notice or, if she noticed, didn't pay a second's attention to the warning.

"Let's start with this morning's little escapade," Daddy said.

"That shows I'm hot blooded?" Mavis asked, more than a hint of pride in her voice. The girl was so crazy, she wanted to be known as hot-blooded. I couldn't begin to imagine why.

"Shows you have the makings of not knowing up from down," Mama said. "Doesn't say a thing about the temperature of your blood."

"Now, I wouldn't say I agree with you on that one." Daddy might just have said that to cheer Mavis, who looked completely disappointed over not having hot blood. "But doesn't matter one way or the other cause whether that's a good example or not, I know Mavis has some of that Meniere hot blood running her veins. Isn't that right, Hazey?"

Mavis perked right up, stopped leaning against the table and sat with the rest of us, not looking even a little angry about her punishment anymore. I was happy about that. No one likes to sleep next to a girl who's liable to kick you half a dozen times, tossing and turning before she settles to sleep. "Tell something else about me that shows my hot blood," Mavis said, her mouth so full of an oatmeal raisin, the words slurred and bits of cookie edged her mouth.

"Something else. Let's see." Daddy sipped coffee and pulled a cigar from his pocket.

"Do you have to light that thing in my kitchen?"

Daddy bit the end off the cigar but didn't light it. "Hot-blooded people don't much care what other folks think. They just do what they please. Go on their merry way."

"That's me?" Mavis asked.

"Sure it's you," I said.

We all three looked at Mama to see if she would say different. She just kept sipping coffee, looking only half interested in the conversation now that Daddy had decided not to light his cigar, least not right away.

"Take Marydale for one good instance," Daddy said.

Mama stopped swinging her foot. Mavis put down the cookie she was working on and sat straighter.

"Most white girls your age would care enough about what folks say to think twice about playing with a colored girl so much. But not you." His voice was soft, not mean but not joking anymore either.

Mavis crumbled cookie on the table, then pushed crumbs into a small pile. Mama didn't fuss about the mess.

"See what I mean, Mavis?" Daddy said, his voice still soft as Cleo's fur.

Mavis wet her pointer finger and passed it in the crumbs, then in her mouth. "Marydale's all right."

"Sure she is. Marydale's one all right little colored girl. Don't let me hear anyone say different."

"She can't prove I'm hot blooded. Tell something else about me," Mavis said.

I've never seen anyone so determined to be hot-blooded.

"Baby, your daddy can't tell more cause he doesn't know what he's talking about," Mama said.

"That so?" Daddy asked.

"Hot blood. Cold blood. Lukewarm blood. Thing I'd like to know is where you get those ideas. Anyone in this family have something wrong with their blood, it's got to be you."

"See, girls. There's your mama's hot blood rising up. That's hot blood talking, if ever I've heard any."

"Now we've got talking blood, do we?" Mama's foot started swinging again. "If my blood could do half the tricks you're claiming, I'd sell it, make myself a mint."

"You could sell it at Mavis's and Marydale's peanut stand," I said.

"What peanuts you talking about?" Daddy asked.

"Vivien Leigh has the biggest mouth in Louisiana, biggest mouth in the entire world." Mavis swept the rest of her crumbs off the table and into

her palm, then stomped out the room, angry again. I could only hope she'd
be sleeping before I got to bed.

Daddy looked at Mama, who shrugged one shoulder slightly. She didn't
know any more about the peanuts than he did.

"If Aussie wasn't here so often, Mavis might get to seeing the problem
with Marydale hanging here so much," Daddy said in that same soft, serious voice he'd used with Mavis.

"Aussie's here on Thursdays. Once a week to clean. That's it. Hardly call
that often." Mama uncrossed her legs, planting each foot solidly in front of
her chair.

"Times she comes hauling Marydale from here. Times she brings some
trinket Mavis has forgotten at her place. Those times can't all be
Thursdays."

"Aussie's my cleaning lady. That's all."

I looked at Mama, searching for some sign of embarrassment at what I
knew to be nothing but a falsehood. All the talk that flowed between them,
Thursdays and other times too, gave the lie to Mama's words. But her face
was set regular, no extra color, no frown that wasn't normal. My mama
wasn't usually a lying woman. Maybe I was the one wrong, mistaking truth
for lie. Maybe everyone talked with their cleaning lady the way Mama
talked with hers.

"Girls could help out more," Daddy said.

I wrinkled my nose. Hadn't he dropped that idea yet? No one noticed
my face or, if they did, didn't say anything.

"I need Aussie," Mama said. She picked up her cup, then set it down
again. "Once a week isn't much."

"If that's all there was," Daddy said. "If you'd set limits. That's all I'm
saying. Set limits."

"Mavis is just a baby," Mama said.

"All the more reason for her to see your limits. Make it easier for her to
see the need for limits of her own."

"I've known Aussie a long time."

"Sure." He put the cigar in his mouth, switching it from side to side.

"I've known Aussie longer than I've known you."

"But I'm the one you married." He lit the cigar, puffing to get it started.
The first smoke ring floated across the table, disappearing as it reached
Mama.

13

BUTTERFLY GLASS

"MAVIS. VIVIEN LEIGH. TIME TO GET MOVING." Mama rubbed my back.

"What's the matter?" I mumbled, my brain not accustomed to getting up with the sky still a pale rose, the sun not even fully risen.

"Canning day," Mavis said next to me.

"I know," I said, even though I'd asked the question and had shut my eyes again.

"Wear long pants," Mama reminded before she left us. Smells of pancakes and bacon and coffee drifted from the kitchen. No one can pick figs on an empty stomach or one filled with nothing but soggy Sugar Pops.

Mavis hopped out of bed, ran to the bathroom and back before I stretched myself into a sitting position. She sat on the bed to pull up her pants, which reached above her ankles and were snug at her waist and across her bottom too. She was ready for the next size up, but this was the only pair Mama hadn't stored for summer.

"Better get yourself dressed," she said, bending to tie her tennis shoes.

"I am," I said.

"Mama'll be after you soon," she said.

I couldn't say anything to what was the plain truth, so I swung myself over the end of the bed and went to the bathroom. I was almost done washing my face when Daddy banged on the door.

"Hurry it up, Little Miss. Don't make me late for work."

"No, sir." This was earlier than usual, even for canning day, if Daddy hadn't done his bathroom business yet.

I wasn't more than a minute longer, but when I came out, Daddy was leaning against the wall, looking as if he'd been waiting halfway to tomorrow. "About time," he said. "Sure hope those builders hurry up my bathroom."

He shut the door before I could ask since when was the new bathroom going to belong to him. The bedroom would be mine. But the rest of it, den and hall and bathroom, belonged to the whole family, not just to Daddy. Didn't it?

I pulled on a shirt and pants that were as short and tight on me as Mavis's were on her. Only reason I had to wear long pants was Mavis fell from a branch a couple of years ago and scraped up her legs good. Probably could still find bloodstains on that tree, if you looked carefully. Mama decided Mavis wouldn't of gotten bruised so bad if she'd been wearing pants instead of shorts. Mavis gets hurt, I end up wearing pants in the hottest month of the year. Mama wouldn't listen to my saying I wasn't careless as Mavis, knew better than to go falling out a fig tree, had no need to be wearing pants in August.

By the time I got to the kitchen only one pancake was left on the platter. But Mama was flipping more at the stove, so that was okay.

"Pig," I said to Mavis, serving myself that last pancake.

Mavis yawned. "I'm hungry." She yawned again. How could anyone manage to stuff so many pancakes into her mouth when she was yawning so much?

"Pig," I said one more time.

"Leave your sister alone," Mama said. She carried a plate of hot pancakes to the table and took the platter we'd emptied back to the stove.

Mavis lifted two from the new stack. Our family can eat more pancakes than anybody I know.

Daddy came in and helped himself to four right off. "This all there is?" He gave himself eight strips of bacon to match his pancakes, two for one.

"More's coming. Much as anybody wants," Mama said from the stove.

"Bacon too?" I asked.

"You girls go easy on that," Mama said.

We weren't the ones mounding bacon on our plates. I looked over at Daddy, but he was too busy eating to take notice of any looks I sent his way. He finished his pancake stack and another just like it, then left for the oil refinery.

While me and Mavis finished our breakfasts, Mama washed dishes. The window in front of the sink filled with pink dawn. The rooster clock above the door said five forty-five, but it seemed earlier.

I ate slowly, not wanting the rest of the day to start. Already I could feel the August heat seeping into the house. When Mama and Aussie got to canning, the kitchen, whole house, would be near unbearable.

Mama wiped the stove, then counter. "You girls almost finished? Time to get moving. I told Aussie we'd be there before six."

We carried our plates and glasses to the sink for Mama to wash. While she finished in the kitchen, Mavis and I squeezed last drops of pee into the toilet. Mama didn't like us bothering Tante Yvette's bathroom on canning days, so always made us go before we left home. Most days Tante Yvette didn't mind us in her bathroom. But this being fig day, she'd have to let Aussie and Marydale use her bathroom too, if she let us use it.

Tante Yvette's husband, who'd been dead many more years than I'd been alive, had hated coloreds more than anybody in the world. Mama said so. Even nice coloreds like Aussie and Marydale. After breathing in all that hate for so many years, Tante Yvette just wouldn't be comfortable letting a colored sit on her toilet. It's the reason she only has a cleaning lady come a couple of hours at a time twice a week, Tuesdays and Fridays. Cleaning lady who's at your house only couple of hours can hold her bathroom needs for when she gets back to her own home. Tante Yvette does keep a special drinking glass, pink with yellow butterflies painted all over it, in case her colored help gets thirsty.

When her cleaning lady quit couple of months ago, Tante Yvette asked Mama to ask Aussie if she'd be interested in the job. Mama asked that very Friday afternoon when Aussie came over to drag Marydale back to her own home where she properly belonged.

They sat on the back steps, watching Mavis and Marydale carry the tools they'd taken out Daddy's shed. No one bothered asking those girls what they thought they'd do with saws and hammers and wrenches and who knows what else they'd hauled under the willow tree that day. All Mama said was put it all back and put it in the right place unless they were looking to catch it from Daddy. Neither Mavis nor Marydale wanted to chance catching anything from my daddy, so Mama and Aussie could visit without bothering with whether, for once, those girls were doing what they'd been told.

"Tante Yvette's girl quit on her," Mama said.

"One of Aristide Mouton's girls," Aussie said.

"Clara Sue."

"She be third child in that family."

Mama tugged her dress over her knees and smoothed any wrinkles might've snuck up on her during the day. Mavis and Marydale marched past, each carrying one end of Daddy's nail box. God knows what those girls had been doing with the thousands of nails Daddy kept in that box.

"Those Mouton girls, they be good workers. Be some of the best workers in Ville d'Angelle. That's what folks say." Aussie paused a few seconds, giving Mama time to agree or not. But Mama didn't say yea or nay, so Aussie took that as reason enough to keep talking. "Sure be a shame Miz Yvette lost herself such a fine cleaning girl. Sure be a shame for Miz Yvette."

"She was wondering if you'd be interested in taking up the job." Mama didn't look at Aussie, instead watched Mavis and Marydale troop back to the willow.

"No, ma'am. That's not for me." She watched the girls too, not looking at Mama any more than Mama'd looked at her.

"Didn't think it would be."

"Tell Miz Yvette, Aussie send a thank-you for thinking about her. Yes, she do. But can't see going to work couple hours, me. Go, come back. Next day, go, come back. Me, I can't see that at all, no."

"Tante Yvette has her ways."

"She be like all the old people. They all have their ways and don't nobody better be messing with their ways if they know what's good for them."

"That pretty much describes Tante Yvette." Mama smoothed her skirt again, though far as I could tell there weren't any wrinkles possibly still hiding on her. "I've told her it'd make more sense, be easier on everybody, if she just had somebody coming once a week, stay four or five hours. Wouldn't take more than that to keep her house sparkling."

"Old folks don't leave much dirt."

"She won't listen to me. Twice a week is all she can see."

"Old people have their ways."

"Cutting her nose to spite her face is all that's going on." Mama plucked a weed snuggled against the edge of the steps. That weed thought it was safe, growing against the steps in a tiny wedge no one'd ever see. But Mama spotted it and now it was dead as its bolder cousins who'd grown in the light of open day.

"Some folks be more set in their ways. Don't matter if their ways be smart or easy, foolish or hard. Don't matter to those folks at all, no. They be having their ways. That's all they be knowing, them."

"She'll have a rough time finding someone good as Clara Sue."

"Rough time," Aussie agreed. "Some folks don't mind rough times long as they keep their ways, them. Expect Miz Yvette be one of those people."

"Expect you're right," Mama'd said.

They'd been right too, because Tante Yvette went the whole summer before finding another colored to do for her. Rosemary was still in high school. Once school started, she'd come a couple of hours on Tuesdays and Fridays. Bus'd drop her off and her daddy'd pick her up on the way back from work. She could only come on Fridays till school started, but Fridays were better than nothing. "Beggars can't be choosers," is the way Mama'd put it when she hung the phone from hearing Tante Yvette's news a couple of weeks ago.

On fig day, though, we were the beggars, asking Tante Yvette to share some of her sweet figs. She wasn't the one begging anything.

In the car Mama let us roll the windows down soon as we put on our sunglasses. Pants in August, even before six in the morning, give a person need for as much breeze as she can get.

At Aussie's Mama honked twice. They came out before the second honk had faded into quiet. Marydale carried a piece of toast in one hand and rubbed sleep out her eyes with the other. Aussie settled into the front seat, a wooden bucket between her feet. After we said our good mornings, we were quiet, it being too early for talking even for Mama and Aussie. Mavis and Marydale were too busy yawning, and Marydale chewing too, to do any talking.

Before Mama killed the engine, Tante Yvette poked her head out the door. "Morning, Hazey." She wiggled one finger at us. Tante Yvette never had children of her own so was never quite sure how to act with anyone under twenty-one.

"Morning, Tante." Mama took a few steps toward the house, her keys dangling in one hand. "You're up early."

"Up with the chickens. You know that, Hazey. Don't let the chickens get a head start on the day. " She stepped out the door to stand on her top step and pointed at the fenced coop at the side of her house, where two scraggly chickens pecked corn the rooster had missed. "Remember that, girls, and morning to you."

"Morning," all three of us answered, though Marydale wasn't one of the "girls" Tante Yvette was talking about and was old enough to know it. But we were too polite, even Tante Yvette was too polite, to say anything about that.

"Morning to you too, Aussie," Tante Yvette said.

Aussie looked up from the buckets she was hauling out Mama's trunk. "Nice day for picking figs," Tante Yvette said.

"Yes, ma'am. Sure be a nice day for that." Aussie hung two buckets on each arm, then, with her free hands, carried the bushel baskets. She disappeared around the corner of the house. Marydale and Mavis, each carrying two buckets, lagged behind.

Mama stared after them, then took a few steps toward Tante Yvette as if there was something more she had to tell her. I couldn't imagine what it'd be. Neither could Tante Yvette, I supposed. So we just waited. But Mama didn't say a word.

"That Aussie's sure a good worker," Tante Yvette said when she'd grown tired of waiting for Mama to get her words out.

"She is that," Mama said.

"You're lucky to have a hardworking colored being your cleaning lady. Count your blessings there." A beam of morning sun shone on Tante Yvette's cap of white tight curls. She might've been a Catechism saint with a halo glowing the way they always did in religious books.

"Nobody works better than Aussie." Mama's voice was a little louder than usual, but not so loud that Aussie would for sure hear her from the back of the house. It was medium loud. Maybe Aussie heard. Maybe not. "We better get picking," Mama said, her voice normal again.

"Lots of figs this year," Tante Yvette said. "Lots of them."

By the time Mama and I got to the fig trees, Aussie was sitting in one of them, her bucket near half full. Aussie was a fast picker. Marydale and Mavis were sharing a tree and doing more eating than picking. When I looked in their bucket, it held three sorry-looking figs and that was all.

"Good fig picking this year," Mama said.

Aussie nodded from her perch.

"One of the best years in a long time, don't you think?" Mama asked.

"A good year," Aussie said. She shifted her weight on her branch so she could reach behind for the figs she'd had her back to.

Mama walked to the third tree and started picking, first from the bottom branches. Then, when she couldn't reach figs from the ground, she climbed her tree just like Aussie had climbed hers and Mavis and Marydale theirs. Left me to be the bucket dumper. Until then, I concentrated on finding figs at the bottoms of trees no one was picking.

"Ready," Aussie called. She handed her full bucket down to me. I handed an empty one up to her. I dumped her figs into the first bushel basket, readying the bucket for the next person who'd need an empty one.

"Ready," Mama called. I ran to her tree and exchanged her full bucket for an empty one. "Get yourself a tree to climb. It'll be a while before we need to dump again."

Mavis and Marydale should've been ready soon. But all the should've-beens in Heaven won't make one pie of anything. That's what Mama says and I guess she's right. Those girls were chattering like two blackbirds and not paying half a bit of attention to filling their bucket.

I emptied Mama's pail, then climbed a tree of my own. Mavis and Marydale were the only ones doing any talking. Mama and Aussie and I stuck to our jobs, not wasting time yakking our heads into distraction.

My bucket was near half full before Mama said anything. "Remember we're picking for Deacy too."

"I thought T.J. and Malcolm were going to do some picking this time," I said.

"You don't see them, do you?" Mama said.

"Them boys need to be helping their mama," Aussie said.

"They help some," Mama said.

"Some's not enough when you be carrying a baby, specially a change-of-life baby." Aussie was sure the expert on that.

"That's right," I said.

"Sure not enough when you got a husband dancing in north Louisiana."

"Uncle Everett's chopping lumber, not dancing," I said. Even Everett knew better than to think about dancing without Deacy up in Monroe.

"Deacy's doing just fine." Mama was not partial to anybody criticizing her own sister, not even Aussie.

"Some folks sure got themselves a different picture of fine," Aussie said, her mouth aimed at the sky as if she was talking to the top branches of her fig tree or to God instead of to Mama.

"My sister's fine," Mama said.

"She'd be better if she wasn't stuck with so many no-account boys," I said.

"Keep your mind on your picking," Mama said.

"Might be missing the best ones, if your mind's not fixed on the figs," Aussie said. "Your mama be right there." The way she said it made me wonder how many other things Mama was wrong about. Must've made Mama wonder the same.

"Enough chitchat. We ladies are here to pick, not gab. Hear me, Vivien Leigh?"

"Yes, ma'am, I hear." I was the one who'd been doing the least talking of anybody in these fig trees. So why did my name get called out?

"Good workers work. They leave gossiping to others. Remember that, Vivien Leigh," Mama said.

"Sure," I said and plucked a fig from the tree into my mouth, a consolation for being picked on so much. I liked preserves better because they were so much sweeter, but fresh figs were tasty too.

Mavis and Marydale weren't paying a lick of attention to anything but each other. While Mama and Aussie and I picked without a word, those girls kept their talk going, back and forth, back and forth, back and forth. The soft buzz of their voices filled the air like background music for those of us busy with the real work of the world.

By the time the sun looked like it did when I usually got out of bed, we'd filled both bushels and all but one of the buckets. Mama and Aussie carried the baskets to the trunk, leaving us girls to finish filling the last pail.

"How much figs your mama giving Miz Deacy?" Marydale asked. Now she was working the same tree her mama'd just left, dropping figs into the shirt she'd pulled out her shorts and held out like a tray in front of her. Marydale wasn't interested in long pants in August, no matter the blood and bruises she was risking. I had to agree with her there. I only wished Mama'd listen to me the way Aussie listened to Marydale. But then I wasn't a change-of-life girl and nobody thought I knew anything worth listening to.

"Tante Deacy'll get much as she wants," I said from my tree. It had been picked nearly clean and I was having to scramble to the topmost branches to find even a few figs to put into Mama's kerchief she'd handed me before carrying our loads back to the car.

"Don't seem right. Sure don't." Marydale lowered herself to a bottom branch, then jumped. She dumped her fig-filled shirt into our bucket.

"That's right," Mavis said from her tree. "How come we have to do the picking for the whole world?"

"That right. For what we have to do that, us?"

"You girls better hope Mama's not hearing your selfish ways." From my perch I peered over Tante Yvette's roof and spied the tops of Mama's and Aussie's heads, arranging bushels and buckets in the car. Mavis and Marydale were safe for now.

"Tante Deacy has boys to pick for her." Mavis jumped from her tree, shirt pockets bulging with more figs than she'd picked all morning in the tree with Marydale.

"Nobody can rely on those boys. You know that." I pulled up to a higher branch and sat, swinging my legs.

"That sure be God's truth," Marydale said.

"Still don't know why we have to pick for everybody, the whole world practically." Mavis dropped figs one by one from her pocket and into the bucket. Her figs were squashed from being mashed together, but that didn't matter since Mama would make preserves of them all.

"Tante Deacy and her family aren't close to being the whole world," I said.

"It's not fair is all," Mavis said.

"Not fair at all," Marydale added.

"You girls'll understand when you're more grown," I said in my most adult voice.

"You think you know everything," Mavis called from the tree she'd climbed.

"Nobody know everything but God. God be the only one know everything," Marydale said.

"You're not God either," Mavis said.

"No, ma'am. Only God be God," Marydale said.

"I never said otherwise, did I?"

"You be thinking you God, that's a sin. Biggest sin there be," Marydale said.

"Big, fat, mortal, send-your-soul-to-Hell kind of sin," Mavis said. She threw a fig in my direction. It grazed my branch. I couldn't tell whether that's what she'd intended or whether she'd tried hitting me and missed. Mavis doesn't have a good arm; far as I knew she might've been aiming for my heart and only gotten the branch by mistake.

No use taking a chance on letting her think she could fire things at me without paying a price. I hunted till I held a handful of figs. The first one caught her bottom as she wriggled higher up the tree.

"Hey. What do you think you're doing?"

"I don't think. I know." The next one got her left shoulder.

"Cut that out." Mavis ducked behind a branch, probably gathering ammunition.

A fig pinged the back of my leg. I swirled to face Marydale. "No fair. Two against one's no fair."

"You bigger than us," Mavis called from behind her branch.

"Better aim too," I said, hoping Marydale's hit had been beginner's luck. I lobbed one that clipped Marydale's neck. I had some waiting for Mavis, if she ever dared show her cowardly little face.

Now figs were flying every which way, hitting branches, leaves, sometimes flesh. "Give up?" I yelled.

"Never," Mavis yelled back. She let out a war whoop any time one of her figs or Marydale's got me.

"We never give up," Marydale said. "We be Roy Rogers and Dale Evans." Aussie didn't have a TV, but Marydale'd caught enough on ours to know lots of famous stars.

"King of the cowboys. Queen of the cowgirls," Mavis added.

"King and queen never be giving up," Marydale said.

"I regret I have only one fig to give for my country," I said and aimed my last ammunition at Mavis's chest.

The fig smacked just above her belly button. "What's that supposed to mean?"

"You'll get it when you're older."

A fig flew from Marydale's tree to my foot.

"What in God's name is going on here?" Mama stood at the edge of the fig trees, hands on hips, mouth stiff and mean.

"We were just fooling," I said. All three of us clambered down our trees.

"Wasting other people's fruit is no fooling," Mama said, hands still on hips, eyes still glaring. We looked down at our feet. Even Marydale.

"Miz Hazey be right. No sin greater than wasting other people's figs." Aussie had walked up behind Mama, but no one had paid her any attention.

"What about if you be thinking you God?" Marydale asked. If I'd been closer, I'd of kicked her.

"Then you crazy. Crazy people can't be top sinners cause God just turn the other cheek on them folks. God can't be bothered with crazy people," Aussie said.

"What about killing somebody? That'd have to be worse than fig throwing," Mavis said.

"That just depend," Aussie said. "Could be a reason for a killing."

"Could be a war. Lots of people be killing in a war. Or maybe it be an evil devil. It be evil devil coming after me, I shoot him quick." Now that her mama was conversing, Marydale didn't have to look at her feet anymore.

"Me too," Mavis said. "I'd shoot that devil man dead."

"Nobody can shoot a devil," I said. The ignorance of those girls about everyday, common things never ceased to amaze me.

Aussie picked up the bucket, which was near three-quarters full, and headed toward the car. "Just shows nothing's more sinful than wasting figs don't belong to you."

Mama stared at Aussie's back as if trying to decide whether she was making fun of her, making fun of us girls, or serious. Maybe all three. Mama turned back to us before we had the good sense to run after Aussie.

"You girls march to the house and apologize to Tante Yvette for wasting her figs."

We trudged single file—Mama, followed by Mavis, Marydale, then me—to the front door. Tante Yvette answered on the first knock. She must've been waiting right behind the door because Tante Yvette's an old lady and can't move that fast. Maybe she'd been spying out her bedroom window and seen the fig fight and now was waiting for us. What could an old lady do to you? I didn't want to imagine.

"Girls have something to say to you, Tante," Mama said.

"Well, step in, Hazey. Don't let this sun heat up the house."

The parlor was especially dim after the brightness of outside. She didn't have space for much furniture, but what she did have was dark too, fought off any light that tried to make its way into the room. We lined up in front of her, Mama to our side.

"Guess you girls here to say your thank yous," Tante Yvette said when none of us gave sign of remembering how to talk.

"Yes, ma'am. We sure be wanting to say thank-you for all them good figs. So sweet and juicy. And when Miz Hazey and Mama cook them into preserves." Marydale rubbed her belly and closed her eyes. "I be tasting them figs already, me."

Mama nudged my shoulder. I didn't look at her or Tante Yvette either. Instead I found a red rose from the dozens in the pattern on the sofa and counted petals.

Mama nudged my foot this time, pushing me a little forward. Tante Yvette pulled back, maybe afraid I was losing my balance and not wanting to be in the way when I fell. "Speak up, Vivien Leigh," Mama said.

"We wasted figs, throwing them at each other, and we're sorry." The words came in one long breath. Tante Yvette leaned toward me and frowned, maybe because she was angry about the figs, maybe because she didn't like me talking so fast.

"Sure, we're sorry," Mavis said.

"Sorry as sorry be," Marydale said.

"That's all right, I'm sure. No harm done." She peered at each of us, me, then Mavis, then Marydale. "I don't expect you wasted many." It was part statement, part question.

"No, ma'am. Hardly any wasted figs. Most of those figs heading for the preserve pot. Wasted ones don't amount to much at all. Not at all. Just a little snack for the birds." Marydale held one bare foot out, just her heel touching the floor while the ball of her foot wriggled from side to side, carefree as if she'd never had a fig fight.

"Fine then." Tante Yvette straightened. "No harm done." She smiled at Mama, then looked at us again. "You girls want lemonade, fresh squeezed?"

Of course we did. We sat on the front steps and drank the lemonade and ate gingersnaps. Marydale got the pink glass with yellow butterflies. Tante Yvette didn't offer Mama lemonade because then she would've had to offer Aussie some and she only had one butterfly glass. Instead the ladies inspected Mama's trunk, packed with Tante Yvette's figs, and talked about how this was the hottest summer any of them could remember, which particularly for Tante Yvette covered many, many years. They talked about the moon, whether it was best to pick figs right before or right after a full one. They talked about news of a subdivision being planned down the street from Buddy Benoit's Amoco. Yet with all the words coming out their mouths, a person couldn't help but notice the talk wasn't smooth and easy like when it was just Mama and Aussie. This talk jerked, slowed to an almost stop, speeded ahead to catch up with itself. Nothing smooth and easy about any of it.

We brought our empty glasses to Tante Yvette's kitchen counter, then piled into the back seat, which was hot as the dickens even though we'd left the windows down. Tante Yvette doesn't have a carport to protect visitors' cars or shade trees in the front yard to park under. Heat sizzled my skin through my pant legs. I shifted, crossed my legs, but could not escape the fire eating them and my bottom too. Marydale didn't complain, which surprised me because her bare legs must've been blistering.

Gravel plinked against the car as Mama backed out the drive and into the street. I waited for her and Aussie to start their easy talk, get my mind off this burning back seat. But the talk never came so I spent the whole ride home suffering and wondering why Tante Yvette didn't get herself another butterfly glass, at least for fig days.

1 4

NUMBERS
DON'T LIE

WHEN WE GOT HOME, Tante Deacy was already in the kitchen, measuring sugar into Mama's canning pot that extended across two stove burners. Mama and Aussie carried the bushels in and left the buckets for us girls. Everywhere you looked in our kitchen, all you saw were figs.

"You folks sure did a nice job picking," Deacy said.

"Yes, ma'am. Don't think anybody ever picked themselves so many figs in a morning." Marydale hadn't picked enough to earn a brag, but truth didn't stop that little colored girl from making herself sound like the lead picker of us all.

Mavis and I ran to change into shorts because no one was risking a bloody leg falling in the house. When we got back, Mama had lined three kitchen chairs in front of the back door, away from the stove and counter and table where the ladies would be working. She gave each of us girls a bowl for our laps and a paper sack for between our legs, then set a bucket of figs next to each of us. Marydale was already plucking stems and putting figs in the bowl, discards in the sack. Lots of figs didn't have stems, so all we had to do was drop them into the bowl. But we had to inspect each fig, make sure it didn't have rot spots, not even little tiny ones. Fig pickers can't bother stopping to check for things like tiny rot spots. The checking has to come later and that was our job.

When a checker's bowl was full, Deacy carried the picked-over figs to the sink. She washed every speck of dirt off those figs, dropped them in the colander she'd set up in the sink, shook the colander to get rid of extra water clinging to the fruit, then dumped the figs into the preserve pot. Aussie'd added water to the sugar and was stirring it over two small flames. Heat up a preserve pot too fast and you burn your figs.

"How's Ti-Tante doing?" Deacy asked from the sink.

"Same as always," Mama said.

"Them old folks don't change themselves much, no. You know that, Miz Deacy." Aussie's voice sounded far off with her back to us the way it was. She couldn't turn from the pot even for a second. One thing you have to do when you're preserving figs is keep stirring. Stop for a second and you have yourself a burnt pot and figs that carry a scorched taste even if they weren't sitting on the very bottom.

Nobody said anything for a while, each of us too busy with our jobs for talking. I myself was working fast as I could so I could be out that kitchen soon as possible. Even with Aussie's wide back blocking half the stove, the heat from the pot was already adding to the heat of the day for a sorry combination. My shirt stuck to my back even with me sitting right in front of the open door.

"From the looks of all these figs, I guess you folks didn't miss my hands today," Deacy said. She was sitting at the table, giving herself a break and sipping a glass of iced water, which did look good.

"Can always use an extra set of hands," Mama said. She was aggravated because none of Deacy's no-account boys had showed up to help.

Deacy rubbed the backs of her wrists against the cold sweat on the outside of her glass. She pressed those wet wrists against her cheeks, already flushed with the fire of canning. "I just couldn't find it in my heart to wake the boys." Her voice was a whisper of apology. "Growing boys need their sleep," she said louder, not quite so much I'm-sorry in her voice.

"And girls? Don't girls need as much sleep?" Mama asked from the sink where she'd taken Deacy's place washing.

I listened especially carefully because it wasn't often you'd hear Mama defending our need for sleep. It was something to hold up to her on Saturdays, once school started, when she dragged me out of bed to wash the car or do some other chore.

"Soon them girls be needing more rest than them boys. They be coming on their time soon and they be needing their rest then. That be for sure," Aussie said.

"Time for what?" Mavis asked.

"Time for nothing," Mama said.

"Time for you to be a woman," Aussie said.

"Me and Mavis, we both ready to be a woman. We sure ready for that." Marydale bobbed her head up and down, agreeing with herself, not waiting to see whether anyone else did too.

"That's right. We're ready," Mavis said.

"You girls are still babies." I dropped four plump, stemless figs into my bowl. "Besides, you won't be women till after me. You have to wait till I'm one before you can be one."

"Person be a woman when God say it's time. Some people's time come when they be nine. Some people's time don't come till they be thirteen, fourteen, fifteen," Aussie said.

"We be nine before you be fifteen," Marydale said.

"Years before," Mavis said. She and Marydale grinned at each other as if they'd proven something. I ignored the both of them because if there was one thing I knew for sure and didn't have to argue over with Mavis and Marydale, it was that I'd see womanhood before either of them.

"Your daddy isn't ready for more women in his house," Mama said. She pulled out another big pot and dumped the latest colander of cleaned figs into it. That meant the preserve pot on the stove was full and these would have to wait for the next batch. If a person stuffs too many figs in a preserve pot, they don't cook right, don't get enough sugar coating or something. I pay close attention to fig preserving because that's one thing I want to know how to do when I'm grown. I don't expect Mama'd be willing to come to my house when I'm old and married just to can my figs, and preserved figs are something I plan to be eating the rest of my life. They're that good.

"Too many women drive a man crazy," Aussie said, still stirring, stirring.

"Everett's lucky that way, I guess." Deacy took another swallow of water. The ice cubes were nearly melted, just tiny crystals still floating in her glass. She didn't look ready to get up from her break. Not that Deacy was like her lazy boys. Not at all. It was this heat and that baby working her.

"Everett just has me to worry about in the women category." She looked at Mama, whose back was turned, culling another bushel of figs straight from the basket into the colander. "Isn't that right, Hazey?"

"If you say so."

"Not if I say so. That's how it is. Pure and simple. Doesn't matter what I say. Isn't that right, Aussie?" Deacy was bound to have someone agree with her.

"Always matters what a person says, Miz Deacy."

"I don't know what's wrong with you ladies. I sure don't." Deacy passed a hand across her forehead. She pulled a napkin out the holder on the table, pleated it into a fan, and waved it across her face. "What would you say if I told you I got a letter and a check, a check mind you, from my husband yesterday? Just yesterday, something came."

"I'd say thank God the man hasn't totally forgotten his obligations. That's about all I'd say," Mama said. She emptied the colander into the pot with the other figs waiting their turn for the stove.

"Of course he hasn't forgotten his obligations," Deacy said. "That's what he's doing up there in Monroe. Trying to take care of his obligations."

"Man have a wife carrying his baby, that man belongs at home, not up north in Monroe." Aussie pronounced each syllable of "Monroe" so distinctly, she made it sound like some foreign place, not just a city in Louisiana, up north, but Louisiana all the same.

"Aussie, you have spoken God's truth," Mama said. Now that Deacy was here, Mama didn't have to defend her and her wayward husband. Instead, Mama could agree with Aussie, which is what she'd probably wanted to do back in Tante Yvette's fig trees.

"Yes, ma'am. My mama always tells God's truth. I be doing the same. Always be telling God's truth." No one bothered over that piece of story. We all knew Marydale told the truth when the feeling came on her and not any other time. Trouble was, the feeling didn't come often enough to suit anybody with any intention of following the Eighth Commandment.

"Everett's trying to make a little extra to take care of me and the boys and this new baby. That's all he's trying to do." She wanted to convince Mama and Aussie, maybe to keep herself convinced. I wasn't sure what had happened between Deacy's cold Sunday good-bye to Everett and today. Maybe nothing but time going by. Maybe Deacy'd spent so much time believing Everett, she couldn't stick with not believing him for more than a few weeks at a time.

Mama and Aussie grunted their disbelief at the exact same moment, but no one laughed, not even Mavis or Marydale.

"So how much was that check?" Mama asked.

Tante Deacy told and that brought a choking sound from Mama. "Deacy, what's that, about five dollars more than he made at the IGA?"

"Forty-five more. It's forty-five more."

"For forty-five lousy dollars the man has abandoned his wife, left her to raise his sons, to go through a pregnancy that's getting harder with each passing day." Mama sucked in a deep breath and let it out in a whistle puff of air. "Forty-five dollars," she said again as if she couldn't believe the number. But, like Daddy says, numbers don't lie and this number, this forty-five, wasn't going anywhere.

"Would fifty make it okay?" Mavis hadn't examined a fig since this conversation started. The girl was too easily distracted. I could listen and throw out bad figs and sing "Yankee Doodle" in my head all at the same time.

"Far as your mama's concerned, fifty thousand wouldn't make it okay," Deacy said.

I knew that wasn't true. For fifty thousand dollars, Mama wouldn't mind if Daddy spent time up in Monroe. She'd even pack his bags for him. Course, she'd expect him home every weekend. Plus, she wouldn't let him be gone more than a year or so, I imagined.

"I'm not arguing with you, Deacy." Mama sounded as if she'd spent too much time arguing with her already. I wondered where I could've been when all this fighting was going on. Missing something big like that really made me mad. Mama says only dogs and lunatics get mad. I don't care. I'm not a dog or a lunatic, but I get mad as either of them when I miss out on excitement in my own family.

"So how's Uncle Everett doing up in Monroe?" I'd heard enough about the check and was ready to move on to that letter.

"Doing okay," Deacy said. She dipped her fan into her glass, then patted the back of her neck with the wet napkin. "Aussie, you ever seen such a hot day in your life?"

"Sure be hot," Aussie said. She had her hair rolled into a knot on the back of her head, but beads of sweat still glistened, rolled down the creases of her neck.

"How's that batch looking?" Mama asked. She'd stopped fig washing and was lining mason jars along the counter.

"Look to be needing more pot time," Aussie said.

"Next time Uncle Everett comes down, you can give him a couple of jars of preserves," I said. Everybody knew Everett loved his fig preserves. He ate them straight from the jar, put them between slices of bread for sandwiches and on top of vanilla ice cream in place of hot fudge, though that last way wasn't very appetizing to my way of thinking.

"These figs are not going to Monroe," Mama said, back at the sink, washing figs again.

"Now, Hazey. Just a jar or two. Not much."

"Everett Comeaux wants figs, he can get himself down here. None of these figs are traveling any farther north than Aussie's house up the road."

"We sure don't be living far north, us. No, ma'am, we sure don't," Marydale said.

"You know how Everett does love his figs." Deacy stood, rubbed the small of her back.

"Yes, ma'am. We do know Mister Everett be loving his fig preserves, him." I don't know why Marydale kept butting into this conversation, which was none of her concern. No one was talking about her uncle's entitlement to fig preserves. The girl just couldn't keep her mouth shut longer than a fast minute.

"Deacy, girl, some days I wonder how we could be blood related. For as little sense as you show some days, I sure do wonder," Mama said.

Deacy walked to the counter and lined up the mason jars into a four-across square. "He's still my husband." She moved one jar to the back of the counter. "Don't any of you be forgetting that, about him being my husband." Mama didn't say anything, even though there was a lot more to get done and Deacy shouldn't have been wasting time playing with mason jars. "Well, isn't he?"

"Isn't he what?" Mama shook the colander, then poured figs into her waiting pot, which was about full to the brim.

"My husband. Isn't that what we're talking about?"

"No one in this kitchen be saying your husband not your husband, Miz Deacy. No one saying that at all, no." Aussie turned off the burners and carried the preserve pot to the table, setting it on holders Mama'd spaced exactly right.

"If no one's saying that, then what are they saying?" Deacy carried two jars and a ladle to the table.

"They're saying what you already know," Mama said.

"And what's that, if I may be so bold as to ask?"

"That forty-five dollars isn't enough to move a man away from his family, up to Monroe, Louisiana."

I'd never been to Monroe, but Mama made it sound the nastiest place on earth. Hoped I never had to go there for any reason.

"Folks always talking about what doesn't concern them, what's none of their damn business." Deacy carried more jars to the table while Aussie filled them with sweet figs.

Mama measured sugar and water into her largest mixing bowl, ready for the next batch. We worked steady at our jobs, even Mavis and Marydale routing figs from their buckets to their bowls. We were a team, smooth and together. Everybody had to hold up her end or else the figs wouldn't get preserved. I didn't mind working when everybody else was too and when the results would be preserves to last all fall and winter and spring and most of next summer too.

After the first set of jars was filled, Deacy and Aussie tightened lids while Mama washed out the preserve pot, ready for the second batch. Most canning days we ended up with three batches. But we'd picked so many figs this day, even without Deacy's help, I wouldn't be surprised if we went up to four, maybe even five batches. With us having so much extra, didn't make sense for Mama to begrudge Everett a jar or two.

"Folks should learn to take care of their own business and leave the rest alone," Deacy said.

"That be a lot to be asking some folks," Aussie said. "Some folks, they don't be stretching into everybody's business, they don't know how to get along, them."

"How many people you know like that?" I asked.

"How many? How many? Let Aussie think now. She sure don't want to be telling no lie." She rubbed her temples as if her brain hurt from so much thinking. "I couldn't name them all if I be in this spot from now to God's kingdom come on earth."

"You could name every single person in Ville d'Angelle before kingdom comes." It wasn't often I got to correct Aussie.

"Sure could. Just show how many people be big-nose people." Aussie filled herself a glass of iced water and passed the whole glass across her face. I knew that felt good. Then she poured one for each of us girls. The water was so cold, it sent chills up my arms. Wished I could lie in a tub full of water that icy. But Mama'd think that was nothing but a tub of foolishness, even on the hottest day of the year, which this surely would prove to be.

"You girls excited about school?" Deacy asked, smiling as if that would be enough to make all of us in the kitchen forget what we'd been talking about. She was at the sink, rinsing now, while Mama stirred the second batch on the stove and Aussie measured sugar and water for the third. "School starting Wednesday."

"We know," I said.

"Yes, ma'am, Miz Deacy, we sure be knowing that sorry fact," Marydale said.

"Marydale Arceneaux, don't be telling me you don't do just fine in school and love going every single day." It was nice hearing that smile in Tante Deacy's voice. It had been missing most days since the Everett business started.

"I be doing fine, but I sure not be loving it."

"Those Sacred Heart sisters'll be sad to hear that."

"Won't be sad cause I won't be telling them," Marydale said.

"Your girl's too smart for her own good, Aussie."

"Yes, ma'am. She be smart all right." Aussie smiled, passed a hand across Marydale's sweaty forehead, up across her hair plaits, before carrying a bucket of figs we girls hadn't checked yet to the sink, where she inspected them straight to the counter for Deacy to wash.

"Most seven-, eight-year-olds don't know how to keep secrets. Don't even know what needs to be kept secret," Deacy said.

"I can keep secrets," Mavis said. She didn't want anybody thinking she couldn't keep secrets well as Marydale.

"Right," I said with a tone that let anybody listening know my sister couldn't keep a real secret if the future of the entire universe depended on her.

"Me and Mavis, we have so many secrets, we forget more than half of them."

"We've forgotten more secrets than most people have in a whole life," Mavis said.

"So what's the good of having a secret if you've forgotten it?" I said, trying to offer a little sense to the conversation.

"It's too hot for bickering, so stop unless you want a taste of the switch," Mama said. She couldn't stop stirring the pot, so we weren't worried over getting spanked, least not right this minute.

"How's Marydale's grades? I bet she does fine at Sacred Heart." Deacy was changing the subject from secrets to school to save us from Mama's whip. That was nice of her, but she should've known Mama was a bigger talker than doer when it came to whippings. She was Mama's only sister and surely should've known at least that little secret about her, even if she didn't know others.

"She does fine," Aussie said. She carried my almost-filled bowl to the counter and dumped my figs into one side of the sink.

"Straight A's, I bet," Deacy said. All she had to do was reach a hand in one side of the sink and bring figs over to the other to wash. That cold water she ran must've felt good over her hands. Wished my hands had been the ones under that faucet.

"No, ma'am. Not quite." Aussie carried a bushel basket closer to us and filled our buckets to the brim. Mavis sighed. Seemed as if those figs'd never stop coming. I kept reminding myself of the sweet taste of those preserves to keep from wishing we hadn't picked quite so many, left a few more to share with the birds.

The steam from the preserve pot had spread through the whole kitchen. We were all soaking. Were those beads of sweat or steam crawling down our skin? Didn't really matter because one felt hot as the other.

"So what's her worst subject? Spelling? I never was very good at spelling myself," Deacy said. She was happy to keep talking long as the talk wasn't about Everett or her no-account sons or Monroe, Louisiana. "Remember how bad I was at spelling, Hazey?"

"Couldn't spell your way out a hat," Mama said.

"Sure did drive Mama batty. Her so determined I'd spell good as her or my sister. Wasn't meant to be."

"I always suspected you missed those spelling words specially to drive her crazy."

"Who, me?" Deacy's voice floated in a bubble of laughter. "How could you say that about your own sister?"

"Marydale's a top speller," Aussie said. Like Mama before her, she stood next to Deacy, dropping good figs directly into the sink, bad ones into a paper sack sitting on the floor next to her feet.

"Different. D-I-F-F-E-R-E-N-T. Different." Marydale spelled her cleverness into that steaming kitchen for all of us to admire.

"I know who to call next time I need a word spelled," Deacy said.

"Just don't be calling my house looking for a girl who can sit still, be quiet. Don't be looking for a girl like that at my house, no," Aussie said.

"You don't get straight A's in conduct?" Deacy was teasing, knowing full well Marydale couldn't sit still and quiet all day, day after day after day, which is what a person has to do for a top grade in conduct. Least that's what the sisters at Holy Rosary expected and, I suspected, the sisters at Sacred Heart expected the same. But maybe I was wrong. Maybe colored sisters didn't demand much good behavior as white ones. Maybe having a colored teacher would bring a few good things my way.

"I never got myself a single A in conduct all first grade." Marydale didn't sound embarrassed. Just the opposite. Proud as if she'd done something worth bragging over.

"Not even one?" Deacy asked.

"No, ma'am. Not a one." There was that bragging voice again, proud about something anyone with a spoon of foolishness could do.

"That surely does surprise me." Tante Deacy was still teasing. She knew well as the rest of us that Marydale wasn't the sitting-still, being-quiet type girl. But just because she couldn't make A's in conduct didn't mean I didn't have a real chance at pulling up my B's and C's to A's in that particular subject.

"You get marked down for getting up to sharpen your pencil?" Far as I was concerned that had been Sister Katherine's dumbest conduct rule in fourth. Raise your hand and ask permission before walking to the pencil sharpener. She never said, "No, your pencil's sharp enough. You can't go to that sharpener. Write till your pencil end is worn to a dull nub." Sister Katherine always said, "Yes, you may," whenever someone wanted their pencil sharpened. So why the rule? I'd missed out on a couple of B+'s, maybe even an A- or two because of that stupid pencil rule.

"My teacher never marked off for pencil sharpening."

"Even if you didn't ask permission first?" I dropped three figs into my bowl, one into the paper sack.

"Didn't need permission for sharpening a pencil." Marydale looked at me as if I was ready for Pineville, the hospital for anybody who turned crazy in Louisiana. I didn't blame her. That's how I felt about Sister Katherine's rule too. I sure hoped my colored sister had had some training in a school like Sacred Heart. I smiled, thinking of that long line of straight A's in conduct waiting for me in fifth, so many A's the shine off my report card would blind Mama and shock Daddy. Grades weren't like numbers. Grades could change from one thing to another even as you watched.

15

ROLLING
THUNDER

THE LONG, COOLING RAIN everyone had been hoping for all summer came the first day of school. Big drops splatting everywhere. Rain so thick and fast, it turned the pit the house builders had dug for the foundation into a mucky swamp before we were done breakfast.

"Now, it rains," Daddy said.

"We can use it," Mama said.

"Some people can use it. We ourselves could use more of those dry days we've been having all damn summer." He reached for three more pancakes, which Mama'd made special for me and Mavis for the first day of school, but which, of course, we had to share with Daddy. "All summer we get one lousy rainstorm. But let me start building and look at it." He waved a disgusted hand at the window. "Just look at it."

"What do the workers do when they can't be outside?" I asked.

"Go elsewhere, work someplace they've already put up a roof and foundation."

"What if they don't have a place like that?"

"Then they get themselves a day off," Daddy said.

"We should have a day off too if the first day of school is miserable like this," I said. I wasn't usually superstitious, but this much rain felt like bad luck.

"That's right. It's too wet for school," Mavis said.

"How do you girls expect to learn anything if you don't go to school?" Mama flipped the last pancake and carried it to the table on the spatula.

"Wouldn't be for always. Just the first day. If it's raining hard, really hard, the first day gets postponed," I said.

"Postponed till sunshine," Mavis said. She smiled, thinking of the possibility of no school today. I don't know what she was worrying over. Second grade was nearly easy as first.

"Far as Vivien Leigh's concerned we could postpone school till next September." Daddy carried his plate and cup to the sink and leaned against the counter, his hands pushing against the sink, staring hard at the rain slapping the panes. "Much as the girl'll be learning this year, she might as well skip the whole thing."

That would've been fine with me, except I'd miss Clorise, hearing more Lena Guilbeaux jokes, watching Willie LeBlanc get himself into more trouble than you'd think possible for one human boy. Besides, Mama wouldn't abide my skipping an entire year of school, no matter the color of my teacher. Wouldn't abide it at all.

We fifths were quieter than usual because none of us knew what to expect from a colored sister. Was she a colored or was she a sister? We wore starched uniforms and loafers and, after a summer of no shoes and raggedy shorts and shirts, felt tied up. Sometimes I wonder what she must've thought of us that day as we trudged in with starched white collars, girls' brown skirts hanging to midcalves so mamas wouldn't have to be buying larger uniforms before next May and boys' cuffs rolled up twice for the same reason.

She sat behind her desk and every once in a while glanced at us straggling in, one or two or three or four at a time, depending on what bus we'd ridden. With it raining so hard, we didn't have a choice but to wait in the classroom for Mother Ignatius to ring her bell, signaling the beginning of a new school year. We clustered in small groups in the back of the room that smelled the same as any other first school day, fresh chalk and newly sharpened pencils perfuming the air. Only difference was a large map of the United States tacked to the front board. Didn't look brand new, so she must've brought it from her old school, which must've been a colored school. The states all looked to be there, though, so I guessed it didn't matter where it had been before. But even with the regular school smells and a regular school map, our problem was still there. How could it be a regular school day with a colored sister sitting behind the teacher's desk?

We snuck quick looks at her, no one staring long enough to risk being spoken to. She didn't seem as curious about us. Her head stayed bent over some papers and her fingers flew across them with a thick black pen.

Surely she wasn't writing up a test. This was the first day of school and we didn't know a thing yet. Nobody could get angry at us for not knowing anything on the first day of school. Why didn't I think to ask Marydale whether colored teachers gave tests the very first day?

At eight-thirty exactly—I didn't have a watch, but Clorise did and announced the time for the rest of us and, even without her, I would've known it was exactly eight-thirty because Mother Ignatius was never late, never early—Mother began ringing her bell in sixth. Her office was tucked in the far corner of sixth grade, which she taught, because it was so convenient. Her office wasn't much of an office, just sheets of fiberboard squaring off the corner, a rectangle cut through one panel and covered by a dark green drape donated by the Coussans for a door. Not much of a door. Not much of an office. But Mother Ignatius couldn't complain, being a nun and nuns having renounced all worldly goods, including nice offices.

Mother Ignatius started our rainy school day by stepping out that office with her golden bell, large as a first-grader's reader, and ringing it to bring the sixths to their desks. She held the bell by its shining wooden handle and swung it up and down by her side. When the sixths looked to be under control, she propped open the door separating fifths' class from sixths' and rang us to our desks. She smiled since this was first day, but didn't speak, just let her bell do her talking.

After she'd belled us to our seats, she opened the door to fourth grade and rang those children to order. She worked her way down the schoolhouse, which unfolded in a long single line, the people who built it many years back not being able to imagine anything but six classrooms, one after another in a straight line.

Her bell faded till she reached first, at the opposite end of the building from sixth. I felt sorry for those babies, remembering how scared I'd been the first time I heard that bell, sounding as if God's avenging angel was working her way right to me. It had been all I could do not to run out the back door. But I'd stayed, knowing even at age six, there was no escaping an avenging angel.

After what seemed forever but was probably no more than a minute or two, the ringing stopped. Mother Ignatius had left all the doors open in the wake of her passage and now stood in the door frame between third and fourth. She welcomed us to the new year, said she knew we all planned to work hard, do our very best every day. I watched Willie ball pieces of paper and line them along the pencil-holder groove at the front of his desk, and knew Mother Ignatius was wrong, at least about some of us. After she said those few things, she led us in the Nicene Creed, an Our Father, and one Hail Mary. Then she walked back the way she'd come, leaving teachers in first and second to close their own doors. The others she closed herself.

When she walked back through our room, we all looked at her, even Willie, searching for hints about how we were supposed to act, what we were expected to do. Her free hand raised in a half wave, then lowered so quickly, I wasn't sure it had moved at all. Was it a warning? A request for quiet? An apology? Nothing? She smiled again but still didn't say anything. I think she must've been sad, felt sorry for us having to have a colored sister. That's sure the way each of us felt, sitting in those desks, waiting for what we could not imagine. The door to sixth swung closed and we were left alone with a colored sister blacker than the clouds hovering over school and home and all of Ville d'Angelle.

Sister Cecilia Elizabeth Patrick was her full nun name, but we could call her Sister Pat. That's the first thing she said or at least the first thing I understood. Turned out she was from Brooklyn and I decided that was one place I was never going. If everybody from Brooklyn talked like Sister Pat, it'd feel like a foreign country.

There were three absolutes in Sister Pat's room—no interrupting when someone else was talking, no sneezing or coughing without covering your mouth, and no gum. I think she added that last rule because she spied Willie with a wad in his cheek.

"Since this is the first day, I'm allowing all of you with gum to dispose of it in a piece of paper and then into my trash can." She looked right at Willie. He stared off into space as if he hadn't heard a thing.

She walked between two lines of desks toward Willie, who slouched in the back row. Her blue habit brushed my elbow as she swept past.

When she reached Willie, she folded her arms across her chest. "I'm talking to you, young man," she said, her voice teacher mean.

Willie still didn't say a word. The corners of his mouth twitched and any minute he'd break into that grin he wore when he didn't know what else to do.

Don't smile, Willie, I prayed to myself. She wouldn't know the grin meant he was worked up inside about something and didn't know how else to show it.

"Give me that gum," she said and held out her hand.

Willie didn't move. His mouth stopped twitching. He was too scared to even grin. Willie knew what nuns could do to you.

Quick as a lick, she grabbed Willie by his arm, pulled him out his desk, and marched him down the aisle. By the time he came to his senses they'd reached the front of the room.

"My daddy says he won't abide a colored touching on me," Willie said and yanked his arm free.

The rest of us fifths stared at the floor, scared about what would happen next, but excited too.

Sister Pat grabbed Willie again, this time holding both his upper arms. She leaned so close to him, he must've been able to smell the blackness of her. "You tell your daddy there'll be no gum in my classroom. Take it out." She held him a few more seconds, then let go, but didn't stop glaring at him or leaning into him.

Willie took out his gum real slow, as if he was under a spell, and rolled it in the paper she gave him, then flipped it to the trash can. "Was getting old, anyhow," he muttered as he walked back to his desk.

"Was brand new, Willie LeBlanc, and everyone knows it," I said.

Everybody laughed. Even Willie and Sister Pat. Then she went to the board and wrote out a poem that she made us copy in our notebooks and that was the first of many, many we'd write out before Christmas vacation. She wrote:

The Dream Keeper by Langston Hughes

Bring me all of your dreams,
You dreamers,
Bring me all of your
Heart melodies
That I may wrap them
In a blue cloud-cloth
Away from the too-rough fingers
Of the world.

"This is going to be a long year," Willie whispered under his breath while he finished copying the poem.

I'd never heard of Mister Hughes, but I expected he would've understood exactly what Willie meant.

That night and every night for the first week I got the third degree from Daddy during supper. "What did Sister Cecilia Elizabeth Patrick say today?" He never called her plain Sister Pat because it sounded too friendly and he didn't want anybody thinking he approved of a colored sister in a white school, though how anyone could think that of my daddy, I could never imagine.

"Nothing much," I said.

"She had to say something. Never heard of a teacher, even a colored one, going all day without saying nothing." He never missed a chance of reminding me things in fifth weren't right and natural.

I stabbed four peas with my fork. "Get out your readers. Time for spelling. Stuff like that."

"Any kids giving her trouble?" he asked with some hope.

"No more trouble than regular. She takes care of what trouble there is. Same as all the sisters."

"For Heaven's sake, Floyd. Stop trying to stir up a mess," Mama said. "The school year's just started."

"Just asking," he said. "A father's sure entitled to ask after his daughter's schooling."

"You're not fooling me any, Mister Floyd Dubois," Mama said. She pushed her chair back and carried the bowl of leftover peas and platter of chicken to the kitchen counter.

By the end of the week Daddy eased up on pestering me about school. Maybe he was disappointed I never reported trouble. Sister Pat never let on that she was staring at a roomful of white kids instead of colored ones like she should've been. So I couldn't tell Daddy otherwise. More likely, he got discouraged because she knew all the capitals of all the states, even places like Idaho and North Dakota, and could recite lots of poems without looking up a single word. Her colored nun brain worked well as any white nun brain I'd come up against. She was solid proof it didn't matter whether colored brains looked the same as white ones.

Daddy could've lived with all Sister Pat knew, though, if it hadn't been for the other thing. He couldn't stand the thought of Sister Pat in Yankee Stadium, not just once but lots and lots and lots of times. She saw Joe DiMaggio hit during his streak that Daddy called the most amazing feat in baseball, better than Babe Ruth's home runs. After I told him that, Daddy didn't want me talking too much about school or Sister Pat. Fine with me. To Daddy she was nothing but a colored dressed like a nun. But she never acted any different from the other sisters at school. So that's how we fifths treated her—like just another sister liable to smack your knuckles with your own ruler if you forgot your spelling homework. Nobody messes with sisters and we fifths knew that.

The rain that started with school kept coming. Didn't seem we had one dry minute in nearly two weeks. I got so tired of wearing my yellow slicker and lugging an umbrella everywhere, I was ready to bury them both in that gold hole of Mavis and Marydale's. Work on the extension had halted completely, the workers not able to do a thing till the ground dried out and the rain not stopping long enough to dry anything. Daddy grew grouchier and grouchier, mad at the rain, mad at us, mad at everything.

Friday, Mama and Aussie were at the kitchen table, drinking Coca-Colas and eating Fig Newtons, when the bus dropped us off. Aussie had come over for closet cleaning. Mama'd spent Thursday with Deacy, who'd come down with a virus. She made up some meals T.J. could warm without bothering poor sick Deacy. Mama'd come home Thursday afternoon saying Deacy was still tired but feeling better, no thanks to Everett. Didn't seem right for Mama to blame Everett for a virus attacking hundreds of miles from Monroe, Louisiana. He had sent that forty-five dollars, but the money wasn't enough to buy his redemption, far as Mama was concerned. And until he was redeemed, he could be blamed for anything.

"You girls have a good day?" Mama asked.

We hung our raincoats and umbrellas on hooks at the back door. Mama'd laid a towel on the floor to catch the puddles that were already forming.

"Sister Terese gives too much homework." Mavis got herself five Fig Newtons and a glass of milk. "Even on weekends."

"Sister wanting to smarten you up. Girl doesn't get herself plenty homework, she's not any smarter when the sun sets than when it rose up." Aussie reached for another Fig Newton.

"Marydale doesn't have near as much homework," Mavis said.

"She goes to a different school." I grabbed a couple of Newtons for myself before Mavis gobbled them all.

"So?" Mavis said.

"So, different school means different type teachers means different type homework." I didn't want to come right out, with Aussie sitting there, and say colored children naturally don't have as much homework as white children since coloreds don't have to know as much, learn as much as whites. You'd think Mavis could figure that without being told direct.

"Me and Marydale, we're both second-graders. Right?"

"That be right," Aussie said.

"We should be equal on homework, then. Fair is fair." Mavis popped another Fig Newton, not just a bite, but the whole thing. Girl has the biggest mouth I've ever seen on a seven-year-old.

"You're too little to be talking fair," Mama said.

Mavis bulged her eyes at Mama to show her disagreement. Even Mavis knew better than to try talking with a mouth crammed full of sticky Fig Newton.

"Marydale gets plenty homework, her," Aussie said.

"Marydale says she finishes her homework while she's eating her snack. Doesn't sound like plenty to me." Mavis had chewed and swallowed fast so she could use her mouth for talking.

"No need for you to be worrying over your neighbor. Worry about your own work," I said.

"Your sister's right," Mama said, her voice surprised I could be so wise.

She wouldn't have smiled at me if I'd told her that was one of Sister Pat's favorite sayings. "Don't worry about your neighbor. Do your own work," Sister Pat said at least twice a day and often more than that. Mama wouldn't approve my getting a saying from a colored, no matter how good the saying might be.

"Sister Terese's trying to cram all second grade into one week. That's what it looks like to me."

"Girl, you be complaining much as my own baby," Aussie said.

"What does she have to complain over? Homework you can finish during snack time?" Mavis snorted her disgust at Marydale's easy time. What did the girl want? To learn as little as a colored and not a fact more?

"Little Mavis, you know how Marydale likes her food. Lord, that baby of mine starts eating when she walk in the door and don't stop till her daddy gets home, no. Girl's mouth don't get more than a minute's break between snacking and suppering."

"Now are you satisfied?" Mama asked.

"Marydale says she hardly has any homework." Mavis's cheeks were starting to puff. She was determined to have Marydale without as much homework as herself, maybe because if she admitted Marydale might not be telling God's exact truth about homework, she'd have to face up to the possibility that Marydale might not be telling God's exact truth about other things.

"Marydale likes her schoolwork so much, don't seem like any time at all gone by when she doing that homework. Girl loves school that much, her." Aussie couldn't let herself say, or even hint, that Marydale was telling another one of her fibs when it came to homework and how much she did or didn't have. Aussie and Mavis, two peas in a pod over Marydale.

"These girls love their school too," Mama said. "If I told them they had to stay home all year, couldn't go to school, all of Ville d'Angelle would hear the crying." She didn't want Aussie thinking we didn't love our school every bit as much as Marydale loved hers. That hardly seemed worth an argument to me. But I could see Mama felt different.

"Wouldn't hear me crying. Least not if Marydale was home too," Mavis said.

"Marydale be at school, be learning what she supposed to be learning," Aussie said.

"How about you get yourself started on some of that homework instead of just fussing about it." Mama wasn't asking a question. She was saying, Get busy if you want to stay out of trouble.

Mavis let out a big sigh, but pulled her writing worksheet out her book satchel and got to work on her cursive c's, which were not nearly as hard as the q's she'd get later in the year.

"Sister Terese's trying to shovel all our cursives into our heads by the end of next week, I bet."

"You're only on c," I reminded her.

"Stop picking on me. Mama, you tell her to stop picking on me."

Mama gave me one of her looks, which I ignored because giving your sister obvious information does not count as picking. But I did pull out my geography notebook and start on my United States map even though it was just Friday and I had all weekend to finish the coloring. By the end of the year we'd know the capitals and at least ten other facts about each state. Gave me a headache just thinking about knowing so much.

"My baby sure be loving her school," Aussie said.

"Well, so do these girls." Mama's voice had an edge to it that kept Mavis quiet, though she did look up from the line of c's trailing across her paper.

"Children always be loving their school. Yes, ma'am. That's God's truth. Children at Sacred Heart be loving their school. Children at Holy Rosary be loving their school. All the same. All them children be loving their school just the same." Aussie shook an ice cube into her mouth and cracked it, so loud it sounded like thunder booming across our kitchen.

"Not exactly the same," Mama said.

"Yes, ma'am. Just the same," Aussie repeated.

"How can you say that? It's not the same. Will never be the same. Two schools, different as night and day." Different as black and white, Mama was thinking, but was too polite to say out loud.

"Children go to one school, learn their A-B-C's, 1-2-3's. Go to the other school, learn the same. Nothing different in your A-B-C's, 1-2-3's."

"It's different still. Different teachers. Other things too."

Aussie shrugged. "Not so different." It was as close as she could get to reminding Mama out loud about the colored sister teaching one of her own girls.

"It's always been different. Always will be." Sounded like Daddy talking out Mama's mouth.

"Different. Same. Don't matter to God and if it don't bother God, it sure don't bother Aussie."

Mama got up to put away the milk carton Mavis had left on the counter. She didn't say anything to Aussie because even Mama couldn't insist on being bothered by something that wasn't bothering God.

Aussie bit into another ice cube, rolling thunder across our kitchen again.

16

SHEETS AND CROSSES

SATURDAY BROUGHT THE FIRST RAYS of sun since school had started. When I got up at seven-thirty, only a strip of light shone in my window, but that strip was more than I'd seen in nearly two weeks. Even though we'd only been in school eight days, I'd lost the sleeping-late habit. My brain already knew I wasn't allowed to stay in bed till nine, ten, later if I was lucky. Those hours were for summer and summer was gone in a storm of rain that hinted of hurricane season edging closer.

About noon, men delivered lumber, which Mama had them stack under the carport after she backed her car down the drive. One of the workers said the wood'd be out of her way in no time. Mama joked it'd be a lot longer than that if this weather didn't give us a break. The worker said he imagined that was so, then got in his emptied truck and drove off, probably to pick up another load of lumber for somebody else waiting like us for the rain to stop, for the ground to dry.

But the men hadn't even had time to reach the lumberyard and reload when clouds covered the only taste of sun we'd had in many days. By two, rain was falling, not hard and fast, but slow and steady, the kind that would last the rest of the day and into night, maybe even into the next day.

After we'd picked up our room and saved our clean laundry and wiped off the kitchen table and chairs, Mama couldn't think of anything else for us to do. All that rain must've clogged her brain because Mama wasn't usually at a loss for finding work for me and Mavis, mainly me.

I spent the rest of the afternoon reading a biography of Dolley Madison. When the White House nearly burnt to the ground, she saved lots of important papers, even a portrait of George Washington. She was brave, much braver than I'd ever be, especially over a picture and a stack of papers, no matter how important. The British had invaded the capital and she risked her life to rescue things that weren't even alive. Afterward she said she only did what was right. I am always amazed by people who know right from wrong so easily. If she had burnt in the fire along with those papers, been captured by the British and tortured, would her running in after them still have been the right thing? Is something right forever, wrong forever, no matter what? I lay on my bed watching rain drizzle down the window and wondering what Dolley Madison would say about that.

Next day Tante Deacy and Malcolm and Austin drove over after dinner. T.J. stayed home to get schoolwork done. Deacy said high schoolers get ever so much more homework. But the truth was, T.J. stayed behind because he figured we wouldn't be offering food so soon after dinner. I know my cousin and his stomach and his thinking. He can fool his mama but not me.

Daddy took Malcolm and Austin to the shed to help him sharpen knives, ours and Deacy's too. He only invited them back there because he felt sorry for them not having a daddy at home anymore. He certainly didn't expect any real help out of either of them. My daddy's not that stupid. Mavis followed, saying she could help much as Malcolm and more than Austin. No one paid her any attention since, as usual, she didn't know what she was talking about.

Mama threw out the remains of coffee and made up a fresh pot, then sat at the table with Deacy and me to wait for it to finish brewing. The old pot was close to half full but a lady carrying a change-of-life baby gets herself special treats all the time, from every direction, from everybody she knows.

"Got myself another letter," Deacy said.

"From Everett?" Mama asked.

"Who else?" She was right about that. We were not a letter-writing family. Only time we got personal mail was at Christmas and even those pieces were only cards, not real letters.

"Another forty-five extra?" Mama said, spitting out the number like strings of squash caught between her teeth.

"More than that."

"How much?"

"Still forty-five, but with news." Deacy smoothed her dress over her belly ballooning with her change-of-life baby. "Says he'll be home for Thanksgiving. That's not far off."

I wondered what had happened to those promises of visits home nearly every weekend.

"So one turkey's coming home to eat another turkey." Mama got up to pour coffee into cups.

"Don't be that way, Hazey."

"What way? What way am I being?"

Deacy sighed, then looked at me and rolled her eyes. I grinned, since Mama's back was still to us, pouring coffee. Deacy grinned back, then rolled her eyes once more before Mama turned back to the table.

"How's that colored sister treating you?" Deacy asked, going for a subject change.

"All right, I guess." Adults couldn't believe there really hadn't been any difference between this sister and all the other ones I'd had in earlier grades except this one was colored and the others weren't.

"Sure glad my boys aren't in fifth." She pulled a church fan from her purse, still there from morning Mass, and opened it to get some breeze going.

"It's not so bad," I said.

"Everett wanted to know if the sheets have started anything," Deacy said.

"What could sheets do?" I said. "Nothing but cover a bed." I waited for more explanation, but none was offered.

"Everett heard something? How could Everett know anything up in Monroe?" Mama had taken to saying the name like Aussie, each syllable too distinct to belong to a real place.

"He's got friends. Hears things."

"His friends don't write letters and don't, for sure, spend money on long-distance phone calls." She tapped the handle of her cup with one finger. "Your husband always did like pretending he knew things before anybody else. Why is that?"

"Working that IGA, he did hear things. Lots of things." Deacy fanned a little faster and tugged on one of the aqua beads on her necklace. I considered whether it might be real turquoise, but decided probably not.

"He's not working the IGA now."

"This is stuff he heard before Monroe."

"That's old, used-up news. You tell Everett to get his tail back to Ville d'Angelle before he starts spreading rumors he expects anyone to believe."

"Once the sheets start, they won't stop. That's for sure."

"Sheets. Sheets. What's all this about some dopey old sheets?" This conversation wasn't making an ounce of sense. The key was those sheets, but what did sheets have to do with anything?

"Don't you have something better to do than spy on two old ladies?" Mama asked.

I looked down at the table, pretending I was invisible.

"Floyd hasn't said anything," Mama said when I didn't answer.

I let out my breath slow as an invisible girl should.

"Some of those hotheads wouldn't know how to stop, if something got started," Deacy said.

"I think things'll stay peaceful. They're nuns, after all," Mama said.

"Wimples don't stop sheets. Especially Baton Rouge sheets. You know that well as I do." Deacy went to the stove for another cup of coffee. I was surprised by how much her belly had spread in just a few weeks. That change-of-life baby was growing faster than anyone I knew. Soon she'd sprinkle magic all over her family, including her cousins, I hoped.

"This is a little place, just a blink on the highway, a dot on the official state map. Nothing anybody'll bother over. Nuns'll teach a year. Be gone in June. That's all there'll be to that." Was Mama forgetting her bet? The money still nestled in my top drawer. If no one asked for it at the end of the school year, would keeping it for myself be cheating or stealing? What would Dolley Madison say about my keeping all that money? Right or wrong?

Deacy refilled Mama's cup too before easing back down into her chair. "When it comes to coloreds, no peace is guaranteed. You know that."

Mama sipped. "I'm not wasting my time worrying over sheets."

"Me neither," I said. But no one paid me any mind.

"Got enough other things to worry over and you've got more than me," Mama said.

"I sure do." Deacy dropped a third sugar cube in her cup and stirred with one of Mama's delicate coffee spoons. "I sure do," she said again.

After Deacy and her boys left, Daddy drove us to Borden's in Lafayette for ice cream treats. The rain had stopped with Tante Deacy's arrival and hadn't started up again, but drops still clung to trees, leaves, bushes, blades of grass. Everything sparkled like just-polished silver. Mama was willing to allow cracks in the windows since Sunday Mass was long finished. Those cracks let the smell of fresh, damp earth into the car and, even though I wasn't a farmer and hoped never to be one, I liked the smell of everything washed clean.

We were lucky because when we arrived at Borden's, a family was just leaving and so we got a booth without waiting. Borden's ice cream is worth a long wait, but some days Daddy won't allow waiting and hustles us into the car to lick our cones while he drives home one-handed. My daddy never has been much on the patient side.

I ordered my regular, double-dip cone with chocolate on one side, butter pecan on the other. Those special Borden cones—a single stem to hold at the bottom, but two separate cups, one for each scoop, at the top—made eating two flavors better than at places where they piled your choices one on top of the other. At Borden's you could lick chocolate all the way to the bottom before starting on butter pecan. Or you could take a lick of chocolate, lick of butter pecan, lick of chocolate. Or you could eat half the chocolate, half the butter pecan. No end to the number of ways you could eat a Borden's double cone.

Mavis and Daddy had hot fudge sundaes and Mama went for a root beer float. I took my time licking because even if everyone finished before me, I could carry my cone into the car and finish on the way home.

Daddy spent the first half of his sundae fussing over the rain slowing down our house extension.

"It's not like we don't have a roof over our heads," Mama reminded.

"Once I start something, I like to finish it. That's all. You know that about me." He scooped a bite with nuts. "Ever known me to leave something part done once I start?"

"No, sir. Not you. You start something, you finish it."

"You bet your life on that one." He grinned at Mama, who grinned back, though I couldn't figure what they thought was worth the smiles.

But since they were in a joking mood, I thought I'd throw in the funniest thing I'd heard lately. "Know what Uncle Everett says?"

"No. What does our Monroe man say?" Daddy asked.

"He's all worked up over what some sheets are planning." I giggled, then licked chocolate. "Can you imagine worrying over old sheets?"

I expected Daddy to laugh, but he didn't even smile, turning instead to Mama sitting next to him. "Everett hearing something?"

"Old IGA news is all," Mama said. "Wouldn't put any weight to it."

"I haven't heard about any boys riding."

"Riding where?" I asked.

Mama shivered. Her float must've been colder than usual. "Let's don't even talk about it."

"Facts is facts, Hazel." He scooped another spoonful of ice cream and fudge, dipped back for nuts, sundaes being about the only time Daddy'd let different foods mix in the same bite he took to his mouth. "Them boys are just protecting their own. That's all they're doing."

"Nothing in Ville d'Angelle belongs to those Baton Rouge boys." She stirred her float with the straw. "There's more to it than that. Lots more."

"What boys? What riding?" I asked again.

"Nothing to worry yourself over," Mama said.

I wasn't worrying, just curious. But didn't look like anyone was going to kill themselves to satisfy my curiosity.

"We are talking God's servants here," Mama said. She pushed her float toward the center of the table, done even though her glass was still a third full.

"We are talking uppity niggers."

"Floyd."

"Uppity," Daddy said again, as if that was the word Mama was objecting over.

"You don't think anything'll happen, do you?" Mama asked. Two lines of worry split her brows and her eyes were shades darker than normal.

Daddy shrugged. "Haven't heard. That's all I can say. I haven't heard."

Mama wasn't much comforted. Those two lines flitted between her brows for the rest of our Borden's trip. Some of that was over Mavis catching a disease from pulling gum off the underside of our booth table, where nasty people had put it, and rolling it into a big ball with her hands. But not all of it. Not even most of it was over Mavis.

Monday morning was rich blue sky and cool temperatures, least cool for September. Not a cloud marked the blueness. The rain of the last weeks might never have been. Overnight, the promise of fall had arrived.

This being the third week of school, Mama didn't have anything special waiting on the breakfast table. Daddy'd eaten and gone before me and Mavis were up. He didn't mind being late for Mama's pancakes, but nothing else was worth the explaining he had to give to Mister Jack, his boss.

Mama made lunch sandwiches, Spam for me, peanut butter and jelly for Mavis, while we ate cereal. "Daddy must be happy to see sun," I said.

"Just so it lasts," Mama said.

"It'll last," I said, more hoping than knowing. Southwest Louisiana was not known for its dryness, this past summer being the exception to anything I could remember.

"Maybe. We'll see," Mama said, her doubt plain for the listening.

Mavis and I both finished early enough to be standing by the road when the bus drove up. One good thing about school uniforms, you don't have to waste time deciding what to wear each morning. Mama waved to us from the side yard where she was weeding her garden. Mavis waved back before stepping on the bus. I ignored Mama, pretended she was waving just to Mavis and not to me too. I was in fifth and much closer to grown than Mavis and didn't wave good-bye to my mama when all I was doing was going to school.

Later I tried to remember whether anything that morning had clued what we'd find at school. Nothing. Everything from Mama waking us to Daddy being gone to work to breakfast cereal to Mama's wave was normal as ever. No hints of what school would bring.

The bus dropped us off at Holy Rosary before going another several blocks to drop off the public school children. Nothing different about that either. But when we got to the back playground, something was plenty different. Instead of kids clumped here and there, playing tag or hopscotch or just talking, they were spread in an almost perfect circle, two and three abreast, staring at something in the middle.

Sister Terese and Mother Ignatius huddled near the back door, glancing every so often, but not really paying much attention to the children. I couldn't hear what they were saying but knew it meant trouble. The smell of worry filled the school ground. I didn't have to see what those kids were staring at to know that. But smelling worry, knowing something was terribly wrong didn't make me want to see the middle of the circle any less.

I ran up to where the fifths were standing and found Clorise and Lena. "What is it? What's going on?"

Clorise shoved me to the inside of the circle. In the middle, burnt into the grass, was a giant black cross. You wouldn't think grass so wet could've burnt so black, but it had. Whoever did it had crisscrossed sticks in the shape of a cross. The sticks had burnt first, drying the grass and letting it burn too. Now that I was closer the stench of burn filled my nose, gagged my throat. I tried to pull back, but the fifths pushed against me, pressing me closer to the foul smell of that cross of ashes.

I was saved by Mother Ignatius's golden bell. She rang and rang till all the classes were lined in their proper spots on the playground. We fifths should've stood right in the middle of the cross. But we snaked our line around so no one had to stand on burnt grass, each of us knowing the devil had dipped his pitchfork on our playground.

"Who did it?" I whispered to Clorise, who stood in front of me.

"The Klan, stupid," Willie answered next to me from the boys' line. Willie LeBlanc has the biggest set of ears anyone's ever seen and should be in the record books.

"What?" I said.

"The KKK. Do I have to spell it out? Boy, girls are sure stupid." He smirked and hunched away from me, ready to run if I decided to punch his arm.

But I was too busy thinking to bother punching anyone, even Willie LeBlanc. We'd read about the Ku Klux Klan, the white-hooded-sheet wearers, when we studied the Civil War at the end of fourth. But nothing in those history books had said anything about crosses in a schoolyard. Burnt crosses weren't supposed to come to Holy Rosary. I leaned against Clorise, making sure no boy's big ears could catch my words. "Willie says it's the Klan. Do you think so?"

Clorise nodded, her eyes on Mother Ignatius.

"At school, though? Do you think they'd do this at our school?"

Again, the nod.

"Why? Why do you think?" The questions sounded stupid even to my own ears. Clorise didn't answer, just turned to me with a look that said, Girl, if you can't figure it out, you don't belong in fifth.

This time it was my turn to nod.

When we were all quiet as we ever got, Mother Ignatius led prayers, same ones as always—Hail Mary, Our Father, Nicene Creed. "I believe in God, Father Almighty, Maker of Heaven and earth…" The people who burnt that cross must not've been Catholic, must not even believe in God. If they'd been believers, surely they would've known better than to risk going up against holy ground. School sat on church property, which made it holy, not holy as the church itself, but still holy. Those cross burners were messing with God's stuff—his school, his playground, his nuns. I dug fingernails into my palms till my hands hurt. If I hadn't been so angry, seeing my school scarred that way, I could've almost felt sorry for what would surely happen to the poor folks who'd sinned against God and Mother Ignatius.

"Guess Sister Pat won't be in a very good mood this morning," Willie joked to anyone who'd listen just before we trooped to the front door, following fourth into the building and trailed by sixth. "Guess she won't care who's chewing gum this morning." He slumped into his desk, still grinning.

17

STARS, NEVER CHANGING, FOREVER AND EVER

TEACHERS ALL TRIED ACTING as if nothing was different about this day. Sister Pat wrote four-digit multiplication problems on the board. When we'd done those, she made us take out our spellers. After that it was reading groups, then recess, then more work, then lunch, then more work. Same thing went on in the other classes, far as I could tell.

"Sister Katherine say anything about the cross?" I asked Austin during morning recess.

"Nothing," he said.

"Not a thing?"

"That's what I said." He ran off to meet his friends, who were racing across the yard with no purpose in mind that I could fathom.

Mavis said the same when I cornered her during lunch. Sister Terese had assigned three cursive letters to be finished by tomorrow, but Mavis didn't think that was related to the cross. I agreed.

By last period—art, since today was Monday—I was about ready to believe the cross didn't mean anything more than pieces of burnt grass that'd have to be reseeded and might always carry more green newness than the grass next to it. Sister Pat passed out pictures of boats she'd cut from magazines or maybe very old books because a teacher would never cut from a brand-new one. But there weren't enough pictures to go around, so we had to share.

I got stuck with Willie. I didn't mind too much, though I would've preferred pushing my desk next to Lena's or Clorise's, sharing a picture with one of them. But Willie was a good drawer, the best in class. It was the one thing he did really well, so he probably wouldn't bother me too much or fool around and get us in trouble. I might even pick up a few drawing tips.

But this day held no more luck for me than it had for the back playground. Sister Pat handed us the most complicated boat, ship really, I'd ever seen. Looked like something that traveled the oceans when Columbus did. Masts and sails and lines crisscrossed each other so it was impossible to tell where one ended and the next started. Except when you looked at the picture, none of it seemed jumbled or out of place, everything fit just right. I knew from the very beginning, before I even picked up a pencil, the ship that would end up on my paper would never look like the one in the picture, wouldn't even look like a close relative.

Next to me and Willie kids were drawing a sailboat. Anyone can draw a sailboat. In front of us Clorise and Elvie had a canoe. It did have hundreds of intricate designs, but there were so many, no one would notice if you left off one or two. Even with the designs, it was still just a canoe. Easy.

I thought about raising my hand, asking why we'd gotten the hardest picture. But I thought better of it just in time. Willie'd make some smart comment about not seeing anything particularly difficult about it and why did I think it was so hard when he thought it was about the easiest thing he'd ever been asked to draw. I let my hands rest in my lap instead of waving either of them to catch Sister Pat's eye and pretended I was studying the ship before getting started. Really I was waiting for Willie to start, hoping I'd pick up a clue about how to begin.

But Willie wasn't any more eager than me. Maybe he was stumped too.

"Hard to know where to start," I said in the quiet voice Sister Pat allowed during partner work.

"The beginning is always the hardest," Willie said. He chewed the inside of his cheek, thinking. I hoped he wasn't drawing blood. If blood started oozing from between his lips, though, Sister Pat might change her mind about the no-gum rule. Chewing gum had definite advantages over chewing cheeks.

I waited, studied the picture, watched Willie out the corner of my eye, waited some more. Finally he picked up a pencil and drew lines every which way across his paper. I could see no relation to the ship propped up with books we'd arranged across the crack separating our two desks. But for each line he drew, I tried to draw an exactly identical one on my paper. If we both ended up with nothing but a mishmash of crossing lines, no resemblance to a ship at all, it'd be Willie's fault, not mine.

We were half finished art period before a ship began appearing on our papers. Seconds earlier, there'd been nothing but random lines, intersecting for no apparent reason. Now two ships were emerging, one on my paper, the other on Willie's.

"Looks pretty good," I said.

"It's not done."

"I know that." I was tempted to say more but couldn't spare the breath, being too busy following Willie's pencil, which now flew across his sheet, sure of where it was going, what was needed next.

"Nice," Sister Pat said, peering over our shoulders.

I couldn't stop for a thank-you. Willie was going that fast. I didn't bother looking at the magazine picture now. It was all I could do to keep up with Willie. By the time he put his pencil down I had no idea what I'd see when I looked at my paper. I was surprised by how good my ship was. It wasn't good as Willie's. My lines were jerky, unsure compared to his smooth, even strokes. Still, anybody could tell the drawing was a ship, which was more than you could say about most of my art projects.

"This is really good," I said.

"The mainsail is too wide," Willie said, squinting first at his drawing, then at the magazine, then at his picture again.

"Looks okay to me."

"Too wide," he said again.

I didn't argue. He knew I wouldn't. When it came to drawing, Willie was the expert. He knew that. So did everyone else.

Sister Pat was at the other end of the room, studying other kids' boats. She leaned over a desk, slid her finger across Gloria's paper, showing where a line belonged or maybe where one didn't belong. Sister Pat wasn't a bad drawer herself, though not good as Willie. Gloria asked a question I couldn't hear and Sister gave an answer I also couldn't hear, but it must've satisfied Gloria because she picked up her pencil again.

"Sister Pat's pretty nice, don't you think?"

"She's okay for being colored." Willie's head bent over his drawing, shading one side of the sail that bothered him so much.

I watched but didn't try to copy. This was the best thing I'd ever drawn and I wasn't taking any chances on ruining it. "She knows an awful lot of stuff. She's been places too. New York."

"Don't be stupid. New York doesn't count cause that's where she's from." He erased part of his shading, then held the picture an arm's length away to study.

"If the place you're born is big as New York, it does so count."

"Where you're born never counts."

"That's the dumbest thing I've ever heard."

"Then you haven't been listening or looking very hard." He put the picture on his desk and smoothed it with one finger, trying to decide whether he was satisfied or not.

"What's that supposed to mean?"

"Means a nigger teacher in a white classroom is the dumbest thing you'll ever see or hear. If you don't know that, you're the dumb one."

"Is she a nun or is she not?" I glanced around to make sure Sister Pat hadn't worked her way to our side of the room, unbeknownst to us. But she was still too far away to hear us.

"No one's saying she isn't a nun."

"It's a sin to call a nun nigger."

"Says who?"

"God's Commandments. That's who." That stopped Willie for a while. He was as bad at Catechism as he was good at drawing. "It might be a mortal sin to call a nun that."

"But you're not sure." He tapped a fist on my desk three times lightly as if he'd won the argument.

"It's either a major venial or a mortal." I raised an eyebrow, daring him to question my sin classification.

"So maybe God made that rule never expecting a colored nun would end up teaching in a white school."

"You forgetting God knows everything, past, present, and future?" We'd memorized that bit of information every year since first grade and even Willie's brain must've soaked it up.

"I'm not forgetting nothing."

"God knows everything. He knew this would happen when he made up that rule." Sister Pat stooped next to Lena's desk, her profile to me. The corners of her mouth lifted in a smile. Lena must've told one of her jokes. What's black and white and red all over? A newspaper. What's red and green and goes a hundred miles an hour? A frog in a blender. Or maybe it was a new joke, one I'd never heard before. Lena collected jokes the way some people collected bugs.

"That cross out back says it all." Willie lowered his voice, quieter than partner talk, just over a whisper. "If she ever forgets she's a nigger, all she has to do is look out at that cross." He grinned, his mouth so close to my face, I could see a speck of apple peel from lunch snagged between two bottom teeth.

Sister Pat ordered us to put our desks back in their proper spots. When the shuffling quieted, she had me and Willie and Elvie bring our drawings to the front of the room, where she tacked them on the bulletin board propped against her desk. In all my years of schooling I'd never had a drawing singled out for special attention, least not in a good way. Clorise patted my arm as I walked past her desk, on the way to mine. She knew what a terrible drawer I'd been my whole life and was shocked as I was by the ship with my name on it that flapped on the bulletin board. It was all Willie's doing and I should've thanked him. But I didn't want to see his mouth open, even in a short welcome, because all I'd see would be that disgusting apple peel, wedged between his teeth like a torn strip of flag.

Mama was waiting behind the school buses when the dismissal bell rang. She picked us up some days when she was out running errands or we had dentist or doctor appointments or for a special treat. I didn't know which it was today.

We weren't even a block from school when her questions started. If I'd looked out the back window, I would've seen kids still climbing their bus steps, sisters nudging slowpokes, helping the little guys who'd dropped their school bags or coloring papers or whatever, a string of waiting parents' cars much longer than usual.

"The sisters let you play out back or what?" she asked.

"Recesses were all in front," I said and wondered how she already knew about the cross.

"You think Mister Dugan's going to arrest anybody?" Mavis asked from the back where she was stuck because I'd spotted Mama first and beaten her to the front seat.

"Who's he supposed to arrest?" I asked. Jerry Dugan had been sheriff of Ville d'Angelle for long as I could remember, since before I was born even, and he'd never arrested a single person far as I'd heard. Why would he start arresting people now?

"The people who burnt up our playground. That's who."

"First he'd have to find them, now, wouldn't he?"

"So?"

"So, no one knows who did this. That's what." Sometimes, most times, my sister was dumber than beans. "Think someone'll step right out and say, 'Me, I'm the one. Arrest me, Sheriff.' That what you think?"

"Sergeant Friday could find out."

"That's TV. Nutty old TV, not real life." I grabbed sunglasses from the glove compartment, tossed a pair to Mavis and put the second on myself, then rolled the window half down. "Nothing's easy as they play on TV."

"I think you're wrong about those troublemakers not admitting anything," Mama said. I hadn't thought she'd been paying me and Mavis any mind. "Type persons who burnt that cross have bragged themselves halfway to Mississippi by now. And each time they told the story the cross got bigger, the flames higher, the sisters more scared."

"Sisters aren't scared of nothing. They've got God on their side," I reminded.

"Even sisters get scared some days," Mama said.

I thought about that a while. I didn't think Mama was right. I myself had never seen a sister look close to scared. But maybe it was possible. I was still a child and hadn't seen everything yet.

"Nobody was acting scared today," Mavis said. For once, she was right.

"Nothing but a regular day," I said.

"Can't be regular with that cross blocking your way to the back," Mama said.

"What do you think will happen now?" I asked.

Mama glanced at me as she turned into our drive. "They'll dig up that burnt place, plant new grass. After that, I don't know." She parked the car at the far side of the drive so workers could come and go as needed. "I'm not sure anything'll ever grow right across that burn. Seems I've heard tell burnt ground never holds seed like it should."

When Daddy got home close to suppertime, he knew more about the cross than we did. Someone—I was never clear on who—had been out to measure it. Turned out to be thirty feet, two inches on the long end, fifteen feet exact on the short one. No one claimed bragging rights to the cross, least no one from Ville d'Angelle. Didn't surprise me any. Only a crazy person'd go up against God and Mother Ignatius and if a person went crazy in Ville d'Angelle, we shipped them right out to Pineville. I knew that for a fact because it had happened three or four times to Mrs. Guillot's sister. There just were no people living in Ville d'Angelle crazy enough to burn that cross.

"Are the Concerned Citizens doing anything about this?" I asked at supper.

Daddy stabbed a forkful of green beans, fresh from Mama's garden. "What would they be doing with this mess?"

"If you're a Concerned Citizen, seems to me this'd be something to get concerned over," I said.

"Girl makes sense there," Mama said.

Daddy chewed, didn't say anything.

"Thing I'm wondering is whether this is just the beginning, wondering what else we'll see before Christmas." Mama pushed her mounded rice and gravy closer to her pile of beans, but all that rearranging couldn't hide the fact she'd only taken two bites, three at most, since we'd sat to supper. Mavis was making up for her, shoveling rice and beans and fish patties into her big mouth so fast you'd think we all sat ready to snatch food off her plate if she didn't get to it first.

"Lots of people wondering the same thing," Daddy said.

Mama didn't get on him for talking with his mouth full of rice. Her mind must've been fully occupied with that cross, which unlike the rest of us she hadn't even seen yet, far as I knew. Sometimes, though, things you haven't seen are scarier than things you have seen. Makes me think once Everett sees his change-of-life baby, he'll realize there was nothing to be so worried about. Nothing at all.

"Some people saying maybe it's time to pull children out Holy Rosary," Daddy said. He spooned another pile of beans to his plate. Daddy sure loved Mama's garden green beans.

"Pull us to where?" I asked.

"Public. Where do you think?" Daddy said.

"We don't get any tuition back. Money we've spent on uniforms," Mama said.

Daddy shrugged, the most indifferent to the possibility of losing money I'd ever seen him. "No rule against wearing uniforms in public school. Wouldn't lose that money."

I could see myself, the butt of a thousand jokes because I had to wear a Catholic uniform to public school. I looked to Mama for relief from what was beginning to sound too much like a thought-out plan on Daddy's part.

"Anybody talking about safety?" Mama asked. She managed to get one measly bean off her fork and into her mouth.

"Some," Daddy said.

"So what do you think?"

He took another bite, chewed and swallowed before answering. "I don't think the cross burners'll do anything in the light of day." He pushed his empty plate away, balanced his chair on its hind legs. "That's what I think, but I'm not sure, can't be sure."

Mama stuck out her lower lip so it covered her upper one. "Deacy's keeping Austin in, unless Everett says otherwise. I told her it was her decision, leave Everett out of it. Person up in Monroe can't be giving advice on matters down in Ville d'Angelle."

"I'm sure your sister was happy to get that little piece of free opinion." Daddy looked at me. "Meniere women can't even manage to stay out each other's business."

Mama smiled as Daddy'd expected her to. "Even with that cross, I can't get myself to believe there's danger lurking on the school ground."

"The fire got put out easy," Mavis said. I wondered where she'd heard that. Before I could ask, she carried her dishes to the sink and said, "I finished my homework, so can I run down to Aussie's, take Marydale's baby doll back?"

"What's her baby doll doing at our house?" Daddy asked.

"She forgot it. That's all," Mavis said. "I'll be fast."

"Right," I said, my voice saying I meant just the opposite. Neither of those girls knew the meaning of *fast* when they got to playing, which I knew they'd do the minute Mavis walked into the Arceneaux yard.

Mama stood, carried her dishes and Daddy's to the sink, then began clearing serving bowls off the table.

"Marydale hates to sleep without her baby," Mavis said.

"You tell her to think about that next time she leaves her things here," Daddy said.

"Sure, I'll tell her." Mavis reached under the table, grabbed the black baby she must've been holding between her feet during supper, and ran out the back door, even remembering to hold the screen so it wouldn't slam. Her feet slapping the ground echoed in the kitchen, but only for a short time.

Daddy pointed a finger at the back door. "That's what we have to worry about. Holy Rosary is everybody's business." He wagged his finger at the door again. "This is our business." He walked over to the door, stared out at the new construction, maybe at the spot Mavis had been just a minute ago. "What would the cross burners think if they saw Mavis running down the road, a colored doll flopping in her hand?" He turned to Mama, who was filling the sink with hot soapy water. "Think about that, Hazel."

Mama shook her head. Was that a sign she refused to think about anything or that she couldn't believe what she was being forced to think about? I couldn't tell which. "Mavis is just a baby. Nothing but a baby."

"Cross burners don't stop for babies, don't stop for nothing."

I was positive Daddy was right there. They hadn't stopped for God's holy sisters. Why would they stop on account of Mavis, who didn't have a single drop of holy blood in her entire body?

After supper dishes were done, Mama and I joined Daddy in the parlor for a TV special about Little Rock. That TV show cleared up a lot of questions for me. By the end of it I knew all about coloreds determined to go to Central High School. The reporter interviewed two girls, white ones, wearing cheerleader costumes, big C's on their chests. The girls had come up with the cheer they greeted colored children with each morning. "Two, four, six, eight. We don't want to integrate."

I knew that cheer. At Holy Rosary we gave the cheer to our mamas when they brought us special treats and to bus drivers who took us to the park for the end-of-the-year picnic. Except we said it different. "Two, four, six, eight. Who do we appreciate?" Then we yelled out the name of the person we appreciated. Integrate had nothing to do with that cheer. But those Arkansas cheerleaders acted real proud of themselves, like they'd thought up the cleverest chant ever.

The TV showed colored children getting off the bus, an alley of police sent by President Eisenhower himself walling them off from whites heckling them left and right. "Why do those colored children want to go to Central High anyhow?" I asked. "They have their own school, don't they?"

"Sure they do," Daddy said. "They want to go cause it's a white school. Only reason there could be."

Would I have had the nerve to stick myself between two long lines of colored police while other coloreds yelled at me to go home? Never. So where did those Negro children find their courage? Why did they bother? And why weren't all those white people at work? They looked normal as anything, could've walked the streets of Ville d'Angelle without attracting attention. But I couldn't imagine anyone from my town taking off work to stand at the high school and scream at teenagers.

"Think those coloreds will give up and go back to their own school?" I asked.

"Doesn't look like it," Mama said.

Daddy switched off the set when the program ended and grabbed a *Popular Mechanics*. "People in Arkansas let things go too far and that's the price they're having to pay." He didn't sound one bit sorry for those people. What would he do if Arkansas problems came raining down on Louisiana? Would Mister Jack let Daddy and the other men off work to stand around the high school? Not that I could see. Then Daddy would have to choose: his job or yelling at colored children. I couldn't guess which way he'd go.

By the time Mavis got home it was close to eight, her bath time. I was sprawled on the bed, reading *The Virginian*. I'm not usually partial to cowboys on TV or in my books either, but this one wasn't bad. "What happened to 'fast'?" I asked. Mavis stripped in the corner, getting ready for the tub.

"Aussie wanted to know everything about the cross. How big? Where? The smell. How the grass looked. Everything."

"Why?"

"She didn't say. Just kept asking me about a million questions. What did the sisters do? The white ones? The colored ones?"

"What did you tell her?"

"Everything." Mavis slipped into her pink terry-cloth robe, which used to drag the floor but now hung at her knees. The sleeves, which had started out way too long and rolled over double at the cuffs, reached just above her wrists now. She needed a new robe but wouldn't hear of it. That robe was one of her favorite things and she wasn't letting go of it till she couldn't possibly squeeze into it. One thing you had to say for Mavis, she was loyal, even to her clothes.

When Mavis went to the bathroom, I went to the back steps to sit a while. The air had cooled from the heavy heat of July and August but didn't have the true smell of fall here to stay. That would come in a few weeks, late October if things stayed normal. But this had not been a normal summer. September wasn't turning out to be a normal month. No reason to believe the rest of this year would be any more regular than the last months had been.

I stared at the sky, trying to find constellations. The Big Dipper was the only one I could make out, as always. In our science book dozens of pictures, each one plain as day, are drawn with stars. Those pictures cheat some, though. They use lines and without the lines connecting the stars, the pictures wouldn't be nearly as clear. People who invented constellations must've had powerful eyesights and even more powerful imaginations to take smatterings of stars and make pictures, whole stories from them.

Cleo climbed the steps to snuggle against my bare legs. I stroked her back, scratched behind her ears. "Pretty baby. Such a pretty girl."

She purred her thank-you.

"How many stars do you see, Cleo?"

She purred louder.

"Millions? Me too. Millions and millions, always there, never changing, forever and ever."

18

YELLOW
GLASSES

EVERY DAY THAT WEEK I went to school expecting
something to have happened during the night. I wasn't sure what—another
cross, a letter tacked on the front door, clogged toilets, I didn't know. But
my expectations stayed just that, never blossomed into anything real. I
guessed the sheets had had enough excitement for one week. The rest of
us certainly had.

At home there was no more talk about public school, least not that I
heard. But I was sent to bed at nine-thirty on school nights, which left at
least an hour and a half for Mama and Daddy to discuss matters without
my knowing. I'd lie in bed, Mavis snoring softly next to me, and strain my
ears, trying to hear parlor conversation. This wasn't like August when
Daddy'd paced and yelled, in a frenzy over colored sisters teaching at Holy
Rosary. With the hum of TV and snores, all I caught now were bits, scattered words that made no whole. Trying to weave sense out of a smattering of unrelated phrases wore me out and soon I fell asleep, no wiser than
Mavis, who didn't bother trying to listen through walls. Still, I comforted
myself with the thought that a move to public would have to be made public before it actually happened. I was safe till then.

By the last day of September, a Thursday, most of us at Holy Rosary
were ready to believe we were out of danger. Nothing else had happened

that we could see. There weren't dozens of burnt crosses scattered across the playground as Willie had predicted. There weren't even any nasty notes hammered on the front door as I'd secretly feared. There was just fall, nearly settled in for good and none too soon, relieving us from the smothering hotness of summer, fending off the cold drizzles of winter.

During morning recess Clorise, Lena, Elvie, and I decided on hopscotch. Some of the boys kept running across the blocks we were trying to draw in the dirt with a stick. "Get away from here," I yelled. "Go back to your side."

"Ooh, ooh. I'm so-o-o-o-o-o scared." Kenneth Poitier clasped his head between both hands and sashayed around our squares.

"We'll give you something to be scared about." I looked around till I spied a clod of dirt. My aim was true and it splattered across his white shirt. The other girls grabbed dirt clods and threw till all you could see were clouds of dust rising from the ground like smoke from a campfire.

Course the boys didn't just stand around, politely waiting for more dirt to smack up against them. They scooped dirt and threw too. By the time Sister Bernie came running, not one of us would be able to wear our uniforms a second day without washing.

"Girls, girls. Boys, boys." Sister Bernadetta Magdalena, who said it was okay to call her Sister Bernie, was the other colored nun and when folks wouldn't let her teach first, she was put in charge of recess. She wasn't like Sister Pat at all. She was light skinned—had a white grandpa, Daddy said. She talked funny, but not like Sister Pat. She talked like people on TV.

Sister Bernadetta Magdalena was all right. She just didn't know what to do with kids over seven. She was lots more comfortable with the little guys. They loved her too. I could tell from the way Mavis talked. I know whites aren't supposed to love coloreds. But those little kids didn't know better. All Mavis talked about on the bus ride home was the new game or paper trick—how to make a cup from folding paper, no scissors even—Sister Bernie taught her that day. Mavis stopped her talking when we got home, though. Some days Mavis gave signs of knowing up from down, despite her stubborn intentions to the contrary.

"They started," the boys yelled. "Vivien Leigh did."

"It's their fault," we yelled back, me loudest.

"Children, children." Her chin quivered like it did when she didn't know what to do next. She looked over her shoulder, hoping some other nun would come to her rescue. But no one appeared. She was in charge of recess, though she lost control more days than not. After more arguing and screaming, she finally managed to get the boys back to their side of the playground where they should've stayed in the first place.

Lena won the line toss. Clorise went after her, then Elvie, then me. I usually managed to toss my rock closer to the starting block, but I was distracted today. A regular nun wouldn't have taken half the sass dished out by those boys, or by us girls either, I had to admit if I were being all the way honest. Did that mean Sister Bernie was only half a nun? I tried to think of a white sister who'd been timid as Sister Bernie but couldn't come up with a single name.

"Sister Bernie sure doesn't know how to run the playground," Clorise said, almost as if she'd been reading my mind.

"You'd think she'd know which side belongs to the boys, which to the girls," Lena said, hopping out from her first circle of blocks.

"It's the end of September. You'd think she'd know by now," Elvie said. "Don't you think so, Vivien Leigh?"

I shrugged, squatting next to the squares, clutching a rock in one hand, leaning my weight on my empty hand, which lay flat on the ground. "I suppose," I said.

"She's colored," Clorise said, as if there was a chance the rest of us hadn't noticed and as if that was explanation enough.

"She's a sister too," I said.

"Nobody's saying she's not a sister. It's just that she's colored too." Clorise stepped on a line in her second go-round. Just the tip of her left heel, but on the line all the same. I hoped Elvie made it to block four where Lena's rock sat. Otherwise I'd have to jump to block five, landing on one foot, an almost impossible leap to safety.

"At least with Sister Pat, you know where things stand." I stood, stretching my legs for my turn. "No doubt but that she's a holy sister."

"No doubt at all." Elvie hopped safely out her second turn and tossed her piece into the third block.

"Hope you make it," I said.

She nodded, concentrating on the leap to block five even while knowing my selfish motives for wishing her luck. Elvie stepped back several yards to get a running start, but it didn't do her any good. She sprawled between blocks four and five.

My luck wasn't any better. Same for Lena and Clorise. By the time Mother Ignatius rang her bell, ending recess, I was about to take my third try with not much hope of being any more successful than I'd been the first two times.

"We made it too big," I said as we walked to the fifth's line.

"Those stupid boys messed us up," Lena said.

"Who could measure anything right with those stupid boys?" Elvie said, loud enough for Kenneth to hear. He crossed his eyes and lolled his tongue at her.

"What's skinny and ugly and has eyes like a sick frog?" Lena asked.

"Kenneth Poitier," Lena and Elvie said together.

"Ha, ha. So funny I forgot to laugh," Kenneth said.

"We're still the ones who made it too big," I said, but in a whisper because Sister Pat was leading us back to the classroom and did not allow talking in line once we started walking. Besides, Lena and Elvie and Clorise weren't in the mood for taking responsibility for our part in this, so it didn't matter whether they heard me or not.

When the bus dropped us off home, Mama's car wasn't in the drive. Bringing Aussie home from cleaning day is what I guessed. I watched the two workers who looked like ants scrambling along the floor beams of our new addition, moving fast as they could.

"Sure could use a glass of iced water," Mister Tom called out, looking at no one in particular. His stomach hung over his belt buckle so far, I doubted he could see his feet. But Daddy said he really knew building. "How about you, Clay? You in the mood for a tall glass of iced water?"

"Yes, sir. That'd hit the spot all right." Clay spoke with nails sticking out both sides of his mouth. But you could understand him just as well as you could've if his mouth had been empty. He'd told me his tongue had learned to work its way around whatever he was holding between his teeth at any particular moment. After he said that I'd gone to my bedroom, stuck five pencils in my mouth, and tried reciting the Pledge of Allegiance. Mavis said I sounded like someone reciting the Pledge of Allegiance with five pencils in her mouth. Takes practice, I guessed.

"Want me to get you iced water?" Mavis asked.

"Why, Mavis Dubois. You back from school already? Didn't even hear you sneaking up the drive," Mister Tom said.

"I wasn't sneaking. Just walking regular."

"Bet you could be sneaky if you had to," Mister Tom said.

Clay grinned but kept hammering.

"Sure, I can be good and sneaky." Mavis dropped her school bag next to me and ran to the back door, slamming the screen, knowing Mama wasn't around to give her what-for.

"Your sister sneaky as she says?" Mister Tom asked. He sat on the edge of what would soon be the floor of my new bedroom and smoked a Camel. He could do that because he was boss, Clay just a helper. Learning the trade is how Clay put it. And because Clay was still learning, he had to keep hammering till the water arrived while Mister Tom got to enjoy a longer break. I am being a boss when I'm grown. Anything less isn't worth the trouble.

"How sneaky is that Mavis?" Clay asked. He was down to three nails in his mouth. I hoped he'd chance a sit and smoke after he hammered those three. Mister Tom wasn't really mean, pretty nice actually. He wouldn't mind. Clay's face was red and sweaty, even with his shirt off and a bandanna tied around his head. A break was definitely what he needed.

"Not sneaky as she claims." I rolled a pebble between my feet, trying to decide whether to stay here or go inside. "Not sneaky as most grown-ups," I added. I wanted Mister Tom to know he wasn't putting anything over me, even if he was over Mavis. I wasn't angry at Clay, who didn't have any choice about following Mister Tom's lead.

"They're making girls smarter nowadays. You notice that, Clay? Notice how smart they're making girls?"

"Smart all right," Clay said.

"Must be those vitamins mamas give their babies. Think it could be the vitamins?"

"Could be, I suppose," Clay said.

"I never took vitamins," I said, not sure whether I had, not caring either.

Mavis banged the screen again. At least this time she had the excuse of full hands. She carried a tall, pale yellow glass in one hand and one of our regular blue glasses in the other. She gave Mister Tom the yellow, Clay the blue.

"Where'd you get that yellow glass?" It wasn't one of our regulars, everyday or Sunday. I'd never seen it before and hadn't heard Mama planning on getting new glasses. Probably something I'd missed from being forced to bed at nine-thirty.

"On the counter," Mavis said.

"It's new," I said.

"Guess that makes me the lucky one. Get to drink out a brand-new glass," Mister Tom said. He drank the water down in one long gulp, his Adam's apple bobbing with each swallow. Prickly whiskers stuck out from his Adam's apple, making him look part porcupine.

"That was good, sweetheart. Just what the doctor ordered," Mister Tom said. He cracked an ice cube with his teeth, then sucked.

"What doctor?" Mavis asked.

"It's just a saying." I hated strangers knowing how dumb my sister was.

Mama drove up then. She waved but didn't stop to talk, just nosed the car as far into the carport as the lumber allowed and went in the back door. Mavis ran after her, no doubt hoping there were Oreos in that Simoneaux Market bag she carried into the house. I waited for Mister Tom and Clay to finish their ice, then carried the glasses to the kitchen table. Mama doesn't like her glasses left outside. Besides, maybe there were Oreos in that bag.

Mavis sat at the table, an open bag of Fig Newtons and a glass of milk in front of her. Fig Newtons are okay, but not when you're hoping for Oreos.

"How was school?" Mama asked, her back to me as she dug potatoes and carrots from the bin under the cabinet, then carried them to the table, then went back for a paring knife and bowl, and finally a third time for a paper sack to hold the peelings. She settled next to Mavis, catty-corner from me and my pile of Newtons and my milk.

"Rhonda Robineaux's mama's letting her have a fancy birthday party," Mavis said, not bothering to finish swallowing.

"How fancy?" I asked, my own mouth clear of leftover cookie.

"Party dresses. Party hats. Balloons hanging from the ceiling. Blowers with colored streamers on the ends that fan out when you blow them. Rhonda's cousin from New Orleans had some for her birthday is where Rhonda got the idea."

"How do you hang balloons from a ceiling?" I couldn't imagine Mrs. Robineaux allowing nails or even tacks hammered into her ceiling. I didn't really know her except to say hello at church, but I couldn't imagine any mama allowing such a thing.

"Sounds like a fine party," Mama said. She held the sack between her legs, dropping potato peelings into it.

"Tiny sandwiches with crusts cut off like you get at weddings. Chocolate cake big enough for everybody to get two pieces at least. Three different kinds of ice cream. Three." Mavis paused for breath or maybe just to imagine all those good things spread out in front of her. "And cherry Kool-Aid. Much as you can drink."

I puckered my lips at the thought of cherry Kool-Aid and chocolate cake and three kinds of ice cream mixing in someone's stomach. "So when's this big affair supposed to happen?"

"I said. Her birthday." Mavis bit a corner off a new cookie, then licked the filling that showed through.

"Which is when?"

"March tenth. But the party's on the fifteenth, a Saturday."

"That's not till next year," I said.

"So?"

"So how can anyone get excited about a party that's a year away?" I slipped my shoes off and raised my feet to the edge of my chair, my heels just balanced on the tip of the seat cushion.

"You'll be surprised how quick next year'll get here," Mama said, not looking up from the carrot she was peeling.

"Rhonda's mama's only letting her invite eight girls. But Rhonda says I'll probably be one of them." Mavis scooped more filling with her tongue. "I sure hope me and Rhonda don't have any fights before March fifteenth." She stared at that scooped-out Fig Newton and looked about as worried as a seven-year-old mind could get.

Mama's head was bent to her sack, but I caught the smile she swallowed fast as it showed.

"You in the habit of fighting with Rhonda Robineaux?" I asked.

Mavis shrugged one shoulder. "Things happen sometimes. I don't know."

"Well, if you're going to have a fight, do it before Christmas. She'll forget about it by March."

"You think?"

"Sure."

"That's okay then." She jumped from her chair, took three giant steps to the back door, and ran out to bother Mister Tom and Clay. Mavis Dubois does not know how lucky she is to have me paving the way for her.

"Anything going on at school for you, Little Miss?"

"Nothing much." I told about the dirt fight, being sure she understood it was all the boys' fault for being on our side of the playground.

"I was wondering how that uniform got so filthy," Mama said.

I stared down at my white blouse, speckled gray and green. My skirt didn't look so bad since dirt doesn't show against brown near much as it does against white.

Mama carried her bowl of peeled vegetables to the sink for washing. "Try to stay away from the boys tomorrow. I don't want to have to be washing and ironing two uniforms for you Saturday."

"There won't be trouble, if they stay on their side of the yard." I swept cookie crumbs into my hand and dumped them in Mama's sack of peelings. "They'd stay over where they belong if Sister Pat was in charge of recess. I know that."

"She pulls a pretty tight rein, does she?"

"Just like the other nuns. Except for Sister Bernie." I rolled Mister Tom's yellow glass from the corner of the table where I'd set it. "Sister Bernie's the most nervous holy sister I've ever seen."

"Nervous?"

"Jittery. Her chin trembles a lot. She doesn't seem to know how to get control, be in charge."

"Probably act different if she were at a colored school. Sister Bernie knows she doesn't belong at Holy Rosary." She chopped carrots on the cutting board and dropped the pieces into the pot of boiling water on the stove. Drops of water splattered against the pot and stove.

I shook my head, but Mama didn't see. I couldn't imagine Sister Bernie as anything but a scared rabbit no matter where the convent sent her, unless the place had nobody older than seven running around.

I held Mister Tom's glass across my eyes. Everything turned yellow. "When did you get new glasses?"

"What glasses?" Mama dropped the last of her vegetables into the boiling water.

"These yellow ones." Even Mama looked a sick yellow through that glass. "I don't like them."

Mavis slammed through the screen.

"Watch that door," Mama said.

Mavis grabbed another Newton, stuck it in her mouth, and stretched on the floor like a log with a cookie in its knothole. Mister Tom must've told her to stop bothering so he could get his work done. Clay didn't mind company at all and still got twice as much work done as Mister Tom. But we all knew who was boss and so that was that.

"What don't you like?" Mavis asked.

"The new glasses. They're the color of vomit."

"Gross." Mavis giggled. "Vomit glasses."

"Only a couple and they're no business of yours." Mama carried the yellow and blue glasses to the sink. "I haven't even had a chance to wash this out."

"Mister Tom drank himself some new-glass germs then," Mavis said.

"You gave Mister Tom this glass?"

"It was on the counter. Looked clean." Mavis raised to her knees, dipped her hand into the sink, and lifted the glass out. "Still looks clean cause all Mister Tom had was water." She stared through the glass just as I'd done. "Do you think Mister Tom'll get sick from store germs?"

"Doubt it," I said. "Store germs aren't near as powerful as human germs or animal germs."

"What makes you the big expert on germs?" Mavis asked.

"Science." Mavis wouldn't get a science book till fourth, so she couldn't argue over that.

"Do boys have more germs than girls?"

"Probably," I said.

"Grown-ups more than kids?"

"Maybe." We were edging into territory my science books hadn't covered yet. "Do you know when a person sneezes, those sneeze germs fly across a room, can land on somebody standing way on the other side of the room?"

"I don't believe that."

"Believe or not, it's true. You could stand next to Mama, sneeze my direction, and I'd be covered with your germs."

"Snot can't fly that far."

"Not most of it. Not the wet, sticky part. But the germs are teeny-tiny. They fly farther, faster. You can't see them or feel when they land. But they're there and they're powerful."

"Germs," Mavis said. She put the yellow glass on her mouth and sucked to hold it there without using her hands.

"You better hope Mister Tom doesn't have himself too many germs cause now you're full of them."

She stopped sucking. The glass clattered to the floor, bouncing once before rolling toward me. She was lucky it didn't crack.

Mama turned to us from where she stood, seasoning meat at the counter. "You girls be careful with that glass. Hear me?"

"We have plenty of glasses," I said.

"I like the blue ones better anyhow," Mavis said.

"That's fine cause these yellow ones aren't for you. Neither the yellow dishes or the yellow cups. Nothing yellow is for you or your sister or me or your daddy." She pounded the round steak with a mallet, tenderizing it so that after it was cooked it'd fall apart on your tongue, the way Daddy liked it.

"Who's going to use these glasses and that other stuff then?"

Soon as Mavis asked the question, I knew the answer. But I still half expected Mama to prove me wrong.

"Aussie and Marydale'll use them the most," Mama said. She whacked the meat again and again.

"Why can't they use the blue ones, same as us, same as always?" Mavis's cheeks puffed, though not so wide as her chipmunk look.

"If the yellows are dirty or something, they can. Just, these'll be their special dishes." Mama pounded, louder and harder than usual.

"Like Tante Yvette's butterfly glass," Mavis said.

"Not the same at all." Mama slapped that meat so hard, I was surprised it didn't split in two. "I told you, they'll use our blue things if their yellow ones are dirty."

"So why bother?" I said.

"Yellow's Aussie's favorite color. Bet you girls didn't know that," Mama said.

"Marydale hates yellow." Mavis was making up a story and anyone could tell, but I didn't say anything.

"Marydale will get used to it. She'll have to." Mama slammed the mallet hard against the meat, again and again and again. "Times have changed, Baby, and the sooner Marydale gets used to it, the better off she'll be."

"What did Aussie say when you gave her the yellow glass?" I asked.

"Nothing much. Just how she liked yellow. Nothing at all really."

I tried to imagine Aussie saying nothing at all, nothing much. The picture wouldn't come. Instead, all I saw was Aussie, rolling that vomit glass between her big hands, covering it with words about her having a special glass in this house she'd been cleaning since before any babies were born, before any colored sisters took a liking to teaching in a white school, before sheets and crosses, before near everything.

I looked over at Mavis. Very, very slowly, the last traces of puffiness melted and I was surprised by how much older she seemed with flattened cheeks. Guess I really hadn't noticed how much older Mavis was getting.

19

FREEDOM ROAD

THE WALLS WENT UP THE WEEK before Thanksgiving. Later, much later than Daddy had expected, but that couldn't be helped. Most every day of October was rain soaked. By the beginning of October Mister Tom and Clay didn't have much to do before the walls could go up. But they couldn't do that little bit without a couple of days of dry weather, something October wouldn't let us have.

Hurricane Hilda struck the third of November and she delayed things more. Daddy was completely and absolutely disgusted. "Rain all October. Now what? Hurricanes all November?" Mama and Mavis had run to the store for supplies. Daddy and I were filling gallons of washed-out plastic jugs with water.

"Hilda isn't supposed to be too bad." I was careful to keep the disappointment out my voice. I couldn't admit this to anyone, not even to Clorise or Lena, but I loved hurricanes. I knew they were dangerous, people lost their homes, sometimes died. Hurricanes were truly terrible, yet I couldn't help loving them. It was the evil in me and I did confess my sinful feelings every time a hurricane came. Father Strauss gave me an extra Hail Mary for penance. Nothing more, far as I could tell. Since my evil thoughts only cost me one small prayer, I didn't feel too pushed to control them.

"Bad or not, she could show the good grace of going up to Texas, across to Mississippi instead of straight at us." Daddy never cared what happened to folks in Texas or Mississippi or even north Louisiana, except for Uncle Everett of course. He capped the fourth container and handed it to me to shove to the far corner of the counter.

"Guess Hurricane Hilda doesn't care about my bedroom."

"You'll be an old woman before you ever sleep in that new room."

I swallowed my laugh because Daddy's voice wasn't the joking one. But it was hard not to smile when I pictured old-woman Vivien Leigh—cap of gray curls, wrinkled and age-spotted hands, leaning on a cane—hobbling to the bedroom she'd been waiting on since she was ten.

"Should I start the tub?" I asked when Daddy'd filled the last of the jugs.

"Don't forget the sink."

I didn't need to be reminded. The electricity would go out, which meant our water well wouldn't pump, which meant we'd be without water for at least a couple of days, maybe a week or more. When a hurricane was on the way, we had to put in as much water as possible, guarding against running out altogether. That time the electricity stayed off eight days, our water tasted near putrid by the last glasses. Mama reminded me and Mavis we should be grateful to have something to drink, happy we'd planned so far ahead. But it's near impossible to be grateful when you're gagging on water.

The tub and bathroom sink were both filled by the time Mama and Mavis got home. We carried sack after sack into the kitchen.

"We got the last three Evangeline Maid loaves," Mavis said.

I'd been hurricane shopping with Mama and knew what that meant. The store would've been a madhouse. People grabbing things off shelves, things they never normally ate, for fear the store wouldn't restock for months after the hurricane struck. Those fears never turned out true. But people couldn't seem to remember that from one hurricane to the next. Even Mama came home with three cans of anchovies once. Anchovies! Who could care if we ran out of that?

"Did you get treats?" I asked. All I'd seen Mama unpack so far were canned goods, crackers, and peanut butter.

"Seven bags of cookies," Mavis said.

"Seven?" I couldn't believe our good luck.

"Sure," Mavis said as if we kept seven bags of cookies in the house all the time. "Chips too. What else, Mama?" Mavis would've been too caught up in the excitement of desperate people flinging food into their carts, hurrying down aisles as if the hurricane was blowing at their necks, to notice every single thing Mama pitched into our basket.

"Enough so we won't starve." Mama stacked canned meats on one section of the counter, vegetables on another, peanut butter and jelly on a third. She liked having everything at hand during hurricane weather to avoid fumbling in a dark cabinet in a dark kitchen, though we had two hurricane lamps that gave a fair amount of light.

"Where's your daddy?"

"Hammering plywood across the shed window and checking outside for stuff." A hurricane wind going strong could pick up a hammer, a saw, probably even a person and toss them around like a boll of cotton. A couple of years ago a hurricane grabbed hold of the Amoco sign at Benoit's and didn't drop it till it reached the Benoit front yard, which is on the other side of town, more blocks than I could guess. Buddy Benoit was so amazed, he called the television station in Lafayette, that being the closest station to Ville d'Angelle. They sent out a camera and Buddy Benoit and his front yard and his Amoco sign all got themselves on TV. It wasn't clear whether the reporter was more impressed by a hurricane strong enough to rip an Amoco sign off its steel moorings and carry it across town or by a hurricane smart enough to hold on to that sign till it reached the front yard of the man who owned the station and the sign, both.

We'd had our shed window smashed a couple of times when Daddy hadn't covered it with plywood. But a broken window couldn't match up against Buddy Benoit's Amoco sign, so we never got ourselves on TV.

After Mama finished stacking food on the counter, our kitchen practically looked like a supermarket itself. No matter how long Hurricane Hilda lasted, we wouldn't run out of food. That is the lesson hurricanes offer over and over: Be prepared and never take anything for granted.

Rain started minutes after Daddy came in from hammering. Not the soft, easy rain of October. This was a pounding rain from the first drop, a rain with purpose behind it. I knelt in front of our bedroom window and watched water splatter the glass. The wind hadn't fiercened up yet, but that would come soon. There'd be no school tomorrow, Thursday, or the next day. Maybe not even Monday or Tuesday, depending on how bad the flooding got and how soon bus drivers were willing to chance a ride across hurricane-soaked roads.

At supper Mama forced milk on everybody. Milk'd go bad while the electricity was out and if there's one thing Mama hates, it's wasting good food. Right after Mavis and I finished the dishes and Mama filled both sides of the sink with fresh water, the lights went out. Daddy was ready with a kerosene lamp, so we weren't in the dark for long.

We sat in the parlor, the lamp and a transistor radio on the coffee table. The radio told us some things we'd already guessed. Electricity was out from Morgan City to Opelousas, New Orleans to Alexandria, maybe beyond. The radio also told us some things we didn't know. Hilda's winds were proving stronger than the forecasters had predicted. One hundred thirty or forty miles an hour was the best guess now. The eye was expected to cross Morgan City about eleven. Depending on how fast it moved inland, that'd put the eye in Ville d'Angelle about midnight or one. The radio didn't tell us that. Daddy did. The radio didn't much care when the eye passed over Ville d'Angelle.

"Anybody for a snack?" Mama asked. The radio'd decided it was tired of hurricane news and had switched to Cajun music, the Lafayette Playboys.

Mavis stood right away to follow Mama into the kitchen. The girl had a hole in her stomach. Food fell out fast as she shoved it in. Only way to explain Mavis Dubois's steady, never-ending eating.

Mama took the lamp to the kitchen, leaving me and Daddy in the dark. "When are you lighting the other kerosene?"

"When we need it." Daddy flipped off the radio, which only gave us four stations on its best days. With this weather, we were lucky to still have one working. Daddy didn't care much for any music, but especially Cajun. Too much accordion and fiddle and not enough guitar is how he explained it.

"When will that be?"

Even in the pitch black of the parlor I could feel Daddy's shrug. "Tomorrow maybe. The day after. No use to burning two lamps at the same time."

"If we had the second lamp, we wouldn't be in the dark."

"If we burnt all the kerosene in both lamps, we'd have no light at all."

"Hurricanes never last that long."

"This one was supposed to be nothing but a baby storm. Now she's blowing one forty." He paused, letting the wind raging at our house under-line his words. "Hurricanes are nothing but surprises. One surprise after another."

I was done arguing, though I still didn't see the harm in turning on our second lamp. Mama led Mavis back to the parlor, a tray in one hand, the lamp in the other. After she'd set both on the coffee table, we helped our-selves to milk—again—and chocolate chip cookies.

"We got any ice cream to go with this?" Daddy asked.

"Ice cream's gone, Daddy," Mavis said. She didn't add she'd eaten the last of it, but no doubt she had.

"Think, Floyd. Was I getting ice cream that'd go bad with melting?"

"We'd have taken care of that ice cream for you. Right girls?"

"That's right," Mavis said. "We wouldn't let ice cream go to waste."

"All I'd need," Mama said. "Three vomiting fools and us with no water or electric."

"Two," I corrected. "I wouldn't have eaten so much to make myself sick."

"Mavis, you ever been sick from ice cream?" Daddy asked.

"Not me," Mavis said.

"Think tonight would've been the first time?"

"No, sir."

Daddy turned to Mama. "See? Would've been fine. You should've gotten Mavis and me ice cream to go with these cookies." He snapped a cookie in half and put both pieces in his mouth at once. Mavis gets her eating ways from Daddy. "Plain vanilla would've gone good."

"I think somebody in this family would've gotten a major bellyache from too much ice cream. I'm not saying who. Just somebody," Mama said.

"Hazey, you can find the most foolish things to worry over."

"Unlike you, I suppose?"

"When I worry, it's about something worth worrying over. That's right."

"There's another good one." Mama held an arm up like a cop stopping traffic. The lamp threw a monster shadow of her arm across the room to the opposite wall. "Stop, world. Before you worry over anything, check with Mister Floyd Dubois. He'll tell you whether your worry is worth the time. You might be wasting worry on something not worth a spider's web." She lowered her arm and shook her head slowly, unable to believe Daddy's nerve. When Mama got started, she could keep going for some time, especially if Daddy pushed the wrong way.

But tonight Daddy wasn't in the pushing mood. He stood, took the lamp, and walked down the hall to the bathroom, leaving darkness behind. I felt my way around furniture to the window. If I pressed my face to the glass, I could make out the front-yard magnolias swirling in a wild, mad dance with each other. The hurricane partnered them in a way that couldn't happen during a regular storm, no matter how violent.

If a hurricane ever blew the roof off, we'd run to the bridge crossing the canal back of the house. That'd be the safest spot, Daddy said. I wouldn't mind spending a hurricane under that bridge. Sometimes, when I wasn't trying to control my evil thoughts, I hoped it would happen. The four of us huddled under the bridge, blankets wrapped around us, wind and rain whirling over us, everything gone unhinged.

Daddy came back with the lamp and even though it didn't throw much light, it was enough to make it impossible to see the dancing magnolias.

But the wind still roared, beating against the house so hard, I thought there was a chance I'd see the underside of the bridge this night.

That didn't happen, though. Instead, the eye passed over us at midnight, just as Daddy'd predicted. Mavis and Mama were already asleep. But Daddy and I stayed up for it. We stepped outside. The night wasn't so black, more yellow now, and nothing moved, not a leaf or branch or twig. The whole world took a deep breath and held it.

Cleo stayed on the sofa, refusing to come out. No other animals stirred either. Even the birds had disappeared, probably hiding under the bridge. Animals are too clever to fall for a hurricane's eye. They know the calm is a trick, trying to tempt them into the open where the sudden return of ferocious wind and rain can trap them unawares. With the first drops of rain Daddy and I went back inside, at least as clever as any wild animal.

The sun was fierce next day, chasing any cloud that dared show its face. Nothing is ever blue as sky the day after a strong hurricane. After we'd helped clear the yard of branches and other debris, me and Mavis took off our shoes and socks and tromped through puddles and even walked down the middle of the road, more bayou than street now, with water reaching above our knees. We were halfway to the Blakes before Mama called us back. Don't know why she did, though. Cars couldn't even try to drive on our road yet. Even Daddy didn't bother calling Mister Jack with an excuse for staying home. It was hurricane time and Mister Jack knew that. No one expected anything ordinary when a hurricane landed. Us wading through a stream flowing where a common road had run just yesterday. Daddy home all day on a Thursday. Mama leaving a bag of peanut butter cookies open on the counter for anyone to help themselves whenever they felt like it. Nothing about a hurricane day had a string of ordinariness in it.

The sun stayed out the rest of that week and into the next, so the waters cleared quickly. We had electricity by Sunday morning, faster than usual, so it turned out the forecasters were partly right and Hilda wasn't such a bad hurricane after all.

By Thursday of the next week we'd had enough dry weather to let Mister Tom and Clay raise the walls on my new bedroom. On Friday the walls for Daddy's den and the second bathroom went up. On Monday and Tuesday after that it was the roof. Now let the rains come. There was a roof over our new rooms, so what did we care.

The workers didn't come over on Wednesday, day before Thanksgiving. Tuesday night, Mister Tom called Mama to say they'd be working another house, trying to get a roof finished. Mama said fine on the phone. But when she hung up, she told Daddy they were probably spending the next day giving early thanks. Daddy laughed and said nobody could be grateful as builders looking at four straight days off with the promise of stretching it into five.

Mama didn't mind the workers staying away Wednesday. She and Aussie'd have their hands full with Thanksgiving cooking and didn't need to be bothered with hammering and sawing and other such distractions.

Aussie and Marydale got to the house about eight-thirty. Mama already had me chopping celery at the table when they walked in the back door. Chopping is about the main job the day before Thanksgiving. Mavis was playing paper dolls in our room since she couldn't be trusted with a sharp knife. I knew that was true but couldn't help being put out by her getting out of work so easily.

Mavis must've had both ears listening because the door hadn't even latched shut when she called from the bedroom. "That you, Marydale?"

"Sure. Who you think?" Marydale half skipped, half scooted across the kitchen floor.

"Where your manners, girl? You say a hello to Miz Hazey." Aussie glared at Marydale, pretending menace.

"How do, Miz Hazey." Her scoots and skips had gotten her just outside the parlor.

"Been a while since you've been here, Marydale." Mama looked up from the bowl of sweet potatoes she was peeling. "Let me look at you."

Marydale stood straight, but couldn't keep still, one foot still insisting on sliding back and forth across the other one. "It's still me."

"I think you've grown three inches since summer," Mama said.

"I be close to tallest girl in my class."

"I believe that," Mama said, still staring at Marydale as if she were a total stranger and not just the same colored girl Mama'd known her whole life. "I do think you're growing up, Marydale."

"Yes, ma'am. I'm in second."

"Miz Hazey knows that, her. She knows you be same grade as Mavis," Aussie said.

"Marydale," Mavis yelled from the bedroom.

Tired of waiting on Mama's inspection, Marydale fled to Mavis's voice. Aussie didn't bother reeling her in this time.

Aussie pulled out a cutting board and sharp knife—she knew where every single thing was stored in our kitchen—and began peeling and chopping onions.

"I sure wish onions weren't so powerful," I said. My eyes watered even though Aussie and I sat on opposite ends of the table.

"They be telling you they fresh. That's what powerful onions be telling you." Aussie peeled and chopped and cried, never letting a tear stop the peeling or the chopping or the talking neither.

"Who all is coming tomorrow?" Mama asked. She stood at the counter, her back to us, mashing pumpkin for pie.

"Evie and Little Aussie. Rest of the girls. Henry's side—Big Mama, Little Daddy, Henry's sisters and their men and their babies, many as can find their way to the house." She paused to wipe a sleeved arm across her eyes.

"Your side coming?" I asked.

"My side going to Lake Charles, cousin Florece." She sniffed, Thanksgiving in Lake Charles being too disgusting for words. "My side coming Christmas."

"Why don't you let both sides come at the same time?" I asked.

Aussie let loose one of her deep-down, rumbling laughs that filled the kitchen, spilled into the rest of the house, lifted dust off furniture and tempted mice out their cubbyholes. "Girl, first thing you learn when you marry is your side be your side and his side be his side." She looked at Mama's back. "That right, Miz Hazey?"

"God's truth," Mama said.

"Your mama's right. God's truth and no one else's." Aussie slid chopped onions into a bowl and covered it with waxed paper, an elastic band stretched around the rim of the bowl to keep the paper in place.

I tried to remember Mama's side and Daddy's side at the house all at the same time. My First Communion a few years back? Had that been the last time? I strained to remember a nearer time but couldn't.

"Guess you'll be thankful the Landrys won't be sitting down with the Arceneauxs tomorrow," Mama said. She carried spices from the shelf to the counter, adding this and that till mashed pumpkin would taste like pie. A pinch of this, a tad of that and you had pie. A baking miracle.

"I be thankful for lots more than that, Miz Hazey. Lots more," Aussie said.

"I'm thankful this year's about done," Mama said.

"This be a hard year we give ourselves."

"Harder than January promised," Mama said.

"Harder than anything," Aussie said. She stood, stretched one arm above her head, then another. "Onions give a person the dry mouth."

"You want some cider? Just opened last night. Or water? Which will it be?" Mama asked.

"Cider feels like Thanksgiving. That's what Aussie thinks."

Mama wiped her hands on a towel, opened the door of the top cabinet, snaked her arm through a maze of glasses to pull out a yellow one. She rinsed it and poured cider near to the brim before carrying it to Aussie, who reached out a hand, black as a hurricane night. Aussie looked at that yellow glass, looked at Mama, back at the glass, then raised the cider to her mouth. She drank half in one long, uninterrupted swallow, her throat muscles the only thing moving. "I be looking at a long list of thank-yous for my Jesus. Yes, ma'am. Aussie sure be looking at a long list."

"Like what?" I asked.

"Me and my family feeling good. Nobody got any bad sickness, no bad spells. We got our work. Henry and me. I got my ladies." She lifted the glass to her face, stared at it a moment. "I be grateful I be having such nice things to use when I come to Miz Hazey's. Such nice yellow glasses to use." She didn't chuckle like she did when she was being purposeful, teasing sassy, just took that nice yellow glass to her mouth and drank till nothing but cider dregs lined the bottom.

"The year's about done," Mama said softly, almost as if she wasn't talking to me or Aussie or anyone of particular consequence in that kitchen.

"Year be done, but not forgotten. Nobody be forgetting this year we give ourselves in Ville d'Angelle." Aussie pulled a pan from a hook, cut pats of butter to drop in, and put it on a stove burner. Onions sizzled when she poured them in. Once she got her onions and my celery cooking, she carried her cutting board next to Mama, who was cutting crusts off bread for stuffing. Mama passed crustless bread to Aussie, who cut them into small squares, sixteen to a slice. There was a lot of bread, just like there'd been lots of onions and celery, because half this stuffing would be going home with Aussie.

"I'm gonna find the Freedom Road, the Freedom Road, the Freedom Road. I'm gonna find me that Freedom Road. Oh Lord, yes, I am," Aussie sang.

I'd never heard the song and wondered if it was a colored hymn from her church. Aussie had a strong, low voice and was in the Saint Paul's choir. But she didn't often sing in our house. She only sang when the spirit moved her. Guess Thanksgiving must've put her in the spirit.

Mama likes good singing herself. But she didn't join in. Didn't hum along. Didn't even pat a foot accompaniment. Just kept whacking off crusts and sliding them to Aussie singing about her Freedom Road.

Aussie stopped singing when the bread was done, ready for the oven.

"Nobody's ever free," Mama said, again sounding as if the words weren't aimed at anyone in particular.

"Everybody's free. Even coloreds are free since the Civil War," I said. I took a deep breath, smelling Thanksgiving spreading in the house.

"Your mama be right. Nobody's free. On this poor earth nobody be free. Amen." She rinsed out her yellow glass and filled it with water, which she drank down without stopping once.

How could Mama and Aussie have gotten through school without learning about the Civil War, Robert E. Lee, Ulysses S. Grant, Sherman's March? Didn't those ladies know we were all free? Every single person in this country was free, except for criminals of course. I would never want to be a criminal, cooped in jail. "I'm grateful for being free," I said.

Aussie looked at me a few seconds, then let one of those laughs roll out, over me, over Mama, whipping through the house, covering Mavis and Marydale and even Cleo who'd hidden behind the sofa, thinking there she'd be safe from a colored lady's laugh. But she wasn't.

20

GIVING THANKS

MAMA AND AUSSIE WORKED through the day, baking
and cooking and even talking, though not near as much as they used to, it
seemed to me. Sister Pat and Sister Bernie and the sheets with their crosses
and those yellow glasses had wedged a wall between Aussie and Mama that
might never come down. But sometimes their mouths forgot things had
changed between them and that's when their tongues got to running fast
as if Sister Pat had never left Brooklyn.

"We getting us a paved road before summer comes," Aussie said, rolling
out her third piecrust. Mama's crusts were okay. But Aussie's made you
think Heaven's couldn't be any tastier.

"Where'd you hear that?" Mama asked.

"Henry got told by Mister Fred."

"Fred Fortier? Fred Fortier doesn't know a thing about our road."

"Mister Fred says he be digging up the street before long."

"I'll believe that one when I see it." Mama layered sliced sweet potatoes,
brown sugar paste, and pecans in a glass dish, ready for baking in the
morning. "Can't believe two words out of Fred Fortier's mouth."

"He's fair to Henry."

"That I don't doubt. Fortiers are all fair folks. Just that Fred, in particular, gets carried away with what he thinks he knows." Mama covered the

sweet potatoes with waxed paper and stuck the dish in the icebox. "Reminds me of my brother-in-law."

"Mister Fred always be fair. That's something many folks never learn, them. How to be fair. The Monseigneur always be preaching on the Commandments—tell the truth, don't kill or steal, love God, honor your father and mother. But he never talk on fairness."

"There isn't a Commandment for fairness," I said. We'd had to memorize the Ten Commandments since second grade and I knew, for a certain fact, fairness was not one of them.

"Fairness be one of those hiding Commandments." Aussie flipped dough into a pie pan.

"I never heard of any hidden Commandments." Cleo jumped on my lap, tempted into the kitchen by Thanksgiving smells.

"There's plenty hiding Commandments. Be nice to people and wild animals, which sometime be the same. Give to the poor folks. Tithe your church. Where's the Commandments for those things?"

"Aussie's got you there," Mama said. She smiled at me, at Aussie, pleased, it seemed, to have me gotten by Aussie.

I stroked Cleo and wondered how God could've managed to leave out so many important things from his Commandments. Somehow it seemed likely those things Aussie'd listed were covered by the holy laws, just weren't in the open, plain for the seeing. Hiding Commandments, like Aussie'd said.

"Sisters teaching you God's Commandments?" Aussie asked.

"Sure," I said.

"Marydale already knows all her Commandments."

"How many does she obey?" Mama asked, a laugh lining her words.

"That be the hard part, right Miz Hazey? For sure, that be the hard part."

"Nobody's perfect," I said. I held my hand still, resting across Cleo's back. Cleo looked up at me, her unblinking eyes green as Willie's favorite marble shooter, hypnotizing me into scratching behind her ears.

"All my girls know their Commandments. Know them real good. But they sure don't be perfect, them."

"You'd think things'd get easier as you grew older. Right and wrong would be clear as glass, easy to tell apart, easy as anything," Mama said.

"Easy as black and white," Aussie said.

"Easy as that," Mama agreed quickly.

"Nothing in this life be that easy. Nothing at all," Aussie said.

Mama nodded her agreement. I was disappointed to hear the two of them being of the same mind on this so fast. I'd looked forward to knowing the right way to act as I got older. I didn't appreciate hearing things weren't going to get easier, clearer, only muddier and more confusing. Made being grown seem not nearly so tempting. What's the use to getting grown if you're still plagued with questions of right and wrong?

Mavis came in the kitchen to get snacks for her and Marydale even though their stomachs should've still been full from lunch. "We have any more peanut butter cookies?"

"Grab the cookie jar for your sister," Mama said to me.

The jar was three-fourths full before Mavis stuck her greedy hand in and pulled out half the cookies. "Mama, look how many Mavis took."

Mavis looked at her hands, both of them bulging with peanut butter cookies. "They're for the two of us. For the whole afternoon." Even Mavis saw the need for explaining all those cookies.

"Everybody deserves something special for Thanksgiving," Mama said.

"That's true. Little Mavis, you and my Marydale eat up all those cookies and if you still want more after that, you come back to this kitchen cause I know Miz Hazey be giving you more treats. Many as you babies can eat."

"We aren't babies, Aussie."

"You always be our babies. Right Miz Hazey?"

"Always," Mama said.

"Babies always and forever. Babies, babies, babies," I chanted, following Mavis out the kitchen, across the parlor. She ran to our room, slammed the door, and called for Marydale to brace up against the door with her to keep me out.

I pushed at the door but couldn't budge it more than a crack.

"Leave us alone or we're telling," Mavis called through the slitted opening.

I could've pushed more but didn't want to start anything the day before Thanksgiving. "Babies, babies, babies," I sang in a loud whisper. "Babies forever and ever."

I let go the door all of a sudden and that tiny crack widened into an opening large enough to let me slip through. But I wasn't interested anymore. Instead I curled on the sofa, Cleo snuggled across my stockinged feet, and read *The Yearling* all afternoon. I'd done as much chopping as this Thanksgiving deserved.

Thanksgiving morning was bright and clear and blue as any late-November day had any right to expect. By the time Mavis and I got dressed for breakfast Mama'd been to Tante Deacy's and back, taking the turkey she and Aussie had dressed yesterday so Deacy could stick it in her oven. Rice dressing was cooking on the stove—rice in one pot, pork and beef Mama'd ground with seasonings in another. Sweet potato casserole was in the oven. The smell of pork and onions fought with the brown sugar in the sweet potatoes over which would rule the kitchen. White potatoes and a few eggs were boiling for salad. Two pumpkin pies, two pecan pies, two lemon meringue pies lined the counter. Except for not having a turkey, we could've had a pretty good feast in our own kitchen. But when I said that, Mama said we were going to Deacy's because that's what Deacy wanted and Deacy deserved getting at least one thing she wanted and I was to keep my mouth shut about the whole thing.

I widened my eyes at Mavis across my bowl of cornflakes. Mavis widened her eyes back, knowing well as I did that my little comment did not deserve such a hot harangue. Even all those pies wouldn't sweeten our Thanksgiving if Mama stayed in her mood. So for the rest of breakfast I didn't say a thing and neither did Mavis. All that quiet must've been just what Mama needed because by the time we packed the car, she joked she didn't want to see a single thumbprint on any of her pies, which Mavis and I held balanced on trays across our laps in the back seat.

Daddy drove slow as he ever did because the trunk held sweet potatoes and rice dressing and green bean casserole. Mama held the potato salad bowl between her feet, the relish tray on her knees. We were a traveling restaurant, a food accident waiting to happen if Daddy braked too suddenly, turned too sharply. I rearranged my pies so the lemon meringue sat in the middle, right where my face would likely land if that food accident happened.

"Everett got home okay?" Daddy asked, turning carefully, much too carefully, from our road to the main highway into Ville d'Angelle.

"Finally. Past midnight," Mama said. She shifted her shoulders, all the movement her food-guarding duty allowed.

"Must've been tired. That long drive from Monroe must've worn him out."

"And Deacy? How about Deacy? How worn out do you think she was?" Mama looked out her window. "Woman expecting her fourth, her fourth mind you, baby needs to be getting to bed way before midnight. Everett certainly knows that. So why didn't he leave Monroe earlier? Tell me that."

No one dared answer Mama. We were all hoping—even Daddy must've been hoping—for a good Thanksgiving, not a repeat of breakfast with Mama jumping us for no good reason.

"We're talking four, five hours tops," Mama said, answering her own question since none of the rest of us were brave enough to do it. "What was he doing in Monroe till eight, nine o'clock? Probably later, knowing how Everett drives."

"For God's sake, Hazey, give the man a break, cut him some lead, would you."

Mama stretched her neck, rubbed the back of it with her free hand.

"He is your sister's husband."

"Don't remind me."

"Looks like somebody better be reminding you."

I looked at Mavis, who was looking out her window so I couldn't tell what she thought of all this.

"He is Deacy's husband. Here or in Monroe or anywhere else, he is still her husband. That's all you have to keep telling yourself," Daddy said.

"You sound like Deacy."

"A Meniere woman making sense for once." Daddy was trying to joke Mama out her mood. But the way she turned back to her window, her neck still and stiff, told us all the joking in the world wouldn't work this day.

When we pulled into the drive, we had to park behind Uncle Everett's truck instead of pulling right up to the door.

"Man could at least have bothered using the garage."

"Maybe he didn't want to wake anybody when he got in last night." Daddy was bound to be on Everett's side, maybe because he felt sorry for him.

"It's two-thirty. Who's still sleeping at two-thirty in the afternoon? Even Everett must be up by now, could've moved his truck out the way. But I guess that would've taken too much consideration for someone besides himself." Mama wasn't letting anything get between her and the deep and abiding anger she'd built against Uncle Everett these past months.

Daddy killed the engine. Austin and Malcolm ran from the backyard, where they no doubt had been sent to keep from getting underfoot. Daddy went over to Mama's side, handed Austin the potato salad, Malcolm the relish tray. Mama walked to the back of the car with Daddy to rescue the food from the trunk. Mavis and I were stuck in the back seat till someone remembered to help us. But if no one remembered and we were stuck in our car all afternoon, that would be okay because we had the pies.

"Poor Uncle Everett," Mavis said as we watched Malcolm and Austin run back to the car, hands empty and ready for more. No way those boys would forget about the pies.

Inside, T.J. and Uncle Everett were watching a football game, cheering the team with the dark uniforms. I didn't expect the TV watching to stop just for us and T.J. didn't look away from the screen for even a split second. But Everett had different ideas.

"Looky here, will you," he said. "If it ain't the two prettiest girls in all Louisiana." He stood and motioned us to him, both hands cupping the air at his side.

We didn't have a choice but to move into his arms for hugs. His shirt-sleeves were rolled up to just below his elbows. His arms were darker, thicker than I remembered. He squeezed us against his chest, stealing our breaths. "Floyd, you be watching out. These beauties'll have boys batting down your door like bees at the honeycomb before you know it. Yes, sir, before you know it."

He finally let us go and Mavis and I smiled at him. What else can you do when a grown-up spouts foolishness? God help my change-of-life cousin. She was getting herself born with a daddy grown crazy from axing too many trees up in Monroe, Louisiana.

"Hear what I said, Floyd? These girls of yours are getting themselves too pretty. Too pretty by far."

"Must be they take after the Dubois side," Daddy said.

Everett laughed, louder and longer than Daddy's tiny joke deserved.

Mama'd already joined Deacy in the kitchen, where the Thanksgiving work would get done so my lazy, good-for-nothing cousins and my Monroe uncle and the rest of us could stuff ourselves. Daddy took a space on the sofa between T.J. and Everett. He asked the score, which Everett told and also about this play and that. Then it was halftime, my favorite part. I loved the way those marching bands spelled out things or made pictures with their bodies. Once I saw a band make a covered wagon and roll that wagon all across the football field.

"Can you believe that?" I'd asked Mavis, who'd been watching with me.

She hadn't answered. Just shrugged and went on watching that wagon, wheels rolling across the field. She was too young to be amazed. Those band people couldn't tell what they looked like from where they stood. All they could see were the instrument players right next to them, in front and to the side. None of it could look like a wagon to them. But if one, just one, of those marchers took a wrong step, turned right instead of left, the whole wagon would fall apart. Each of them depended on the others to do the right thing, to know the right place to go and then to go there.

A band strutted across Deacy's TV screen, doing such a high-step march, I knew they'd be really good. T.J. went to the kitchen, more interested in begging food from his mama and mine than in watching this band make up words and pictures. The boy had no appreciation for the fine and artful things of life.

I grabbed the sofa space he'd left behind so I could get a real good view of the band. The first thing they made was a turkey and did it look good, even its wattle flopping like it should. This band would be good all right.

"How was the drive?" Daddy asked.

"Cops everywhere. I'm lucky I didn't get myself a stack of tickets."

"You'd of been in the doghouse then, my friend. All that Monroe money going to pay speeding tickets." Daddy grinned. "Deacy would never let you hear the end of that one."

"Deacy doesn't let me hear the end of it anyhow. Don't need to add speeding tickets to her list."

Tante Deacy had some Meniere spunk, though not much as Mama, so I knew Everett was speaking the truth.

Tigers—the word, not the animals—stood still while the band played some song I didn't recognize.

"LSU looking good this year," Daddy said. "You been following them up in Monroe?" He drug out those Monroe syllables because he'd gotten into the habit of saying the word like Mama, who'd gotten the habit from Aussie. If Daddy'd realized he was talking like a colored lady, he would've clipped Monroe into closer to one syllable than three.

"Sure I been following them," Everett said. "Monroe's got itself some newspapers, TV stations, radios."

"I was thinking that far north, people'd follow the Razorbacks."

"Not that far north. Still Louisiana."

The band was moving again. TIGERS disappeared, but I couldn't tell what'd take its place, more words or a picture.

"So you been getting the cold shoulder or what?" Daddy asked.

"Cold shoulder, cold bed, cold everything." He leaned closer to the set to get a better view of the majorettes.

"Guess you manage to keep warm up in Monroe," Daddy said, his voice rougher than usual.

"Man just trying to get ahead, do better for his family, sure don't deserve the deep-freeze treatment," Everett said, still staring at the majorettes.

An alligator. Plain as day. The band marched around the field on those little alligator legs, swishing that long alligator tail.

"Women don't see the importance of money sometimes," Daddy said.

That wasn't true, but I was too interested in the human alligator to bother telling him. Wasn't I put in charge of the colored sisters bet money?

Didn't that show I knew the importance of money, of deciding fairly who earned that money, who lost it? And wasn't I closer to woman than man? But I didn't say any of that because it was Thanksgiving and Daddy was just trying to make Everett feel better and there was an alligator kicking its legs, first one side, then the other, in perfect unison, doing a cancan dance on the fifty-yard line. I almost called Deacy to see it, her being such a dance lover. But I didn't, figuring she and Mama needed to finish in the kitchen so it wouldn't be dark before we sat down to turkey.

My first disappointment was I got put between T.J. and Tante Yvette at the dinner table. T.J. stuffed his face so fast, anybody watching was bound to gag on their own bites. Tante Yvette had loose false teeth that rattled when she chewed, clacking like castanets. You couldn't even ask her to try to keep her teeth quiet because that would be disrespectful. At least that's what Mama said and with her sitting catty-corner across from me, I couldn't dare say anything.

Tante Deacy led grace, it being her house, then started passing platters. I had to hold off on the green beans and corn bread stuffing till I got to seconds. I didn't have room on my plate for all that food.

"Girls, you outdid yourselves this day," Tante Yvette said to Mama and Deacy.

"Mama had me chopping most all of yesterday," I said, not wanting anyone to forget my contribution to this feast.

"You'll be fixing up the whole dinner before you know it," Tante Yvette said. Click-clack. Click-clack. Turkey and cranberry mold got chewed.

"Give us some warning before that happens," Daddy said. "Give us a chance to stop at Vern's for hamburgers."

Everybody laughed and Mavis laughed so hard, she choked. Served her right.

"Vivien Leigh will be a fine cook one of these days," Mama said when Mavis recovered her breath. "She's learning all my secrets."

"Sure am," I said. "And when I make up my first lemon meringue pie, I'll remember who said what at this table." I glared at Daddy, who loved lemon meringue pie much as Everett loved fig preserves.

"You give these ignorant fools what-for, sweet girl," Everett said. "I want you to remember I didn't laugh or make any jokes this day cause I know you're going to be the finest cook in all Louisiana before long."

"Thank you, Uncle Everett." I sat up straighter as was befitting the future best cook, not to mention one of the two prettiest girls, in all Louisiana.

"She's got good cooking genes. Her grandma made the best *maque choux* I ever tasted." Tante Yvette cut a bite off her turkey. "Always wished I'd gotten that recipe before she passed."

"Wish Deacy had picked up a few of those Meniere cooking lessons. What's the matter? Did you ladies think she was too pretty to ever have need of cooking secrets?" Everett reached for more sweet potatoes.

Heads all turned to Deacy, who hated her cooking insulted almost as much as she hated her dancing insulted. "One look at that paunch and anyone could tell you haven't starved in your years with me."

"Big difference between starving and good cooking." Everett reached for more turkey. "What did you do to this turkey, Hazey? Tenderest bird this mouth ever tasted."

"I was just thinking it was a bit off," Mama said. We all knew she didn't believe a word of that, just said it to put Everett in his place.

"My kind of off," he said.

"You'd be the expert on something being off," Deacy said.

"What's that supposed to mean?"

Table talk stopped. Even Tante Yvette's clacking teeth stopped.

"You know what it means well as I do. Well as anybody else sitting at this table." Everett had been gone too long for Deacy to be the same now as before. She'd never be tough as Mama, never deny she was Everett's wife, but she'd never be the old Deacy again, no matter how often Everett promised to take her dancing. Long as no one was attacking Everett, she didn't feel any obligation to defend him and his Monroe adventure.

"Repeat after me, Deacy. My husband is trying to make a little extra money for his family. Everett is working his butt to bone cause Deacy couldn't manage, at her age, to keep from getting pregnant with a baby no one needs, no one wants." He spoke slowly as if Deacy was too retarded to get his meaning otherwise. But he was wrong about that. Every person at that table, even Mavis, got his meaning strong and clear. I wanted to cover Deacy's belly with my hands so her change-of-life baby wouldn't hear what her Daddy'd just said.

"Take it easy, Everett. Take it easy," Daddy said.

"Hell, I wish I could. Take it easy. Man, easy stopped a long time ago for me." He stabbed a chunk of turkey and sweet potatoes and shoved the whole thing into his mouth, staring at his plate while he chewed, his jaw jutting stiffly between chews.

"Easy. The man thinks he doesn't have it easy." Deacy rested her hands flat on her wide belly, maybe trying to cover her baby's ears like I'd wanted to do, and spoke to the ceiling. "Tell the man to try taking care of three boys and being pregnant and being alone. Tell him to try that and then talk about who has it easy."

"Since I walked through that door, I've gotten nothing but your damn feel-sorry-for-me attitude. Aren't you done yet?"

"Ten weeks and four days. A lot can build up in a person in ten weeks and four days," Deacy said. Her palms still lay flat on her big belly, but her fingers fluttered like caged butterflies, searching, searching for a way out.

"In that time a person can get his eyes opened. See that he's always belonged outdoors, swinging an ax, pulling and pushing his end of a two-man saw." Everett put his fork down and grabbed hold of his plate like he was protecting pure gold. "Man can learn in ten weeks and four days that he never belonged in somebody else's IGA, stacking lima beans and corn and pulling old bread off shelves. Never was meant for that life."

"What about his wife, his family? What can a man learn in ten weeks, four days about them?" Deacy's voice was soft now, quiet as a feather floating in the night.

My brain hurt from trying so hard to think of something to say to change the subject at this table. Nothing came to me, though. That was my second disappointment this Thanksgiving. Nothing came to anyone else either. We'd become nothing but the audience for Deacy and Everett, each sitting at one end of the table, opposite each other. They were on their own for changing the direction of this talk.

"Well, Everett, can you tell me that? Answer me that?"

"It's a hard question, Deacy. A hard question."

"It's the easiest question in the world."

Deacy might've thought that, but Everett must've disagreed because he didn't answer. He let go his plate, picked up his fork, and got to work on his food again.

"So what do you hear tell about that Little Rock business?" At last Daddy'd thought of some other conversation topic.

"Nothing much. Same as you hear, I expect."

That broke the spell and everybody started talking at once. Tante Yvette talked over my dead grandma's *maque choux* with Mama. Austin and Mavis argued over whether Sister Bernie knew a thousand playground games, Austin saying no and Mavis saying probably even more than that, probably closer to two thousand. Even T.J. talked, trying to scare me and Malcolm about how much harder high school was, how much meaner the teachers were. That got Malcolm to talking about how much harder public was than Catholic.

"We did four book reports already. Read the book and wrote the reports," Malcolm said. "How many reports have you done?"

"I'm in fifth, not seventh."

"So how many?"

"I read four books in a week, less than a week."

"Just as I thought. You haven't done a single book report this entire school term." Malcolm made it sound like I'd been in fifth for two and a half years instead of two and a half months.

"That's not Vivien Leigh's fault," T.J. said. "She's got herself a nigger teacher."

"That is not true," I said.

"What do you mean, that's not true? Sure it's true. She got herself fired or something?" T.J. asked.

"You cannot call a holy sister nigger."

"Says who?"

"Says my mama and your mama and every other grown-up in Ville d'Angelle who has themselves one ounce of Catholic blood." I stabbed a pecan with my fork. "And if you don't know that, you're the most ignorant fool ever been allowed in ninth grade anywhere in the world, public school and Catholic school combined."

"Looks to me like our cousin got herself turned into a nigger lover," T.J. said to Malcolm.

I was so mad. Why did I get put between Tante Yvette and T.J. with Malcolm next to him? "You say that word one more time T.J. Comeaux and I'm telling your mama. I swear I am."

T.J. giggled, that high-pitched laugh a boy in high school should be embarrassed to own. He whispered something to Malcolm, which got Malcolm laughing too. I turned to my plate to show the food was lots more interesting than the company at this Thanksgiving dinner.

After a few bites I looked up. Everyone was still talking and eating and acting normal, looking to be having a good time. Everyone but me and Deacy, who still sat with her hands across her stomach, though her butterfly fingers had stopped fluttering. She didn't take her eyes off Everett, watched him pile more green bean casserole on his plate, watched him laugh at something Daddy said, watched him reach across Malcolm on his left for the rice dressing bowl without bothering to say excuse me.

Mama reached her hand across the table to pat Deacy's shoulder. "You ready for seconds yet, sister?"

Deacy started as if she'd forgotten the rest of us were there, gathered around her table to give thanks. "I think I'm full." She looked at her plate, holding almost as much food as when dinner'd started. "I must be full."

"Leave room for dessert," Mama said. She patted Deacy again before picking up her fork.

"Dessert. Sure. Dessert," Deacy said like a woman in a trance.

"Tante Yvette, you ever know Deacy to pass up the sweetest part of a meal?" Mama asked.

Tante Yvette had to finish clacking her mouthful before she could answer. "Deacy's had a liking for the sweets since she got her first chewing tooth."

Deacy smiled, which was what Mama'd been after, but the smile looked old and pinched, a faded slash across her face. "Tell you ladies the truth. I just don't much feel like anything sweet tonight." Her eyes watered, but no tears spilled. Mama wouldn't let her cry, not on Thanksgiving, and Deacy knew that. But she didn't eat a sliver of pie, not even pecan, her favorite.

When we left, Uncle Everett gave me an extra-long, extra-hard squeeze. He wasn't going back to Monroe till Sunday, so I'd probably see him again. But still he gave that extra hugging, maybe to let me know he'd always like me even if I never learned to cook any better than Deacy.

We dropped Tante Yvette at her house before we drove home. Our car headlights beamed a path to her front door. We waited till she'd turned on her parlor light and waved us on our way.

"That was sure a good dinner," I said. My stomach hurt with all the food I'd forced into it.

"It was okay," Mama said. Since she'd made most of it, I thought maybe she was just being polite.

"Company could've been better," Daddy said.

"Some of the company," Mama said.

"Looks to me like that change-of-life baby is bringing Tante Deacy nothing but bad times," I said.

"Don't say that about that innocent baby ever again," Mama said sharply. She half turned in her seat to face me down. But there wasn't anything to face down because I wasn't intending on starting a fight. I was too full and too sleepy from all the food for that.

"One thing I'll say. I've had better Thanksgivings in my time. Lots and lots better," Daddy said.

None of us could disagree with that.

"All that talk about cooking got me thinking too," Daddy said.

"Watch out when Floyd Dubois gets to thinking," Mama said.

"Next year you let Aussie fix her own dinner. She does hers. You do ours. Vivien Leigh can help." He paused, waiting for Mama to object. When she didn't, he added more. "Turkey fixed with colored hands can't help but bring bad luck."

Mama turned to him. I couldn't see her expression but knew it must've been disgusted with the plain stupidity of that idea.

The rest of the drive home nobody said anything more. We were all too busy trying to imagine a Thanksgiving without Aussie's melt-in-your-mouth piecrusts and her listing out reasons for being thankful from the past year. How could we celebrate Thanksgiving without Aussie reminding us how much we had to be grateful for? Daddy wanted too much from us sometimes. Just plain too much.

21

WITNESSING
LIFE

MOST TIMES MAMA PRACTICALLY has to shake me awake. Nothing gets me up, especially in the middle of the night. But all the food I'd stuffed into myself kept me on the edge of wakefulness, unable to sink into deep sleep. So when the phone rang and rang and rang in the middle of darkness, I woke.

After I'd lost track of the number of rings, Mama got out of bed and padded to the parlor. She muttered under her breath. I strained to hear but couldn't. Even when the ringing stopped and Mama spoke into the receiver, I couldn't make out her words. The only way I could tell she'd hung up was by the footsteps I heard leading past my room to hers.

I expected to hear the bed groan with her weight. Instead, I heard drawers opening, the closet door squeaking, sounds of Mama getting dressed. I sat up, wishing my alarm clock hadn't broken so I could check the time. From the darkness yawning around me, I knew it wasn't close to sunrise. Two or three in the early morning was my best guess. Where was Mama going at two or three in the morning?

She and Daddy were talking in such low whispers, I couldn't understand what he said, much less Mama. I threw back my side of the covers, careful not to pull any off Mavis, and reached under the bed for my slippers. After I'd tied the belt of my robe, I tiptoed out the room, not that snoring Mavis looked ready to jump up.

Mama, all dressed, stepped out her bedroom door same time I stepped out mine. "Where you going, Mama?"

"What are you doing out of bed? Do you know what time it is?"

"Two or three?" I guessed.

"Two thirty-five to be exact."

"So why are you dressed? You going somewhere or what?" I followed her to the kitchen, where she started water boiling for coffee.

"I can't do anything without my coffee."

I knew that was true. Mama could not start any day, especially one beginning at two thirty-five, without a cup of Community, best coffee in the world.

"Who called?"

"Everett."

I waited for her to give me a full and complete explanation of what was going on at two thirty-five in the morning. But it was too early in the day for Mama to be in a talking mood without prodding on my part. "What did he want?"

"Deacy made him call, tell me they were leaving for the hospital." Mama's coffee beans waited in the filter on her pot so the minute water boiled, she'd be set.

"Tante Deacy having her baby already?"

"Looks like." She poured the first several drops of water evenly across the filter, letting all the ground beans soak before she started pouring more generously.

"The baby wasn't supposed to get here until after New Year's," I said.

"Guess the baby was tired of waiting."

I could understand that easily. Us Menieres were never known for our patience. But I hoped this baby wasn't rushing things too much. "You think the baby's going to be okay?"

Mama poured herself a first cup of coffee, even though water was still dripping through the grounds. "Only God knows for sure."

"What do you think, though? Think Tante Deacy's baby'll be all right?" I knew God wouldn't be saying yea or nay about my change-of-life cousin. But if I could get a good answer from Mama, that'd be better than nothing. I'd be able to get back to sleep if Mama told me she thought Deacy's new baby would be fine. But Mama was never one for easy assurances. She drank her entire cup of coffee while I sat, waiting an answer. When she got up to pour herself a half cup more, I ran out of the little bit of Meniere patience I owned. "I think that baby'll be just fine," I said, answering my own question since Mama wouldn't bother.

"Do you?" Mama asked.

"Sure. Just tinier than most babies." I remembered Clorise's cousin from Mississippi who'd been born earlier than he was supposed to be. Glenny was five and still too skinny, but nothing else was wrong with the boy, least not that Clorise could tell last time she saw him. I hoped, hoped hard, Mama'd agree with me fast as she'd ever agreed with Aussie about anything.

"I hope you're right. That's all I can say." That was hardly the fast and sure agreement I'd been looking for, but it would have to do.

Mama hustled me back to bed after she rinsed out her cup and put on her coat. She wasn't happy over sitting in the waiting room with Everett, but she had to go because Deacy was her sister, her only and truly loved sister. Deacy had been at the hospital when I was born and Mavis too. Mama had been there for T.J. and Malcolm and Austin and now would be there for this change-of-life baby, Everett or no Everett.

When I got myself properly covered, my pillow plumped just right, Mavis turned to her side so she'd stop snoring, I tried to relax myself back to sleep. But sleep wouldn't come. I couldn't stop thinking about Deacy's new baby, pushing her way into the world too soon. I wondered if the luck a change-of-life baby carried got thinned when she was born too soon. I wondered if the baby had been listening when her daddy said nobody wanted her and decided to get herself born then and there just to show him. I wondered if I'd get up in the middle of the night to go to the hospital when Mavis had herself a baby. I laughed out loud once, just thinking about dumb old Mavis having a baby. That single laugh cleared my brain of all those baby thoughts and soon I was asleep.

I didn't get up till close to ten the next morning. Mavis was watching *Romper Room* even though she was nearly too old for that baby show. "Mama back yet?" I asked.

"Not yet." Her eyes were fixed on Miss Sue, who was holding up her magic—magic, right, sure, tell me another one—mirror to see all the boys and girls who'd watched the show that morning. I let my next question wait because this was Mavis's favorite part and she wouldn't pay a second's worth of attention to me. Once, just once, Miss Sue had called out Mavis's name and, ever since, my sister had been waiting to hear her name called out again. Girl would probably still be listening to *Romper Room* in fifth grade, still waiting for Miss Sue to call out her name on TV.

Miss Sue put down her mirror, waved good-bye. At least Mavis didn't wave back anymore.

"Mama call from the hospital?" I asked. I squatted next to Mavis, who lay on the floor less than a foot from the set. The girl was bound to make herself blind. I am not, definitely not, taking care of a blind sister, but no use telling Mavis that. She'd only move closer to the TV just to show me she could.

"Daddy said things were moving slow. That's what Mama told him."

"How much longer before our cousin gets herself born?"

"Might be another boy."

No use trying to explain to Mavis how I'd figured for sure it'd be a girl. "How much longer?" I repeated.

"That's all Daddy said. He didn't say anything about how much longer." *The Price Is Right* came on then and I lost Mavis's attention even though she had less idea than I did about what anything cost or didn't cost.

I wandered into the kitchen for breakfast and Daddy, who might know more than he'd told Mavis. He was on his knees, scraping glue from the floor where three more tiles had come undone. Mama'd been after him since school started to get those reglued and now he'd finally decided to do it. Maybe the thought had come to him that Mister Kidder could take it on himself to inspect our house again. But the bank couldn't take back its money now, not with walls and roof all in place. I was certain about that, but maybe Daddy wasn't.

"How much longer before Tante Deacy has her baby?"

He looked up from his scraping. "Only God and maybe Deacy's doctor know."

"Mama didn't say?"

"Might come as a surprise, but your mama does not know everything."

I didn't say anything to that. Of course I knew Mama didn't know everything. She did know many things, though. When Deacy's baby was getting herself born just wasn't one of them, if Daddy was to be believed.

My bread had popped out the toaster and I'd buttered both slices and sprinkled cinnamon sugar over one of them when the phone rang. Mavis answered and when Daddy and I heard, "She did?" we both ran to the parlor, neither of us trusting Mavis's message taking.

"Give me that phone," Daddy said, stern enough to close off any arguing Mavis might be inclined to offer.

"Tante Deacy had her baby?" I whispered to Mavis.

"Yep."

"A girl?"

"Yep."

"Everything's okay?"

"Yep." Mavis had been watching too many cowboy shows again.

I waited patiently as any Meniere ever had for Daddy to get off the line. "Everything's okay?" I asked again, this time aiming my question at someone who wouldn't give me a horsey answer.

"Baby's fine. Girl. Itty-bitty, your mama says. But fine. Deacy's tired, but fine. Everybody's fine."

I was happy to have predicted the whole thing myself. "Having a baby's hard work."

"Talk to your mama about that one." He went back to the kitchen floor and I followed.

"When do we get to see the baby?"

"When she goes home."

"Can't I go to the hospital?" I sprinkled cinnamon sugar on my second piece of toast.

"Hospitals don't let children in to look at new babies." He swept glue scrapings into his hand and dumped them in the trash. "Too many germs." He stared at my hands and I did too, but no visible germs danced on my fingertips.

"I'm her cousin."

"Hospitals don't care about that."

I sat at the table with my toast and milk. "What's her name?"

"Don't know." He squeezed glue on the floor space he'd cleaned, then on one of the tiles. "Maybe she doesn't have a name."

"Tante Deacy would have a name." Maybe Everett wouldn't of wanted to pick a name any more than he'd wanted to have the baby in the first place. But Deacy would. I was sure of it.

"Baby's in an incubator, oxygen tank thing. Maybe Deacy's wanting to hold her close before naming her. That's what your mama did." He smiled, probably remembering how cute I'd been when I was born.

"I can hardly wait to hold that baby myself."

"Something real special about new babies all right. Real special." He squeezed glue on the floor for the second tile.

"Guess that'll be especially true for this change-of-life baby." I pulled crusts off my toast and put one in my mouth, saving the softer center for last.

"Change-of-life babies aren't always for the good, you know."

"This one will be," I said with more confidence than I'd felt these last few weeks. Whistling in the dark, Mama would've called it.

"Not even close to grown and already you've got that Meniere know-it-all attitude." He pressed the second tile to the floor. "Looking at you now, it's hard to truly recall what a fully adorable baby you were."

"What about me? Was I adorable too?" *The Price Is Right* was finished so Mavis had come to the kitchen, probably hoping to beg a handout, cookie or piece of leftover pie, something.

"You looked like a wet rat," I said.

"You were fully adorable," Daddy said so quickly, her cheeks barely had time to puff. "You smelled sweet too, smelled brand new."

"Bet Vivien Leigh stunk like a skunk," Mavis said.

"She smelled good as you did."

"If you smelled sweet, I smelled sweeter," I said.

"You did not. Daddy, did she?"

"For God's sake, both you girls were sweet smelling and fully adorable, one the same as the other." He stood and stretched kinks out his legs and back. "What I want to know is this. What happened between then and now? Tell me that, if you please." He stared at us, pretending to expect an answer. But even Mavis was smart enough to know he was teasing, asking a question that didn't deserve an answer. Nobody can stay a sweet-smelling, fully adorable baby forever.

Mama walked through the back door just then, so we could stop this ridiculous conversation.

"How's the baby? Does she have a name yet? When's she coming home?" I stopped, waiting for Mama's replies.

"Would somebody give me a minute to catch my breath?"

When I was young, I used to stare at Mama when she said that, expecting her to snatch escaping breath with a hand and shove it into her open mouth. Course now that I'm older, I know better.

Mama hung her coat in the hall closet. I let her pour a cup of coffee, cut a slice of leftover Thanksgiving lemon meringue pie, and take a bite and a sip before I pestered her again. "So tell us," I said.

"Everything's fine far as we can tell. Baby's itty-bitty."

"Cause she got born too soon," Mavis said as if she was the world's biggest expert on when babies should get themselves born.

"That's right," Mama said. "Born too soon." She rubbed a finger across each eye but couldn't rub away the blue circles under each one.

"Bet Everett's strutting like a barnyard rooster," Daddy said.

"Everett's being Everett," Mama said. She made his name sound like a new curse word.

"What about a name? What's her name?" I asked again. I was tired of calling my new cousin change-of-life baby. I wanted a real name to go with this real baby.

"Baby probably doesn't even have a name yet," Daddy said. He stood at the sink, rinsing his brush and scraper.

"Course she has a name," Mama said. She cleared her throat. A baby's name should always be called out in a strong voice, at least the first time it's called out. "Angelina Christine Comeaux. That's her name. Baby angel, baby Christ is what it means, according to Deacy."

It was a beautiful name I loved at first sound. Baby angel, baby Christ. What a wonderful name for a change-of-life baby, a name sure to bring even more good luck her way.

"When is she coming home?" I asked.

"Deacy'll be back next Tuesday, probably. But the hospital'll keep the baby longer. She needs that extra oxygen."

"How much longer?"

"Two weeks. Maybe three."

"I can't wait that long," I said. I'd been waiting since summer, but now three more weeks seemed impossible. I wanted to meet that new cousin now, right away. "Can't I go to the hospital?"

"I already told you hospitals don't let pipsqueaks in. That nursery isn't some freak show," Daddy said between bites of leftover pecan pie he'd sliced, one piece for himself, one for Mavis.

"If you're ten or older, this hospital lets you visit in the afternoon, three to four," Mama said.

"I'm ten," I nearly screamed. "I can go. This afternoon. I'm going this afternoon."

"What about me?" Mavis didn't bother swallowing her bite before starting her whines. "I'd be good. Wouldn't make any noise." She puffed her cheeks, crossed her arms across her chest. "I want to see that baby too."

"I know you'd be good as anything, Baby. But ten's the rule, the hospital's rule and no getting around it." Mama was kind as could be, probably feeling sorry for Mavis. Even I felt a little sorry for poor old Mavis, who had the misfortune of being born too late to be ten on this particularly glorious November Friday.

She stomped back to our bedroom, cheeks puffed their fattest, not even bothering to finish her pie. But even the fattest cheeks in Louisiana wouldn't force the hospital to change its rules. Daddy pulled Mavis's leftover piece to his side of the table. While I watched him chew the last bites of her pie, I tried to decide what to wear that afternoon. I wanted to look just right when I met Angelina Christine Comeaux for the very first time.

But as it ended up I didn't get to the hospital that afternoon, didn't get to go till Saturday at three after I'd helped Mama wash, wax, and vacuum the car, all of it without any help from Mavis. Mama was full of excuses for why I couldn't go Friday, the day my cousin was born. The real reason, of course, was she wanted to let Mavis calm down about the whole thing. One day wasn't enough to calm Mavis, who hadn't even been very interested in Deacy's change-of-life baby until she found out I could go to the hospital and she couldn't. Mavis did manage to get herself pancakes and bacon for breakfast and a trip to Borden's for afternoon ice cream with Daddy while Mama and I went to the hospital. I didn't care. A peek at my new lucky cousin was worth a dozen Borden's double cones at the very least.

"Tante Deacy'll be happy to see me," I said as we pushed through the wide front doors, glass top to bottom, at Lourdes Hospital in Lafayette.

"She'll be happy, all right," Mama said.

A gray-haired woman guarded the round information desk sitting in the middle of the lobby. "Girl ten or not?" the woman asked, her voice so gravelly I knew she was a smoker. I peered across her desk and, sure enough, two ashtrays overflowed with butts.

"Sure I'm ten, near ten and a half," I said.

Mama yanked my hand. "Girl's got a big mouth, but she is ten."

The lady laughed, a scratchy sound like fingernails across a chalkboard. "Elevator's back that way." She pointed to the left, behind her desk.

Mama tugged me to the elevators, the lady's laugh following us down the lobby. "Hospitals don't allow smart-mouth children. Guess I forgot to tell you that part."

I ignored her, just pressed three when the elevator swished open, three for Deacy's room, three thirteen. The doors opened to pale blue walls, pink trim. Carpet was the opposite, dark rose with pale blue piping. Everything pink and blue for new babies.

"Which way are the babies?" I asked.

"We'll see Deacy first."

I didn't argue. This was my first trip to a hospital, first visit to see a just-born baby. If Mama said we had to see Deacy first, that's what we'd do. I wasn't risking getting thrown out of Lourdes for visiting in the wrong order.

Everett was the one who answered my knock. He and Tante Yvette were the only ones in the room besides Deacy, who wore a pink-laced nightgown and matching robe so everyone who saw her would know she'd gotten herself a baby girl at last.

"Welcome, welcome," Everett said. He pushed a chair in Mama's direction, but she ignored him, going to give Deacy a kiss on the cheek and settling on the bed instead, holding Deacy's hand.

"Hazey told me you were probably coming," Deacy said to me.

"I'm ten," I explained.

"Well, come here and give your favorite aunt a kiss."

She smelled all powdered up. That surprised me because I didn't think hospitals let people cover up their natural smells. "You smell great."

"Deacy always was a sweet-smelling woman," Everett said. He'd sat back in his chair since Mama'd refused it and I was too young to deserve it.

Deacy smiled at him, a warm and true smile. Guess it's not easy to stay angry when you've just had a man's change-of-life baby.

"You seen the baby yet?" Everett asked.

I shook my head. "I know her name, though. Angelina Christine. It's a beautiful name."

"Her mama picked it," Everett said.

Course I already knew that.

"She's the tiniest thing I've ever seen. I swear she'd fit in Everett's hand. Fit just like this." Tante Yvette cupped her hand to show what she meant.

"Prettiest thing I've ever seen. That's all I know," Everett said.

"Woman had a baby that small in my day, baby'd die for sure," Tante Yvette said.

"Don't start talking gruesome," Mama said, but her voice was free and light.

"Not gruesome, just the truth. Baby Angelina's fine, though." She pushed up from her chair, pressing at her low back to straighten it once her bottom had lifted. "I'm going down to see her one more time, then Hazey can take me home."

"But we just got here," I protested. We'd hardly been there long enough for Mavis to have earned her bacon and pancakes, much less her trip to Borden's.

"You can stay. I'll drive Tante home. Come back for you." Mama didn't sound like she relished the extra driving, but Tante Yvette was an old woman accustomed to having her own way and Mama knew that well as the rest of us.

Everett led us to the nursery. Bassinets lined the room and babies filled nearly each one. I had no idea so many babies were getting themselves born these days.

"They have name tags on their cribs," Everett said. "There she is. Over to the left." He pointed to a special bed covered with a hood contraption, which I guessed was the oxygen Daddy'd mentioned.

"I can't hardly see her." I pressed against the glass, but that didn't do me any good.

Everett waved at a nurse and pointed to Angelina Christine's crib. The nurse smiled, then pulled and pushed bassinets, rearranging till our baby's was right next to the window.

She lay still as possum breath. Her eyes were closed and her tiny lips were slightly parted. I hoped that didn't mean she had caught herself a cold and was having trouble breathing through her nose. Then I remembered her oxygen and knew everything would be fine breathingwise. Narrow tubes were taped into her little heel. She was too small to even try kicking them away, which is what I know she felt like doing. I imagined she almost regretted getting herself born too early even though it did teach her daddy a good lesson, which I hoped he wouldn't soon be forgetting.

When we'd all had our fill of Angelina Christine, we went back to Deacy's room. Mama and Tante Yvette got their purses and left, but only after Mama told me to mind. An unnecessary reminder because what kind of trouble could a girl get into in a hospital?

"Tell the truth, Vivien Leigh. Isn't Angelina the most beautiful baby you've ever seen?" Everett said right after the door shut on Mama and Tante Yvette.

I thought back on her perfect little nose, brows like a smattering of dust above each eye, the exquisite nails, new and round and shiny. "She is beautiful," I said. "A beautiful, beautiful baby."

"Gets her looks from her mama, don't you think?"

"That's what my mama would say."

"For sure. For sure." We both knew that was the least of what Mama would say. Everett reached around the side of Deacy's bed and pushed a button, filling the room with a waltz.

"Where's that coming from?" I asked.

"Hospital tapes it, I guess," Deacy said. "Isn't regular radio, but you can listen whenever you feel like, middle of the day, middle of the night, doesn't matter. Three channels, but this is our favorite, mine and Everett's."

Wait till Mavis heard this one. Music, special music, piped right into your hospital room.

Everett bowed from the waist in Deacy's direction and even though he wore work dungarees and a plaid flannel shirt and even though his stomach pouched over his belt, he still looked quite gallant, the way I imagined Rochester must've seemed to Jane Eyre. "May I have this dance, Madam?"

"Everett, don't be silly. We're in the hospital. What if someone comes in, catches us?" But Deacy's legs were already swinging across the side of the bed, her hands extended toward Everett. He took two long steps to reach her, catching her offered hands with his, pulling her up and against him. His hands lowered to circle her waist, still bulging wide and ungainly from the empty space that had so recently held Angelina Christine. Then, holding her that way, Everett slowly waltzed Deacy around the room, keeping perfect time to the music the hospital so kindly provided. Deacy giggled and said what would the nurses say, what would the boys think. She didn't have to worry over T.J. or Malcolm or Austin because that front-desk lady wouldn't let no-account boys into the hospital no matter what their ages. I didn't know about the nurses.

But with all her protests, Deacy didn't once push Everett away. They danced and danced in that cramped room. I could almost imagine them young and free, Deacy in her finest gown, her cameo cradled in the hollow at the base of her neck, dancing to New Orleans's finest music, not stopping till sun pinked the sky.

Everything would be fine now. Angelina Christine had worked her change-of-life magic to give herself a family, strong and whole, faithful too. That was how I saw things at that moment in that hospital room, watching my uncle twirl my aunt around and around. But what did I know? I was only a child, barely old enough to witness my own life, much less the lives of so many other people.

22

WISHES

TWO WEEKS LATER ANGELINA CHRISTINE was still in the hospital, still living in her special oxygen-filled incubator, but getting stronger and closer to coming home every day. That's what Mama said and Deacy too when I talked to her on the phone or drove over to her place to straighten things up with Mama. Her boys sure couldn't be counted on for straightening anything, and Everett had gone back to Monroe to finish out his job. But he'd be back soon. Everyone knew it and no one was upset with him anymore, except for Mama, who tried not to show it. Angelina Christine's magic was powerful enough to get her daddy back to Ville d'Angelle and to get most everyone to forgive his cowardly run up north, but it wasn't strong enough to erase Mama's memories of what he'd done. There are limits to what even a change-of-life baby can do.

Just a few days before Christmas vacation I came down with one of those winter colds that stop up your whole head till you wish you could chop the thing off. Most mothers would keep their children home. Not mine, though. Unless you had a temperature and looked as if you were dying, my mama believed you belonged in school and out from underfoot. She sent Sister Pat a note saying I should be kept indoors for recess—her only concession to the fact I might be coming down with pneumonia, double pneumonia more than likely.

I sat at my desk, coloring a Nativity scene on the back of the *Scholastic Reader*. It was baby work but I was so sorely bored and miserable, I didn't even care. I tried concentrating on Mary's blue veil but even with the windows closed, I could hear the fifths whooping and hollering and having a time outside. Mother Ignatius was out there too, so since Sister Bernie wasn't by herself, the fifths weren't getting away with anything. But at least they were out there, having themselves as much fun as there was to be had on this ugly day.

While I colored, missing recess at school and game shows at home, Sister Pat scribbled at her desk. I coughed a couple of times, maybe a smidgen louder than regular. She looked up. "Walk around. Exercise your legs." She didn't wait to see if I'd take up her idea, but went right back to scribbling. Sisters *know* people'll listen to them. They don't have to bother making sure.

I eased out my desk, walked to the window, and smoothed my skirt, which now hung just below my knees. By May it'd be just above my knees, short but not indecent. Those fifths looked like they were having a time out there. Sister Bernie flapped her arms like one of Tante Yvette's chickens, trying to get somebody's attention. I giggled, then remembered how bad I felt and let out a long sigh, practically a moan.

Sister Pat dropped her pen. "How about checkers?"

I was pretty good at checkers, since I played Mama each Sunday. Sister Pat set up the board on the corner of her desk. She said I could pull Clorise's desk next to hers, but I said no thanks, I'd stand. Clorise was very particular about her things and would say I messed her stuff up, even though it wouldn't be true.

Sister Pat let me go first, which was only fair since I was a child and a sick one at that. She got a few of my pieces. I got a few of hers. She got the first king. Mama says when a player gets a king, things get interesting. But I picked one up soon after she did, so it was a pretty even match.

"Any big plans for Christmas?" Sister Pat asked.

"Ham and roast dinner at our house. Mama'll fix it. She does it every year. My Tante Yvette'll be there and my Tante Deacy and Uncle Everett with their boys and, I hope, baby Angelina Christine, though of course she won't be doing any eating."

"Course not," Sister Pat said. I'd told the class all about my change-of-life cousin, not actually planning to mention she was a change-of-life baby because then someone would be bound to ask what that meant and I wasn't fully sure I knew. But then Willie had raised his hand.

"My mama says your cousin is a change-of-life baby," Willie said. "Just like me," he bragged.

"That's right," I said, answering with a voice that dared anybody to show their ignorance by asking what that meant.

Sister Pat moved her king to the middle of the board, a bold place to be. I preferred the edges, where it felt safer. Mama says I have coward blood and maybe I do, though not too much of it I hope.

"Compared to most families around here, yours is on the small side," Sister Pat said.

"Sometimes I wish there were more of us. Not just me and old Mavis. But that's how it is. Maybe we'll have more someday. I don't think so, though. I don't know really." I always talk too much when I'm nervous. Even after four and a half years in a Catholic school I could count on one hand the number of times I'd been alone with a nun, and not one of those times had been with a colored one.

"I come from a big family, four sisters and three brothers. A real Catholic family," Sister Pat said.

I looked up from the board, surprised. I'd never thought of sisters having families. They just seemed to have sprung full grown in navy robes.

"Mavis is all right," I said. I braced my palms on the edge of her desk and leaned forward. "But she's an awful pest."

"That's what my sisters said about me." She chuckled softly and moved a piece, then put it back and moved a different one instead. "I was the middle sister. A good place to be to pester everybody else."

"Mavis and me fight too much. That's what Mama says."

"Mavis and I," she corrected.

I knew that. Just forgot sometimes.

"We fought day and night. Especially my sisters. Not so much my brothers." Sister Pat shook her head and got this dreamy smile on her face. "My mother used to say we kids never gave her a minute's rest. She was right too."

Imagine nuns pinching and screaming like Mavis and me. I tried to picture Sister Pat as a little girl, pulling hair when she was serious fighting. All I could come up with was a short nun. I couldn't seem to get Sister Pat out of her nun clothes and into regular kid clothes. Hair pulling was impossible to picture.

"This will be my first Christmas home in five years," Sister Pat said after she jumped two of my pieces.

"I didn't know nuns went home for Christmas," I blurted. I looked down quickly at the board, pretending to concentrate on my next turn.

"Every once in a while they let us out." When I looked up, she was smiling, so I relaxed.

"Guess all that noise'll seem funny." I'd been inside the convent a couple of times. Even though it was right next to the school, it was another world—everything hushed and worn and solemn. No one thought about acting up in a convent. Nuns couldn't even talk after supper unless it was a real emergency, like the convent was on fire, and even then they had to whisper.

"It'll just be home. No funnier than you going home," she said.

"Guess I'd even miss Mavis, if I left home," I said.

"Guess you would. Just like me."

I blushed. It wasn't right, a colored saying I was just like her. But I didn't say that because some things you can't say to a nun, especially a colored nun, no matter how nice she's being to you.

She jumped another of my pieces and added it to her pile. "Some things I don't miss, though."

"Like what?" The question jumped out my mouth before I could clamp my lips.

"Always being in the colored part of Brooklyn. When you're a nun, color doesn't matter as much."

I could see that. Being a sister was stronger than almost anything, even than being colored. You might mess with a colored girl, but you wouldn't mess with a sister, colored or not.

"My family will be happy to see me in one piece."

"Why?" I asked quickly, hoping I was about to learn some secret, dangerous nun ritual I could pass on to the other fifths.

"Your turn," she said.

I'd forgotten about checkers but looked at the board to pretend interest. "Why wouldn't you be in one piece?"

"You southerners have yourselves a reputation."

"We do?" I was surprised anyone bothered thinking about us, floating among the bayous in a state that never even got a mention on the evening news, something Arkansas managed nearly every night.

"Lynchings, things like that," she said.

"That's stupid." I moved the first piece I saw so maybe I wouldn't get in trouble for saying that to a teacher, even though I was in the right and knew it. Those Brooklyn people didn't just talk funny, they had strange ideas. Maybe they watched too many cowboy movies. Maybe that's all there was to do in Brooklyn.

"Even if I didn't get myself lynched, they were sure I wouldn't be able to understand a word you people said."

"We speak good." I shifted weight from one foot to the other.

"They thought most Cajuns spoke only French and those who did speak English had such an accent you couldn't make out half their words," she said.

"What'd they say when you told them we speak good as anybody?" I said.

"No one would mistake Cajuns for New Yorkers, I told them. But after a while listening comes pretty easily." Sister Pat jumped my last king and the game was over. "I'm not sure they believe me yet."

I could hear things quieting down outside, which meant Sister Bernie was lining up the fifths to return to class.

"I used to have trouble understanding you. We all did," I confided as I stacked the checker pieces in a box, red on one side, black on the other. "But now it's just like listening to anybody else."

"We all like to do things our way. That goes for talking too," Sister Pat said.

No doubt she was right about that.

I went back to my desk and watched the fifths, red cheeked and laughing, file back. While I waited for them to settle down, I finished copying the day's poem in my notebook.

Prayer [1] by Langston Hughes

I ask you this:
Which way to go?
I ask you this:
Which sin to bear?
Which crown to put
Upon my hair?
I do not know,
Lord God,
I do not know.

Looked to me as if some days Mister Hughes, who was probably Catholic, was confused as me about where to go, what to do, which way was right and which not.

When I got home that afternoon, I went straight to bed, didn't even bother with a snack, which I always have right after school. Mama took my temperature and thank goodness I had one so she would have to let me stay home next day. I slept off and on most of that afternoon. Mama fixed a supper tray with saltines and chicken noodle soup and Coke and served it to me in bed. I wasn't hungry for much of it and wished I'd felt well enough to enjoy the service I was getting. Once Mama decided you were really sick, she knew how to treat you just right.

Even Mavis was nice as she ever got. She fumbled in the dark for her pajamas and slippers and robe, not turning on the light because she thought I was sleeping, which I had been till she opened the door and which I still was, halfway. She didn't come back to the room that night, which meant Mama'd opened the sofa bed. Mavis loved sleeping on that sofa, which was double-bed size, same as ours, but felt bigger. Sometimes she begged Mama to let Marydale spend the night with her on the sofa bed. Mama said not to be ridiculous. Daddy would not abide a colored girl sleeping in his parlor, even if the colored girl was nice as Marydale.

I felt better next morning. My nose was still packed solid but I wasn't chilled and hot at the same time. I hoped Mama wouldn't take my temperature since I didn't think I had one, at least not one that'd keep me home. But when Mama came into my room, she had a tray with buttered toast and orange juice and didn't mention school once.

"You feeling any better?" she asked.

"A little," I said, dragging out that "little" to sound sick as possible. "Mavis still here?"

"Bus came close to two hours ago." That meant it was going on nine-thirty. I was safe.

Mama sat on the edge of my bed while I ate. It was Friday, her grocery-shopping day, but she'd put that off if I didn't want to stay home by myself. I said, in that same pitiful voice, I didn't mind. I'd read or watch TV or something.

"You going to see Angelina Christine too?" Mama tried to stop by the hospital every chance she got to Lafayette, which is where she'd been doing her big Friday grocery shopping since Everett quit working the IGA and cut off the only family obligation we had to that store.

"You didn't hear last night's news," Mama said. "I'd forgotten."

"What news?" Why do things always happen when I'm not around to keep track?

"Angelina Christine came home yesterday afternoon."

"When can we see her?"

"When you've been well enough to go to school for at least a couple of days."

I didn't protest, knowing babies were especially sensitive to germs. The same germ that gave me nothing but a cold could jump on Angelina Christine and knock her back to Lourdes. Still, I was disappointed I wouldn't hold my cousin soon. I'd only seen her once since my first

Saturday visit. That second time she'd had her eyes open, looking straight at me in particular, though Mama'd said no one could tell for sure what or who she was looking at because babies can't focus their eyes till they're older. Angelina Christine was fine. Nothing to worry about with her. Nothing at all.

Mama got me situated on the sofa, TV on, before leaving for her groceries. Mavis would be aggravated to see me moved to the parlor. But fair's fair. She'd gotten it last night and all because of me too. Now it was my turn.

Mama'd only been gone about half an hour, *The Price Is Right* had just ended, when the front door opened and in stepped Deacy, baby Angelina Christine in her arms.

"Stay away from me," I said. "I've got germs. Bad ones."

"Can't you say hello?" Even from my sofa bed I could see Deacy's eyes were shining too bright.

"Mama's not home. Gone grocery shopping."

"Today's Friday?" Deacy fiddled with the baby's blankets, untucking so she wasn't wrapped so tightly.

"Sure," I said. "Today's Friday."

"You probably think I'm addled." She fanned herself with the edge of the baby blanket, though the parlor wasn't warm, was on the chilly side, if anything. "Time floats into nowhere when you've a new baby in the house."

"She keep you up last night?"

"Not at all. Angelina Christine's a good baby. Aren't you, sweets?" She cooed at her daughter. "A real good baby." She stared at Angelina Christine, not speaking for several seconds. "Vivien Leigh, I want you to look here at this baby. Look at her eyes." She stepped around the front of the sofa bed to get to my side. I held up a hand to warn her off, but she came anyway. Germs didn't scare Deacy the way they scared Mama and Daddy.

She sat on the edge of the bed and laid Angelina Christine right next to me, removing her outdoor coverings till only the swaddling blanket and her long baby gown were left.

"I shouldn't touch her with all my germs," I said.

"Where'd you learn to be so scared about germs?"

I shrugged. Who knows where a person learns fear, what deserves it and what doesn't?

Angelina Christine had her eyes closed when her mama set her down. But now she puckered her mouth and yawned and, if her arms hadn't been bundled to her sides, would've stretched them like a person does just waking up. She finished her yawn, then opened her eyes, which were blacker than I remembered. Of course, I'd only seen her through the nursery's plate-glass window, so maybe she'd always been black-eyed and I was the one who hadn't been able to see clearly.

"Watch this," Deacy said. She passed her hand across Angelina Christine's face, six inches or so from those black, black eyes. The baby didn't blink or turn her head or anything.

"Your hand's boring," I said.

"She's too new to find anything boring." Deacy wiggled her fingers, now drawing her hand so close to her baby's face, she practically touched her, then pulling back so she was about two feet away from that tiny nose. Nothing got Angelina Christine's attention.

"Maybe she'd like something more colorful." I looked around for something she might like, but Mama didn't keep bright, interesting things in the parlor. I ran to the bedroom and grabbed my own Raggedy Ann off the bed. I was too big to play with her anymore, but she had been my favorite when I was little and I was keeping her to give to my own daughter when I had one.

I sat next to Deacy, who still wiggled her hand at her baby. "Here. Try this. Maybe she'll like it better."

Deacy took Raggedy and passed it across Angelina Christine's face, touched it to her nose, waved it back and forth, close, then far. None of it interested that baby, who'd managed to free one hand from her blanket and was patting her nose as if to make sure it was still in the right place. She wasn't really doing that, just seemed to be, because baby Angelina Christine was too young to even know she had a nose.

"Know something, Vivien Leigh?" Deacy's voice was barely whisper loud. "Know what I think? I think my baby's blind. Blind as old Miss Paula Haas who can't see well enough to wipe her own behind."

"No." I shook my head, back and forth, back and forth, a poor imitation of Raggedy Ann in Deacy's hand. This change-of-life baby couldn't begin life with that kind of luck, so bad she'd have to spend her whole life pulling away from her poor start. I wouldn't let that be.

"I've been studying this baby all night." Deacy passed a single finger across her baby's line of vision. Now that she said that, I noticed the circles under her eyes, circles darker than Mama's had been the morning she'd returned from the hospital. Behind us the opening credits for *Truth or Consequences* flashed and the theme music played. I didn't even like that show but couldn't bother turning off the set.

"Babies can't focus. Everybody knows that," I said.

"But they can see. Even a just-born baby can see."

"The doctors would know if she was blind. The hospital. Somebody would've said something." The truth-or-consequence buzzer rang. I wanted to tell Bob Barker to shut off his stupid bell. "Nobody said anything, did they?"

"Maybe they didn't notice. Hospital nurses are too busy changing diapers, giving feedings to notice whether a baby's blind."

"I know she wasn't blind the last time I saw her." I remembered Angelina Christine in her hospital bassinet, looking straight at me, knowing me right away for her cousin who'd be teaching her the ways of the world because her brothers could not be relied on for such information. I think she even smiled at me, though Mama said it was only gas since babies that young can't smile.

"Well, she's for sure blind now," Deacy said softly, her finger rubbing Angelina Christine's cheek. I could imagine that finger, rubbing that soft cheek all night, Deacy alone with her baby, afraid darkness would never end.

"The hospital wouldn't give you a blind baby." I was sure that had to be true. I wished with all my might for Mama to get home right now, right this terrible minute.

Sometimes wishing does make something come true. Not often, but sometimes and this was one of those lucky times. "Deacy, that you in there?" Mama called from the kitchen.

Deacy didn't answer, so I did. "We're in here, Mama."

"Vivien Leigh, don't you be touching that baby." The refrigerator door opened and I could hear Mama putting groceries away. "Don't you be giving that baby her death of a cold."

"No, ma'am," was all I said, not mentioning my poor cousin might have a lot more to worry over than a stuffed-up nose.

Mama finished bringing in her groceries and saving them too, before she stepped into the parlor to join me and Deacy, Angelina Christine on the sofa bed between us. "Are you sure you should be taking the baby out so soon? Her just being out of the hospital and all?" She walked closer and closer till she stood right over the three of us. I watched Mama watching the baby, waiting for a clear sign that the baby was fine or that she wasn't.

"She can't see, Hazey. My baby can't see," Deacy said.

Mama looked at her, at me, at the baby, back at Deacy. "What do you mean she can't see?"

"Just that. My baby's blind, I tell you. Blind." Deacy lifted Angelina Christine and pushed her toward Mama. "My baby. My poor, poor baby."

I expected the tears to start then but Deacy, who'd cried when Everett moved up to Monroe, when each of her boys made their Communions and when I made mine, even when her dog ran away, didn't seem to have a single tear for her poor, blind baby.

"She can't be blind," Mama said, cradling the baby close, looking into her eyes to see whether those eyes were looking back at her. Deacy and I waited for Mama to laugh, to say we were both crazy, that this baby could see just fine. We waited for her to laugh at our silliness, to laugh away the panic we'd laid in her arms.

"Did the doctor say something?" Mama asked. She held my cousin in the crook of one arm and wiggled the fingers of her free hand in front of the baby's eyes. Funniest blindness test I'd ever seen, but it was the exact same one Deacy had used. We stayed that way a full two minutes—Mama wiggling her fingers, me and Deacy on the sofa bed, waiting for the decision.

"She was born so early," Mama said at last. "Babies that young don't have eyes that focus soon as full-term babies."

I'd said the same or practically the same.

"It's not just the focusing, Hazey. She's not seeing, not seeing a single thing."

Mama plopped next to me, hard and sudden as if her legs couldn't hold her anymore. "Take her to the doctor, Deacy. Take her now. I'll come."

"Oh, Hazey. My baby. My poor, poor baby." The tears came now, more tears than I'd ever seen from one pair of eyes at one time. Deacy wiped a hand across her cheeks, then wiped that same hand, damp with her tears, across Angelina Christine's eyes, maybe hoping her tears would give her baby sight. But a blind baby doesn't get sight back from anyone else's tears, not even her own mama's.

Mama took her car, driving while Deacy held Angelina Christine in her lap. As they drove off, I watched from the front parlor window, hugging Raggedy Ann tight as I ever did when I was still a baby myself. I wished the doctor would find nothing wrong with that baby's eyes, but I'd already had one wish come true and one wish a day is more than most folks get. If only I'd saved my wish. If only, if only.

23

FIRE

TURNED OUT THE OXYGEN's what did it. Too much or too little, too weak or too strong, I never understood exactly. But the same thing that saved baby Angelina Christine's life stole her sight and there was nothing even the smartest doctor could do about it.

I felt sorry for her. We all did. At school Sister Pat offered special prayers when we did our morning devotions. Even Willie kept his head bowed over Angelina Christine.

The rest of her was fine, which was what Mama kept reminding Deacy. We should all be grateful the rest of her was healthy as a horse, Mama said. But Deacy couldn't be grateful. She was too busy thinking on having a blind baby who'd never get to see her grandmother's cameo locket with its curl of hair or her mama's face or any color at all.

I guessed that cameo was safely mine now. What would Angelina Christine want with something she couldn't see? Not that I was happy she was blind just because it meant I'd be getting the cameo. Every night when I said my evening prayers, I added a special request. "Dear God, please let Angelina Christine see, even if it means she gets the cameo." I wasn't being selfish when it came to my cousin.

Deacy was right about Angelina Christine being a good baby. She hardly ever cried and when she did, she shut right up after you gave her a bottle or changed her diaper or covered her with a blanket or finally figured why she was howling. She didn't act at all put out by being blind, but that might've been because she was too young to know anything about seeing or not seeing, even though she was a change-of-life baby and knew a lot more than most babies. Aussie said so.

Our first day of Christmas vacation was a Thursday. Might seem odd to start a vacation in the middle of the week that way, but it was all in accordance with the secret calendar nuns carried in their heads—so many days off for holy days, so many days for government holidays, so many days of schooling required by the board of education. Add and subtract it all and you ended up with a vacation starting on Thursday, still Aussie's day.

Daddy'd eased up on letting Aussie go, but he had gotten Mama to cut back to using her only every other Thursday. "A compromise to keep the peace," Mama called it. "Giving in," Mavis said, but she didn't go puff cheeked over it.

Happened that our first day of vacation was one of Aussie's days too. She and Mama did general cleanup in the morning, then baked in the afternoon. Molasses and cinnamon and ginger smells filled the house. Christmas is truly here when Mama starts making her gingerbreads. She gives them to friends and relatives as gifts. Daddy says she gives them to total strangers she meets on the street. Mama laughs when he says this, knowing it's just a joke and Daddy says it hoping she'll keep more of those gingerbreads for us because they taste good as Double Chocolate Devil's Surprise.

The only reason all those gingerbreads taste so good is because me and Mavis and Mama and Aussie test the very first one to come out the oven, making sure the spices are just right, the oven temperature set properly, everything in perfect gingerbread order. Some years Marydale got to test the first one too. But her vacation didn't start till Monday, so she missed out on this year's bread, still warm when Mama put slices on plates for the four of us gathered around the kitchen table.

We each took a bite, chewed slowly, our tongues searching for mistakes. I never found any. Mavis neither. But all of us, Mama too, looked to Aussie to make sure our tongues hadn't deceived us, that the gingerbread wasn't as perfectly delicious as we'd thought.

Aussie closed her eyes while she chewed, letting every part of her mind concentrate on that one bite of gingerbread. After she swallowed, she opened her eyes to announce the verdict. "Fine as I ever tasted, me. Never been better gingerbread crossed these lips."

The rest of us nodded as if we'd all come up with the same conclusion at the same time. This was gingerbread fit for the angels.

Mavis brought a second bite to her mouth, then closed her eyes to chew.

"What do you think you're doing?" I said between bites of my own.

"Girl tasting better. That's what she be doing, her," Aussie said, probably flattered Mavis was copying her. If Mama joined them, shutting her eyes to eat gingerbread, that'd prove every person at this table, except me, was crazy.

"Does it taste different?" I asked, curious in spite of myself.

"Yes," Mavis said, eyes still closed. "You can taste ever so much better." She opened her eyes to reach for another bite. "This is the way Angelina Christine will always eat. Things'll always taste better to her."

"Small comfort for not seeing," I said.

"Least she won't have to fight her brothers over television," Mavis said. Deacy's boys were always fighting over that set, even though there were only three channels to fight over and one of those was fuzzy half the time.

"Poor baby won't ever get to watch TV," I said. The more I thought about Angelina Christine's blindness, the sorrier I felt for her. She had never watched TV too close like Mavis always did and yet she was blind and Mavis wasn't. Blind without ever seeing Miss Sue on *Romper Room*, watching that mirror sparkle while Miss Sue pretended to look through your set, right at you and called out names and, if you were lucky, called out your name. At least my cousin could listen for her name. At least the oxygen hadn't stopped up her ears.

"That baby be seeing things nobody else sees. More than likely, that's what be happening," Aussie said.

"What do you mean?" I helped myself to a second slice of gingerbread and Mavis did the same.

"Second sight. That's what Aussie's talking about. That baby might be having herself second sight. See things nobody else sees. Know things nobody else knows. See and know more than ordinary folks with two working eyes."

I considered that. Could it be that baby Angelina Christine would end up feeling sorry for the rest of the world because we saw only solid things and she saw second-sight things? I thought about never seeing a single thing. Not just television, which I guessed a person could manage to survive without, but everything. Sunsets and hurricanes. Raggedy Ann and spinning tops. Kaleidoscopes and paisley skirts. Her mama's fine jewelry and especially the cameo. Her own dear face. Never to see any of that. "No," I said, so loud Mavis jumped. "Second sight won't make up for her blindness."

"A baby with second sight be closer to Jesus. That's what Reverend Hope says, him."

"Your priest mentioned Deacy's baby in his sermon?" Mama asked. She was so surprised, she held her forked gingerbread in the air, suspended between plate and mouth.

"Yes, ma'am, he sure did. Not just a mention neither. The whole sermon got itself preached on that baby."

"Our cousin got herself a whole sermon?" Mavis made it sound better than getting an entire package of Oreos for herself.

"Whole sermon was about that sweet baby, the Lord's own child. She be a blessing to your family, to everybody. Sweet sweet child of Jesus. Lord, Amen."

"Why'd your priest sermon on Angelina Christine?" I wasn't sure I liked the idea of my cousin on public display in a colored church.

"He was moved by the Lord. You know that." Aussie gave me one of her looks that asked where my brains had gotten to. "Every time a priest, Reverend Hope or any other priest, gets ready to sermon, he be visited by Lord God. When the priest's standing on that altar, in God's own house, Jesus be whispering in his ear. The whole time Jesus saying, 'Tell my people this,' or, 'Tell my people that.' And that's what the priest does, him."

"So why did God want Reverend Hope talking about Angelina Christine?" I asked.

"Why?" Aussie repeated.

"Sure. Why? Why's my cousin any business of the entire congregation of Saint Paul's Church?" I was being bold, but Mama didn't rein me in. Maybe she was wondering the same.

"Nobody on this earth know why God be doing one thing and not the other." She gave me another of those looks. "Don't you learn in Catechism that nobody can know the mind of God?"

"I learned that," Mavis said just to show me up. No Catechism teacher in the universe would bother talking about God's mind with second-graders.

"Sure you did, baby," Aussie said. Aussie was so accustomed to accepting everything as truth that came out Marydale's mouth, she was happy to do the same for Mavis.

"Did the reverend mention anybody else in his sermon?" Mama asked. .

All three of us leaned closer to hear Aussie's answer. Had our names been said out loud in Reverend Hope's sermon? Deacy's or Everett's or

Austin's or Malcolm's or T.J.'s? But then why would God whisper "T.J. Comeaux" in a priest's ear?

"Just Angelina Christine. That the only name crossed the reverend's lips last Sunday."

We all relaxed back in our chairs. Mavis kicked the table leg, truly disappointed God had not whispered her name in Reverend Hope's ear. I was a little disappointed myself.

"He should've at least mentioned Everett, held him up as an example of what happens when a man abandons his wife and family." All that anger Mama had bottled against Everett could come out now. No one dared stop her.

Aussie nodded, inviting Mama to tell her more.

"If Everett hadn't left home, gone to Monroe, handed Deacy that heavy burden, Angelina Christine wouldn't of been pushed out her mama too soon. I feel that to be a true fact. Feel it in my heart."

Aussie kept nodding like she knew it for a true fact too.

"If that baby hadn't been born too soon, she wouldn't have needed extra oxygen, could've made do with what the rest of us breathe."

"Made do," Aussie echoed. She rocked back and forth, her whole body pulling at Mama, yanking out words Mama wouldn't have said to her own sister.

"If Everett Comeaux had stayed where he belonged, that baby girl would have her true eyes."

"Amen, Jesus. Amen, Amen," Aussie said, still rocking to Mama's words. Those Amens in our kitchen put the final seal of disapproval on poor Everett, who would never be welcomed in our home again, least not by Mama's warm and open heart. I felt sorry for him, but not near as sorry as I felt for Angelina Christine, second sight or no second sight.

The next several days, building to Christmas, were too exciting for me to spend much time feeling sorry for Everett, who planned on being home Christmas Eve—for good, I guessed—or even for Angelina Christine. Mama and Mavis and I—Daddy too when he was home—were too busy with cooking and hanging ornaments and shopping to make room for much of anything else.

Christmas was my absolute favorite time of year and not just because of the presents either. I loved the whole time before, everybody working hard to get ready. Decorating. Baking. Wrapping. All of it. I loved Midnight Mass every year, Mama sending us to bed at eight, waking us at ten forty-five to dress in our fancy new Chaisson's Christmas outfits, then stepping outside, cold and shivery in the night air, driving to church with a million stars showing the way. Not knowing what you'd find next to your shoe under the tree on Christmas morning. It was a fairy-tale time. Even grown-ups felt it, smiling at things they would yell at any other time, allowing extra cookies nearly anytime you asked.

Christmas was special, would always be special, even though I didn't believe in Santa anymore. Last year Mother Ignatius came to our class-room right after Thanksgiving and told us Santa would not be distributing gifts to us at the Christmas party. Instead we'd pull names and buy a gift for the schoolmate whose name we pulled. The presents would mean more, coming from a real person instead of a fantasy figure. She knew we were all old enough to realize Santa wasn't real. She was right about that. We'd all suspected Santa wasn't real. How could one person deliver all those toys to all the world's children in just one night? Made no sense. Still, she didn't have to call him "fantasy figure."

But even without Santa, Christmas was the best time of year. Least I'd always thought that. But then two days before Christmas we were awak-ened in the middle of the night, and I had to rethink my idea about Christmas being so wonderful it made everyone, grown-ups included, act better than they usually did.

A ringing phone in the middle of the night usually means bad news. I've known that since I was Mavis's age or younger. We should all have remembered that when Everett called about Deacy going to the hospital. This night was no exception. Mama got to the phone first and I'm not sure whether it was her calling to Daddy or the ringing itself that woke me, though in looking back on it, I seem to remember hearing both, the ring-ing and the yelling.

"It's a fire, Floyd. A fire at the school," Mama called.

"I'm on my way." Daddy was a member of Ville d'Angelle's volunteer fire department. He didn't get to drive the truck, but was a full-fledged member and kept his special fire-fighting clothes and other equipment in the hall closet. He'd been a firefighter for long as I could remember, but he'd only been called to four fires, not counting this one. Not all the vol-unteers got called to each fire and Ville d'Angelle was too small to support many fires. But he still got to ride the engine in the Christmas parade every year.

I was in the hall and behind Mama before her words, all her words, sunk into my brain. "A fire at which school?" I asked, praying she'd say public or even Sacred Heart, but knowing she wouldn't.

"Holy Rosary," she said. "Hurry, Floyd. Hurry," she called, trotting back to the bedroom.

She didn't have to tell me things looked bad. I knew that already. But why my school? And why just two days before Christmas, the most special time of the year?

Daddy rushed out the front door minutes later.

"Is the convent on fire too?" I asked.

"I don't know," Mama said. She pulled her robe tighter to fight the cold air Daddy'd let into the house.

"If a nun dies, she goes straight to Heaven," I said.

"For God's sake, nobody's talking about dying. Where do you get these ideas?"

If a nun died in Ville d'Angelle, we'd have ourselves our own personal saint. There are millions more saints in Heaven than the famous ones we all know. Saint Anne and Saint John and Saint Theresa and Saint James and all those others we've heard of are just a drop in God's holy bucket. The ones we don't know are just as holy, maybe holier, than the ones we do know.

I wouldn't mind having a saint who belonged just to me and my town instead of to the whole world. Not that I was wishing a sister to die in the fire. Who would I wish dead? Mother Ignatius or Sister Katherine? Absolutely not. Sister Bernie or Sister Pat? No, no, no. Besides, most folks in Ville d'Angelle, my own daddy included, wouldn't pray to a colored sister, saint or no saint. And if they did die, all the nuns at Holy Rosary, where would God put them? On the colored side of Heaven or the white? They would've taught together, lived together, been martyred together. Wouldn't that mean they belonged in Heaven together? Maybe God had a special part of Heaven set aside for just those kinds of circumstances. Or maybe God didn't care where you stayed in Heaven, didn't mark some parts COLORED ONLY and others WHITE ONLY.

I wondered which classrooms were burning. I hoped not mine. "How did the fire start?" I followed Mama to her room and sat next to her on the bed.

"Probably won't know till it's put out." She rubbed a hand across her forehead like she did when she got one of her bad headaches.

"You going back to bed?"

"Who could sleep now?" She reached across me to turn the alarm clock our way. Four-thirty. Too early for even Mama to be up.

We sat next to each other that way, neither of us saying anything, for a good long while. Then Mama stood all of a sudden. "I'm going to see that fire for myself," she said.

"Me too," I said.

"Well, if you're coming, hurry yourself. Get Mavis up. I'm leaving in five minutes." She was already at her bureau, pulling out underthings.

"Wake up." I shook Mavis's shoulder. "Wake up now. The school's on fire and we're going to see it."

She moaned and groaned, but I wouldn't let off shaking until she opened both eyes and sat up. "What school?" she said when she was finally sitting and had rubbed the sleep out her eyes.

"Holy Rosary. What do you think?" I threw Mavis's clothes at her. "Get dressed. Hurry or Mama'll leave us."

"Why's our school burning?"

"Nobody knows. Maybe we'll find out, if you hurry yourself up."

And for just about the only time I could remember, Mavis did just that. Actually listened to me and hurried herself up. When Mama called us a few minutes later, all she had left to do was tie her right shoe.

We were halfway to school before Mama bothered turning on the heater. The engine was too cold before that to give us anything but frigid air. Even with the heater going full blast, not much warmth reached the back seat.

When we got to Holy Rosary, seemed like just about the whole town had had the same idea as us. Jerry Dugan had deputized ten or fifteen men and stationed them every couple of yards in the street across from the school. Unless you were a firefighter, you couldn't cross that line of men. But the fire was so big, even across the street, you could see fine, feel the heat of it charring the very air you breathed.

Mama stood between Mavis and me, holding our hands as if we were babies, waiting our chance to run to the flames. I tried to spot Daddy, but from where we stood all the fighters looked the same. It was near bright as day with that fire, but the light wasn't normal or natural. The shining held evil pure as I'd ever seen. I shivered under its glow.

Firefighters gave up on saving even one room of my school and instead turned their hoses and attentions to the convent house, dousing the walls and roof, hoping the water that hadn't been able to save Holy Rosary would at least save the sisters' home. Now that water wasn't pouring on it, the schoolhouse flames reached higher and higher, flicking the sky with hot, angry tongues.

"I've never seen such a thing," Mama said to no one in particular.

"Never," someone behind us answered.

The fire held us all in its trance, none of us willing to turn away for fear of missing something. When it seemed the fire would never end, a loud crack, like thunder but even louder, exploded and the roof collapsed. For a short while the fire burned brighter than ever, but then the collapse checked the flames, at least a little, so they weren't reaching quite so high or appearing quite so fierce.

The crowd seemed to relax a little. Mama stopped gripping my hand so tightly, though she still didn't let it go. I looked around, searching for faces I knew. There was Willie, hands shoved into his pockets, his mama's hand resting on his right shoulder. Behind them were Lena and her two brothers and their mama, Lena looking sober for once and not as if she had a joke running through her mind. Willie's daddy and Lena's daddy were with my own, fighting fire off the convent. I looked for Deacy or one of her boys but didn't see any of them. The only nuns I spied were Mother Ignatius and Sister Katherine, rough beige blankets from the fire truck thrown over their shoulders. Everyone else had gone for Christmas, maybe home like Sister Pat.

By the time the sun rose all that was left of my school were a few flame flickers, ashes and smoke, and the stench of burnt wood. The convent was saved and that was something at least. The crowd broke up as the firefighters rolled their hoses back on the truck. Now that the sun was up I could tell Daddy from the rest of the fighters easily. Every once in a while I spied him, shoulders hunched to his work.

"Where'll we go to school?" Mavis asked. "Sacred Heart?" she asked when Mama didn't answer.

"Course not," I said, answering for Mama. No way Daddy, or even Mama, would let us girls go to a colored school, even if it was Catholic colored.

"Where then?"

"Public," I said.

"Public?" Mavis didn't want to mix with all those children whose parents hadn't bothered giving them a holy education. She didn't want to go to Catechism on Saturdays and for a couple of weeks in the summer in a worn-out butler building without enough air. Neither did I. But what could we do about that now? Nothing that I could think of. At least for the rest of the school year, that fire had pushed us out from under the umbrella of holy schooling and into the world, unprotected by the comforting idea that we were better than children who went to Ville d'Angelle Public School. The fire didn't just burn a building. It burnt each of us who'd depended on it always being there, never changing, telling the world we were a town who cared enough to offer a good Catholic education to anyone who bothered to ask. Now we were reduced to being no better than other small towns who were too lazy or too cheap to offer their children Catholic schooling.

We turned to walk back to our car and fell into step with Willie and his mama.

"Did you see the cross?" Willie asked as we walked behind the grown-ups and Mavis, still holding Mama's hand.

"What cross?"

"Next to the front of the school." He turned and walked backward, pointing in the direction we'd just come. "Wasn't very big, so maybe it was already gone by the time you got here."

"The sheets again," I said, spitting out the words.

"KKK forever," Willie said, but he didn't sound pleased about it.

"Baton Rouge sheets." I kicked a rock off the sidewalk and into someone's front yard and didn't care if I got caught. "I hope they burn in Hell, burn in fires hotter than this one ever got."

"God damn those sheets," Willie said, partly because he meant it and partly for the thrill of saying words that would've earned him several ruler whacks from Mother Ignatius or Sister Pat.

We reached our car first. "Have a good Christmas," Mrs. LeBlanc said.

"You do the same," Mama said, though she knew well as Mrs. LeBlanc that the sheets had made it impossible for any of us to have a good Christmas.

"See you," Willie said.

"Sure. See you," I answered, though neither of us knew when or where we'd be seeing each other again now Holy Rosary was gone.

As Mama eased out our parking space, I pressed my forehead against the back glass, staring at where Holy Rosary had once stood. Mother Ignatius huddled with Sister Katherine, both of them looking smaller and weaker than they ever had, and stared at the black ashes where only hours before a school, a fine wonderful school, had stood. But all the staring in the world wouldn't bring back my school, wouldn't change what had happened this day. Mavis got up on her knees and pressed her forehead against the window too.

"What will happen next?" she asked.

"Nobody knows," I said. "Nobody at all." Maybe Angelina Christine, with her second sight, knew. But she didn't count because she was too little to talk, to tell anyone exactly what she knew.

Mavis put her head on my shoulder and I put my arm around her, hugging tight as I could. We stayed like that all the way home, long past the time we could see any trace of Holy Rosary's ashes out the back window.

24

COLORED, COLORED, ALWAYS COLORED

MY FIRST DAY IN JANUARY at public was as awful as I'd expected even though I wasn't made to wear my Holy Rosary uniform. Not knowing where the bathroom was, getting lost going from the principal's office to my room, not knowing anything. Mama'd said I'd survive, but I wasn't sure. At least public used the same books as Catholic, so I wasn't completely lost. I was two chapters ahead in math, which made me feel good because I knew all the answers to Mrs. Nunez's questions. And even though she never called on me—probably because she couldn't remember my name—those public children must've thought I was a genius with my hand always in the air. I was behind in history, but only by half a chapter, which wasn't too bad.

The new school was lots bigger than my old one. Every grade, including fifth, had two sections, not just one, and each section was about fifteen kids larger than Holy Rosary's single class had been. Most of that first week, before my classroom got enough desks, I had to share a seat with a girl named Charlene Domingue since the teacher had us in alphabetical order. Charlene wore the same pink sweater with tiny pearls on the collar and around buttonholes every day. I thought it must've been a Christmas present. But when I asked, she said, "This old thing? Are you crazy? I don't even remember where I got it."

That was not a polite answer and I would've been in my rights to tell her so. But I didn't. Charlene was a public school child and now I was too. Soon, I was afraid, I would sound just like her, the good manners those nuns had drilled into me lost forever.

Only Lena and Willie were with me in Mrs. Nunez's room, the rest of Holy Rosary kids having been put in the other fifth. We all three of us looked dazed even to ourselves. What are we doing here, scattered among so many alien children? our looks asked.

Four of us Holy Rosary fifths got sent to Catholic schools in other towns. Those other schools would've been happy to take all of us. But for different reasons—money, transportation, inconvenience—most of our parents wouldn't consider sending us out of town to get an education, even a Catholic education.

Clorise was one of those who got sent to Mount Carmel in New Iberia. When she called to tell me, she tried to pretend she was sad about that, but I knew better.

"I wish I was going to public with you and most everybody else," she said.

"Do you really?" My question invited her to tell the absolute truth, which is all best friends are supposed to give each other.

"Sure," she lied. "Can you believe Gloria's going to Mount Carmel too? At least you're rid of her."

I waited for her to admit going to public was ever so much worse than having Gloria Richard in your class. I pulled the phone cord till its corkscrews were straight as Mavis's hair.

"We'll still be best friends. Best friends forever," she said.

"Sure," I lied back. "Forever."

Even while we were making that false pledge, both of us knew it was an impossible promise to keep. How can you stay best friends when you don't even go to the same school?

I never saw Sister Bernie again, nor Sister Pat, who heard about the fire while she was up in New York, spending Christmas with her ordinary family. That's what her letter said.

We'd been in public close to two weeks when I got the only personal mail, addressed to me alone, I'd ever received. Mama had it waiting on the kitchen table when I got off the bus. "You got a letter," she said the second Mavis and I walked through the back door.

"Who'd be writing to Vivien Leigh?" Mavis asked as if I'd be the last person in the world anybody'd think of writing to.

"Lots and lots of people, stupid." I looked at the return address. C.E.P., 3351 Falstaff Avenue, Brooklyn, New York. Only one person I'd ever known from Brooklyn and C.E.P. could only stand for one name.

"Mama, she's calling names again," Mavis said.

"Facts are facts," I said.

"Girls," Mama said, but only gave me, not Mavis, a funny look.

I couldn't tell whether that look was about me calling Mavis stupid or about me getting a letter from a colored sister. Before I could find out which, I went to the parlor with my mail.

Mama and Mavis talked over school in the kitchen, but once I opened the letter, their voices faded and I could almost hear Sister Pat saying the words she'd written on the paper, talking in the way that had seemed so funny in September and now didn't seem funny at all. The letter wasn't very long and was written on a single sheet of beige stationery bordered with a gold stripe.

The last paragraph said, "I am saddened by what happened to Holy Rosary. I know you loved your school. So did I. You will do well in public. You are a very smart girl and have a full and kind heart. I will never forget you, will love and pray for you always. Sister Pat." There was a P.S. "Every night I pray for the souls of the arsonists. You should also."

I didn't know Sister Pat thought I was smart and had a full, kind heart. This was about the best compliment I'd ever had. For a nun to think you were smart meant you really were. And even though I wasn't sure what my heart was full of, I was certain it was full of something good that one day would find its way to the surface and lead me to do right most days.

But I wasn't going to pray for the souls of the people who started the fire. I didn't think Sister Pat should either. That probably meant I had a long way to go before I was holy as her. That didn't bother me. Who ever heard of a child being near holy as a nun? Besides, I was certain her own family agreed with me. "The people who lit that fire will burn in Hell," her family'd probably said. "Count your blessings you weren't in that school or in that convent. You would've gotten yourself burnt to death or lynched, maybe tarred and feathered."

That last part's not true, I wanted to tell them. No one would lynch a sister. Not in Ville d'Angelle. But how could I make them believe that now? How could I still believe when all I saw in my dreams, for days and weeks after Christmas, were crosses and flames, the price of crossing the invisible line?

I thought about writing at least one letter to Sister Pat, telling her none of us started that fire, none of us would've done her harm. She would've liked to know I made myself learn some of Mister Hughes's poems by heart. "I ask you this: Which way to go? I ask you this: Which sin to bear?..." But I was afraid someone would find out I was writing to a colored sister. My heart was full and kind, but not brave, at least not that brave, not yet.

Right after my night prayers asking for eyesight for Angelina Christine I added another request. "Dear God, tell Sister Pat none of us fifths, not even Willie LeBlanc, wanted Holy Rosary to burn or her to come to harm or even to have to leave without saying good-bye." God isn't a telephone, but I hope he gives her my message because I think she would feel better if she knew that.

I never asked the other fifths whether they'd gotten news from Sister Pat. But the week after I got my letter Willie was standing next to me in the cafeteria line.

"You miss Holy Rosary?" he asked quietly so the boys in front and behind him wouldn't hear.

"Some," I said, not wanting to admit out loud the ache in my stomach when I heard the name of my old school. "You?"

He shrugged. "Sister Pat was all right," he said. "For a nun and for being from Brooklyn and being colored like she was. She was all right."

I nodded agreement, smiled to know she'd sent even Willie LeBlanc a personal letter. Wonder what Willie's daddy had to say about that?

Through January and February Mister Tom and Clay were inside, hammering and sawing, covering every part of the house with dust by the end of each day they worked, which wasn't often enough to suit Mama, who didn't like them juggling us among other jobs. She said that wasn't the way to get work done. But Daddy'd struck a good deal moneywise and them not being at our house every day, once the walls and roof were up, was part of that deal.

You'd think the burning school would've made Daddy more eager than ever to get rid of Aussie. Just the opposite.

"Why don't you see if Aussie could get herself over here every morning after Tom manages to get work done? Help clear out some of the filth," Daddy said after supper on Valentine's Day when dust was especially thick in the air, settling so fast, even the cards Mavis and I'd gotten at school that day were dirty.

"Weren't you the man who didn't want her here at all?" Mama asked.

Daddy folded back the front page of his newspaper to find the continuation of the article he'd started. "No need to let Aussie go. She's not a bad colored. Not at all."

Mama looked up from the button she was sewing on one of Daddy's work shirts, opened her mouth as if to say something, then closed it again when she changed her mind and settled for a slight shake of her head.

When me and Mama were alone in the kitchen next morning, I asked why she thought Daddy'd changed his mind.

"Who knows?" she said.

"Is it cause the school burnt and Sister Pat and Sister Bernie left?"

"Maybe."

"Is it cause now he thinks everything can go back to the way it was last summer before the colored sisters came?"

"I don't know. Maybe." She rinsed her coffee cup and set it upside down on a towel. "Why do you need to know every single thing about why something gets done or not? It's all right to have a few blanks in your life, here and there."

That wasn't very generous on Mama's part. How was I supposed to get grown if I didn't learn what was what? How could I choose my life's path if no one bothered telling me what was wrong with this way as opposed to that, why this was the right way to go and the other not? I scooped Cleo from between my feet and rubbed my nose into her fur, soft and warm especially in this dead of winter.

It was near the middle of March before the extension got all the way completed so we could move in. I wouldn't of minded sleeping in my new room before the wallpaper got pasted or the curtains hung, but Mama wouldn't hear of it. She wouldn't even let us use the toilet till the paint dried in the new bathroom. But on the fourteenth of March, when all that had happened, I got to sleep in my own room. Daddy pretended to check my head for gray hairs, the add-on had taken so long, but he didn't find a one. I wasn't that old yet.

I wouldn't whisper this even to Cleo, but the first night was scary. Except for when I'd been too sick to know anything, I couldn't remember sleeping without Mavis next to me. Who'd of thought I'd miss Mavis's snoring and hogging blankets and trying to steal part of the bed that clearly belonged to me? Still, there it was.

I wondered how Mavis was doing in her bunk bed in the room that was now hers alone. I had argued over the unfairness of her getting new furniture, but not with all my might since I was the one with the whole new room and knew well as anybody who was getting the better deal.

I didn't have a clock in my room yet, though Daddy'd promised me a working alarm. But I knew it was past midnight when I was still awake. The night was clear, the moon so round and full, it seemed ready to drop into my arms any minute.

After everyone had been settled for a long, long time, I sat half up, my elbows resting on the windowsill that still smelled of fresh wood and paint, and found the Big Dipper. Maybe by the time I finished fifth I'd be able to see more constellations, but I doubted it. I counted stars, thinking that might help me fall asleep. So many stars. A person could spend her whole life doing nothing but counting stars and still not number all of them. A person could spend her whole life trying to understand people, why they did what they did, and still not understand most of what goes on around her. At about star two hundred fifty, I finally fell asleep.

The next morning, Saturday, Mavis started in pestering about having Marydale spend overnight, this time in her new bunks instead of on the sofa bed. Daddy wasn't home and Mavis was lucky about that. She might've gotten herself spanked for even asking such a stupid question.

Mama was calmer than Daddy would've been but didn't leave any doubt about her answer. "Marydale is not spending overnight in this house." Her voice wasn't loud, but hard and strong, not the voice of someone who would let her mind be changed. "Not ever. Not tonight. Not tomorrow. Not next week. Never."

Mavis banged her cereal spoon, splashing milk out her bowl and onto the table, then ran out, slamming the screen and not even looking back when Mama said to be careful. I expected Mama to go after her, make her come back and clean her milk spill, remind her about door slamming not being allowed in this house. But she did none of that, just let Mavis go and wiped the table with a dish towel herself.

"She's sure mad," I said.

"She'll get over it."

"Good thing Daddy's not home."

"Mavis is his baby. Some days he can't get angry with her."

"He would over this. He's getting awful tired of her not understanding about Marydale, even after all this time." I slurped the last milk from my bowl. "Mavis doesn't know anything."

"Mavis knows a lot. She just doesn't want to admit to what she knows yet."

"Mavis is stubborn as knotted hair," I said.

By ten-thirty Mavis still hadn't shown her face in the house. "Go find your sister. Tell her I have bread pudding just out the oven."

I put down my Nancy Drew, only thirty pages from the end, and went to find the moron. She wasn't by the canal. Not under the willow tree or in the back shed. I yelled and yelled, but of course she didn't answer. Finally I thought to look under the house. There she was, digging with a spoon under the middle of the parlor.

"Why didn't you answer?" I knew she'd heard. I'd spent enough time under the house when I was younger to know she'd heard every call out my mouth.

I crawled in till I was next to her. The place was cool and damp and dark as when I used to go there regular. Only now I had to bend my neck to keep from bumping my head on the underside of the floor.

"Marydale is nice, but colored. Can't you get that through your head?"

She stabbed her spoon into the ground, then flung dirt to the mound next to her.

"Colored, colored, always colored," I singsang. "Mavis Dubois, don't you know what that means yet?"

She kept staring down at her dirt, trying to pretend she wasn't hearing a word I was telling her, but her squinty eyes gave her away.

"Nobody says that's right or good." I remembered Sister Pat's letter, her trips to Yankee Stadium. I wasn't a baseball fan, but when she'd described DiMaggio rounding first, sliding for second, fans screaming, I'd wished I'd of been there to see it too. Wouldn't have mattered whether you were colored or white, you would've wanted to see that. Makes me think coloreds and whites want the same things more times than not. Live a regular life, then die and go to Heaven, freed from all pain and sorrow, everyone freed for good. But a person would have to have more courage than I could summon to say that to anyone grown in Ville d'Angelle.

Mavis kept pretending I wasn't there.

I reached across the hole to sink my nails into the fleshy part of her bare arm. She whimpered and slapped my hand, but I wouldn't let go. "Sheets get hold of you, that's how much it'd hurt. Hurt more, lots more." I let go. "You remember that."

She rubbed her arm where my fingernails still marked. I waited for her to run tattling to Mama or go puff cheeked or start crying like a baby. But she didn't do any of that, just stared at the hole she'd spooned. We sat there, neither of us saying a word for a long time.

"Does it still hurt?" I asked when enough time had gone by for Mama's bread pudding to have cooled completely.

"Not much," she said. "Not like sheets."

"I didn't mean to hurt you bad."

She kept rubbing her arm. "I know."

"Mama has bread pudding. Come on." I turned to crawl out. Behind me I could hear Mavis, her hands and knees hitting the ground as she followed me to sunlight and bread pudding.

We'd just finished our last bites when Marydale flew through the screen door, careful not to let it bang when she saw Mama at the stove. "How do, Miz Hazey."

"Morning, Marydale. Want some bread pudding?"

"No, ma'am. My mama's making cakes for Little Aussie's birthday and I'm helping and I'm here to see if Mavis can help too."

"Is that baby a year already?"

"Yes, ma'am. Just about."

"Only help Aussie'll get from you girls is bowl licking," I said.

"Just be sure you're back here by two forty-five," Mama said.

"Rhonda Robineaux's birthday," Marydale said. As usual, she knew as much about what was going on in my house as I did. Mavis had managed an invitation to Rhonda Robineaux's eighth birthday party, having succeeded in avoiding fights serious enough to get her name scratched from the list. "I sure won't let Mavis forget to come home for that party. No, ma'am. I sure won't. Mavis might be sharing some of her party favors."

"I didn't say for sure." Mavis sounded more put out than she usually did with Marydale. Maybe that pinch under the house had done the girl some good. But Mavis would have to be awfully put out to pass on a chance to lick one of Aussie's cake bowls and I didn't blame her.

At two-thirty Mavis still wasn't back home. No surprise there. The girl would forget to come home altogether some days. Especially with this being the first time she'd been to Marydale's since Christmas, the winter being too cold and wet for Mama to allow her to walk there, she was as likely to forget Rhonda Robineaux's party as not.

Mama sent me to drag my sister home. If it had been up to me, I would've let her stay at Marydale's long as she wanted. If she missed the party, too bad for her. She was nearly done second grade and it was time she learned to take care of her own business. I did not intend to spend my entire life making sure my sister didn't miss her important events. But no use telling Mama that. Mavis was her baby as well as Daddy's and got special treatment and unless Mama got herself a change-of-life child, that would never change.

I didn't mind the walk to Aussie's. A breeze cooled me as I kicked gravel along the side of the road. A few marshmallow clouds floated lazily in a pale blue sky. March was always my favorite month. We're done with winter, not yet burdened with the threat of summer. It's the only month when the weather is properly balanced.

Henry's truck was gone, so I knew he was probably working as he did most Saturdays. Him being one of the only coloreds, he was one of the last in line to get a Saturday off. Henry didn't mind, him being a hardworking man all his life. Even Daddy said Henry gave a boss a good day's work for his money.

In the kitchen Marydale and Aussie and Mavis sat around the table. A fan next to the stove blew heated air out the room. Fresh slices of chocolate cake sat in front of each of them. I parked myself across from Aussie and waited for her to offer me a slice, which she did.

"I thought this was for Little Aussie's birthday," I said.

"We baked ourselves four cakes. Mavis and me frosted this one all by ourselves for eating this day."

I took a bite to stop myself from saying Aussie wouldn't serve a cake frosted by those girls for company even if the company was only family.

"Viven Leigh, you be wanting yourself some milk?" Aussie asked.

"No, thanks. Cake's plenty." Milk would've tasted good, but I was used to milk from the store and Aussie only served milk fresh from the cow. Mama said it was pasteurized same as the milk I poured from the carton each day, except Aussie's was fresher. I guess I just didn't care for fresh milk because I could not accustom myself to the taste of milk that hadn't been out of the cow longer than a day.

"This cake sure be tasting good." Marydale fished for a compliment.

As usual, her mama was more than happy to oblige. "Be about the best cake this mouth ever tasted."

Marydale looked at me for the next compliment.

"Cake's not bad." I wasn't about to exaggerate like her mama had.

Mavis didn't say anything, just kept her head bent to the cake. If you looked carefully, you could see a slight bruise where I'd pinched her that morning.

"Guess it be time for Rhonda Robineaux's party," Marydale said. "If Mavis gets herself enough treats, she's sharing with me."

"I never said I was sharing." Chocolate frosting dotted one corner of Mavis's mouth.

"You might. You said you might."

"Well I'm not. I'm keeping all my treats for my own self." She rotated her plate in a tight circle on the table. "I am," she said again, daring any of us to say different.

The three of us stared at Mavis, who looked down at the table and traced a yellow tulip painted on the oilcloth.

"You could be keeping most of those treats. The best treats be yours to keep. You could just give me one." Marydale sounded as if she might start crying any second.

"I'm not sharing those treats." Mavis sounded as if she wanted to cry too.

"Your mama didn't raise you to be no selfish child," Aussie said gently. "No, ma'am. Miz Hazey didn't raise herself no greedy babies."

The only sound in that kitchen was the constant whirr of the fan blade trying to cool all of us as we waited for Mavis to give in, to agree to share with Marydale as she always had since she'd been tiny as Little Aussie, a baby not afraid of a single thing. But Mavis didn't give in, didn't even try to defend herself against Aussie's words.

"I've got to go now or I'll be late." Mavis pushed herself from the table. The edge of her cake slice, with thick frosting she'd saved for last, sat untouched.

Marydale jumped from her chair, ran to the back of the house, and then to the kitchen again. "Here." She shoved her baby doll toward Mavis.

Mavis stood, her arms dangling at her sides, making no move to reach for Marydale's doll baby. "You need your baby and I don't want her."

"I not be giving her away. Just lending her for a visit. She can sleep in the top bunk and you can pretend it be me up there. Your best friend."

Mavis's right arm twitched as if it was going to reach out for the doll. Instead she rubbed the spot I'd pinched that morning. "No." She ran out the back door and around the house.

Mavis didn't understand anything. She didn't know how to stay away from the bold places where people pointed at you, stared because you didn't act the way everyone expected you to act. That was the only lesson I was trying to teach her that morning. Instead she'd gone off the other end, practically joining Daddy and his Concerned Citizens. Maybe when she got older, she'd understand better, learn there is comfort in staying away from the extremes. Though holding back, afraid to be first, to be different, offers its own dangers. I know that's what Sister Pat would say.

"I'll take your baby," I said. My arm stretched to grab the doll, erase the looks on Marydale's and Aussie's faces. "Mavis is having one of her crazy spells," I said and offered Aussie a grin to apologize for my sister's behavior.

Aussie didn't offer anything back. She put an arm around Marydale's shoulders and squeezed. Marydale stared at her baby doll as if she'd never seen her before.

"The doll baby be staying here," Aussie said. "Guess you better be getting yourself home, Little Miss."

She didn't have any right to call me that. I should've told her too. But this was her house, not mine, and coloreds have rights in their own houses, same as whites do everywhere. So I didn't say anything, just left. By the time I reached the road Mavis was nearly home, her feet raising a cloud of dust as she left me and Marydale and Aussie behind.

When I got home, Mavis was already stripped to her underpants and in the bathroom, cleaning herself with a wet washcloth. She didn't look as if she was about to cry anymore. She wanted to go to that party, wear her best dress, stuff herself with tiny sandwiches and three kinds of ice cream and chocolate cake and cherry Kool-Aid, play games, and get a bag of favors when she went home. Rhonda had promised all that and Mavis wanted all of it.

I followed her to my old room when she'd finished cleaning and sat on the bottom bunk while she dressed. "Marydale's sure mad at you."

She passed a brush through her hair twice, leaving a fist-sized knot in the back, then put on a headband Mama'd bought her special, just for the party. "So?"

While she faced the full-length mirror Daddy'd hung on her door, I buttoned the back of her dress. I didn't remind her there'd been a time she would've gladly promised to share anything she was getting with Marydale, a time she would've done anything to keep Marydale from getting mad at her. "Aussie's mad too," I said.

"Do you think Aussie'll still like me?" Now she sounded sad and worried as she'd looked at Aussie's.

I remembered Aussie's cold look, her cold words sending me home. "I don't know if she'll still like any of us."

Mavis slowly twisted a few strands of hair around her pinkie, the whole time her eyes holding my own in the mirror.

Mavis spent most of the next afternoon under the willow tree, filling in the gold hole she and Marydale had spent so much time digging last summer. I still felt kind of bad about stabbing her with my nails under the porch the way I'd done, so I brought her lemonade and four chocolate chip cookies around three-thirty.

"Why are you filling in your hole?"

"I want to. That's all."

I looked at her arm to see if my marks were gone and they were. Even if you knew exactly where I'd wounded her, you couldn't tell. "Thanks for not telling Mama about yesterday morning." I don't know what had been more of a shock—her not tattling or her cheeks staying flat.

"That's okay," she said.

"Marydale'll be mad when she sees you've filled up the hole."

"There isn't any gold in here." She started on her second cookie.

"Does Marydale know?"

"She knows. She just doesn't know I've decided to fill in the hole." She chewed and swallowed, kicked a clod into the hole.

"She'll be really mad," I said again.

"This is my property. Mine. Marydale knows that."

"If she doesn't, it's time she learns."

Mavis nodded, her mouth too full to say anything. Even with her mouth stuffed with chocolate chip cookies, her cheeks weren't puffed fat as she used to make them. I tried to remember last time she'd done that and was surprised I couldn't. I smiled, remembering how funny she used to look and, somehow, knowing she'd never look that way again. My baby sister was truly growing up.

The next Sunday was Easter. Azaleas still bloomed but didn't look their best. Magnolias in the front yard and lilies along the side of the house were in full bloom, though. Next to Christmas, I love Easter best and not just because of all the chocolates, especially the Gold Brick eggs. Easter is the story of how dying doesn't have to be the end and if dying isn't the end, nothing can really be the end. Jesus died on Good Friday and everybody was sad and crying. Then on Sunday he said, "I'm back. Back forever. Resurrected." I wanted to think even regular people could be like that, resurrected. Mama said of course that's true. Isn't that what I've been taught in Catechism, year after year after year? But that's not what I meant. I don't think you should have to die first to get resurrected. I think resurrection should be a second chance to get something right. Mama says I am a confused child and I imagine she's right.

Since this was Easter week, Aussie didn't come to clean, being busy getting ready for her own Sunday visitors, the Arceneauxs since the Landrys had come for Christmas. The next Thursday wasn't her scheduled week. In April she only came once. Mama said that was fine because Mavis and I weren't home to dirty the place. I always remember to wipe my feet before I step into the house, although I know Mavis doesn't.

But on the first Wednesday in May Aussie was sitting on the front steps with Mama when Mavis and I got home from school.

"This isn't Thursday," Mavis yelled soon as she was off the bus. "You coming on Wednesdays now, Aussie?"

"You girls act like you've been raised on a heathen farm," Mama said. "Say hello."

I hated when she lumped me with Mavis that way. I hadn't been the one yelling like a maniac right off the bus. And what was a heathen farm, anyway?

"Hello," Mavis said. "So are you coming Wednesdays now?"

"Wednesdays would be fine. Any day, really. Nothing holy about Thursdays." Mama patted her skirt, looked at Aussie sideways.

"No, ma'am. Like I says. Thursdays, Wednesdays. Don't matter. Don't work. None of those days." Aussie stared at the road, maybe thinking how a person could end up almost anywhere if she started walking down that road, took just one step followed by another then another then another.

"You wouldn't have to come every week or even the same day every week. We could work something out." She smoothed her skirt again, joined Aussie in staring at the road, which led nowhere and everywhere.

"Gots to watch Little Aussie. That's what I gots to be doing."

"What about the lady who's been watching her all along?" I asked from the carport where I sat on my book bag, watching them, Mavis next to me on her book bag, watching too.

Mama looked my way but didn't say anything about my keeping out of grown-up business.

"I done told your mama. That lady can't be keeping up with those extra hours now that Evie's getting herself all the overtime."

"You've always come here, Aussie. That's the only thing," I said.

"Always," Mavis said.

Mama sighed, a low sad sound that billowed over all of us. "Things change."

"Yes, ma'am. You be right there. Things, they sure do change on us."

"Least in the summer, I could take care of Little Aussie when you were cleaning here," I said.

Aussie and Mama both smiled, looked at me as if I didn't understand what was going on in front of my own eyes. But I understood it all, more than those ladies could even imagine.

"I take care of Angelina Christine sometimes," I said, not bothering to remind anybody that if I could watch over a blind baby, I could surely watch over a seeing one.

"Evie doesn't want some child watching her baby," Mama said. "Not when she can have Aussie."

"Don't you want Aussie to keep coming?" Until then Mavis had been quiet, loosening the straps on her book bag, then tightening them again.

"Aussie knows she's always welcome in this house. Always." Mama faced the road again, her words aimed in that direction instead of ours.

Welcome be a strange word. Yes, ma'am, it sure be," Aussie said.

None of us knew what to say to that, so we waited for Aussie to explain. But for once she didn't offer an explanation, let us work on the problem for our own selves. I don't know what Mama and Mavis came up with, but this is what I decided. I knew Aussie didn't lie. So the part about Evie and Little Aussie and the post office had to be true. All of it true. But I also decided Aussie knew about Mavis not sharing Rhonda Robineaux's treats and not letting Marydale's doll baby sleep over and filling in the gold hole without checking with Marydale first. And I couldn't help but think all that and the yellow dishes made a difference in Aussie deciding she couldn't clean for Mama anymore. Not on Thursdays or Wednesdays or any other day of God's week.

"We'll miss you, Aussie. We'll always miss you and that's God's truth." Mama hugged her waist, but kept her eyes on the road.

"Yes, ma'am. That sure be God's truth," Aussie said softly. "God's only truth."

Neither of those ladies wanted that to be God's truth, but it was. And there was nothing, not a single thing, either of them could do to change that fact. They were burdened by too much weight, the ashes of an entire school and the memories of burning crosses. Resurrection wasn't possible, at least not on this day, not for any of us.

At the beginning of summer Mama got Rosemary, the girl who did for Tante Yvette, to come on Saturdays, so Mavis and I didn't get stuck with too much extra work. I shouldn't have cared so much about Aussie not coming anymore. Just, it didn't seem right, waking Thursdays and not hearing Mama and Aussie tossing their words back and forth, steady as rain on our tin roof.

After that Wednesday afternoon in May, Mama didn't let on that Aussie's quitting bothered her any. She did spend more time on the phone with Deacy, but that's the only difference I noticed. Besides, that could've been more connected to Everett deciding to stay up in Monroe after all. Mama said he was embarrassed about having a blind baby, but I think there was more reason for his staying in Monroe than that. He still came home for visits, holidays especially, because no one wants to be alone at Easter or Christmas or even for any of the little holidays like Fourth of July.

He was in charge of the barbecue on the Fourth, which wasn't nearly as hot as last year's had been. Everyone, even Mama, was nice enough to him. But things weren't the same. He and Daddy talked about lumber prices and the IGA extension Mister Alan was building. When she saw Everett's plate empty, Mama offered more of her potato salad he loved so much. Deacy smiled at his story about the driver who got lost hauling a semi full of cut trees. But nobody asked when he'd be back, if he'd be back. Not even Deacy, who held her baby girl on her lap for most of dinner. Everett only took Angelina Christine once and then only for a few minutes while Deacy sliced watermelon and strawberry shortcake for dessert. Everett jiggled his baby on his knee, bouncing her too high. I know she didn't like being shaken so much. But she didn't cry about it, just puckered her brows until a single line split them. Every so often she twisted her neck as if to stare up at her strange father, though of course she couldn't stare at him or anything else. Soon as desserts were served Everett shoved Angelina Christine back to her mother. Was he afraid that tiny baby would point a second-sight finger at him, draw down a curse on his head that'd pay him back for forcing her out her mama's womb too soon? No one, not even his own daughter, cared if Everett stayed in Monroe forever.

When we got home from Deacy's that Fourth of July afternoon, I pulled Mama and Daddy's betting money from my top bureau drawer. Mama was surprised I offered it to her, almost as if she'd forgotten I had that money. Not likely, though, because Mama wasn't one to forget much. She said I could keep the money. She didn't want it anymore.

"All of it?" I fingered the coins and bills clutched in both fists and watched Mama's face.

"Sure," Mama said, not smiling, not frowning, her face not changing at all that I could tell. "Why not? Keep it for when you want something really special."

I tried to think of something special enough that'd make spending this money all right. But I couldn't think of anything right off, so I just put the money back where it had been all these months, nested in the box of shells Clorise, my once-upon-a-time best friend, had brought back from Biloxi, Mississippi.

Mama didn't bother making me recite all the changes that had taken place since the colored sisters came to town. She could've listed them well as I could. Mavis growing up, learning white girls are never best friends with colored girls, least not in Ville d'Angelle. Aussie stopping working for us even though she'd been coming to our house forever and ever, longer than I'd been alive. Holy Rosary burning to the ground so that, once workers cleaned up, only an empty space was left to show it had ever existed, been a part of our town. Everett moving to Monroe for what looked to be for good. And then, of course, there was Angelina Christine, sweetest blind baby ever there was. She was still too young for anyone to tell whether she had second sight like Aussie and Reverend Hope predicted, but I was pretty certain she did. After all, she was a change-of-life baby.

I knew what that meant now too. It meant when a woman thought she was done having her children, a change-of-life baby told her that wasn't so. She'd have to change for that new baby, or else. That's what Deacy's baby said to all of us. Change or else. Most of us, including me, had done just that. I still didn't want my sister being best friends with a colored girl and I certainly wasn't crazy enough to be a Communist, but then I also didn't want to be a Concerned Citizen and I knew twenty-five capitals, not counting Baton Rouge, Louisiana.

Some, though, my daddy among them, would fight any change from colored sisters and change-of-life babies both. Fight till Hell froze and past then. But that didn't mean they'd stop the change. This past year we'd gotten a whiff of what was heading our way, heading everybody's way. Change so powerful even a burnt school building wouldn't stop it for good. And now it was up to each of us to change too. I hoped Mama could convince Daddy of that, convince him before he got mowed over by a force stronger than all the Baton Rouge sheets lined up opposite. Because even sheets can't stand up forever against the power of colored sisters and change-of-life babies.

Epilogue

LOOKING BACK ON THE YEAR of the colored sisters, I wish
I hadn't been such a coward, had mailed Sister Pat at least one letter. But
when you are a child, being brave is nearly impossible when no one else is.
I have tried to atone for that childhood cowardice by following the course
Sister Pat must have envisioned for me, a smart girl with a full and kind
heart who learned at age ten that the legacy of a Concerned Citizenry can
only be desecration of the soul.

How could anyone have thought history would turn back its pages,
return to the customs and traditions existing before the colored sisters
arrived? Holy Rosary was never rebuilt, the Concerned Citizens' pockets
having been emptied by paying Miss Boudreaux's salary. When Mavis was
a junior, students of color enrolled at Ville d'Angelle High. No one said
or did anything about that. Not even Baton Rouge sheets. The world had
changed and all of us had changed with it. If you had a Concerned
Citizen heart, you could no longer feel easy admitting it. And if you had
a full and kind heart, you could no longer feel easy failing to follow where
that heart led.

I still have Mama and Daddy's betting money because nothing special
enough ever seemed to call for the spending of it. I keep the money in my
jewelry box now, Deacy's cameo resting atop the bills and the bills atop

Sister Pat's letter, all of it—letter and cash and cameo—intrinsically linked to that colored sisters year. Each time I lift the jewelry box lid, I am reminded anew of the price we once paid for our self-imposed circumscriptions. This person you can love, that person not. This person can be your best friend, receive your most intimate secrets, that person not. We were all victims of our world, prisoners as much as jailers. We all needed a second chance to get things right. And that was the ultimate gift we received from Sister Pat and her convent comrades: resurrection and emancipation, though there are still those who prefer the ease of imprisonment to the challenge of freedom.

Letters I never mailed to Sister Pat were written again and again on my mind's tablet. You pointed the way to go, answered Mister Hughes's question, I imagined telling her. Many of us follow the path you illuminated with navy robes and DiMaggio tales and state capitals, city after city after city reminding us of the boundless, magnificent world open to those willing to step out of darkness and into the sunshine of a golden, glorious day.